MASTER OF SANCTITY

Boosting power to his legs, Telemenus hurried on and turned right between two ramshackle workshops. Directly ahead was an impromptu ork barricade of barrels and upturned battered crates. The greenskins were pinned down by heavy bolter and sniper fire from two squads of Scouts beyond the curtain fence, making them easy targets for the Terminator. He fired half a dozen shots, trying his best to cut down the orks with one salvo. There was a single survivor from the burst, who turned in shock at the metal-and-ceramite giant bearing down. At close range Telemenus could not miss, his next burst of fire tearing the xenos in half.

'Gate secured,' he declared.

A WARHAMMER 40,000 NOVEL

MASTER OF SANCTITY

THE LEGACY OF CALIBAN BOOK TWO

GAV THORPE

BLACK LIBRARY

A Black Library Publication

First published in Great Britain in 2014 by
Black Library,
Games Workshop Ltd.,
Willow Road,
Nottingham,
NG7 2WS, UK.

10 9 8 7 6 5 4 3 2 1

Cover illustration by Fares Maese.

A CIP record for this book is available from the British Library.

UK ISBN 13: 978 1 84970 518 9
US ISBN 13: 978 1 84970 519 6

See Black Library on the internet at

blacklibrary.com

Find out more about Games Workshop and the world of Warhammer 40,000 at

games-workshop.com

Printed and bound by CPI Group (UK) Ltd, Croydon, CR0 4YY

It is the 41st millennium. For more than a hundred centuries the Emperor has sat immobile on the Golden Throne of Earth. He is the master of mankind by the will of the gods, and master of a million worlds by the might of his inexhaustible armies. He is a rotting carcass writhing invisibly with power from the Dark Age of Technology. He is the Carrion Lord of the Imperium for whom a thousand souls are sacrificed every day, so that he may never truly die.

Yet even in his deathless state, the Emperor continues his eternal vigilance. Mighty battlefleets cross the daemon-infested miasma of the warp, the only route between distant stars, their way lit by the Astronomican, the psychic manifestation of the Emperor's will. Vast armies give battle in His name on uncounted worlds. Greatest amongst his soldiers are the Adeptus Astartes, the Space Marines, bio-engineered super-warriors. Their comrades in arms are legion: the Imperial Guard and countless planetary defence forces, the ever-vigilant Inquisition and the tech-priests of the Adeptus Mechanicus to name only a few. But for all their multitudes, they are barely enough to hold off the ever-present threat from aliens, heretics, mutants – and worse.

To be a man in such times is to be one amongst untold billions. It is to live in the cruellest and most bloody regime imaginable. These are the tales of those times. Forget the power of technology and science, for so much has been forgotten, never to be re-learned. Forget the promise of progress and understanding, for in the grim dark future there is only war. There is no peace amongst the stars, only an eternity of carnage and slaughter, and the laughter of thirsting gods.

PART ONE
PISCINA

RETRIBUTION

An angel lay fallen and broken.

Sapphon, High Interrogator of the Dark Angels, Finder of Secrets, Master of Sanctity, looked at the chipped, weathered faced of the statue and grimaced. It was not a good omen.

Clad in the black power armour associated with his calling, Sapphon was a darker figure amongst the shadows of the desecrated shrine building. His helm was masked with the visage of a skull, his chestplate adorned with the Imperial aquila, against which rested a large pendant formed as a winged skull; a conversion field generator known as a rosarius gifted to him by the arch-cardinal of Canoptary Prime as a symbol of unity with the Ecclesiarchy. Auspex scans had indicated no threat within the crumbling temple but the Chaplain carried his weapons ready, bolt pistol in his right hand, his eagle-headed mace – a crozius arcanum – in the left.

The continuous smoke of fighting and wildfires blotted

the night sky outside the broken walls and the depths of the nave were pitch-black. Despite this, Sapphon was able to easily navigate around the toppled statue with the assistance of his suit's auto-senses, his already superior vision and hearing boosted to a preternatural level. Audio pick-ups conveyed the crunch of rubble pulverised under armoured boots, echoing through the ruined nave of the basilica as five warriors of the Deathwing spread out around their leader.

The elite of the Chapter wore Tactical Dreadnought armour, known amongst the brethren as Terminators, painted in the ivory of the First Company. Each Terminator suit was an artificer-created technical marvel larger even than standard Adeptus Astartes power armour, combining the mobility of an infantryman with the protection and firepower of a vehicle. Millennia of upkeep and adaption made each suit unique, whether it was the added armour banding around the greaves of Brother Decemius's armour, or the reinforcing studs that strengthened the left pauldron of Brother Fidellus's battleplate. On the left shoulder each of them bore the Crux Terminatus, an honour held by only a tenth of all the Space Marines across the Imperium; a symbol of devotion and courage so lauded it was worn where normally the Chapter symbol would take pride of place. This insignia, the winged sword of the Dark Angels – the blade enigmatically broken in the case of the Deathwing for reasons lost to antiquity – was worn on the right shoulder instead, bright red against the pale bone colour.

Two, brothers Namnos and Decemius, were armed with immense power fists, capable of punching through solid ferrocrete, ripping apart tank armour and pulping flesh and bone, paired with twin-barrelled storm bolters that could lay down a hail of explosive bolts in devastating bursts. Their leader, Sergeant Caulderain, bore a power sword as a mark of his rank as well as his storm bolter. Brother Fidellus was designated squad guardian, his thunder hammer and storm shield dedicated to close combat, while Brother Satrael carried the heavy weapon; for this mission a six-barrelled assault cannon that could lay down a curtain of fire so intense it would obliterate anything caught in the fusillade.

They were the elite by training too, each of them a veteran of many battles. To them had been given the honour of pushing into the ork-held city blocks that surrounded the old Chapter buildings at the heart of the capital of Piscina IV, Kadillus Harbour.

The basilica had once been the pinnacle of the Dark Angels presence in the city. Now it was a near-empty shell, stained glass windows shattered, tapestries and statues exposed to the elements. Everything was marked with soot from flamer sweeps used to incinerate ork spores. Other than this routine cleansing everything else had been left as it had been at the end of the last war for Piscina; a memorial to those that had fought and died to protect the worlds from the brutal horde of the beast Ghazghkull Mag Uruk Thraka and the equally terrible ork warlord Nazdreg.

The noise of rubble shifting on the storey above drew the Chaplain's attention. His bodyguard responded too, beams from armour lamps shining up through the ravaged floor. There was a flash of movement to Sapphon's right – something pale. Definitely not an ork. Another flicker to the left betrayed someone ducking behind the pedestal of an ancient bust depicting Chapter Master Ezerius. Sapphon glimpsed a woman's face, middle-aged, camouflaged with haphazardly applied grime. There was a glint of silver; possibly an old goblet or salver half-tucked under her cloak.

'Looters,' snarled Sergeant Caulderain. 'No mercy!'

'Do not fire!' snapped Sapphon as four storm bolters and an assault cannon were lifted towards their targets.

'Brother-Chaplain, our orders were exact,' said Caulderain. His storm bolter continued to track along the upper storey as the rag-clad woman pushed herself further along into the shadows of the alcove. 'Supreme Grand Master Azrael has assumed martial command of the Piscina system. Curfew is to be enforced with ultimate sanction.'

'And I am here, at your side, and I tell you not to fire, brother-sergeant,' Sapphon said calmly. 'Look at them. They are starving. If they can exchange detritus of the past for a few loaves, we should not punish them for trying.'

'They despoil a mausoleum of the Chapter, Brother Sapphon.'

'The ghosts of our dead do not need silver and gold to feast any longer, sergeant,' Sapphon replied, still keeping his temper in check. 'If you are eager to fire your weapon, let us push into the east quadrant where there will be sufficient orks upon which you can unleash your wrath to duty's contentment. Move on, there is nothing for us here.'

'As you command, Brother-Chaplain,' said Caulderain. He lowered his weapon and the Deathwing squad followed suit.

They crossed the nave and exited through the remains of the east transept, passing through smashed doors to descend a flight of time-worn, bullet-pitted steps to the cratered street outside. Five more Deathwing – Squad Daeron – waited fifty metres to the north at a junction with the east-west arterial route leading into the ork-held sections of the city. Behind them loomed the massive bulk of a Crusader-pattern Land Raider painted in the livery of the First Company, its sponsons laden with the multiple barrels of hurricane bolters, twin assault cannons jutting above the assault ramp at the front.

The surrounding buildings showed obvious signs of ork infestation. Windows and rooftops were augmented with jagged metal plate barricades, firing holes had been smashed through the walls and every flat surface was daubed with pictograph graffiti. Mouldering piles of effluent, oil slicks, scraps of bone and other detritus stained the rubble strewn across the road. Smoke residue marked doorways and window frames, charred remnants of bonfires heaped amongst scattered rubbish. Fungal lobes and fronds of various bright colours splayed from cracked walls and crevices in the ferrocrete roadway, some taller than Sapphon, others diaphanous webs that trailed in the wind.

Trenches and turrets, slant-walled towers and pillbox fortifications cut off many of the side streets and alleys leading from the main thoroughfare, while gantries and ladders criss-crossed the roofs far above, allowing the orks to swiftly redeploy from one area to the next. No doubt they had similar rat runs in the sewers beneath the city; Grand Master Belial was leading the rest of his First Company on a subterranean cleansing sweep.

Yet for all their barbarous conversion, these city blocks were empty, abandoned overnight it seemed. The orks had thwarted yesterday's assault by elements of the Fourth, Seventh and Tenth Companies and Sapphon concluded that the aliens had drawn back in anticipation of a more devastating attack to follow. They were cunning, in a feral kind of way. He had never believed orks to be the unthinking brutes portrayed in a lot of Imperial propaganda and reports of their activities across Kadillus Island had reinforced the Interrogator-Chaplain's opinions. He remembered the last time the Chapter had come to this world in force; long days and nights in the wilderness and abandoned mines outside the city conducting search-and-destroy operations for ork lairs and fortresses. Now, after years of believing Kadillus purged, the Dark Angels had been called back to find the world aflame once more. Most of the Chapter was out in the East Barrens and scouring Koth Ridge again; due to political weakness and instability cleansing patrols by the local defence militia had faltered and allowed the orks to grow in size and numbers in the absence of the Space Marines.

The East Quadrant of Kadillus Harbour was the last hiding place of the greenskins within the city walls but it was proving a tough proposition for the sons of the Lion. Orbital bombardment was impossible without risking the docks, and more importantly the geothermal energy station situated there. Kadillus was nothing more than a huge volcanic mound and a missed lance strike or plasma warhead could set off a chain reaction that would destroy the entire island in one cataclysmic eruption. Only a few square kilometres, the former residential district was a warren of close-built edifices ideal for defence and ambush. Coupled with the canny and spiteful attitude of Piscina's orks, it was a death trap.

For ordinary Space Marines, at least. For the Deathwing, whose entire purpose on the battlefield was to venture into battle zones too deadly for their brethren, it was simply another mission.

The Crusader led the advance, crunching across the rubble on broad tracks, turning the shattered masonry to gravel and dust. The two squads of Deathwing followed with determined strides, forming a protective semicircle ahead of Sapphon. The Interrogator-Chaplain's command relays were coded into the sensoriums of the Terminators, giving him a real-time, three-dimensional overlay of the area across his vision. However, there was so much decaying material – the dead of both sides from yesterday's fighting and many months of previous battles – it was impossible to get any definitive organic trace. Tattered ork banners, vermin and deliberately-erected scarecrow effigies buffeted by the wind confounded motion detectors. Smoke trails from dozens of fires betrayed the orks' crude but effective counter-measures for thermal scanning.

'Eyes and ears and instincts,' Sapphon told the Deathwing warriors. 'All targets are hostile. Three gunships are standing by on fire missions. Previous attacks have not neutralised air defences so they are to be a last resort only. We will establish ingress to the one kilometre mark and resupply by Thunderhawk armoury insertion. Squads from Third Company are waiting at the advance mark to secure the axis of attack at my signal.'

'It would be better if we had the Ravenwing to scout for us,' said Sergeant Daeron. He spoke with a guttural Anolian accent, further distorted by poor vox-quality – a side-effect of his truly ancient Cataphractii-mark helmet. 'We are all but blind here.'

'Trust Sammael to send word of uprising on Piscina but not remain to deal with it,' said Brother Trateon, Squad Daeron's heavy flamer operator. He chuckled. 'Just a quick, "Better look at this!" and then they're off again chasing Emperor-knows-what.'

'I trust Sammael enough to know that he would not quit battle on Piscina had there not been more pressing matters,' Sapphon said, choosing his words carefully. There had been much debate concerning the Second Company's recent activities but Sapphon had chosen to keep his theories to himself; even amongst the Death-wing it was wise to keep mention of the Fallen to a minimum.

'Is that so?' said Sergeant Daeron. His voice dropped a fraction. 'Perhaps they found evidence of our "eternal friends"?'

In a Chapter that was built on concentric levels of ignorance and secrecy, euphemism and innuendo were to be expected, but Sapphon disliked some of the more flippant terms used to describe the traitors he and the Deathwing were tasked to capture. He let this incident pass but resolved to speak to Daeron in private later.

'Orks, brothers,' the Chaplain said evenly. 'We are here to slay orks. Further speculation is simply wasted breath and wagging tongues.'

'As you say, Brother-Chaplain,' said Caulderain, his tone conveying his displeasure at the casual talk. 'Keep eyes keen and weapons ready, these green bastards killed three battle-brothers yesterday and sent another eleven to the Apothecaries.'

Reminded of the Chapter's recent losses, the warriors muttered invocations and commendations to the souls of the dead and fell silent. The crunch of the Crusader's tracks echoed back from the desolate buildings.

A little more than one hundred metres ahead the smoke from many fires was thickening, gathering above the broken-backed tenements in an ork-made thun-derhead, the glow of flames visible on its underbelly. Jury-rigged power lines criss-crossed some of the roofs, sparking and flaring – another crude attempt to outsmart the auspexes of the Space Marines. It was working, in a fashion; the sensorium display was a mess of signals.

'Nothing says "find us here" as nicely as an obvious attempt to hide one's presence,' said Sapphon. He signalled the Land Raider. '*Lion's Fury*, move ahead fifty metres. Draw their fire.'

'Affirmative, Brother-Chaplain,' replied the tank's commander.

The ten Deathwing Terminators stopped, the two squads splitting, weapons covering the windows and roofs ahead. Sapphon followed Caulderain and his warriors to the left. Vision magnified, he scanned the piles of rubble and detritus for signs of ambush. Some orks were capable of uncharacteristic patience on occasion, hiding for hours and days at a time in order to spring their attacks. Nothing indicated any waiting enemies beneath the debris.

'The eyes of the Chapter are upon us, brothers,' he reminded his companions. 'It is to us that they look to lead the way. We shall blaze the path for them to follow, in deeds and in thought.'

'Yes, let's show them how to kill orks,' said Daeron. 'It seems some of our brothers have forgotten.'

It was a second flippant remark from the sergeant and Sapphon expected better from one of the Chapter's senior warriors. There was almost a hint of a challenge in Daeron's attitude, subconscious defiance perhaps.

The chime of a private vox-channel being opened rang in Sapphon's ear.

'Brother-Chaplain, why do you remain silent?' asked Sergeant Caulderain. 'His attitude is unbecoming of the Deathwing.'

'I will remind the brother-sergeant when the time is appropriate,' replied Sapphon. 'A vox-channel on the cusp of battle is not the place or time for such remonstration.'

'I do not know what poor spirit ails my brother, but he seems to be testing you, and he is certainly testing my patience, Brother-Chaplain.'

'Daeron has served the Dark Angels for three hundred years and more, and is one of the bravest and most dedicated Space Marines I have ever known.' A flicker of movement to the Chaplain's right made him pause. A moment later it resolved in his auto-senses into a rag caught on a coil of razor wire.

'My point exactly,' the sergeant continued. Sapphon suppressed an exasperated sigh. 'It is out of character for Daeron to speak so lightly of his duties. I fear it is a sign of a greater malaise within the company. It is a sign of disrespect that should be dealt with immediately and firmly.'

'Do not think me a Scout of the Tenth Company, to submit willingly to such instruction, brother-sergeant,' Sapphon said sternly, his annoyance growing.

'No insult was intended, Brother-Chaplain. I merely reflect that Brother Asmodai is far stricter in h–'

'I am not Brother Asmodai!' The response was uttered a little more hastily, with more vehemence than Sapphon had intended and he winced in reaction. It was simply paranoia speaking; the silent fear that Sapphon kept hidden from his brothers. Caulderain said nothing but Sapphon could imagine the reply that remained unspoken: *if only you were.*

'Movement, balcony, sixth storey, forty metres on the right!' snapped Brother Decemius. Sapphon felt a surge of relief, swiftly replaced with focus and purpose.

Sapphon looked up to see three orks peering over a bullet-pitted balustrade, each carrying a basic-looking rocket tube or launcher. Their grimacing faces were highlighted a moment later by converging flares of storm bolter-rounds. The ferrocrete balcony exploded into shrapnel and dust, tumbling the wound-riddled corpses of the orks to the street.

'More on the lower floors on the other side of the street,' Sapphon said, firing his pistol at lean shapes lurking just inside shattered windows and broken doorways. '*Lion's Fury*, engage. Make the xenos fear our retribution.'

'Affirmative, firing all weapon systems.'

While the Deathwing continued to pour fire into the building to their right, the Crusader's tracks spun as it turned to the left, assault cannon and hurricane bolters elevating as it did so. An ear-piercing whine cut across the roar of storm bolters as the multi-barrelled main weapon spun into action, followed by the rippling crack of hundreds of rounds being spat forth. The hurricane bolters added their fury, filling the sky with the gleaming trace of bolt propellant as the Crusader's fire stitched along the second and third storeys of the building, tearing ragged holes in the ferrocrete and laying waste to the aliens within.

Incoming fire whined down onto the Space Marines from further along the street; bullets and energy pulses from small arms, little to worry the Terminators. The cracked rockcrete of the road splintered and sparked from impacts as Sapphon ordered the tank and two squads to advance another fifty metres.

Something dark blurring against the clouds beyond the smoke caught Sapphon's eye.

'Incoming mortars and artillery. Continue the attack.'

Two seconds later the mortar bombs exploded short of their target, throwing grit and fresh rubble against the hull of the Crusader. Haphazard artillery strikes erupted around the battle group, smashing into buildings and leaving smoking craters in the road ahead and behind the

Deathwing. Still firing, ork bodies slumping against windowsills and toppling into the street, the First Company veterans continued with their steady, purposeful strides.

They came to a crossroads, the two squads now flanking the Land Raider as it concentrated its fire ahead and they dealt with the survivors to each flank. Airburst shells flung fragments of shrapnel that clattered harmlessly from the thick ceramite of the Tactical Dreadnought suits. Bullets pinged and las-bolts shrieked equally ineffectually. A mortar bomb exploded right next to Sapphon. The conversion field in his rosarius activated in a millisecond, transforming the incoming mass and shockwave of the explosion into pure energy. Half a second later a blazing white halo of power enveloped the Chaplain for a moment as the energy-build up in the rosarius flared into luminescent existence.

He fired almost without thinking, picking out available targets on instinct, every bolt sent from the Chaplain's pistol finding its mark in green alien flesh. Rockets screamed and corkscrewed down onto the advancing warriors, sputtering with smoke, warheads throwing flame and shrapnel in all directions but unable to pierce the layers of ceramite, plasteel and adamantium that protected the Dark Angels finest.

Sapphon stopped and checked behind the squad. Power armoured Space Marines were following-up the Terminator advance three hundred metres behind, clearing the buildings of any greenskins that had been missed by the devastation unleashed by the Terminators. The blossom of fire and smoke from frag grenades announced their progress into the upper storeys, while an occasional survivor was discovered and dealt with by bursts of bolter fire, almost inaudible amongst the din of the Deathwing's and Crusader's fusillade.

'Resupply drop in seventy metres,' Sapphon announced. The reticule and distance imposed over his right eye highlighted the dropsite selected by the Techmarines. The Chaplain was down to a third of his ammunition, and he knew that the Deathwing had been burning through their supplies with equal ferocity. Still, there were bolts enough to see them safely to the rendezvous.

Recalling Daeron's earlier words, the Chaplain had to concede that the absence of the Ravenwing had caused problems for the rest of the Chapter. The Darkshrouds and Land Speeders of the Second Company would have made short, bloody work of the greenskin horde that was now boiling up onto the rooftops to fire at the advancing Dark Angels.

'This is Chaplain Sapphon – commence supply insertion at grid point beta.'

The Chaplain barely heard the acknowledgement from the Thunderhawk pilot who had been circling overhead at a safe distance from any ork anti-air guns. Now Sapphon's audio pick-ups detected the roar of plasma engines growing louder as the gunship came in on its subsonic run.

They were barely fifteen metres from the drop point when the Thunderhawk swooped in. Battle cannon and lascannons blazing it circled once, weapons chewing rents and craters into the sides of the buildings surrounding the drop point. Sapphon watched the hatches and assault ramp opening, but instead of hovering for the drop, the Thunderhawk landed in a billow of heat and dust.

'What are you doing?' Sapphon demanded as he and the Deathwing broke forward, weapons firing to cover the approaches to the settling gunship. 'This is a combat drop!'

A Space Marine in the markings of the Third Company appeared at the top of the ramp and raised a fist to Sapphon as armourium servitors started to plod towards the street, ammunition hoppers slung over their shoulders, power packs hung on crane-like arms.

'Sorry, Brother-Chaplain, but we have an urgent request from Master Issachar. He is having difficulties at the Imperial commander's palace. He's asked that we take you to him immediately.'

'Difficulties? There is not an ork within a kilometre of the palace. Trouble with the Piscina Free Militia?' The planetary defence force was under curfew and subject to the disarm commandment as much as any other citizens of Kadillus Harbour, but some groups had opted to resist the Dark Angels efforts to restore order.

'Not exactly, brother.' The Space Marine shook his head. 'It is Brother-Chaplain Asmodai.'

THE ENEMY WITHIN

'You are making a mistake of monumental proportions.' The words were forced through gritted teeth, laden with threat but tempered with an attempt at calm.

Asmodai looked down at the man who had spoken: Colonel Brade of the Piscinan Free Militia. His face was flushed, wrinkled features contorting between fear and anger as he struggled to contain the duelling emotions. His uniform, which was frayed on the collar and cuffs, stained with much old blood both human and ork, was soaked with sweat. A bead of perspiration ran down the tip of the man's bulbous nose and dripped to the floor.

Asmodai could actually hear the man's heart hammering in his chest, the quick double-thud as clear to the Chaplain as the hiss and whine of servos as he shifted his weight and his armour responded. Through olfactory filters he could smell the man's fear, new sweat with the old, clouded by a fragrant pomade slicking the planetary defence officer's thinning hair.

The Dark Angel's gaze flickered for a moment to Brade's fists, which were gripping his belt as if it were a lifesaver thrown to a drowning man. On the colonel's right hip hung a holster in which sat a heavy pistol. Now and then Brade's hand twitched as though subconsciously he wished to draw the weapon. Fortunately for Brade his conscious mind was winning that particular battle.

Brade's blue eyes were mad, staring, locked to Asmodai's, at least locked on the red lenses of the Chaplain's skull-faced helm.

'Your opinion is irrelevant, you have received instruction and you will obey,' said Asmodai. He pointed an armoured finger at the colonel's side arm. 'You will begin by disarming. You will then surrender to my custody to await investigation into your conduct.'

'You have no authority here.' Brade's voice wavered, betraying his insincerity.

'Authority is not granted by legal writs and contracts,' said Asmodai. 'My authority derives from the Emperor, for I am a battle-brother of the Dark Angels, descendants of the First Legion. We are the Adeptus Astartes, his chosen warriors.'

Brade opened his mouth to argue but Asmodai cut him off, stepping forward, the closeness of his immense bulk silencing any protest. The Chaplain waved a hand to encompass the hall in which they stood. The high arched ceiling was stained in places by soot from the grand fireplace that dominated one wall. The hall had once been a banqueting suite, now turned into a command station by Brade and his subordinates. Supply crates had been turned into tables and desks, littered with maps, rations packs, heavy duty vox-casters, weapons, spare energy cells and all manner of other materiel required by a command staff. The frescoed walls were covered with more charts, communiqués, casualty lists, cracked or static-filled comms-screens, recon reports and assorted paraphernalia.

There were sixteen other men in the room; fifteen of them Brade's support officers and the other Master Issachar of the Third Company. All were watching the confrontation.

'Do not speak to me of authority. This building was once the demesne of Imperial Commander Sousan, was it not? Where is she now? Slain, by a mob of her own people. You, and you alone, Colonel Brade, took it upon yourself to install her successor, involving yourself in the political struggle that has seen this world fall to alien invaders and heretics. You are a traitor and will be dealt with accordingly.'

Brade's anger burst through the dam of his terror.

'Traitor?' The commander screamed the word. 'You call me traitor? It was your warriors that came here and attacked us! It was your glorious Chapter that capitalised on the ork resurgence to murder lawful, faithful citizens of Piscina. It was not I that instigated rebellion, Chaplain Asmodai, it was you. And you dare call me traitor?'

The colonel's claims that a force of Dark Angels had killed a large number of civilians, though as yet uncorroborated, were known to Asmodai. Brade's incarceration would facilitate a more thorough inquiry into the events that had plunged Piscina into madness, and would also serve to stifle the rumours still running rampant across Kadillus Harbour – rumours that Asmodai and the other members of the Inner Circle were working hard to keep from the ears of the battle-brethren.

'From your own lips you are condemned,' said Asmodai. He wagged an armoured finger at Brade. The colonel retreated but Asmodai gave him no space, following up with long strides. 'It is only in deference to your efforts against the orks that you are still alive. Treachery such as yours, the wanton defiance of your Imperial commander appointed from Holy Terra, makes you an enemy of the Imperium. Few such foes have opportunity to speak in their defence when confronted by the Dark Angels.'

Brade turned to Issachar, opening his arms as he implored the Dark Angels captain.

'You must see that this is madness? The orks are still active within the city and there are many of our people too afraid of the Adeptus Astartes to ever surrender to the Dark Angels. If you depose me they will only see further injustice and fight all the harder.'

'His opinion is also irrelevant,' Asmodai snapped before Issachar could offer a reply. 'The rebels will be killed if they continue to resist, and the orks will be cleansed. These are not matters for debate. I would no more allow a potential traitor to continue to command military forces in this city than I would invite the orks to a parley aboard the Rock. Hand over your weapon and relinquish command before I take sterner action.'

'My opinion is irrelevant?' Issachar said the words slowly, as though he was only just catching up with events. 'I am commander of the Third Company, tasked with securing these palaces. Brother, you overstep your remit if you think you can remove one of my allies from his duties.'

'Do not take false umbrage at my curt manner, Master Issachar,' answered Asmodai, irritated by the captain's defiant tone. 'Our orders are direct from the Supreme Grand Master. I am well within my authority to have Colonel Brade removed from power and to subject him to questioning. The palace grounds have been secured for several days. I do not understand your tardiness in prosecuting further attacks against the rebels and greenskins.'

There was a buzz as the command channel activated. Issachar strode across the hall to confront Asmodai, his manner making his intent clear even though his words were for the Chaplain alone.

'Do not seek to teach me my duty, Asmodai.' Issachar growled, amplified by the vox-net to sound like an attacking cudbear.

'This is no matter for a simple Company Master,' said Asmodai, seeking to make sense of Issachar's objections. 'While I bow to your judgement on purely military decisions, the acts of Colonel Brade and his men are treasonous, and that is a poison that can infect the minds of others, making it my responsibility. The Piscinan Free Militia are a tarnished, spent force of no strategic value. I do not understand your concerns.'

'And that is your problem, Asmodai.' Issachar shook his head and his tone was sad. 'We have enough enemies to fight without you creating more. Brade is correct – he is best placed to negotiate surrender from the remaining Free Militia still fighting against us.'

'There will be no negotiations. Those who oppose us will be crushed. You allow clear judgement to be clouded by indecent camaraderie with these defence forces. You are mistaken to place any trust in their loyalty or ability, brother-captain.'

'But this is *my* decision, not yours, Asmodai, and I will not have you undermine my command.'

Asmodai was stunned by Issachar's hypocrisy, actually lost for words by the arrogance of his battle-brother. His silence lasted only moments though, as outrage at the Company Master's accusation brought forth fresh words.

'Do you think it is acceptable to defy *me* in front of outsiders?' Asmodai's anger bubbled up like blood from a wound, giving his words even greater vehemence. 'I am the Master of Repentance! None is more loyal to the Chapter and the ideals of the Lion than I. It is not you that stands judgement over others, it is I! I was willing to forgive your disrespect as a momentary lapse, but this insubordination will be punished. I have made my will known – it is your duty to enact it.'

A loud bang had both Space Marines spinning towards the near end of the hall, their weapons ready. The great double doors swung in, revealing Chaplain Sapphon, his robes and armour dirtied by blood and grime from recent battle. The Master of Sanctity strode into the room and headed directly for Asmodai. For a split-second the Master of Repentance thought his superior would strike him, but instead Sapphon laid a hand on Asmodai's arm, gesturing for him to lower his crozius.

'Master Issachar, forgive this intrusion,' said Sapphon over the command link, glancing at the captain before fixing his look on Asmodai. 'If you would excuse my brother and I, there is urgent news to discuss. Brother Asmodai, accompany me to the antechamber.'

Asmodai took in a long, deep breath, agitated by the interruption.

'This matter will be raised with the Supreme Grand Master, Issachar,' Asmodai warned.

Issachar said nothing. The captain stalked away, waving for Brade to join him at a crackling hololith vid unit showing the western half of the city.

'Brother Sapphon, why are you here?' Asmodai asked, genuinely confused. 'I heard no report that the Deathwing assault had been concluded. Have we secured victory?'

Sapphon said nothing in reply, but simply pointed back through the doors. Bemused, Asmodai followed his superior out of the hall.

MISPLACED ZEAL

'Walk with me, brother,' said Sapphon. He released his helm with a hiss of escaping air and turned his head to look at Asmodai beside him. Warriors from the Third Company kept watch at the corridors and archways leading from the passage ahead, while messenger boys of the Free Militia scurried back and forth bringing reports for Brade and carrying orders to the defence forces still operating across Kadillus Harbour.

Sapphon spied a disused room ahead, its shattered window poorly boarded, the remnants of table and chairs piled to one side. There was no door but the chamber was secluded enough for Sapphon's purpose.

'Remove your helmet, brother, and let me look at your face while we speak.'

Asmodai did has he was bade, revealing features almost as skeletal as those on the mask he removed – sharp cheek bones, sunken eyes and a shaven head. His skin was much darker than bone, save for scar tissue that carved pale streaks on his forehead and left cheek. Dark eyes stared at Sapphon without hint of shame or circumspection.

'Why did you come to the Imperial commander's palace, brother?' Sapphon asked, placing his helm on the cracked mantel above an ash-choked fireplace. 'Specifically, why are you not with the Ninth Company as I ordered?'

'My greater duty was here, when I heard that Brade had returned to the scene of his treachery,' said Asmodai.

'Your greater duty was to lead the Ninth in battle against the orks at Koth Ridge and the East Barrens. Perhaps you felt that task beneath one of your station?'

A snarl curled Asmodai's lip.

'Do not suspect me of arrogance, brother. And do not confuse humility with meekness.'

Sapphon ignored the rebuke.

'I know you, Asmodai, so show me the respect due to my position by not trying to coerce me. You use anger to get at the truth. You rile your subjects until they speak in haste or betray themselves with unconscious twitch or tic.' Sapphon dropped his voice, so low that even a Space Marine like Asmodai would be forced to concentrate to hear it, demanding attention. 'I am not in the wrong here.'

'If you have accusation, brother, make it plainly.'

'For the remainder of this conversation you will refer to me by my rank, not as brother,' Sapphon said sternly. Asmodai's brow furrowed, but Sapphon gave him no opportunity to voice dissent – another favoured tactic of the Chaplain was to browbeat his victims with a continuous tirade. Seventeen hours without pause was, according to Chapter rumour and illicit wagers, Asmodai's longest rant to date. Sapphon continued effortlessly, his words slow and measured. 'You will address me as "master", and you will restrict your answers to a simple affirmative or negative. You will remain silent on all other concerns until I give you permission to speak of other matters. Am I clear?'

'Yes, Master Sapphon,' replied Asmodai, lips and jaw barely moving to form the words.

'Colonel Brade's actions will be scrutinised in due course. It is not the place of the Adeptus Astartes to form trial and jury of members of planetary defence forces.'

'I spoke of no trial, master. Only tha–'

'Must I make you swear an oath of silence?' Sapphon asked quietly. He had caught the rebuke and lowered his tone before it left his lips, refusing to rise to Asmodai's bait. Any amount of shouting and remonstration would have no effect on the thick-skinned Chaplain. Sapphon was determined that, just for once, Asmodai would think about his actions from some other perspective than through the warped prism of his zealotry.

'No, master.' Asmodai stood stock still, hands clasped at his chest, eyes following Sapphon like a hawk watching its prey as the Master of Sanctity started to pace in front of the fireplace. The Chaplain's immobility was in direct opposition to Sapphon's need for movement.

'Your uncompromising nature is lauded by the Supreme Grand Master, and in battle there are none that would not fight beside you. Your efforts against the oldest foe are remarkable and your dedication exemplary. However, why must you seek confrontation so readily? Are there not foes enough in the galaxy for us to fight?'

Sapphon could see Asmodai was straining to speak, to defend himself, not realising the questions were rhetorical. The Master of Sanctity did not care; it made a change that Asmodai was the one feeling discomfort. He continued, head bowed, not looking at his subordinate.

'For all your accomplishments, and your seniority, the Inner Circle chose me to succeed as Master of Sanctity.' Sapphon looked at the other Chaplain. 'You are unstable, Asmodai. Worse, you are destabilising. You are a catalyst for dissent, and the harder you react against the infractions of others the more they will resent you for your lack of fraternal understanding.'

The other Chaplain looked as though he was going to explode, the blood vessels in his neck pulsing with the twin beats of his hearts, a particular scar above his right eye almost pure white against reddening flesh. Still Sapphon would not allow Asmodai to speak.

'There are two places where you are of use, Asmodai. The first is in the interrogation cell. The second is on the battlefield.' Sapphon strode to the door and looked left and right theatrically before turning back to Asmodai. The Chaplain's eyes were narrowed, jaw twitching with indignity. There was no verbal or physical abuse that Sapphon could employ that would make his companion repent of his actions, so only the threat of further humiliation remained. 'I see neither, and yet here you are. I ask again, why are you not with the Ninth?'

With no specific charge to defend himself against, Asmodai was confronted by the truth behind the question. He answered as if the words were being dragged out of him under pain of death. His fingers flexed into fists and splayed out again in a slow rhythm.

'Because I disobeyed your orders, master.'

'Yes, brother,' said Sapphon. It pleased the Master of Sanctity to see Asmodai flinch at the use of the more familiar term. 'When confronted with this fact, does it matter the reason for disobedience? How would you deal with such insubordination? The same insubordination of which you have just accused Master Issachar, I might add.'

Asmodai swallowed hard and finally – finally! – looked away, casting his gaze at the ground for a moment, the first sign of shame he had shown since Sapphon's arrival. He did not speak, and Sapphon took this as a good sign.

'You make me appear weak, brother,' Sapphon admitted. Asmodai looked shocked at the revelation. 'And, compared to you, in some ways I am. The brethren take liberties in front of me that would not enter their minds in your presence. They speak out of turn. They are flippant. But, they never disobey orders. Only you dare to go that far. Do you think I am weak, Brother Asmodai?'

'Yes,' said the Chaplain. 'Punishment cleanses the soul and restores discipline. You are too tolerant. Your indulgences spoil the battle-brothers and engender further disobedience. It is also this attitude that sees you fail in the interrogation cells.'

Sapphon smiled grimly. Whatever personality defects affected Asmodai, dishonesty was not amongst them.

'And you consider my elevation to my role as a mistake by the Inner Circle?'

'I made my opposition clear at the time. The Grand Masters chose to promote you against my objections.'

'And did you swear to abide by their decision?'

Again Asmodai looked uncomfortable for a moment, realising he had been manoeuvred into a difficult admission.

'Yes, master,' is all he said, offering no defence.

'And so will you now carry out the orders as I lay them out?'

'Yes, master,' said Asmodai. 'I will join the Ninth as soon as transport is available.'

'Leave me. Penance will be evaluated after the planet is secure.'

Asmodai fitted his helmet, the white skull with its shining red eyes a relief to Sapphon after the intensity of the Chaplain's unmasked appearance.

'For the Lion!' barked Asmodai,

'For the Emperor!' replied Sapphon.

The Master of Sanctity watched his companion leave. He shook his head in disbelief and took up his helmet. He was about to depart when Master Issachar appeared at the doorway.

'Why does the Supreme Grand Master tolerate him?' asked the company captain, looking back into the corridor though Asmodai was no longer in sight. 'He is disruptive, antagonistic and volatile. On the one hand Brother Asmodai will seek penance for any misdemeanour whilst on the other blatantly flaunting the demands of his superiors. He is blind to his own arrogance and hypocrisy.'

'He has his uses. Sometimes we must be reminded that moderation and mercy are choices, not necessities. Brother Asmodai answers to a far higher authority and sterner code than the rest of us.'

'Really? You think he fears the Emperor's judgement?'

Sapphon laughed. 'The Emperor's... Of course not. The Emperor loves His sons, and it was this love that the traitors exploited. No, there is a far harsher judge that Asmodai fears. One that holds no love for any creature. Himself.'

As they headed back towards the temporary headquarters in the hall, Sapphon considered Asmodai's peculiar brand of paranoia. His methods were as subtle as a bolt-round to the face, but often his motives were not wrong. Colonel Brade had indeed witnessed first-hand a possible incident involving the Fallen. It was not wise that he be allowed to remain at large. And following the overthrow of Imperial Commander Sousan it would not be long before the Inquisition started taking an interest in what had transpired in the Piscina system. It would be up to the Supreme Grand Master to decide what to do with the Piscinans that had come into contact with the traitors, but the time had come to start limiting any possible damage.

'Have Colonel Brade join me in the Imperial commander's chambers, please,' he told Issachar. Even though ranked a Company Master, Issachar was not a member of the Inner Circle. There was no need to have him involved in anything more than he already was. 'I should make peace.'

Some things were better done without noise and fuss. That was why the Inner Circle had chosen Sapphon over Asmodai.

PENITENT WARRIORS

High above Piscina the bulk of the Dark Angels fleet lay in orbit. Amongst rapid strike vessels, strike cruisers, battle-barges, scout ships and resupply tenders sat the Rock, fortress-monastery of the Chapter. Protected by vast banks of void shields, surrounded by a constellation of smaller asteroids and defence platforms, the Rock dwarfed everything around it. Launch bays and weapon batteries were dug into the kilometres-thick base, which had once been bedrock from honoured, destroyed Caliban. Upon this immense fragment sat the edifice known as the Tower of Angels, spire after spire, hall and gallery heaped upon each other, piercing the firmament. Thousands of lights twinkled from arched windows. Stained glass dappled pitted stone and ferrocrete with many colours. Once renowned as Aldurukh, citadel of the Order that raised the Dark Angels primarch, it was now home to the warriors who carried the gene-seed of the Lion.

Another vessel, a strike cruiser two kilometres long,

moved into the shadow cast by the Rock. A Thunder-hawk gunship emerged from one of the flight bays of the *Penitent Warrior*, a tiny spark soon swallowed by the bulk of the fortress-monastery.

On board sat brothers Telemenus, Menthius and Daellon. Telemenus and Daellon were in full armour, while Menthius was still clad in robes, his hideous burns not quite healed. The latter's face and bared arms were a mess of scar tissue, exposed flesh contorted with strange whorls left by the traitor's psychic attack on Thyestes. His nose was nothing more than shaped metal plate installed by the Apothecaries, while breathing tubes jutted from his throat and down past the collar of his robe. His wheezing was accompanied by a dull ticking of some machine hidden inside the remains of his lungs.

With them was Veteran Sergeant Seraphiel, who regarded them sternly, his helm cradled in his lap.

'It will take time for you to adjust,' said Seraphiel, stroking an armoured finger across the fleur-de-lys painted on the side of his helm in dark red. Telemenus was not sure what the badge signified, but assumed it was some honour the veteran sergeant had earned whilst he had fought in the First Company. 'To be a warrior in the Death-wing is different to everything else you have experienced. Even these last two months of confinement, segregated from your brothers to protect their innocence, will seem as nothing compared to the strain of being one of the Chapter's elite.'

Telemenus allowed his gaze to wander, looking out of the armoured port beside the veteran sergeant. A row of hooded warriors carved a hundred metres high in dark marble sped past as the Thunderhawk banked alongside the Rock, their grim faces lit by red navigational lamps. They moved out of view when the gunship levelled and started its descent towards one of the lower flight bays.

'Telemenus!' Seraphiel's sharp tone tore back the Space Marine's attention. 'Do not think for one moment that your elevation to the First Company signifies an end to your drills and regular duties. What you will learn next will change your whole view of the universe.'

The sergeant's voice drifted away momentarily, caught up in some memory or other. His tone was soft, sad when he spoke next.

'Everything you believe to be of value will be questioned. Every truth to which you cling will be tested. What you are about to face is a sterner challenge than any you have yet overcome.' Seraphiel leaned forward, straining the harness that held him to the bench. 'You think that you gave up everything when you became a Dark Angel? Your childhood? Your name? Your family and past? Perhaps you believe that there is nothing more you can sacrifice for the Lion and the Emperor. You are wrong. Nothing will prepare you for what you are about to learn.'

Telemenus was not so sure of this truth. He did not know by what circumstance Seraphiel had been elevated to the Deathwing, would probably never know, but the change it had wrought on his psyche was writ clear across his tormented expression. The former Fifth Company marksman, on the other hand, had some suspicion of what was to come. He remembered clearly the last events of Thyestes.

The psyker drew a long blade, its edges glimmering balefully with a sickening yellow light. Unperturbed by the bolts shrieking around him, he strode towards the squad. Telemenus could see that his skin was pale like a corpse, the bones of his cheeks showing through torn flesh, eyes red with thick veins.

'Brave but foolish, brothers,' the traitor declared in a rasping voice. His words were accompanied by a gust of air that carried the stench of effluent and rotting meat. 'Your masters have betrayed you.'

Giving up all thoughts of taking the warrior alive, Telemenus emptied his magazine at the ghastly apparition. As before, the bolts did not hit. Nemeon steadied himself again for another missile shot, but was too slow. The psyker thrust his sword in the Space Marine's direction, a blast of churning warp energy flying from its tip to smash Nemeon from his feet. His armour crumbled, turning to dust in moments, exposed flesh wrinkling and decaying beneath.

Apollon fell next, sent spinning to the ground by a fresh wave of psychic lightning that surrounded him with a cloud of energy. Telemenus skirted to his right, glancing at his battle-brother's twitching body.

'It is folly to oppose me, brothers,' the psyker spoke without malice, blood trickling from split lips as he uttered the words. 'Your sacrifice will go unremembered, your glory unrewarded.'

'I am no brother of yours,' snarled Daellon. A swirl of burning promethium engulfed the enemy warrior, setting fire to his cloak and hair. The psyker staggered to the left and raised his empty hand against the inferno. More sickly yellow light spilled from his open palm, pushing back against the gout of flames.

Fingers curling into a fist, the psyker seemed to grab hold of the streaming promethium, lashing it like a whip back at Daellon. The Dark Angel flung the flamer away and dived to the ground as its fuel canister exploded, showering the defile with burning liquid.

'You are all my brothers,' the psyker continued. 'If your blind masters had half the honour you possess, they would tell you the truth. I was once like you.'

'I know you, traitor,' said Telemenus. 'You have shunned the

Emperor and have no honour. You have the filthy heart of a traitor even if you were once a Space Marine.'

The psyker grinned, bearing a few rotted, pointed teeth, even as flecks of promethium continued to burn through the flesh of his face and flickered on his armour.

'Not just a Space Marine, brother. A Dark Angel.'

Menthius and Daellon had heard the declaration too, but they had both been barely conscious. Telemenus had looked the traitor in the face, seen the vile truth for what it was; a Dark Angel corrupted by the evil forces that had turned Legion against Legion at the dawn of the Imperium. Through sixty-three days of travel from Thyestes, separated from their battle-brothers, the three of them had not raised a word concerning what they had seen. Only in momentary glances, in occasional silences or an intake of breath did they share the experience.

He wondered why it had never occurred to him before. Why had he never considered the possibility that evil intent had touched the Dark Angels as it had laid its grip upon World Eaters and Word Bearers, Death Guard and other traitors? Seraphiel was correct in one regard; it made Telemenus reconsider everything he believed to be true. If the Dark Angels had been touched, what of the Ultramarines? There were many rumours concerning the Blood Angels, and the Space Wolves still verged on heresy to this day. What of the Iron Hands, White Scars and the Salamanders, had they too felt the dagger of treachery from within?

'I see that my words stir something in you,' said Seraphiel. 'Questions without answers? Doubts?'

This last word hung in the air like a toxic fog. Doubt. It was doubt that the Chaplains crushed with their words. Doubt was the harbinger of fear, of ambition, of wilfulness. Now Telemenus realised that doubt was also the herald of something even more deadly. Doubt fed itself. Even now he wondered why he and his brothers had not been told the truth. There were secrets in the hearts of the Dark Angels officers, kept from the battle-brothers with cynical intent.

The thought vexed him, made him angry and something of his mind must have showed on his face.

'Yes, doubt is the worst foe, is it not, Telemenus? You cannot hide from it. You cannot slay it with a bolter-round. You cannot flee from it. Only force of will, true strength of character can eliminate doubt.' Seraphiel turned his attention to Menthius. The sergeant seemed to be taking some perverse satisfaction from the discomfort of his fellow Space Marines, though it may have been relief at being able to share a burden long carried without comment. 'Your scars are a badge of honour, testament to a duty fulfilled. They will help you. Whenever doubt creeps in, the doubt of our righteous cause, the doubt that comes with knowing the true purpose of the Deathwing, you can look at those scars and remember the face of the creature that inflicted them upon you. You will know the nature of the evil we seek to vanquish. Against the armour of those scars doubt will be blunted, unable to harm you.'

A chime indicated that they were sixty seconds from docking. The ports went dark for a moment and then bright light flooded in from the flight bay. The four Space Marines released their restraints and stood up, helms held in their hands. There was a clang and a shudder as the Thunderhawk touched down. The assault ramp at the nose of the gunship whined open, revealing a solitary figure in a sleeveless robe of off-white.

'Grand Master Belial awaits,' said Seraphiel. As the

others filed past him he stood for a moment, gripping wrist-to-wrist with each in a warrior's bond. He stopped Telemenus for a moment with a hand on his arm. 'You are a fine warrior, just remember to keep your pride in check. You were one of the best of the Fifth, but now you are the lowliest of the First. You shall stride amongst the greatest of the Chapter, and do so with honour, but never forget that service is its own reward.'

'Only in death does duty end,' Telemenus replied with a nod. 'Your concern is unwarranted, have no worries on account of my accomplishments. The glory I will earn in the Deathwing will make First Marksman a pale achievement in comparison.'

Seraphiel sighed and shook his head. The sergeant waved for Telemenus to follow his brothers and when the Space Marine reached the ramp he glanced back to see Seraphiel sat down, head bowed in thought.

Joining his two companions, Telemenus had opportunity to see Grand Master Belial properly for the first time. The commander of the First Company, Bearer of the Sword of Silence, had until that moment been a distant, rarely-glimpsed figure for warriors outside the Deathwing.

Dressed in ceremonial robes, Belial seemed no taller or bigger than any other Space Marine. His hair was cropped almost to the scalp, chin and cheeks darkened with stubble that indicated he had been in combat and unable to perform the ritual hygienic cleansing expected of every Dark Angel. His face was expressionless as he watched Telemenus come to attention at the end of the short line. On the right breast of his robe was embroidered the scarlet wings-and-broken-blade sigil of the Deathwing, and on the left a shield bearing a cloaked and hooded figure as heraldry. From his belt were hung three large keys, and in its scabbard the famed Sword of Silence; one of the three Heavenfall blades forged from meteoric stone in the Chapter's ancient past.

'You are tardy,' said Belial, staring a hole through Telemenus.

'Brother Seraphiel had parting words for me, Grand Master,' replied the Space Marine.

'Did I ask for explanation?'

Taken aback by the question, Telemenus shook his head in reply. Belial's brow furrowed deeply.

'Speak when spoken to.'

'No, Grand Master, you did not ask for explanation.'

Belial considered this. Behind the newest members of the Deathwing the Thunderhawk's engines built to a roar and Telemenus felt the warm wash of its departure on the back of his neck. He kept his eyes on Belial as the Grand Master examined Daellon and Menthius. The commander of the First scrutinised the latter at length, looking him up and down with a calculating eye.

'Have the Apothecaries cleared you for combat?' asked Belial.

'No, Grand Master.' Menthius cast his gaze ground-wards, as if this fact were somehow his fault. Telemenus could feel Menthius trembling with shame beside him.

'If you cannot fight you cannot train.' Belial crossed his arms, and it was then that Telemenus noticed the tattoos that lined the Grand Master's flesh, from shoulder to elbow, lines of miniscule text on the melan-chromatically-darkened skin. Belial noticed Telemenus's interest and stepped in front of him, raising and flexing his massive bicep so that the Space Marine could see more clearly what was written there.

They were lines from the Liturgies of Battle, scribed with a neat, rounded script. Some were repeated over and over, others written only once. Telemenus wanted to ask what they were for but knew that to speak would invite further recrimination from the merciless Grand Master. However, Belial read the question in Telemenus's expression.

'Lessons not to be forgotten,' the commander said by way of explanation. He turned away and started towards the door. 'Brother Daellon, you will report to quarters and await further instruction. Brother Menthius, you will report to the apothecarion for further treatment. Brother Telemenus...'

Belial turned back, his gaze as hard as flint as he looked at his newest warrior.

'Brother Telemenus, you will report to the Chaplains for two days penance and contemplation for the disrespect you have shown me. Use the time to reflect on the necessity of making apology when you keep a superior waiting. You may also like to think on the importance of first impressions. I will be watching you closely.'

'Yes, Grand Master,' the three Space Marines said in unison.

When Belial had exited the flight bay, all three let out long, relieved exhalations. Menthius slapped Telemenus on the shoulder and grinned.

'You always want to stand out, brother. I think it is safe to say that by the end of the day everyone in the Deathwing will have heard of you.'

'Really, brother?' Telemenus smiled at the thought. 'You think they will be pleased to welcome a former First Marksman into their ranks?'

'You misunderstand me, brother,' laughed Menthius. 'I think you will be known as First Penitent, who earned the ire of the Grand Master before you had even met!'

THE SEVENTH RITE

The door behind Annael closed, plunging him into utter darkness. There was not a single mote of light in the Reclusiam, and turning his head Annael could not even see Sabrael though his battle-brother stood within arm's reach to his right.

'Perhaps Chaplain Malcifer requires new light globes for his chambers,' said Sabrael.

'Shut up,' said Annael, feeling tainted by his companion's poor humour.

This was a grave occasion; the Seventh Rite of the Raven. On completion of the ceremony the two of them would formally ascend to the rank of Black Knights. Sabrael had been glib about the import of this event since they had received the summons ten hours ago. Over that time the two of them had fasted, as instructed, and spent their time in their dormitory, meditating on their duties and the history of the Ravenwing.

It was the culmination of what had seemed to Annael

like exile. They had left behind Squadron Cassiel, but had not truly become Black Knights. This limbo had existed for over fifty days, during which the only other warriors they had seen had been Malcifer and Grand Master Sammael.

Straining every sense, Annael was sure they were alone. He heard neither a whisper of cloth, nor a breath. He licked his lips, telling himself that it was the hot, dry air and not apprehension that was sucking all of the moisture from his mouth.

The darkness seemed to expand, growing deeper and wider, though that was impossible. The longer Annael stared, the more uncertain he became. Perhaps he was not really in the reclusiam aboard the Ravenwing's specialist cruiser, the *Implacable Justice*. It was more likely that he was dreaming, asleep on his cot in their sparsely furnished dorm. Utter blackness such as surrounded him now could not really exist, and the sense of disorientation was but an element of the dream.

Yet he had not had a dream for centuries. The Apothecaries had once explained it was something to do with the integration of the catalepsean node that allowed him to rest different parts of his brain whilst remaining awake that interrupted the usual cycle and rapid eye movement that brought a dream state.

Or at least, he would likely never remember his dreams, they said.

Alone in the dark – for Sabrael was clearly another figment of the dream – Annael was struck by a sudden thought. Perhaps the masters of the Chapter did not want the battle-brothers to dream. He could barely remember those he had experienced as a child so long ago, but he vaguely recalled flights of fantasy, of unfettered exploration and curiosity. Dreams made one wonder about reality, to question the nature of things. Since coming to the Ravenwing Annael had learned that such trains of thought were discouraged amongst the other battle-brothers. Curiosity, initiative, independence were vices, straining the bonds that held the Chapter together. It had been a moment of uncharacteristic inquisitiveness that had brought Annael to the attention of his superiors and consequently redeployment to the Ravenwing.

The darkness was becoming a living thing, tangible, replacing the air, seeping into Annael's lungs. His hearts were beating steadily, and he felt relaxed, comforted by the embracing blackness. He was Ravenwing, and that was to live in the shadows, to be one with the dark nature of the galaxy. To wear the black, to bear the shadow inside oneself was an honour, though a secret one.

And another unlikely moment, a strange instinct that had made him follow wayward Sabrael instead of obeying orders, had now set him on this path. He had thought long and hard during his isolation but had no answers for why he had chosen to save the Imperial commander of Thyestes rather than press the attack against his Death Guard captors. Annael recalled the words of Grand Master Sammael.

'There is a greater punishment in store for the both of you. You have seen a deeper truth than most. It is not honour or glory to act without thought, simply obeying orders for their own sake. I place a great burden upon you, because you have shown the character and strength of will to bear it in silence, resolute and unyielding. I am short of Black Knights and you will serve me in that role.

'Some may think this reward for your ill-discipline, but do not take it as such. As Black Knights you will be subject to the highest demands of body and soul. It is an onerous duty, but one of which you are both capable. When you have passed the

Seventh Rite of the Raven you will understand that the truth is the harshest master to serve.'

The Seventh Rite of the Raven. It would be coming soon. The dream was a manifestation of anxiety, that much was obvious. The darkness was merely a symptom of perfectly understandable concerns. The feeling of disembodiment was only an expression of unconscious helplessness, confronting a past that could not be changed.

Time had no meaning, his subconscious awareness of its passing eroded by the nothingness that surrounded and devoured him. Annael was becoming the darkness. He was becoming the shadow. He wondered if he was real at all and lifted a hand in front of his face. He felt the slightest movement of air on his cheek and was reassured that he had not become completely incorporeal.

'In the void there is nothing but darkness.'

Annael flinched, startled. The voice was soft, but in breaking the silence the words were a deafening shout.

'In the darkness we dwell,' chorused more voices in response.

As his nerves settled Annael was aware that he was not alone. There were others in the Reclusiam with him, though how they had entered without his knowing was beyond him. He had not heard the slightest sound or felt the softest motion.

'The past is shrouded by shadows.'

Annael now recognised the voice of Chaplain Malcifer, clear, unhindered by helm vocaliser or vox. The sound rebounded oddly from the buttresses of the Reclusiam walls, but Annael was pretty sure the Chaplain was standing a few metres in front of him.

'In the shadows we seek the truth,' replied three voices.

The respondents were behind him and Sabrael, no

more than a couple of metres away. Annael could smell
them now as his senses adapted to the lack of vision.
A rustle of a robe, the gentlest breath of air against the
nape of his neck when the others spoke.

'By its nature the truth shall be found.'

'The truth is light.'

At these words, the lamps of the Reclusiam blazed into
life, blinding Annael. Next to him Sabrael raised a hand
to ward away the sudden glare while Annael blinked
furiously, seeing thin, indistinct silhouettes passing to
either side. As his vision recovered he saw Chaplain Malcifer in black robes, the hood that hid most of his face
decorated with the sigil of the Ravenwing. Beneath the
cowl glinted a white skull mask, a symbol of his position
as Chaplain.

To Malcifer's right stood Huntmaster Tybalain. The left
breast of his robe was embroidered with a silver hammer
shaped in the head of a raven, duplicating the corvus
hammers the Black Knights wielded from their bikes.
Tybalain's right cheek was slashed with a white scar from
nose to ear, the puckered edges of the old wound pierced
with a row of twelve dagger-like pins. Annael had not
noticed before – he had never seen the Huntmaster so
close – but there was a miniscule ruby shaped as a drop
of blood at the end of each.

To either side of Annael and Sabrael waited two more
Space Marines in the black vestments of the Ravenwing.
Their faces were hidden but Annael guessed at their
identities: Brothers Calatus and Nerean who were the
survivors of Tybalain's squadron – Brother Demesius
had been killed by the Death Guard during the attack
on their camp at Thyestes; the squadron of Huntmaster
Charael had been wiped out to a man. Thinking on those
events reminded him of seeing his squadron-brothers,

Araton and Zarall, armour oddly tattered, dead and broken on the snow by cruel fate and a vicious enemy. The Ravenwing had suffered savage losses, nearly a third of their number slain and the same wounded, the fighting drawn out and bitter against the renegade Space Marines who had fought to the last rather than be captured. It would be some time before the company was restored to strength and able to hunt alone.

Annael had felt some measure of guilt at his part in it until both Malcifer and Sammael had told him separately that had he and Sabrael remained with Araton they would likely be dead also, slain by the traitor Librarian they had been hunting; a powerful psyker who had slain more than a dozen Dark Angels with witchery and psychic blade during his attempted escape.

It struck Annael that had not the Black Knights suffered such serious casualties, he and Sabrael might not have been elevated into their depleted ranks. Were they truly worthy, or simply convenient candidates for a Grand Master wishing to retain some morale and honour by such appointment? Annael was saved from further thoughts on the matter by a declaration from Malcifer.

'As we wear the black, the Ravenwing must be creatures of shadow. The truth is a fickle, cautious prey, oft hiding in the deepest recesses, reluctant to be drawn into the light. It is our job to fetch it forth, to see it scrutinised. To do so, we must know the spoor of our quarry, be prepared to recognise deceit for what it is – the camouflage of truth. To see clearly in the darkness we must bring our own light with us. That light is knowledge.'

The Chaplain motioned for Annael and Sabrael to kneel. They did so without comment, eyes fixed on him. Malcifer moved to the wall behind the altar and laid a hand on the silver plaque placed there.

'The Hunt began long ago, under the auspices of the Grand Masters in the wake of the Great Treachery. Some of what transpired has been made known to you, from my lips and that of Sammael, who are the bearers of this truth. We told you of the fall of Caliban, our home destroyed by traitors in league with the arch-heretic Horus, thrice-cursed, may his soul burn in torment forever.' Malcifer sighed, his expression one of sadness not anger. He started to walk around the walls of the Reclusiam, trailing his fingers over the plaques bearing the names of the one hundred and seventy-two Grand Masters of the Ravenwing. 'An ancient philosopher once said that the truth is the first casualty of war. He was wrong. In war we see truth everywhere. The truth etched into the faces of the slayer and the slain. The truth of men's hearts and whether they are heroes or cowards. War brings forth the simple truth, of the righteousness of our cause, of our superiority at arms, of our unflinching devotion to the Emperor. These are the only truths that matter. All else is supposition, politics and hearsay.'

Moving out of sight behind Annael, the Chaplain did not speak, the only sound the soft tread of his boots on the stone-laid floor. The footsteps stopped. Annael focused on the altar a dozen metres in front of him; his reflection in the polished titanium, and the black marble sigil of the Dark Angels worked into its surface. Malcifer remained silent, letting his words sink into the thoughts of the two newly-appointed Black Knights. A part of Annael was glad that even Sabrael had been cowed by the gravitas of the moment; he could not bear the thought of the shame if his companion thought it clever to make an improper remark at this juncture.

In the absence of speech from the Chaplain and Sabrael, Annael found himself wondering what it must have been like for those Dark Angels, the ones that had faced the Horus Heresy and survived. How had they continued? What depths of strength, what reserves of courage must they have been forced to reach into to keep true to their oaths in the face of such horror? He remembered how distraught he had felt upon learning of the existence of Space Marines that had become traitors; the shock of being told the manner of the Lion's death was as fresh as if the knowledge had come to him only yesterday. Hearing of it ten thousand years later had been hard enough and he wondered how the Dark Angels of that distant epoch had managed to survive, bereft of their primarch, all they had fought to build lying shattered around them.

'Knowledge is so precious that we must guard it with our lives.' Malcifer's claim struck Annael as odd, that the words meant something beyond the obvious, but he did not have time to ponder why before the Chaplain continued. 'It is a scarce resource, and must be rationed and apportioned accordingly. Knowledge in the wrong hands can be misused. Knowledge not treated with care and consideration will spread itself, changing and mutating itself into deception and ignorance. No truth is there greater than that a little knowledge is a dangerous thing. Better no knowledge than half-truths, for a half-truth is no better than a lie.'

Annael was trying hard to understand the Chaplain's meaning and was not sure whether Malcifer was making some deeper point without wishing to utter it openly. It worried Annael that he might not comprehend the essential lesson being imparted.

The Chaplain completed his circuit of the Reclusiam and took his place between the Black Knights in front of the altar. With a nod from Malcifer, Tybalain and his men turned and filed out of the chamber through a curtained doorway to Annael's right. The Chaplain remained with head bowed, his voice dropping to a whisper.

'It is with deepest shame that I must offer apology on behalf of all those who are guardians of knowledge, and with profound regret inform you that what you have been told before is not the truth.'

Annael felt Sabrael stir next to him, a slow shake of the head and a sigh. The pronouncement surprised Annael too, for he had believed he had been told the truth when he had been inducted into the Ravenwing. Malcifer called into question all of the teachings of the Chapter with that single admission. The Chaplain knew as much; Annael could feel Malcifer studying him, the glimmer of eyes staring at him through the lenses of the skull mask.

'When you have learned that which has been kept from you, you will understand the need for circumspection, as you came to accept the need for secrecy when you were brought into the fold of the Ravenwing.' Malcifer raised his hands to his chest and knotted his fingers together as if in prayer. Behind him Tybalain and the others returned. Calatus and Nerean each carried a long-handled mattock with a head shaped like a bird's beak – the corvus hammers of the Black Knights. The three warriors stood in line in front of Malcifer, as if protecting him, hammers thrust towards Annael and Sabrael haft-first.

'In taking up these weapons you are accepting a binding oath to the Chapter and the Emperor. You will swear that you will uphold the lore of the Black Knights of Caliban. You will offer up your lives in protection of the rites and knowledge of the Order. As Black Knights of the Ravenwing you shall be the eyes and ears of your Grand Master not only on the battlefield but amongst your brethren. You shall guard against heresy and rebellion with every fibre and be prepared to lay down not only your life but your honour in the prosecution of our ancient pursuit.'

This last statement sent a flush of anxiety through Annael; a momentary doubt he had never experienced before. What was service to the Emperor, in the name of the Lion and the Chapter, if not done with honour? He was willing to die in an instant to protect his brothers, to fulfil a mission and protect the Emperor's realm. But to sacrifice his good name? To risk being struck from the rolls of honour, to be expunged from the annals of the Dark Angels in shame?

He looked up at Malcifer past Tybalain and the Chaplain noticed the glance. So too did the Huntmaster, whose hard stare had been fixed on Sabrael but now passed to Annael. The battle-brother felt that gaze fall upon him as if he'd been struck, a scrutiny that bore into him, shredding all defence, piercing the walls of duty, honour and dedication that had armoured his soul against doubt, fear and treachery. All was laid bare in that moment as Tybalain knew exactly what Annael dreaded the most and was contemptuous of his fellow Space Marine's weakness.

Annael wanted to blurt out an apology to the Huntmaster and Chaplain; wanted to abase himself and offer atonement for every moment of doubt he had endured since being chosen as an aspirant of the Lion.

For all that the urge swamped him, every instinct crying 'They know, they know,' and a harder, sterner part of Annael kept his gaze level, matching Tybalain's accusation with defiance. Deep in the core of his soul, beneath any momentary worries and concerns, Annael was a Dark Angel Space Marine. He lived and died at the behest of the Chapter, for the service of the Emperor. If his honour, if his name and legacy, was the price required to defend mankind against unimaginable threat, he would be ready to offer it, as willingly as the blood that was surging through his veins.

Tybalain gave the barest hint of a nod, the corners of his lips twitching into a satisfied smile for a microsecond before his stern demeanour returned.

'Yes, brothers, everything you fear and more may come to pass,' said Malcifer. 'Liar, heretic, traitor.' Annael flinched at each word as though they were the striking of bullets in his flesh. 'These things and others you may be called, in life or in death. By your brothers. By those you have sworn to protect. By those you serve, so that their honour can be maintained at the expense of yours. When you became Dark Angels you left your pasts behind. As you become Black Knights you must forfeit your futures. Are you ready?'

'I am ready.'

The words had left Annael's lips before he had registered Malcifer's question. His voice conveyed his utter conviction. Beside him, Sabrael echoed the sentiment.

'Take up your hammers and your rightful place amongst the Black Knights of the Ravenwing, chosen of Sammael.'

Annael took the weapon proffered by Nerean while Sabrael received the hammer brought in by Calatus. The two Black Knights bowed and received the gesture in return as Annael and Sabrael stood up to join the line at a motion from Tybalain.

'So oath is made and accepted, sworn in secrecy, upheld in silence. Know then, the truth of the Seventh Rite of the Raven.' Malcifer drew back his hood and lifted away his mask, revealing an almost paternal look. 'As Ravenwing you have hunted traitors at the behest of the Supreme Grand Master. As Black Knights you must know the full nature of the creatures we bring to justice.

'During the war some call the Horus Heresy, the traitor warmaster drew Space Marines to his rebel cause. This you know. Now you must learn of the shame we all share, for the Dark Angels were not immune to the thrice-cursed traitor's entreaties. Fair Caliban, the birthplace of the Lion, home world of the Legion, was destroyed not by Horus, but by Dark Angels corrupted by their own ambition, who used forbidden warp-tech in an attempt to overthrow the rightful rule of the Lion.'

Malcifer paused while Annael and Sabrael silently absorbed this revelation. Confused, Annael glanced at his companion and saw Sabrael's brow knotted, jaw clenched. The words sank in and Annael started to comprehend what the Chaplain was telling them. Perhaps sensing Annael's instinctual refusal to accept this truth and all that it engendered, Malcifer made it clear.

'The Space Marines we hunt as Ravenwing were once Dark Angels. Their existence has been kept secret for ten thousand years and they are the greatest threat to the Chapter and all who share the gene-seed of the Lion. We call them the Fallen and until the last has been hunted down and brought to account for their sins, there can be no rest.'

The enormity of it welled up inside Annael. He had suspected something – on entering the Ravenwing the notion that there were levels of knowledge to which he was not privy could not be avoided – but he had never in his wildest moments of doubt envisioned something so catastrophic. For ten millennia the Dark Angels had harboured the secret that members of the Lion's own

Legion, the First, Sons of Caliban, had betrayed the Emperor.

With that realisation came something else: hate. At that moment Annael hated the Fallen more than any foe he had ever faced. Their weakness at a time when they had needed to be at their strongest made a mockery of ten thousand years of strife and struggle. Every achievement, every victory and battle honour won by the Dark Angels was meaningless compared to that ancient shame. Every battle-brother who had died in the Emperor's service was vain sacrifice to the ambition of the Fallen. Thinking of those that had died in blessed ignorance he envied them for a moment, for they had believed themselves inheritors of a pure, noble tradition. Then anger returned, for their belief had been a falsehood, rendered iniquitous by the actions of a selfish few at the dawn of the Imperium.

He understood with pinpoint clarity the importance of the Hunt now. Until that stain was expunged, until there were no more traitorous Dark Angels drawing breath, there was no honour. One of the Chapter mottos sprang to mind, more potent than ever before, and he gave voice to it, hands tightening around the haft of his hammer.

'Never forget.' He raised the hammer, head pointing towards the Chapter sigil on the altar. 'Never forgive!'

THE PRISONER

With the whine of the gunship's engines dying behind him, Annael stood on the landing apron looking at the large, ornate gates in front of him. They were wrought from black metal in the design of a winged sword that was mirrored on each side.

In the dark, cavernous room beyond, he could see ten giant figures swathed in thick white robes. They were standing in the shadows between the guttering circles of flame cast by tall candles set around the chamber's walls. Each figure bore a two-handed sword, held upright across chest and face, the sharp edges of the weapons glinting in the erratic light. The ruddy glow flickered off thousands of skulls adorning the walls and ceiling of the vast sepulchre, gleaming in eyeless sockets and shining off polished lipless grins. Many were human, but most were not: a mix of subtle, elongated features; brutal, bucket-jawed aliens; eyeless monstrosities; horned, twisted creatures and many other contorted, inhuman stares looked down upon the assembled Dark Angels.

Alongside Annael was Tybalain, and on the opposite side of the Thunderhawk's ramp waited the other Black Knights. This was the first time they had come together since undergoing the Seventh Rite and Annael was still getting used to the ivory-coloured trim on his black Ravenwing robes, and seeing Sabrael in the same.

Footsteps at the top of the gunship's ramp drew his attention to the prisoner.

Annael did not know his name, and details surrounding his capture were sketchy. All Annael really knew was that the warrior was one of the Fallen, a former Librarian of the Dark Angels Legion who had been run to ground during the assault on the Death Guard camp at Thyestes; as far as he could tell the other Black Knights thought the same and there was no reason to suspect there was anything more to be known.

The prisoner was naked save for a grey loincloth, his body a disgusting mass of scars, sores, open wounds and bruised flesh. Annael wondered what manner of torture or infection could inflict such wounds, but he knew better than to ask there and then. Such queries would be dealt with by Malcifer after the ceremony of presentation was complete. Thick chains bound the man's arms and wrists, his ankles equally shackled. Annael could see tiny runes etched into the links of the black iron, filled with silver that glittered in a way that did not match the candlelight. His head was bound in a metal hood, inscribed with more runes, pierced with lorelai crystal shards that suppressed his psychic talent.

Behind the prisoner came Malcifer and Harahel, fully armoured, as was Grand Master Sammael following them. Gripping the captured warrior by the shoulders the Chaplain and Librarian forced him down the ramp.

The stench from his rotting injuries was almost over-whelming. Annael remembered a similar stink from the encampment and warriors of the Death Guard; decay run rampant, a foetid aura that permeated everything. The captive reminded Annael of the filthy Traitor legion-naires, his scab-encrusted body and lesion-marked flesh perhaps an indication of what lay beneath the corroded armour of the Death Guard.

The solitary toll of a bell brought the assembled guard to attention, both Ravenwing and Deathwing. The great gates in front of the prisoner opened inwards, another clanging of the bell drowning out the hiss of hydrau-lics and creak of ancient hinges. The prisoner took a few steps forward. The Fallen stopped and looked over his shoulder, heavily bloodshot eyes visible through the slit of his iron hood. The glance was met by the unblinking stare of Malcifer's skull mask. The Chap-lain pointed through the gates and shoved the prisoner another step.

'Where are you taking me?' the prisoner demanded, pulling loose from Malcifer's grip.

Harahel was upon him in an instant, sweeping his legs from underneath with the haft of his force axe. As the Fallen crashed to the ground the Dark Angels Librarian pressed the flat of the blade against the Space Marine's bared chest. Light and heat flared, eliciting a howl of pain from the captive warrior. Annael suppressed a wince – he had never heard a Space Marine utter such a noise and could not imagine the agony that brief flow of psychic energy had imparted.

Cowed, the prisoner did not struggle as Malcifer pulled him upright and dragged him through the gate.

'Guard, dismiss,' muttered Sammael. The Grand Master seemed distasteful of the whole ceremony and was quick to head back to the gunship. At a word from Tybalain the Black Knights followed.

As he strode up the ramp, Annael looked back to see Malcifer and Harahel returning to the Thunderhawk. Behind them the gate swung shut as the robed Death-wing closed around the Fallen; he was their responsibility now. At the last moment, he saw a glimpse of bone-white from a Chaplain's helm and then the group was gone, vanishing into the shadows of the tunnel.

'Better not to know,' said Tybalain, following Annael's gaze.

JUDGED

'Methelas, damned by deed and word.'

As he spoke this judgement Chaplain Malcifer almost threw the Fallen warrior into the hands of Brother Asmodai. The Master of Repentance stepped back as if recoiling from the plague-ridden creature thrust towards him, beckoning for the First Company to take hold of the prisoner. Telemenus suppressed his anxiety and disgust as he stepped forward to seize the captive's arm, Brother Laestus taking the other side. The representatives of the Ravenwing were already hastening away, their burden passed to the Deathwing.

Five of the Space Marines turned and took up position in front of Asmodai, while the others fell in behind the prisoner. Telemenus and Daellon had been counted amongst the guard for no other reason than as many Terminator-trained warriors as possible were needed for the war on the planet below. The newest inductees to the First Company could not serve on the field of battle and so their initiation began with this first encounter with the Fallen. As he felt his fingers sinking into corrupted flesh he wished his introduction had started with something less repulsive. He had seen many grievous wounds and deaths by blade, bolt and blast but the visceral nature of Methelas's condition was hard to stomach at such close range. It was difficult to reconcile the mutated creature with the dauntless armoured warrior he had so thoughtlessly confronted on Thyestes.

At another command from the Chaplain, they started a slow march. The Dark Angels led the Fallen further and further into the bowels of the Rock. Their journey was lit by torches that burned with smokeless flame, held in sconces at regular intervals along the walls.

Other corridors branched left and right. Telemenus knew from recent tuition that they were passing through the tombs of the ancient rulers of Caliban. And yet he could not reconcile the thought of this once being part of the home world of the Dark Angels, torn asunder by the machinations of the Fallen and their diabolic attempt to usurp the Lion. He knew he was on an armoured fortress hanging in space but to hear the testimony of Brothers Asmodai and Sapphon one could be mistaken for thinking that this was still the sacred ground of that ancient world, forever remembered in secret Chapter legend.

They turned left and right on occasion, weaving through the labyrinth of tunnels, surrounded by tablets proclaiming the names of Dark Angels who had died in heroic combat. They seemed to go on forever in all directions. Underfoot, the dust was thick save for a narrow path, having lain undisturbed for many years, perhaps decades or centuries. Small alcoves set into the walls held relics of the past – ornately decorated shoulder pads, the hilt and half the blade of a broken power sword, engraved skulls, a tarnished gauntlet, glass-fronted ossuaries displaying the bones of those who had fallen in battle, a plaque beneath declaring who they were in life. He felt draughts, chill breezes on his face emanating from side chambers, and occasionally heard a distant sigh, or the clank of a chain, all of which added to the macabre aura of the crypt, which did little to ease Telemenus's unsettled mind.

He felt the prisoner recoiling in his grasp and tightened his grip, fearing his charge would attempt to bolt. The slick, oily sensation of psychic energy leaked from the suppressor helm, tainting Telemenus's thoughts, and despite every precaution he kept getting glimpses inside the former Librarian's mind; visions of Caliban as it had once been, debased ceremonies of destruction and obedience to entreat vastly indifferent yet overwhelmingly powerful entities.

'Bear it no mind,' snapped Asmodai, breaking the vague connection with his harsh words. 'The glorified hallucinations of a madman.'

Telemenus concentrated on the task at hand, focusing all of his thoughts into a shield of hatred; it was easy enough when one looked at the depraved creature the Space Marine had become. His soul was as tarnished as his flesh, and the knowledge that the prisoner had once sworn oaths of allegiance to the Lion and the Emperor and then turned on both fuelled Telemenus's disdain.

Turning right at one particular junction, a peripheral movement caught Telemenus's keen eye and he glanced to his left. In the shadows he saw a diminutive being, no higher than his waist, almost hidden in the darkness. It was little more than a small robe, but from the depths of the black hood two eyes glittered with a cold, blue light as the strange creature regarded the small contingent, a gust of icy breeze passed over them. As suddenly as he had spotted it, the Watcher in the Dark faded back into the shadows and was gone.

Distracted by this encounter – and the lack of reaction from the others – Telemenus almost missed the command to halt. They were in a circular hallway roughly two dozen metres across, its circumference lined with windowless iron doors. All of the doors were closed except one. Through the doorway Telemenus glimpsed the interior of the cell, barely five metres square, lit by a brazier in the far corner. A stone slab dominated the centre of the room, pierced by iron rings from which hung heavy chains, and to one side a row of shelves was stacked with various metal implements that menacingly caught the light of glowing coals. There were two more robed Space Marines awaiting them, their faces hidden by heavy hoods, their hands concealed beneath studded metal gauntlets. As one took a step forward, Telemenus caught a glimpse of a white skull face under his hood.

Without any further word from Asmodai the other Dark Angels started to file out by the way they had entered. Telemenus followed after a moment's pause, the last to turn away as Asmodai grabbed the prisoner and with a snarl hauled him into the cell. The crash of the door closing echoed along the corridors, louder and more sinister than the tolling of the bells had been.

RIGHTEOUSNESS

The thing chained to the interrogation slab was not a Dark Angel. It was not even a Space Marine; not even human. It was a grotesque parody of a person. It had two arms, two legs and a head, but the outward appearance, the flesh that clothed it, was nothing but a masquerade.

It called itself Methelas but it deserved no name.

It was a traitor.

This was the simple truth that kept running through Asmodai's thoughts as he paced around the cell, his stare locked on the creature brought in by the Ravenwing.

It was a traitor. It deserved no pity, no mercy, and no remorse.

Asmodai was barely aware of anything else; the sterile stink of the interrogator's implements on the silver trolley against one wall; the breathing of Brother Ezekiel as he stood in the shadows cast by the brazier, his psychic effort concentrated on prying open the traitor's mind. The sweat of the captive was rank, oozing pus-like from the wide pores of his pallid skin. Bile and other fluids dribbled from corrupted wounds.

Asmodai thought of what the thing on the slab represented; ten thousand years of utter shame. It was the antithesis of everything he held to be good and pure. It was the flesh-and-blood incarnation of a malaise that had brought the Imperium crashing down into ruin even as it should have risen to the heights of power across the galaxy.

Traitor, I name thee.

Four words, uttered as a curse so dire there was nothing more filthy or vile in the universe.

Traitor, I name thee.

Four words spoken by the Lion in an accusation so grievous it continued to burn in the minds of his sons ten millennia later.

Traitor. Traitor! TRAITOR!

The thought consumed Asmodai. It turned his world into a tiny vessel; a personal dimension consisting only of him and the assemblage of bones, muscle and organs on the slab before him.

The hatred was always there. Perhaps it had been there when the boy that would become Asmodai had been born; recognised as a gift by the Dark Angels rather than squandered in pointless fighting against siblings and rivals.

TRAITOR! TRAITOR! TRAITOR!

The hate was a calm pool compared to the rage. Every brother of the Chapter knew hate. It was poured into them by the Chaplains during their time amongst the aspirants and Scouts, reinforced with elegy, eulogy, catechism and battle-prayer. Asmodai had unleashed the hate countless times with a specific word, a canticle or phrase implanted through day after day of psycho-indoctrinal therapies. As a Chaplain he knew the hundred and one holy words that triggered that implanted hatred.

TRAITOR! TRAITOR! TRAITOR!

Asmodai's hate was no purer than any other's, but his rage… The rage was his just reward, his true calling. It was the indignity, shame and fear melded as one that had been unleashed in the depths of hive moon Sigma of Ceti Albus. It was the shattering of righteous innocence given vent.

On the slab the thing had a face, plucked from the darkest depths of Asmodai's memories. The face of the creature that had destroyed his world, physically and metaphorically. The face of a traitor.

Malvine Rhemell.

The first Fallen he had met. The warrior, the beast, who had slain his battle-brothers and sacrificed countless millions for his own petty schemes.

The traitor was so much more than that. It was a more fundamental anger that fuelled Asmodai in the cells. An ork warlord was no less cruel, no less destructive. Yet it was in its nature to do so, it had no choice. The eldar seers were every bit as manipulative and self-serving. Asmodai, for all that he despised them, knew their opposition to mankind was driven by the need to survive. Even the rebels and separatists who sought to break from the Emperor's rule were simply misguided, weak-willed and easily daunted.

The Fallen had no such excuse. They had been the Emperor's finest, His chosen warriors, shepherded by His will, led by His greatest general. The Lion had taken them as sons, taught them and guided them. They knew better. They had been better. And they had betrayed everything not out of instinct, or necessity or even delusion. They had, with cold and calculating malice, turned on everything they were meant to uphold and protect and had cast it down.

For that there could be nothing but the purest rage, the most precise and personal affront fuelled by every fibre that made up Asmodai's being.

TRAITOR! TRAITOR! TRAITOR!

He thought of the Lion, dead at the hands of the traitors, of a world destroyed by hubris and a dream of greatness and eternal deliverance quashed. He thought of what the Fallen had done and looked at the creature on the slab.

TRAITOR! TRAITOR! TRAITOR!

What followed came easily.

He stopped only when Master Sapphon intervened. It seemed moments had passed but it was actually several hours. When he was finished, standing at the trolley cleansing his arms of the blood and other fluids, Asmodai could barely remember what had happened. The rage had guided him, letting free every pain he could devise, but his subject had resisted.

This time.

He looked at the bloodied thing on the slab. It had a name again. Methelas. One of the Fallen, who had uttered barely a grunt or snarl throughout Asmodai's gory ministrations. Unsatisfied, the Chaplain scraped clean his forearms while he regarded the traitor. It looked back at him with bloodshot eyes, the crystalline null clamps of the suppressor helm still driven into its temples though the shell of the hood had been removed.

'There is nothing you can do to hurt me, lackey of the Lion.' Methelas grinned, displaying toothless gums. 'I have become pain, I am one with it. My patron inures me to the pitiful weaknesses of flesh.'

'So it would seem,' said Sapphon, standing on the

other side of the cell, his bone-coloured robes a stark contrast to Asmodai's which were almost totally crimson, the red darkening as the blood dried. His face was hidden behind a Chaplain's mask.

Asmodai finished cleaning his hands, leaving crimson swirls in the deep basin atop the trolley. He dried them thoroughly, between the fingers, along the knuckles, every movement a part of the ritual to help suppress the rage. It was still there, held in check only by the presence of Sapphon. Asmodai flexed his fingers, trying to remember the feeling of flesh parting, but he could not. It came only in flashes, the detail washed away by the flood of his ire.

'Nor do I fear death.' The defiance in Methelas's eyes conveyed conviction every bit as strongly as his words. 'I yearn to be united with my master.'

'Perhaps you do,' said Sapphon.

Asmodai returned to the slab, arms crossed. The floor was slick and he stepped around the ruddy puddle to stand beside Methelas's head. The Fallen looked up at him with red-rimmed eyes.

'I can wait for an eternity. Can you?'

The rage was coming back, every word that spilled from the traitor's ragged mouth bringing it back to the surface.

'I will not have to,' said Asmodai, reaching out to take up his Blades of Reason. 'I am only just starting.'

'Brother, indulge me for a moment.' Sapphon stepped towards the cell door and gestured for Asmodai to follow.

With a last glare at his subject, the Master of Repentance replaced his implements on the trolley and followed his superior into the hallway. Sapphon closed the door, sealing away the Fallen.

'You interrupted my work, brother,' said Asmodai.

'Now I will have to start again.'

'It will not succeed,' said Sapphon. Asmodai bridled at the comment but the Master of Sanctity stilled his protest with a raised hand. 'Not for lack on your part, brother. He has aligned himself to the Lord of Decay, his flesh is nothing more than a vessel. No harm you inflict upon it will cause him to repent.'

'Let us test his faith a little more,' said Asmodai. 'It has been but five hours and already your resolve is weakening.'

'I am not weakening, merely assessing our goals and methods.' Sapphon took a long breath. 'There is more to be won on this day than the repentance of a single Fallen. Far wider concerns hinge upon this interrogation.'

'There is no greater goal than to offer mercy to the soul of a repentant Fallen,' replied Asmodai. 'It is the purpose of our existence.'

'And what if through his testimony, Methelas could lead us to find others of his kind,' asked Sapphon.

'A slim opportunity, of little relevance,' said Asmodai. 'They are scattered, leaderless, with little regard for each other. Such confessions are almost always lies. You know this, brother.'

'For the most part, but circumstances can alter,' said Sapphon. The words were spoken calmly but Asmodai felt the tension behind them and stiffened at the implication.

'You think that the Fallen are starting to work together? What do you think is so important about this particular creature? Methelas is part of some grander plan?'

'That much is certain,' said Sapphon. 'While you have been exerting your skills on your captive I have been debriefing Brother Malcifer. I expect you to acquaint yourself with his full account, but for the moment it is sufficient that you understand what is at stake. Methelas was working in concert with at least two other Fallen. In turn, they may have information that will lead us to the greatest prize of all.'

Asmodai was intrigued and for a moment allowed himself to wonder what could be so valuable. There was but one thing – one person – that was pursued above all others. Someone Asmodai desired to find even more than Malvine Rhemell.

'Cypher?' he said, almost daring to hope that the arch-traitor might be delivered to his attentions. 'You have found the accursed one?'

'Not yet.' Sapphon shook his head. 'But Sammael came close. Cypher was here, at Piscina, within the last year.'

'And Methelas knows of this?' Asmodai looked back at the cell door, picturing the captive within. 'You lay this bounty before me, and it is welcome, brother. I shall redouble my efforts.'

Sapphon laid a hand on Asmodai's arm as the Chaplain took a step back towards the cell.

'Do not hinder me further, he recuperates while we delay,' said the Master of Repentance.

'A far subtler knife is required to loosen this one's tongue, I believe.'

The disappointment was crushing. Feeling used, Asmodai turned his anger on Sapphon.

'You taunt me with this information and deny me my right to pursue it further! The Inner Circle may have chosen you for your guile, but in these cells you are not my match. Leave me be and I will deliver this cretin's secrets to you.'

'Did I command you to cease in your efforts, brother?'

Asmodai reconsidered the other Chaplain's words.

'I… It seemed as though you desired it.'

'Not at all, Asmodai. Unleash your every effort, as grievous as you can be. I do not expect your methods to bring success, but I cannot deny your past victories and will not oppose the opportunity for you to prove your worth again. And when you fail, the traitor will be all the more vulnerable because of your perseverance.'

'There is some trickery guiding your actions, I can feel it,' said Asmodai, wary of Sapphon's silvery words.

'No subterfuge, brother,' Sapphon said, opening out his hands in a gesture of innocence. 'You are the one with the talent for prying open deceit and digging through deception. I would not dare to attempt such misdirection against you. Take as long as you need, but when he does not repent I expect you to support my methods to ascertain what we require, whatever that demands of you.'

Asmodai nodded and headed towards the cell door. Sapphon again stopped him.

'Your word, Asmodai?'

Asmodai was keen to begin the interrogation again. The rage was already building, seeking release, and time was wasting.

'By the honour of the Lion's shade,' he swore.

LESSONS OF WAR

'I feel like I'm waddling through damn synth-gruel.'
Actuators whined and servos shrieked in protest as Daellon tried to turn his Tactical Dreadnought armour to face Telemenus. His arms were raised from his sides with the appearance of a toddler trying to keep balance. Without his helmet on – all three of the new Deathwing were helmless for the moment – he looked dwarfed by his powered suit despite his gene-augmented height and build. 'It is worse than when I first put on power armour.'

'Nearly punched your own head off, if I recall,' said Menthius, a grin breaking his half-burned face. Daellon looked shocked that anyone would remember such a thing. 'It was still the talk of the Seventh Company when I joined their ranks four years after you.'

Telemenus did not join in the banter and he barely heard the exchange. Every sense strained as he concentrated on taking a step forward. The bulk of the Terminator armour and its massively powered artificial muscle fibres made him feel as though he was trying to move at some crushing depth underwater; a feat that a trained Terminator was actually capable of performing unlike taking this first step.

'One step,' muttered Telemenus. 'One step. One step.'

He was almost frightened to lift up his foot, feeling that to shift the immense weight around him, to unleash the incredible strength stored in the mnemonic bundles that laced the armour, would topple him backwards and leaving him lying stranded like a flipped beetle. He had already suffered mockery for the past few days over his internment in the penitentium by Belial; to perform badly at this first Tactical Dreadnought trial would see his reputation plunge even further.

Two Techmarines and a gaggle of serf orderlies and servitors lined the walls; they had assisted the three Space Marines into their suits and now watched with amused interest, those capable of emotion, as the Chapter's finest stood around and bickered light-heartedly about who was going to fall over first.

'Trust in the tech-priests, and in their artifices,' growled Sergeant Arbalan. 'These suits are calibrated for your physiques, down to two micrometres. Just walk!'

Their new squad leader prowled the perimeter of the training hall that had been set aside for them, his armoured boots thudding heavily with each stride. Various ramps, low walls, openings and depressions formed an obstacle course running in a circuit over the reinforced mesh of the decking. The ease with which Arbalan moved astounded Telemenus, a distinctive sway to his stride as he circled like a predator, and the battle-brother redoubled his efforts, screwing up his courage to lift his right foot.

'What are you going to do now? Hop?' bellowed

Arbalan as Telemenus's foot rose from the deck almost of its own volition. 'Lean your weight into it. Use your whole body, not just your legs.'

Ignoring the smart to his pride in the sergeant's tone Telemenus focused on the content, daring to unbalance himself. The Terminator suit reacted smoothly as he leaned forward. Actuators whined at his hip and knee and his foot crashed down after half a stride. It reminded the Space Marine of the high-gee drills he had learned in the Scout Company as he was becoming accustomed to his first suit of battleplate.

'Stop! Just stop where you are,' snapped Arbalan. His footfalls sent shudders through the deck as he advanced to stand in front of the trio. The three newest members of the Deathwing froze in place, limbs splayed in immobile comical statues. Arbalan looked at each of them in turn, more with pity than anger. When he spoke his voice was quiet, encouraging. 'You are thinking about this too much. You fill minds with the impression that you cannot shift these enormous weights, that somehow you have to do something differently to carry the bulk. The men who designed these suits more than ten thousand years ago were not fools. I know that it is hard, but try to ignore the armour. There is a technique, for rapid movement, but for the moment all you have to do is walk. Close your eyes if it helps.'

It was hard to put the sergeant's words into practise, as he had admitted. A Terminator suit backpack extended half a metre above the wearer's shoulders and the pauldrons on either side were clearly visible in Telemenus's peripheral vision. The natural pose inside the suit was a little like a hunching gorilla, with spine straight, shoulders back and arms hanging out to the sides, knees bent to bring the weight forward on the hips. It was all but impossible to ignore the mass of the armour, but Telemenus closed his eyes and imagined he was clad in his robe, so light to his muscled build it was virtually weightless.

He had almost completed the picture and was ready to risk another stride when a whoop of excitement from Menthius broke Telemenus's concentration. He heard a rapid clump of footsteps and opened his eyes to see his companion stalking away, boots pounding on the deck. Glancing at Daellon, Telemenus saw that the other Space Marine was on the verge of following Menthius, though with a constant stream of swear words and colourful curses muttered under his breath.

Telemenus saw the audience from the armourium watching him closely and was determined that he would not be the last of the three to master his armour. Such news would soon spread through the company, perhaps even the rest of the Chapter, despite them being deployed across a dozen battle zones on Piscina IV. Fuelled by burgeoning shame and desperation he moved out of raw instinct, and to his delight found himself tramping loudly after Menthius.

Ahead of Telemenus was a wall of mortared blocks three metres high and a metre thick, with a gap in it about three metres to his left. He was approaching with quick strides, propelled by momentum.

He wondered if Arbalan would be offering any advice on how to turn or stop.

PROMISES

The cell door was open, which Asmodai always found slightly counter-intuitive, but Sapphon had refused all petition to rescind Boreas's standing order that the captive's chamber remain unlocked. Though unbarred, the cell was not unguarded; pict-scanners and motion detectors monitored the Fallen at all times, watched by mind-scrubbed servitors that would raise the alarm the moment the prisoner stepped out of his room.

From the corridor there seemed to be a line across the threshold. On the one side, in the cell, was light, glowing gently from a lumistrip in the ceiling. On the outside was darkness. For the Fallen the line between light and dark was as solid as any physical barrier and in fifteen years and more he had not voluntarily set foot outside his cell.

Standing outside in the blackness Asmodai could see the prisoner. He sat on a low bench, as straight as his rack-twisted spine would allow. He was naked but for a gown of ragged material, undyed and stained with blood. Brand and blade marks criss-crossed his withered frame – once the toned muscle of a giant warrior, now a wasted, wiry vision of a Space Marine. His bald, scarred head rested back against the bare stone of the wall, hands on his knees. On a small shelf beside him was a bowl fashioned from wood, a plain tin cup next to it.

He had his eyes closed. They opened the moment Asmodai approached the open door, regarding the Chaplain coolly.

'The sneaking thief returns in the gloom, I see,' said the Fallen, voice hoarse, barely a whisper.

The taunt was a barb ragging at Asmodai's anger, pulling the Chaplain into the room. Asmodai was upon the prisoner in moments. He smashed a fist into the captive's jaw, the blow sending the Fallen's head crashing into the wall.

'Choose your words with deference, traitor,' snarled Asmodai, bringing his hand back across the Fallen's face, knocking him from the bench to the bare floor. Blood sprayed from lips split countless times and dribbled from a nose already mashed to pulp by similar blows.

The Chaplain stepped back, hands raised, ready for the counter-attack but the Fallen did not respond with violence. He shook his head, pushed himself slowly to his hands and knees and then stood up, the movement twisting his face with a grimace of pain.

Asmodai saw the Fallen about to speak and knew from the look in his eyes it would be more disrespect, more facetious jibes. He grabbed the prisoner by the throat and hauled him from his feet, slamming him spinewards onto the bench before he could utter his defiance.

'Curb your tongue, and employ ears to purpose,' rasped

Asmodai, face centimetres from the Fallen's, spittle flying. 'Your falsehoods have been revealed. Your true nature is unmasked.'

Asmodai stepped back, savouring the coming moment of triumph. With deliberate, pain-wracked movements the Fallen sat up, one eye starting to close beneath a spreading bruise.

'Deny it once more,' said Asmodai. 'Deny that you are a traitor to the Lion, and tell me again how you remain the Emperor's faithful warrior.'

'I have little enough breath. To waste it on pointless repetition would be foolish.' The prisoner wiped blood from his chin with a finger. 'Do not let me spoil your ranting, however. I have missed your company, Asmodai, and your tirades. I find they are a pleasant distraction from the boredom of my captivity.'

'So sure, so certain,' growled Asmodai. 'Merir Astelan, the ill-understood son, the innocent victim of confusion and suspicion. Admit your lies now, of free will, and your end will be merciful. Fresh evidence of your crimes has surfaced. Any further denial will result in unnecessary pain.'

Astelan feigned a yawn.

'I was mistaken. The scuttling of the rats makes for more entertaining diversion than your garbled threats.'

Asmodai lashed out, the punch felling the prisoner once more. The Chaplain measured his next blow, driving his boot into Astelan's chest with just enough force to send him sprawling onto his back. The Chaplain lowered himself, knee in the side of the Fallen's neck, forcing his face into the hard floor, a position of total dominance. To insure there was no resistance, Asmodai laid a hand on the traitor's scalp, feeling puckered, ridged scar tissue under his fingertips. He pushed, exerting a fraction of his strength, squashing Astelan's face into the stone just a little harder still, enough to stop him speaking.

'Your conspirator, Methelas, has been captured.' There was no reaction from Astelan. 'Your grand plans have come to nought. The Ruinous Powers that you serve have been thwarted, and Thyestes has been saved. Confess now of your sins and be granted swift release.'

Standing up, Asmodai dragged the other Space Marine back onto the bench, leaving him propped up against the wall. Astelan fixed the Dark Angel with a hateful glare.

'I remember when the Chaplains were first introduced,' said the Fallen. 'They were custodians of the finest traditions of Terra and Caliban combined. No Word Bearer overseer for us, the First Legion. Raised from our own ranks, when we looked to our Chaplains we saw the finest exemplars of the Legiones Astartes, true to oath and noble of bearing.'

'And what do you see when you look at me?' Asmodai demanded.

'A thuggish child dressing up in the robes of his betters.'

Frustration and fury erupted and for several minutes Asmodai gave it free rein, though enough semblance of control remained to leave bones unbroken and organs undamaged. When the rage subsided, Asmodai stood panting over Astelan, foot on his throat. There was blood on the Chaplain's hands and sprayed down the front of his surplice.

'Liar! You are a liar and a traitor!' Asmodai wished that he had the powers of Ezekiel and the other Librarians. What excruciations he could visit upon these faithless dogs if he had the talent to reach into their minds and souls, to break and twist without the crude interaction of flesh. 'Your resistance is beneath contempt. Your denial is meaningless. You are such a twisted serpent you would claim night is day even beneath the scorching light of the sun. Though your flesh may cover the marks of your sin, it festers in your soul.'

Stepping away, Asmodai turned his back on the prisoner, showing he regarded him as no threat at all.

'By past testimony I know that you and Methelas conspired together. His guilt is plain, and yours by association undeniable. Do you now argue against this?'

'Methelas and I parted ways decades ago,' said Astelan, a curled heap of rags and pummelled flesh in the far corner of the cell.

'His taint is plain to see for all. You may hide yours, but he wears his corruption with pride.'

Astelan said nothing. Some might take the silence as admission but the defiance in the prisoner's eyes told Asmodai a different tale. Whatever mania drove the Fallen to deny his corruption it would not be overcome without being directly confronted with the truth.

The Chaplain seized Astelan by a wrist and pulled him to his feet. In the prime of his power he hauled him up as easily as an adult carries a child though even in his decrepit state the Fallen was no small weight. Astelan stumbled as he was half-dragged out of the cell and along the corridor, feet flapping uselessly against the flagstones to leave a broken trail of bloody smears and scattered droplets.

Reaching the chamber where Methelas was held, Asmodai pulled back the cover of the viewing slot and thrust Astelan against the door to look within.

'See with your own eyes,' hissed the Chaplain. 'Beneath the wounds caused by my hand, witness the malaise of the Dark Powers rampant in your companion's flesh. Look! Look and deny that you and he consorted with diabolic powers to overthrow the Lion!'

Astelan said nothing, but Asmodai felt a tremble of recognition in the Fallen. He pulled his captive away from the door to look him in the face. There was horror written there, not guilt.

'I swear I made no pact with the Dark Powers.' There was desperation as Astelan spoke, his eyes drawn back towards the thing on the slab. Swallowing hard, the Fallen returned his gaze to Asmodai, expression hardening. 'He was witch-kind, a Librarian. They are the most vulnerable. If he succumbed in later years to temptation it is no proof against me. I am servant to no power but the Emperor.'

'Lies! Bare-faced lies! Your treachery is without bounds and your duplicity an affront to all dignity of the Emperor.'

For the first time since Asmodai had arrived there was a spark of anger in Astelan when he replied.

'You compare me to that… that thing?' The Fallen thrust a finger towards the cell. 'That abomination is nothing to do with me. I have never denied my part in the rebellion against the Lion, but *that* is not the cause I served.'

'Prove it,' said a voice behind Asmodai.

He turned to see Sapphon stepping from the shadows beyond the small patch of light glimmering from Methelas's cell. The Master of Sanctity gestured for Asmodai to release his grip. He did so reluctantly, eyes boring holes in the treacherous Fallen.

'Prove the truth of what you say,' said Sapphon.

'I have told you everything, but you will not believe me.' A hint of desperation marred Astelan's expression. 'What more could I claim that would convince you?'

'Your words are worthless,' snapped Asmodai. 'Your lips would sooner burst into flames than have truth pass between them.'

'Deeds, Astelan,' said Sapphon. He stepped between Asmodai and the Fallen. 'As my companion rightly says, your words have been proven false already. We found Port Imperial. We know you did not destroy it, and we know that you conspired further with Methelas to overthrow the Emperor's rule on the world of Thyestes.'

Asmodai felt a tinge of satisfaction as doubt wracked the Fallen, his bravado slipping away. The former Dark Angel looked at Sapphon and held out an imploring hand.

'I... I did not...'

Sapphon shook his head and turned away. Asmodai was partly intrigued and partly confused by the interplay between the two. It seemed as though the Master of Sanctity had his prisoner at a disadvantage and yet failed to press home his cause.

'If you will not treat straight with me, I will leave you to the attentions of Brother Asmodai.'

'Wait!'

'Why?' asked Sapphon without turning around.

'What would you have me do?'

'That is not the relevant question.' Sapphon half-turned, all but his face hidden in the darkness. 'What would *you* do to prove you are innocent? If you serve the Emperor as you claim, what will *you* do to thwart His enemies?'

Astelan considered this for a moment. His eyes widened with realisation and a look of hope crossed his face.

'You want me to betray Methelas and Anovel?' The Fallen nodded without waiting for a reply. 'As you wish. They are nothing to me. I shall tell you everything I know.'

'You are going to do more than that if you want to

prove your innocence.' Sapphon moved into the darkness and his voice seemed to drift away with him. 'Much, much more than that.'

MARKSMANSHIP

He had fought in zero-gee vacuum, whirling from one starship to another on a grav-line, and taken the battle to enemies amidst swirling dust hurricanes and in the collapsing core of a hive, but Telemenus nevertheless had to fight back a wave of deep nausea as more data signals, targeter relay reticules and situational analysis symbols swam across his vision. The sensorium of the Terminator suit was even more sophisticated than his power armour's auto-senses, feeding information not only via sight, smell, sound and touch, but directly interfacing via his black carapace implants to provide a three-hundred-and-sixty-degrees impression of the battlespace around him for up to half a kilometre. Added to that was the feed-link to the armour of his fellow Terminators, sub-displays showing their view, micro-channels conducting what came to their ears.

It was like two extra sets of eyes capable of radar, infra-red and ultraviolet; ears that could detect the sound of a bolt shell dropped onto cloth at fifty metres, powerful enough to use the reverberations for echo location; taste sensitive enough to pick up one part in a million for chemical and biological traces; boosted kinaesthetic and proprioceptors alerting him to the physical position of his armour as an outer skin and the relative attitude of his storm bolter and power fist; all combined with an artificial form of extra-sensory perception that tracked millitorrs of static and dynamic pressure differences as well as fluctuating luminosity, temperature and electromagnetic readings.

And if this sensory overload was not enough to contend with, making Telemenus feel as though he was blinded, disorientated and deafened whilst constantly and gently vibrating from head to toe, the tactical analysis data feeds and vox-network made it seem like there was a thousand counsellors alternately whispering and screaming at him with a host of occasionally relevant but often obscure or nonsensical advice.

Closing his eyes didn't help this time, it simply made the neural feeds boost the other sense signals to compensate; a nice sub-doctrine of the armour to account for the fraction of a second whilst blinking and to allow him to fight whilst blinded. Telemenus desperately wanted to ask if there was some way to turn off some of the systems, perhaps filtering out half of them to allow his mind and body to adjust. He couldn't ask, not without showing weakness in front of the others. He was mindful that Grand Master Belial had appeared on the observation gallery above the practice range moments before the Techmarines had activated the armour's full suite of augmented systems.

He tried to focus on a single element: his storm bolter. The targeter feed from the double-barrelled weapon in his right hand registered as a small inset display that felt like it was somewhere above and to the left of his right eye. He knew he could not move his eye to look at it directly, but had to register the link with peripheral vision as he had done countless times before with his old bolter. At the moment the link showed an unmagnified view of the tiled floor.

With the ease of the last hundred hours of in-suit practice, he braced his legs and lifted the storm bolter, the breeze disturbed by this movement feeling like a wave washing against his right leg and arm. He ignored the sensation, fixed on the target globe two hundred metres away at the end of the live fire hall. Telemenus made small adjustments with his wrist to bring the storm bolter reticule directly in line with the tiny crosshairs that marked the centre of his vision.

How different it was to the fluid locate-aim-shoot that had brought him his one hundred thousand bolter kills and the Marksman's Honour of the Fifth Company. It was frustrating and harrowing in equal measure, trying to find the rhythm of the shot amongst the static and distraction of the sensorium inputs. The battle-icons from the transponders of the other two Terminators were blinking furiously, while heat- and motion-sensitive augur relays were trying to attract his attention to the presence of the other Space Marines and servitors watching on.

Battle telemetry was telling him that there was a slight crosswise, three-degree-downwards pressure in the air from the circulation vents. He adjusted his aim by a fraction of a millimetre and opened fire.

The storm bolter was set to a three-round burst. To his heightened senses the short fusillade was a welter of digital information; the light and heat and stink from the bolt propellant, the wash of the bolts through the air, the sound of the initial crack of firing and whisper of air molecules parting.

The target globe exploded into shards of silvery ceramic and a cloud of dust, the motes coiling away from the impact, tiny fragments of the bolt glittering in their midst.

A moment later another target shattered, followed by four more in swift succession as a line of bolt detonations shrieked across the firing range, almost as many projectiles tearing into the wall at the far end as hit the targets. The sudden flashes and roar dazed Telemenus for a split second, and he turned with an angry shout to see who had fired.

'You are armed with a storm bolter, use it like one,' Sergeant Arbalan snapped, the haze of propellant exhaust drifting from the twin muzzles of his weapon. 'If you wish to fight with a sniper rifle perhaps we should send you back to the Tenth Company.'

Telemenus bit back a retort, though his pride smarted at the implication that he was no better than a novitiate. He lowered his storm bolter and took a deep breath, conscious of Master Belial's gaze on him from the gallery above.

'Apologies, brother-sergeant.' He raised his power fist to his chest as a sign of respect – a bow was awkward in Terminator armour, and consequently considered melodramatic. 'I shall adjust my approach to combat as you instruct.'

He noticed a flicker of movement from Belial – was it a shake of the head? – and the Grand Master of the Deathwing turned and left. Telemenus wondered why their captain did not remain to watch his companions at their firing exercises. Had that first impression truly rankled so badly? Telemenus had heard frequently that Belial was an unforgiving perfectionist, but it had never been brought to his attention that the Grand Master was vindictive. As he stepped back from the firing line to allow Menthius to take his place, Telemenus could not help but think that Belial's undue scrutiny was personal in some way.

There was no complaint to be had, for Telemenus was aware that he was falling short of the mark expected of the Deathwing. It nagged him that Daellon and Menthius seemed to be progressing more swiftly with their adoption of the Terminator style of fighting. Stopping beside Daellon he was forced to conclude that the only course of action was to focus even harder and work to impress Arbalan in the hopes that a word of merit would be passed up the chain of command to earn some relent, maybe some respect, from Belial.

ARGUMENTS OLD AND NEW

Washed, wounds tended, garbed in a plain grey robe of a serf, Astelan looked healthier than he had in years. Though in a weakened state after years of deprivation, his body already showed no traces of the beating Asmodai had inflicted; no bruise or cut fresher than a year old marked him.

Sapphon watched the Fallen on the vid-link monitor for a while, gauging his strategy. Next to the Master of Sanctity Asmodai loomed, his desire to lay his hands upon Astelan again emanating like a wash of heat. Sapphon knew that not only was the ongoing hunt for the Fallen reaching a critical juncture, his own reputation amongst the Inner Circle was being set as stake. Though not voiced openly, there were those amongst the highest-ranking Chaplains, Grand Masters and Librarians that believed Sapphon's leadership was lacking, and that a more hard-line approach led by Asmodai would see the search for the ancient foe strengthened.

For the moment the Master of Sanctity knew he enjoyed the support of Azrael, but the Supreme Grand Master could not silence every criticism, and his chief concern was to maintain cohesion amongst the Inner Circle. If the voices against Sapphon were raised openly, there was only so long left until he would be forced to cede his command to the Master of Repentance; a disastrous move in Sapphon's opinion and one he could avoid with a fresh victory here.

'Why do you coddle him like some deserving aspirant?' Asmodai demanded.

'I gave you time with Methelas to extract confession, but none has been forthcoming.' Sapphon allowed his annoyance to show this time, confident that Asmodai could not exploit it. 'You will convey the same regard to me, without these second-guesses, absent of distracting commentary.'

'You do not wish me to participate?' Asmodai was shocked at the thought. He shook his head. 'You think that words alone will bring forth that which we desire? This creature knows nothing of respect or honour. Do not think to treat it like an equal.'

'I will treat him any way I choose!' The sudden outburst caused Asmodai to blink, caught off-guard by Sapphon's anger after so many occasions of tolerance. 'You do not instruct me, brother. If you find your bloodlust running high, I suggest you divert your boredom upon the flesh of Methelas while I conduct serious investigation.'

Sapphon turned away from the monitor and opened the door to the adjoining chamber where Astelan was seated. He looked back once, ordering Asmodai to stay where he was with a meaningful glare, and shut the door behind him.

Like the other cells the chamber was bare rock, though

it housed padded benches, a table and shuttered lanterns. It was often used for solitary penance by the brothers and it had taken some arguing by Sapphon to allow him to bring Astelan out of the dungeons to this higher level of the Rock. All other personnel had been cleared away and warriors from the First Company were on hand at the entrances and corridor junctions to prevent escape or intercept accidental interlopers.

'Do *not* treat me like a fool,' said Astelan as Sapphon sat on the bench opposite him. The Fallen ran his crooked fingers over the leather covering of the bench cushion. 'Do you not think that Boreas offered me comfort, seeking to weaken my resolve with mock kindness?'

'The comfort of the surroundings, such as they are, are to my benefit, not yours,' Sapphon replied. 'I will not treat you like a fool if you offer the same in return.'

Astelan regarded Sapphon for a few seconds, lips pursed in thought. He nodded.

'Our first understanding, it seems,' said Sapphon. He leaned forward to a ewer of wine and two goblets on the table. He poured out measures of the dark red liquid and pushed one towards Astelan. The Fallen glanced at Sapphon with suspicion and then, perhaps remembering that they were treating each other as urbane, civilised companions, took up the wine. He slurped it down a little more eagerly than perhaps he intended, wiping the back of his hand across his mouth as he returned the empty goblet.

'Do you know what the most difficult aspect of my role is?' asked Sapphon. He sipped his drink while Astelan shrugged. 'There is so much I would like to know, about the ancient days when the Lion walked abroad as a man. Or to learn what it was like to follow the Emperor Himself into battle.'

'Ask me your questions, but I do not promise you will like the answers to them all.'

'And therein we discover the problem. You are, by previous statements, now shown to be false, a proven liar, Astelan. I cannot trust a single word that has passed your lips in the last fifteen years.'

'Have I passed any lie greater than those that you wrap about yourself? Those that you spin in the minds of your supposed brothers?' Astelan poured himself another goblet of wine, though he held it in his lap, gazing at his reflection as he swirled the liquid around, rather than taking a drink. 'I lie, you lie – somewhere between the two perhaps is the truth.'

'Let us exchange truths for a moment.' Sapphon knew he had not the endurance or personality to contest headlong with a stubborn foe as Asmodai would, but he had other talents instead of sheer bullish persistence. 'I need the information you are withholding from us.'

'And? What of it?'

'That is my first truth. You do not get another until you return in kind.' Sapphon watched Astelan out of the corner of his eye as he sipped his wine, almost seeing the calculations being made behind the Fallen's eyes. Just as the traitor was about to speak Sapphon interrupted him, keeping Astelan from dictating the conversation. 'And remember that if at any time I tire of our arrangement or I believe I am wasting my time with your machinations, I will have Asmodai make you scream for mercy. I know he can do it. I have heard your cries, Merir Astelan, echoing in the depths.'

The Fallen paled slightly and reconsidered his words.

'I lied about Port Imperial,' he said. 'It was not destroyed.'

'No, no, that is not good enough, Astelan.' Sapphon shook his head sorrowfully and placed his goblet on the table. 'We already know this. We found Port Imperial, and Methelas. You cannot offer me what I already possess. Do not confuse my patience with tolerance. If you continue to test me I will surrender you to Asmodai and seek another means to hunt down your companions.'

'How can I trust you will not set your savage hound upon me anyway, simply out of spite?'

'There are no guarantees except mutual self-interest. This is your last chance, Astelan. I will leave here if your next words displease me.'

Sucking his lips against broken teeth, the Fallen Dark Angel looked between Sapphon and the door, where he had clearly spied Asmodai earlier.

'Tharsis was to provide the recruits, as a new home world under my command,' said the Fallen, avoiding Sapphon's gaze, though not out of shame it seemed. 'Methelas was to use Port Imperial to secure a fleet. Anovel was an Apothecary and we tasked him with recovering arms and gene-seed with which we could create a new force of Space Marines.'

Sapphon nodded, pleased with this confession.

'Very good,' he said. 'Now I reciprocate. When we took you and Tharsis, your companions came up with a contingency of their own. Methelas tried to turn the pirates of Port Imperial into a fighting force.'

'No,' said Astelan. 'They were intended simply as a stop-gap.'

'But they had to make do without your sacred bands as recruits,' said Sapphon. He avoided asking the obvious question – why Astelan and the others wanted to create their own Chapter – and instead focused on the relationship between them. 'Methelas and his warriors were corrupted by the Ruinous Powers. Should we expect the same of Anovel?'

'I swear that I would have no time for such allies.' Astelan leaned forward, straining with earnest attitude. 'When we parted ways they were not as you say.'

'Let us accept that for the moment, and only for the moment, to avoid further debate,' said Sapphon. 'What was your interest in Piscina?'

'What is Piscina?' The question seemed to genuinely confuse Astelan. 'Is it a person? A place?'

'You have never heard of the world before? Did Anovel not mention it to you?'

'Anovel did not say where he was heading, only that he could secure pure Legion gene-seed and the equipment for its implantation. Tharsis was to be the world where we raised our force and started once more on the Great Crusade.'

'You still maintain that myth?' Sapphon sighed. 'I thought we could dispense with the past, claim and accusation, justification and counter-claim. Methelas and Anovel were not interested in ushering forth a new era of the Emperor's conquests and neither were you. You sought simply to restore your lost power, to have an army of warriors at your back to legitimise piracy and personal ambition.'

This time it was for Astelan to shake his head dismissively, unconcerned by the accusation.

'Not you, or Boreas or that vicious cur Asmodai, can grasp the truth even when it is presented so plainly. So narrow have your minds become you cannot see past the bonds placed upon you. The Legiones Astartes once conquered the galaxy for the Emperor. If you only divested yourselves of the shackles weak men placed upon you that time of glory could be restored.'

'Old ground, well trodden, as you say, Astelan.' Sapphon stood up and there was a moment of panic in the Fallen's eyes.

'Where are you going?' Astelan stood up as well, casting a wary glance at the closed door. He offered his hands in conciliation. 'We have only just started. Let not old grievances, well worn by use, endanger the rapport we are building here. Forgive my zeal and not let misunderstandings stifle this progress. Give me a chance to show the nature of my honour, I beseech you.'

'What of Cypher?' Sapphon asked, keeping his manner casual. 'What part was he to play in your scheme?'

'The Lord Cypher?' Astelan's brow furrowed deeply and he shook his head. 'An antiquated role, lauded by the Calibanites. I do not think he survived the cataclysm.'

Sapphon looked for signs that the answer was evasion but it was impossible to say for sure. Astelan's reaction seemed natural, but he had been able to deceive both Boreas and Asmodai, and mislead the greatest Librarians of the Chapter. Whatever the truth, Sapphon had Astelan snapping at the bait he had laid. Now the Master of Sanctity would reel him in and, with permission from the Supreme Grand Master, toss him back into the waters to see under which rock he would swim.

PAST TIMES

The parkland was almost unrecognisable, especially under the cover of night. In the months since Annael had last been in Kadillus Harbour the war-torn city had been further ravaged. What had been a grassy space between tall tenements was now a crater-pocked mess of dirt and weeds. The buildings were abandoned, although that was unsurprising considering the pounding the Ravenwing had given them the last time they had fought here; ferrocrete fascias were heavily cracked, windows and doorways split open, roofs and upper storeys collapsed, the streets choked with rubble. Such was the legacy of defying the sons of the Lion.

The augurs read nothing. The central district of Kadillus Harbour was devoid of life except for the Ravenwing bike squadrons and Land Speeders cruising along the streets on the watch for insurrectionists and looters. Above, the distant screams of jets betrayed the presence of Nephilim and Dark Talon aircraft ready to bring in a crippling airstrike at a moment's notice. The blue haze of Thunderhawk engines illuminated the low clouds as gunships circled the subdued city with lascannons, missiles and battle cannons ready to unleash a torrent of destruction.

'A little quieter than our last visit,' remarked Sabrael as Tybalain signalled the Black Knights squadron to a halt a short distance from the rise at the heart of the park. 'It seems our return is no cause for celebration.'

Annael expected a rebuke from the Huntmaster to follow but nothing was forthcoming. The augurs of his bike, *Black Shadow*, showed nothing out of the ordinary within five hundred metres. The peace unnerved him, for he knew that it was false. There were many that still harboured resentment against the Dark Angels, and those that had ambushed the Ravenwing on the last occasion still had cause to repeat such attacks. Armouries had been looted as full-scale war had torn the city apart, and although the Dark Angels were undeniably in control of the city now – the orks' presence eliminated by the latest offensive led by the Deathwing – there were nightly uprisings that threatened to spill over into more significant armed resistance.

'What do you think will happen here?' Annael asked. 'Once order is restored, there will still be much work to be done.'

'The Adeptus Terra will swing its ponderous might into action,' said Sabrael, 'like a full-bellied grox rousing from slumber. I expect they'll wipe the island clear of everything except the geothermal stations and start again. If they deem Piscina worth rescuing, that is.'

Annael passed his eye along the northern and eastern edges of the park, where prefabricated defences had been erected by servitors from the armoury. Almost a metre thick, the plasteel barricade was two metres high, lowering in short stretches for a few Space Marines to fire over, pierced with vision slits and firing slots in others. It was not manned at the moment; with the Ravenwing returned to finish securing the city and perform counter-rebel patrols the other companies were pressing on through the East Barrens to eliminate the remaining orks.

'Worlds have been reclaimed from worse,' said Nerean. 'It has only been the aegis of the Dark Angels that held back full exploitation of the system. In deference to our recruitment from Piscina Five the Adeptus Terra excluded Piscina from their tithes, but that will not last much longer.'

'How so?' asked Annael.

'Piscina is tainted,' said Tybalain, turning in his saddle to address them. 'The traitors have been here. Who can say if they interfered with the tribes from which we recruited? The mark of the corrupt has been laid upon this star system. The Supreme Grand Master will declare Piscina *diabolia* and no more will the sons of Piscina Five be raised to the ranks of the Dark Angels.'

'Not that such shall be shared with the Adeptus Terra,' added Calatus.

'What of the tribespeople?' Annael was disturbed by this thought. Ten thousand years of tradition and continuity ended in a moment. 'What will happen when we lift our aegis from them?'

'The Imperium will happen,' said Calatus. He laughed; a harsh noise totally devoid of any sympathy. 'The people will wait for the warriors from beyond the cloud to return and they will wait in vain. The next time they see ships descending on their world it will be assessor teams from the Adeptus Terra, or perhaps a Mechanicus survey force. The jungles will be flattened, the minerals drilled from the ground, the people put to work in mines and factories.'

'Is that right?' Annael whispered, picturing the destruction. 'After taking their greatest sons for five hundred generations do we not owe them more than that? Is that fair?'

'Fair?' Tybalain spoke quietly, and it seemed to Annael that the Huntmaster was equally saddened by the prospect. 'Fairness is an illusion. For five hundred generations they have been spared this fate because of the service they have given us. That service is no longer provided and the Emperor demands a different sacrifice.'

To the west, to Annael's right, an undulating halo of light sprang into being; high-powered lamps surrounding a newly-installed skyshield landing pad. As the guidance beams illuminated the cloud layer a Thunderhawk dipped in to an approach pattern from the east, flying low over the city. Augmented Techmarine assistants and their servitors swarmed around the platform as the gunship descended, dragging energy cells, recharging cables, fresh hellstrike missiles and ammunition crates. The blur of a Land Speeder Tornado performing a sweep of the surrounding broken-down factories demonstrated the Dark Angels vigilance despite the recent lull in fighting within the capital.

'The ignorant savages will know nothing better,' said Sabrael. 'In a hundred years, they will not remember the days when they used to be the favoured of the Dark Angels.'

'Perhaps, perhaps not,' said Annael. 'Worlds kept alive the hope of being reunited with Terra for the whole of the Dark Age, who can say that the people of Piscina Five will not also keep the stories in their hearts and wait for the day when the Dark Angels return for them?'

'They will die disappointed,' said Sabrael.

The sound of incoming motors ended the discussion. A group of four Ravenwing bikes rounded a junction to the left, their lamps bright in the night. As they passed Annael saw a flash of metal; the bionic leg of their sergeant. In the gleam of lamps he recognised his old squadron leader, Cassiel. He had not seen the sergeant since they had parted ways on Port Imperial.

'A moment, brother-sergeant,' Annael called out.

Cassiel barked an order to his men and the squadron whirled around, cutting onto the grass from the road to stop a short distance away.

'Brother Annael,' said Cassiel with a nod of respect. He looked past Annael and nodded again. 'Sabrael.'

Annael suddenly realised he did not know what to say. He had greeted the sergeant out of instinct, but hearing Cassiel's voice brought back the memory of their squadron-brothers who had died on Thyestes. Had Cassiel not been in the apothecarion, his leg blown off by a plasma blast at Port Imperial, it was likely the sergeant too would have been amongst the slain. Annael felt keenly the loss of Zarall and Araton, but could not find words to express the sensation. It was made worse by the fact that he and Sabrael had been inducted into the Black Knights, seemingly promoted for their disobedience. None would openly question the will of Grand Master Sammael, but Annael feared that Cassiel did not understand.

'Did you have something to say, brother?' asked Cassiel. 'Brevity would suit, for we have a patrol to conclude.'

Annael wanted to apologise but that would be ridiculous, because it was not his fault the others had died. The Space Marine was unsure of what he wanted to say, but feeling deep within that he should share words with Cassiel that would renew their brotherly bonds. Everything that came to mind seemed to be trite or, worse still, a falsehood.

'It is pleasing to see you in the saddle again, brother-sergeant,' said Sabrael, breaking the awkward moment much to Annael's relief. 'It seems that my plan to drive you around in an attack bike has been belayed by higher authority.'

'An offer that was sensibly rejected at the time, if I can recall,' said Cassiel. He looked at Annael, perhaps recognising his discomfort. 'We all die, Annael. You did not. Some would say that to live to fight on is the first duty of a Space Marine.'

Some would say. It was an odd choice of phrase, from which Annael drew no comfort. It implied that Cassiel did not agree; that perhaps had Annael and Sabrael stayed with Araton and Zarall they would not be dead. Annael agreed with the sentiment, despite assurances from Sammael that this would not have been the case.

'Only in death does duty end,' said Annael, wondering if he really meant the words so often spoken without thought. He knew that there were other circumstances – despicable occasions – when duty had ended before death. 'We seek only to serve the Lion and the Emperor.'

Cassiel nodded without comment, raised a fist in respect to Tybalain and led his squadron away. Annael could feel the others looking at him, the lenses of their helms bright in the glare of bike lamps. Were they judging him, he wondered? Was his death the only evidence he could offer to prove his dedication to the Chapter? Was that the only way to alleviate the blame he felt?

CONCLAVE

The hexagonal chamber was lined with hundreds of shelves and each held hundreds of bound tomes and scrolls. A walkway wound up the walls, spiralling into the darkness beyond the light of the few torches held in sconces every few metres. The fluttering and chirruping of something in the far upper reaches echoed back as Sapphon followed the line of the ramp around and around until it was swallowed by the gloom. Columns carved as towering figures robed and cowled holding all manner of implements lined the room: one with a sword; scales; shield; orb; sceptre; axe; globe; key. On and on the path wound about the Chaplain, every figure different from the last.

'Herein is contained all the knowledge of the Dark Angels.'

The disembodied voice was quiet, leaving no echo. Sapphon was not entirely sure it was a voice at all. He did not detect a trace of accent or a direction of origin. Perhaps it was a thought projected straight into his mind without recourse to his superhuman hearing.

'Ten thousand years of seeking the truth, all held within this one chamber.'

The weight of it all seemed to crush down upon Sapphon. It made the mind shrink from the magnitude of the universe to think that ten millennia of wisdom, ten thousand years of philosophies and edicts, records of battles, names of commanders and the commanded, star charts, interrogations, confessions, penances demanded and delivered, honours and promotions, censures and rolls of heroic deeds could be contained in one space; and still it was but a fraction of the sum of all mankind's existence.

'Find that which you seek and enlightenment shall be yours.'

At first there appeared to be no reason or order to the books, but on closer inspection Sapphon came to the conclusion that the oldest tomes were those furthest away. The state of the volumes grew worse the higher he passed his gaze, and he wondered in what decrepit condition he would find them at the height of the library. Surely it was there he should search, he reasoned, at the very start of the Chapter's records, for the library had not been built, but rather delved into the bedrock of the Tower of Angels.

He walked a few paces up the ramp, running a finger along the edge of the nearest shelf, looking at the titles on the spines of the plas-bound books. Most appeared mundane: ledgers of the armoury and lists of recruits. Such trivia would continue for storey after storey above him. Was this simply a test of endurance and patience, to see if he had the persistence to reach the top of the spiral?

The thought triggered another. A pattern formed in Sapphon's mind. The spiral. He remembered something from the old teachings. There was a lot he had learned, so much to recall, so many canticles and verses of exhortation and admonition that it took him a few moments to dredge up the memory he sought.

It was an instruction from his sergeant when he had been in the Tenth Company; or rather an analogy to teach a combat technique. The sergeant had spoken of a time when the knights of Caliban had trained upon a spiral, perfecting their skills with gun and blade, starting at the outer edge and moving ever closer. The Scouts had not learned upon a literal spiral as the knights of old, but the resemblance remained as they learned first to kill from afar and then at subsequently closer ranges until they mastered the dagger and the sword.

The sergeant had said that the truth was found at the centre of the spiral, eye-to-eye and blade-to-blade with the foe. To master the eye of the spiral was to be a true warrior.

Looking up again Sapphon wondered if the eye lay far above, but his instinct warned him otherwise. He turned about and surveyed the rest of the giant hall. The torches laid bare the books on the walls but the centre of the chamber was swathed in darkness. There was something altogether unnatural about the gloom, Sapphon decided. It was, for want of a better reference, too dark. Though dim the torches should have provided enough light for his enhanced vision to see to the centre of the hall but instead there was only blackness.

Darkness was a warning. He understood the symbolism well after years as a Chaplain. Darkness was danger, a metaphor for the unknown, where prying minds should not wander.

Was it a test of faith?

Sapphon pondered the question. Was it as simple as ascending through the light to pass the test? The darkness was temptation; the unknowable that lured the righteous from the path of loyalty. One who delved into the darkness would become consumed by it. To question, to doubt, was a sin. The light was reason and truth. Whichever way Sapphon examined the situation, it made sense to follow the light, the path of purity.

For all that logic dictated such a course of action, Sapphon

*had never been able to quell his curiosity. Penances and pun-
ishments from the Chaplains had never quashed it. Years
of service as a battle-brother and then as Chaplain had not
dulled it.*

He stepped off the ramp and into the blackness.

I should have stayed in the light, thought Sapphon.

In other Chapters the Master of Sanctity was a position
given to the strongest adherent to the Chapter ortho-
doxy, the exemplar to which the other battle-brothers
aspired. On the face of it, the same was true of the Dark
Angels, but there was a far more vexing purpose to Sapphon's role, which required not unwavering devotion to
the creed but a questioning, anti-authoritarian streak. In
a Chapter that favoured obedience, only the disobedient
could truly discover the roots of dissatisfaction, seeking
the seeds of heresy that had once caused such schism
and destruction.

If only Sapphon had stayed in the light he would
have remained a simple Chaplain and perhaps never
ascended to the mysteries of the Inner Circle. And in that
alternate life he would not now be sat at a conclave of
the Inner Circle arguing with Asmodai about the merits
of allowing two of the Fallen to share the same air.

'If they but pass word to each other it strengthens
resolve,' said the Master of Repentance.

He stood to Sapphon's left but had not once looked
at his superior, addressing his words instead to the few
Space Marines present and the vox-servitors that held
the places of members conducting their appearance
from the surface of Piscina IV. Supreme Grand Master
Azrael had returned to convene the conclave and stood
at the head of the table, his robes over armour still
scratched and stained from recent battle. A few of the

Librarius were present, as was Grand Master Sammael of the Ravenwing and Grand Master Belial. The withered vox-servitors, suspended by pipes and cables from the ceiling of the conclave chamber, were twinned with transmitters and receivers on the world below, so that what they saw and heard was also visible and audible to those that participated at a distance while vox-conducted voices were conveyed back from the surface to move puppet-mouths.

'We are far beyond plain excruciation and interrogation,' replied Sapphon, also directing his address to the other members of the Inner Circle. By tradition debates were not made between individuals, but presented as case for all to consider. In practice, the two Chaplains simply argued by proxy, it being plain that their opinions were irreconcilable. 'This is the closest we have come to bringing Cypher to account for a long time.'

'Astelan and Methelas both deny knowledge of the thrice-cursed. If we bring them together you simply give them occasion to conspire.'

'We will monitor every exchange between them.'

'And are we so learned of the ways of the Fallen that we can trust there is no hidden meaning behind words plainly spoken?' Asmodai leaned forward, fists on the table, focusing his attention on Azrael. 'Who can say what message or bargain they might make through hidden code? They have acted in concert before and will do so again.'

'To what end?' Sapphon kept the exasperation from his voice but he knew that Asmodai had sympathisers amongst his audience. 'Both are locked in the bowels of the Rock. There is no plan they can enact. They cannot communicate with the outside. Any conspiracy in such circumstances is meaningless.'

'It is a blatant disregard to the tenets of interrogation, bordering on giving succour to the enemy.'

This accusation bit hard, but Sapphon was prevented from retort by the Supreme Grand Master, who raised a hand for silence, perhaps realising the Master of Sanctity was quickly losing his famed patience. Azrael looked at the two Chaplains, rugged features half-hidden in the shadow of his cowl.

'Can he be trusted?' said the Chapter Master. Sapphon assumed the question was addressed to him. 'Is Astelan's oath worth anything?'

'It is worth less than the compassion of an ork,' rasped Asmodai.

'Objectively?' Sapphon considered his reply more carefully. 'No. He is a self-serving traitor – a power-hungry demagogue. However, in the context of the position in which I have manoeuvred him, he must abide by a sense of honour or admit his crimes. Such an admission is beyond his comprehension, so for the moment he will strive to show himself aligned to the nobler ideals he pretends to espouse.'

'We have heard much of the risks, or lack, but what is to be gained?'

Even Asmodai knew better than to offer opinion this time, leaving it to Sapphon to justify his proposed course of action.

'There is a causal link between Astelan and events here on Piscina. Although not directly involved, if he wishes to prove his innocence by exposing his co-conspirators we shall learn more of the chain that runs from him to Cypher. Anovel is the missing component, I know it. I believe Astelan when he states he does not know where Anovel is, but I am equally sure that Methelas holds that information. What we cannot prise from Methelas with blade and brand we shall nevertheless loosen with subtler means.'

'Very well.' Azrael swept his gaze across all of the members, both present and by proxy, a fist held in front of him. With his other hand he pulled back his hood, black hair spilling across his shoulders. 'The time of decision is upon us. Let it be known that the war on Piscina progresses swiftly to conclusion with the might of the Chapter ranged against greenskin and rebel alike. However, the conflict has much delayed us in the pursuit, as I suspect was intended by those that instigated the attacks on Kadillus and the destruction of the fortress here. The gene-seed was stolen by Anovel, I conclude, and to what end we already know. I consider the thwarting of this plot to be of the utmost significance, while the Raven-wing and Deathwing can stand ready for fresh duties. You have witnessed argument for and against Sapphon's proposal. Let judgement be made.'

The room descended to pitch blackness so that not even the Space Marines could pierce the gloom. Sapphon raised his right hand, in which he held a white sphere about the size of an eyeball. He placed it into a channel carved into the surface of the conclave table and let it go to roll down the incline into the receptacle at the table's heart. The black sphere in his left hand he placed in a gutter at the edge, where it clattered to his left to gather with other discarded votes in front of Azrael. The clack of balls rolling and dropping into the containers broke the still as the rest of the Inner Circle likewise made their decision known by the white or black.

Sapphon knew Asmodai would vote against. Belial too, most likely. Azrael seemed in favour of the plan, though his vote counted only once, his position no greater benefit in the matter of blind ballot. There were other allies and opponents to be considered but on the face of it Sapphon's proposal hinged on its merits rather than politics.

The lights flickered into life once more. Azrael activated a mechanical arm that swept out from the ceiling and brought forth the ballot bowl set into the centre of the table. The crane clanked and whirred as it carried the will of the conclave to be counted by the Supreme Grand Master. Sapphon looked away, not meeting the gazes, normal and half-mechanical, of the others around the table. The balls clicked as Azrael separated them into two slots before him.

'The white outweighs the black,' Azrael announced. 'Master Sapphon will bring together the two Fallen captives. Brother Asmodai will also be on hand to ensure the security of this encounter. Both will report to me in person within a standard day, at which point I will make further deliberations and decisions cogent with the will of the Inner Circle.'

Sapphon slowly let out a long breath, relieved more than he would care to admit. He turned to Asmodai, ready to offer conciliation but the Master of Repentance was already stalking from the chamber, shoulders hunched, hands balled in fists. One by one the servitors slumped as they were deactivated, while the other Space Marines filed after Asmodai, leaving Sapphon alone with Azrael. The Supreme Grand Master betrayed nothing of his thoughts, his face an impassive mask.

Sapphon nodded, a gesture of gratitude, and then bowed to show his respect.

'Asmodai does not take kindly to your gambles and plots, brother,' said Azrael.

'Asmodai does not take kindly to anything, master,'

replied Sapphon. 'Do not judge him harshly though. He has proven his worth many, many times.'

'It is not Asmodai's worth that needs proof,' Azrael said, pulling up his hood to shadow his features. 'You have one day.'

PACIFICATION

The pacification of Piscina was in full flow and every warrior was needed to combat the resurgent orks and pockets of rebels. Just days after their full initiation into the Deathwing and being accepted onto the combat roster, Telemenus and his companions found themselves readying for a teleport attack against an ork encampment. Though it had been purged years before, the orks kept returning to this place, the site of the tellyporta gate where many of the ork invaders had arrived on-world during the invasion by Ghazghkull and Nazdreg.

'Some residual ork psychic field, perhaps?' suggested Brother Menthius when the subject of the orks' attraction to the area was raised by Telemenus.

'Or some damn spore-carried beacon stench,' countered Daellon.

The three of them waited in the teleportarium situated above the Lower Docks of the Rock. It was a cavernous chamber, the walls lined with faceted plates of plasteel, fashioned with hexagrammic wards that could be activated in the event of a warp breach through the teleportation portal. The teleportarium was far larger than those of any starship, lined by huge conduits to the massive warp drives and antimatter reactors deep in the heart of the star fortress. Such power allowed several squads to deploy simultaneously from orbit, and there were three other such chambers across the fortress-monastery. With such facilities, the entire Deathwing could be dropped as one force into the heart of battle.

The teleporter itself was a wire-framed dome within the heart of the chamber, surrounded by a score of tall spires of girders, wires and dish-like projectors, each linked to its neighbour by a crystal-embedded matrix. The floor within the teleporter was fashioned from a jet-black substance unknown to Telemenus, which seemed to suck in the light, offering no reflection despite the harsh glare. It looked like a sheen of oil, a hint of rainbow-like colours pooled on the surface.

Having been told to muster with the rest of their squad at the appointed hour, Telemenus had roused his companions early, to allow plenty of time for them to arm and armour themselves with the aid of the tech-priests; to be tardy risked further chastisement from Belial or Sergeant Arbalan. As he looked at the inky plate of the teleporter he felt vaguely unsettled by the notion of being disassembled and transmitted, even for a brief instant, through the roiling sea of the warp.

'Or perhaps they simply do not know any better,' said Telemenus, answering his own question to distract himself. 'Orks are stupid and superstitious creatures, let us not attribute to higher meaning that which can be explained by unthinking habit.'

'I think Brother Telemenus has the right of it, after a

fashion,' announced Brother Cadmael from the teleportarium doorway. He was armed with a storm bolter and power fist as the others, but atop the back of his ivory-coloured Terminator suit, running between his shoulder plates, was a cyclone launcher, filled with a dozen light-weight anti-personnel missiles and the same number of anti-tank rockets.

As Cadmael entered he was followed by Sergeant Arbalan, a sword in his left hand where the others had power fists, and after him, the last of the squad, came Brother Arrias with twin lightning claws as his armament.

'Thank you, brother,' said Telemenus.

'After a fashion,' repeated Cadmael. 'The orks return to the teleporter site because they do not know any better, but not out of superstition but necessity. The orks we fight now are perhaps the fourth or fifth generation of such creatures since we first purged Kadillus. There have been systematic exterminations over those years and we have never wiped them out fully, but how can these new generations know the spot where so many of their kind arrived?'

'Hence my explanation,' said Menthius. 'The technology employed by the orks must have been similar in some way to our own, utilising warp power. Such transmissions as must have been necessary to move so many orks and light vehicles to the surface would have a profound effect on the warp-signature of the whole area.'

'A surprise that you did not seek to become a Techmarine,' said Arrias. 'With such technical knowledge you would be a boon to the armoury.'

'A passing interest, not a calling, brother,' replied Menthius.

'Does it matter a damn?' said Daellon. 'They go there. We go there. We kill them. Is that not correct, brother-sergeant?'

'Correct,' said Arbalan. He had not yet fitted his helmet and his gaze moved over Menthius and Daellon and rested on Telemenus for a moment – a fraction longer, Telemenus thought – before returning to the teleporter mechanism. 'Scouts have infiltrated the area around Naaman Heights, the site of the ork teleporter incursion many years ago. The terrain is hilly, broken by scrub and small trees in places. There is a geothermal power plant close to the insertion site, hence there will be no orbital support. Tenth Company squads are placing teleporter beacons as we speak and once we receive confirmation that they are in place we assault.'

The sergeant again looked at the newest three members of his squad and waved his sword at the teleporter.

'Teleportation is highly disorientating, even for those that have experienced it many times. You know the technology, each of us will be passed through a small warp-based tunnel to the planet's surface, but the reality is something else. Think of the moment of sickness a ship's translation causes and imagine that magnified ten-fold. We have no Geller fields, so we are completely exposed to the immaterium for that instant – an instant that may seem to last for several seconds, up to a minute from our perspective but I am told lasts no longer than point-five seconds, objective time.

'When we arrive on the surface we may be displaced and your suit's systems will be momentarily inactive. You must arrive at maximum readiness. Be prepared to assess the situation and engage the enemy without further authority. There is a possibility that I will not survive the teleportation, so chain of command is seniority. Use your sensorium to highlight and destroy immediate threats first – all other objectives and mission parameters are secondary.'

'What happens if there is a malfunction?' asked Daellon.

'Pray,' said Cadmael. 'If you survive.'

'Brother Cadmael has it right,' said Arbalan. He paused for a moment, raising a hand to the comm-bead in his ear as he listened. He put on his helmet and waved for them to follow as he stepped up onto the black flooring of the teleporter. His next words came over the vox-link. 'That was the signal from the Scouts. Beacons and triangulators are in position. I know that you are only just becoming accustomed to your armour but the power plant and surrounding buildings are close terrain and we are the best chance to secure the area from within and allow other companies to clear out the surviving orks. Remember that you are Dark Angels, the Emperor's First. We are the finest, His Angels of Death, retribution incarnate. For the Emperor!'

'For the Emperor!' the others chorused as they spread out across the teleporter bay, a few metres from each other in a circular formation facing outwards.

A schematic of the planned landing site sprang into view as Telemenus connected his sensorium to those of the other Terminators. Their relative positions flickered as green runes.

'Signal locked,' confirmed the Techmarine manning the controls beside a huge bank of digital displays and dials. Energy cells whined into action and lightning crept with bizarre slowness along the hanging cables, looking like serpents of energy slithering along vines. Forks of varying colour and ferocity started to spit and leap between the Terminators, moving from one tower to the others, linking them altogether, binding the Space Marines in a net of cracking energy. The Techmarine lifted a fist in salute. 'Purge the xenos!'

With this thought echoing through his brain, Telemenus felt his whole body lurch, splitting apart and sliding sideways through a dimension in addition to the normal four. He made the mistake of looking down at the black plate a moment before the teleporter fully activated. He was staring down into nothingness; a swirling vortex that existed somewhere between reality and the warp like a giant gullet about to swallow him whole.

His stomach, capable of digesting almost any organic matter, modified to be resistant to poison and toxin, did a somersault as material and immaterial forces intersected somewhere around the Space Marine's lungs. He felt like he was suffocating, his chest a solid piece of flesh.

The displays from the sensorium were wild and contradictory. There was no sensory input; no sound, no temperature, no light or dark, no pressure or gravity, but his directional and attitude indicators were whirling left and right, up and down, trying to get a fix on a position that did not exist in reality.

With a crack of expanding air displaced by his arrival, Telemenus was deposited on the roof of a bunker-like ferrocrete building at the edge of the power plant compound. On the street below him appeared Daellon and Cadmael, while Menthius resolved into existence just ahead. It looked as though Arbalan and Arrias had been lost, but a blip on his sensorium showed that they were actually inside the building beneath his feet. The wind was coming strong from the west, bringing a fine cloud of dust that was adding to the drifts already piled at the edges of the streets.

Still shaken by the warp transition, it took a moment for Telemenus to realise that along with grains of dirt pattering against his armour were bullet impacts. There were orks on a gantry above and to his left firing down at him, with more on a ramshackle tower next to them turning to see what had caused the shuddering boom that still echoed around the geothermal installation. Telemenus fired instantly, stitching bolt detonations across the xenos filth and their surrounds with a hail of fire. It was a clumsy fusillade, with none of the elegance and precision he found so reassuring, but it was effective. Five orks were ripped apart by two bursts, and another three were sent tumbling by a third.

'Assemble, point five,' barked Arbalan.

Telemenus checked the navi-grid on his display and turned to his right to head in the direction indicated by the sergeant. The roof sagged under his weight but he reached the edge of the low building safely. It was roughly two and a half metres to the ground, an easy drop in power armour but Telemenus hesitated, still not certain of himself in his Terminator suit. He felt momentary vertigo as he looked down, the distance exaggerated by the magnification of his auto-senses.

He granted himself a little more time, turning at the waist to fire his storm bolter down at a group of orks hurrying towards them through a gap in the buildings to the left. Heads exploded and limbs scattered through the air, detached by the welter of bolts that ripped along the street. As he moved to reload his storm bolter, his power fist deactivated, its crackling field dissipating with a pop. Telemenus pulled the magnetically-clamped magazine from his thigh, ejected the empty casing and slammed the fresh one into place with practised ease. The power field enveloped his reinforced glove the moment he was finished.

There was nothing for it but to make a leap of faith. Wary of overbalancing, Telemenus stepped out, pushing off with his toes. He crashed into the cracked ferrocrete ground, shattering the surface with the impact but staying on his feet.

Arbalan led the squad ahead, pushing northwards through the power plant, the three veterans at the front, and newest inductees behind them. Telemenus followed Cadmael, scanning the upper levels of the buildings while the other Space Marine was keeping watch at ground level; with a thought Telemenus could switch between the vid-feeds from the other suits and a subconscious part of him was monitoring what they saw as much as what he was directly observing. Pylons and conduits had collapsed across the roofs and blocked some of the streets, but they were little obstacle to the Terminators who wrenched and shouldered aside anything in their path, storm bolters picking off any greenskin foolish enough to come into sight.

'Movement, ground floor window,' announced Arrias. His view flashed up in Telemenus's left eye, showing a shadow passing a window in a long, low row of worker huts ahead.

'Daellon, investigate. Telemenus, maintain perimeter.' Arbalan's orders were spoken quickly but calmly, reassuring Telemenus that the sergeant was in complete control.

The door to the nearest hut had been ripped away in the past, and the hole that was left was not anywhere near big enough to accommodate a Terminator suit. Daellon ducked as best he could and forced his way inside, storm bolter at the ready, lintel and wall collapsing after him as he surged through the bricks. Checking the sensorium, Telemenus stayed outside and kept level with Daellon, watching the windows ahead. There were heat returns on the thermascope.

'All targets hostile,' Sergeant Arbalan reminded them. 'Purge with intent.'

'Affirmative,' replied Daellon and Telemenus together. The two of them opened fire, synchronising bursts between them. Brickwork turned to dust as Telemenus pounded the huts from outside while Daellon let fly through interior walls. A few sparks of las-bolts from a window two dozen metres ahead drew the attention of Telemenus. He returned fire, punching half a dozen bolts through the wall.

'Some kind of sub-level here,' reported Daellon. 'Descending.'

'Wait!' yelled Telemenus, but his warning came too late. The audio pick-ups brought the sound of splintering woods and crumbling ferrocrete followed by an almighty crash.

Daellon cursed without pause over the vox.

'Report,' barked Arbalan.

'Brother Daellon misjudged the load bearing of some internal stairs, brother-sergeant,' said Telemenus, trying not to laugh. For once he was glad somebody else was attracting the negative scrutiny. There was a chuckle from Cadmael and a sigh from Arbalan.

'Daellon, can you climb out?' asked the sergeant.

'Negative, a three metre drop at least. The floor will not hold my weight to pull myself up.'

'No threats detected,' Telemenus added, his auspex sensors encompassing the long row of huts.

'Understood,' said Arbalan. He sounded impatient. 'Daellon, remain in place, I will signal for an armoury extraction team. Telemenus, rejoin the squad.'

The growl of an incoming rocket wiped away any remaining humour. The projectile burst into flame across Arbalan's left shoulder, scattering shrapnel and ceramite fragments. Menthius, beside the sergeant, laid down bursts of fire every few seconds as the other

Terminators advanced. Telemenus picked out targets but could not bring his weapon to bear quickly enough as the orks dashed from cover to cover, running down the side streets between the worker habs, equipment sheds and the main power plant building.

'They are trying to encircle us, sergeant.' Menthius peeled away from the group as he issued the warning, firing off to the left.

'Understood. Menthius, protect our flank. Telemenus, what is keeping you?'

'Covering the rear, brother-sergeant,' said Telemenus. He had been turning every few paces to check the street behind the squad to ensure nothing was moving towards Daellon.

'Is there some problem with your sensorium?' Arbalan sounded angry and Telemenus knew better than to make excuses.

'No, brother-sergeant.'

'Then why are you turning to look when Brother Daellon's sensorium covers our rear?'

'Apologies, brother-sergeant. Increasing speed to your position.'

'Negative. Flank right, and provide covering fire towards the main gate. The Scouts should be making rendezvous in sixty seconds.'

'Affirmative, brother-sergeant.'

Telemenus suppressed a resentful grumble, realising that it was unworthy behaviour. He had made a mistake and the sergeant had corrected him on it. However, he could not help but feel that Daellon's far more catastrophic error had not been taken seriously, while his own minor infraction had brought down instant reprimand.

The rapid-fire snap of the cyclone missile launcher

drew his attention back to the squad as they came into view at the junction ahead of Telemenus. A flurry of missiles streaked from Arrias's back and smashed into the upper floors of the central power station above them. An ork body spun to the ground, splattering into the dirt just in front of Arbalan. Remarkably the ork was still alive; at least for the second between the impact and the sergeant's immense boot crushing the alien's skull into dust-covered ferrocrete.

Boosting power to his legs, Telemenus hurried on and turned right between two ramshackle workshops. Directly ahead was an impromptu ork barricade of barrels and upturned battered crates. The greenskins were pinned down by heavy bolter and sniper fire from two squads of Scouts beyond the curtain fence, making them easy targets for the Terminator. He fired half a dozen shots, trying his best to cut down the orks with one salvo. There was a single survivor from the burst, who turned in shock at the metal-and-ceramite giant bearing down. At close range Telemenus could not miss, his next burst of fire tearing the xenos in half.

'Gate secured,' he declared, checking the sensorium. There were no enemy signals within a hundred metres. A cluster of returns showed where the orks had barricaded themselves within the central geothermal delve site.

The Scouts emerged from the grass and rocks, their cameleoline cloaks shielding them even from the multi-spectral scanner of the sensorium. The ground where they had been was riddled with craters while scorch marks stained the boulders, evidence of the much heavier fire that had repulsed earlier attacks. The Scouts dashed up to the gate, sawing through chain links and cutting through metal spars and plates haphazardly welded across the gap by the orks.

A trio of Rhino troop transports and a Predator tank crested the ridge a few hundred metres outside the compound, moving at speed, their green-painted hulls visible past the overgrown ruins of the buildings that had once formed a small settlement around the power station. The armoured column crashed down the slope, firing at targets some way off to Telemenus's right even as they headed for the newly opened gates.

The hill – Naaman Heights – was named after a renowned Scout sergeant who had been instrumental in the destruction of the orks' teleporter array, and who had died somewhere in the ruins assisting the Deathwing in a similar teleport assault. It was sobering to think of the sacrifices that had been made in those battles. The Dark Angels had desperately clung on in their defence of Piscina until the rest of the Chapter had arrived in force. It had been luck more than anything that had placed the larger part of three companies on the planet at the time the orks arrived. Telemenus realised he had heard nothing of the five-man garrison that had manned the recruiting citadel in the intervening time. There had been no word of them when the Fifth Company had accompanied the Ravenwing here months earlier, and certainly no news during their return.

He decided that it was probably not in his best interest at the moment to be asking such questions, and it was likely they had simply been overwhelmed, either by the orks or traitors in the planetary defence force. Such matters were to be resolved another day; Arbalan would be waiting for confirmation.

'Incoming support, brother-sergeant,' Telemenus reported. 'Awaiting orders.'

'Remain in position, suppress ork activity and assist incoming forces as necessary.'

It felt like a rebuke, to be left out here guarding nothing while Menthius was with the rest of the squad performing the last assault on the central building with the others. All Telemenus could do was listen to the reports over the vox as his battle-brother continued to earn the respect and praise of the First Company veterans while he was left to regret his errors.

A RIDDLE IN THE DARK

'Unhand me!' roared Astelan as two Deathwing Space Marines manhandled him into the cell, heavy chains binding his wrists and ankles clattering along the floor. 'This is not what we agreed!'

They unceremoniously dumped the Fallen into the chamber, darting loathing glares at the other prisoner shackled in the corner, his head encased in a wrought iron cage laced with anti-psychic circuitry. Methelas shifted, manacles clinking as he rose to his feet, eyes fixed on the newcomer. With a clang that made Astelan wince, the door slammed shut, leaving them lit only by a sliver of lamplight from under the door and a narrow, flickering shaft coming through the viewing slot.

'Bastards!' snarled Astelan, hurling himself at the door. He grunted in desperation as he thudded his shoulder again and again into the unforgiving metal-bound wood. Eventually he slumped to the floor, blood streaming from his injured arm, resting back against the wall. He muttered to himself and the cell filled with the sound of metal links being scraped back and forth across the floor.

'Merir?' The voice in the darkness was guttural, edged with the slur of a healing jaw and toothless gums. 'Merir Astelan?'

The noise stopped and Astelan looked up from his labours.

'Methelas?'

'I wondered what became of you.'

'An unfortunate circumstance, as you can see.' Astelan resumed his scraping with the chains. 'I never gave you up, you and Anovel. I want you to know that. I told them Port Imperial had been destroyed. It was no word of mine that took them to you.'

For several minutes the only sound was the skritch of metal on stone.

'By Luther, will you stop that irritation!' snapped Methelas. 'This damn null-psi harness makes my head pound and your pointless scraping is like a rusted dagger being drawn down my brainstem.'

The sound ceased.

'Apologies, brother. They change the chains, now and then, but no sooner than every ten days by my reckoning. Of course, I have not the strength I used to have. Perhaps you could help?'

'Help? With what?'

'Escape, of course.'

'Impossible. Even if we got out of this cell, and even if we knew our way out of these catacombs, we'd b–'

'I know these tunnels and chambers, brother. Do you not understand? This is the crypt underneath the west tower of Aldurukh.'

'Aldurukh? We are on Caliban?'

Astelan let out a long sigh.

'Alas not, brother. Caliban is no more, destroyed as we fought the slaves of the Lion, I have learned. Aldurukh is all that remains of our world. The great shield protected the Tower of Angels from the storm that consumed us it seems.'

'You seem to have learned much since our parting. How interesting.'

'Fifteen years is a long time, brother. Fifteen years under their blades, and not a word of our plan did I speak, but I listened well, piecing together what has happened these ten thousand years.'

'Plan? We had no plan. I know nothing of which you speak. Leave me be.'

'I understand. You do not trust me, I think. Very well, we shall sit here together and not speak.'

The metal scraping began afresh, accompanied by a tuneless humming.

In a chamber on the level above the cell, Asmodai and Sapphon listened to the exchange emanating from a vox-set placed on the small table between them.

'Worse than useless!' snarled Asmodai. 'He is warning Methelas, can you not hear it? Now the witch knows he is not alone, that Astelan has survived here for fifteen years. There is no threat that can undo the hope brought by such knowledge.'

'For one who can labour for hours with the Blades of Reason, and sermonise for even longer, you show a remarkable lack of patience, brother,' said Sapphon. 'Did you think Astelan would win his trust in moments? Put yourself in Methelas's position for a moment and think how he would think.'

'I cannot ever conceive of the vile thoughts of such a creature,' said Asmodai. 'It is utterly alien to me.'

'You really cannot, can you, brother?' said Sapphon,

with some sadness. Asmodai's total lack of empathy was almost unique in Sapphon's experience; even amongst the Adeptus Astartes, a group not chosen for their emotional depth nor trained in anything but the utter suppression of basic feelings. While it made Asmodai perfect in some ways, utterly lacking in compassion or conscience and able to inflict pain and misery without a moment's regret, that same psychopathic propensity limited the Interrogator-Chaplain's ability to exercise other levers of control. He never understood his subjects' fears on anything but an intellectual level, and so could not fully exploit them.

'Are you sure that Methelas is unaware of our monitoring of the conversation?' said Asmodai.

'The Librarium assure me the suppressor-helm curtails all psychic sense. Further, Brother Ezekiel is in the adjoining chamber exerting influence to ensure Methelas cannot extend any supernatural sense. The vox-transmitter is so low-powered not even a Space Marine can detect its energy source. You seem vexed, Asmodai, and I think the security arrangements are not cause but merely symptom.'

The other Chaplain did not reply. His face screwed up in concentration as he listened to the scrape-scratch-scrape-scritch of Astelan abrading his chain links. Sapphon gave up trying to encourage his companion to share any worries he might harbour and took a drink from the jug of water beside the vox-receiver. The gentle ticking of a tape-drive recording device overlaid the sound of metal on stone.

'I knew it!' raged Asmodai, surging to his feet, the sudden movement causing Sapphon to spill water down the front of his robe. 'He betrays us yet again!'

'Wait!' Sapphon dropped the jug and lunged towards

Asmodai to grab his arm as the Chaplain flung open the cell door. 'Do not go down there, you will ruin everything!'

'You are a blind fool, Sapphon. Your tricks have been turned against you.' Asmodai tore free from the other Chaplain's grasp and strode back to the table. With quick fingers he stopped the vox-unit and spooled back the tape. He activated the playback. 'Listen!'

Sapphon heard the last part of the exchange between the two Fallen, and then half a minute of nothing but metallic scraping.

'What do you hear, brother? Sub-vocals? I hear nothing.'

'Listen closely,' said Asmodai.

The Master of Repentance started to tap a finger on the table, just slightly quicker than once a second. After about fifteen taps the rhythm was in Sapphon's head and suddenly he heard the pattern behind the sound of Astelan's scraping. There was more than idle noise; it was a code of some kind, an ancient battle-cryptocom he did not recognise.

'Clever,' said Sapphon, intrigued.

'You admire him?' snarled Asmodai. He thumped a fist on the table, knocking over the vox and recording device. 'He mocks us, treating us as fools, and you have words of praise for him?'

'Stay where you are!' barked Sapphon as Asmodai took several steps towards the open door. 'You will not interfere.'

'The Supreme Grand Master appointed me to oversee this debacle, and I will no longer allow it to continue.'

'I am still your superior!' Sapphon hated raising his voice, but it made Asmodai stop at the threshold. He lowered his tone when he continued. 'Do you not understand what Astelan is doing? By communicating in secret he is feigning allegiance. A lie hidden within the truth. He is probably telling Methelas that we are listening in, and to say nothing.'

'You argue my case back at me,' said Asmodai.

'But listen further. I laud your keen ear for detecting the code, but you did not follow its continuation.'

Asmodai frowned but did as he was told, listening intently to the static-layered noise still coming from the vox. Astelan's scraping stopped after a few seconds. There was the briefest of pauses and then another scraping noise began, almost identical but not quite, the subtle difference nearly lost in the bad quality of the transmission. This also stopped after several seconds and the original scraping resumed.

'Methelas is replying,' said Asmodai, lip curling with anger. 'It is this that I warned against, brother. You did not believe me then, but now allow me to act on proof of your error.'

'No, we must let them talk,' said Sapphon. 'Our best crypto-servitors will decipher the code easily enough. There may even be record of it in the earliest databanks. There can be only one of two outcomes. Either Astelan works against us and with Methelas, or he does not. If the former, we know he cannot be trusted as you claim, and that gives us advantage. And if he has turned against Methelas, this may be the only way the traitor will let slip any information of value.'

Sapphon could see the indecision wracking Asmodai. It was clear that he hated not knowing what was being said between the two, his natural instinct to corral and control anything beyond his understanding. Weighed against that was the logic of Sapphon's argument. After several seconds teetering one way and then the other in the doorway, he eventually relented to Sapphon's will and returned to his stool, arms folded tightly, glaring at Sapphon. The Master of Sanctity righted the vox-devices and sat opposite, meeting Asmodai's glare with a steady gaze.

'Astelan has too much to lose to play me false,' said Sapphon, assuring himself of this fact as much as he sought to convince Asmodai.

'And we have everything to lose if he does,' replied the other Chaplain.

TO CATCH A FALLEN...

After the day allotted to him by Supreme Grand Master Azrael, Sapphon had Astelan withdrawn from the cell, cursing and kicking as he had been deposited. Returned to the cell within the solitarium, sitting with shackled hands in his lap, the Fallen was confronted not only by Sapphon but also Asmodai, and with the two Chaplains Chief Librarian Ezekiel and Azrael himself. The leaders of the Inner Circle wished to witness for themselves whether Sapphon's plan had yielded any useful information, and the Master of Sanctity realised as he looked at Astelan's relaxed smile that he was probably more intimidated by their presence than the Fallen.

'You hold yourself as leader here,' said Astelan, looking at Azrael. 'Your heraldry declares as such also, though it is much changed from the time of the Order that I remember. Does it feel strange to bear devices from a defunct organisation that was based on a world now destroyed, to which you have no connection other than the fluke of being stolen from your family by a roving band of self-righteous murderers?'

Sapphon suppressed a wince and felt Asmodai stir with a growl, but Azrael greeted the question with a deep laugh.

'You have a unique perspective, which I find refreshing,' said the Chapter commander. 'I like "self-righteous murderers", particularly.'

Azrael stepped closer to the Fallen and his smile faded. Without warning, the Supreme Grand Master grabbed the front of the prisoner's robe and drove his fist into Astelan's cheek, knocking him sideways. He pulled him back upright and punched him again, repeating the attack three times more before letting go and stepping back.

'Billions dead on Tharsis,' said Azrael, flicking blood from his fingers. 'All by your command and all for your ego. Do not call me a self-righteous murderer when there is so much blood on your hands. Asmodai, you and your brothers have had fifteen years to finish what Boreas began, and that is time enough. If this creature lies, evades or otherwise refuses to cooperate fully with Brother Sapphon you will kill him, not swiftly and with great infliction of pain if possible.'

Azrael stalked from the room, leaving tense silence in his wake. Astelan levered himself back to a sitting position and grinned, showing freshly bloodied teeth.

'I probably deserved that,' he said. 'It was a rather rude thing to say.'

'Enough of your flippancy,' said Sapphon. 'We know that you communicated with Methelas. What did you learn?'

'And you expect me to divulge that information merely because you ask for it?' Astelan shook his head, wiped blood from his mouth with the back of his hand. He rested his head against the wall and closed his eyes. 'Wake me when you have a more tempting offer.'

'You seem keen for death, and I will grant it,' said Asmodai. Sapphon thought he detected something strange in his companion's voice; genuine happiness perhaps?

'I die a righteous man,' replied Astelan. 'Fifteen years wasted, my friend. I will not repent, not under threat of death.'

'Too much time has been wasted on your account already.' Asmodai flexed his fingers and stepped towards the captive. 'I cannot deny that I will gain pleasure from bringing about your end. Be assured I will make suitable penance afterwards.'

'Wait,' Sapphon said quietly. He looked at Astelan through narrowed eyes, trying to gauge his prisoner's conviction. For fifteen years the Fallen had duelled words and will against the greatest of the Chapter's interrogators and they had not broken him. 'Death is what he wants. Do not grant him that mercy.'

'The Supreme Grand Master commands. I obey.' Asmodai took another step but was stopped by a contemptuous laugh from Astelan.

'Supreme Grand Master?' The Fallen seemed genuinely amused. 'Was "Grand Master" simply not pompous enough?' The humour disappeared, replaced by a sneer. 'Even the Lion, colossus of arrogance and ego as he was, was content with the rank of Grand Master of the Order. Perhaps your commander seeks to outrank even a primarch?'

'He is goading you!' Sapphon spoke quietly but urgently. He looked to Ezekiel for support. 'Brother, you must see it as well.'

The Librarian turned his gaze on Sapphon, one eye a

red-lensed bionic, the other glittering with the flicker of golden psychic energy. Sapphon had faced death and dread on countless occasions and had attained his position by dint of immense willpower, but even he had to look away from that eternal, damned gaze after only a moment.

'I am here to ascertain the veracity of any statement the prisoner makes,' said Ezekiel, returning his attention to Astelan. 'I am a Librarian, not a Chaplain. I do not care to offer opinion on the conduct of his interrogation.'

'Then tell me this,' Sapphon said quickly. 'Is he telling the truth? Is he willing to die rather than tell us what we need to know?'

'Better still, why not prise it out of his head?' demanded Asmodai. 'Rip thoughts from the mind and leave the flesh to me.'

'Not this one,' Ezekiel said with a single shake of the head. 'We tried before. Brother Samiel... It did not end well. There is a shell we cannot penetrate, no matter how hard we try. Something we have never encountered before or since.'

'Kill me or make a bargain,' said Astelan. 'I am happy with either path.'

'That is true,' said Ezekiel.

'You know that we cannot release you,' said Sapphon. 'There is no comfort we will give you. Your continued life is simply a stay of execution – a sentence that cannot be commuted. For what do you bargain?'

'My honour, and a chance to restore it,' said Astelan. He grabbed his chains in his fists and leaned forwards, speaking with earnest intensity. 'We can argue for eternity about my actions but I never swore away my loyalty to the Emperor. I am not like Methelas and Anovel. *I am not corrupt.* They used me. Had I known to what depths they had descended I would have killed them. Let me prove it to you. Let me help you destroy this vile plot.'

Asmodai and Sapphon both looked at Ezekiel.

'Truth,' said the Librarian. 'He believes what he says.'

'How will you aid us?' said Sapphon.

'Enough of this!' Asmodai interposed himself between the Fallen and the Chaplain. 'He is a traitor! We do not negotiate with traitors. There is no good that can come of evil, no matter the intent.'

'Ulthor.'

Astelan said the word quietly and it hung in the air like a stale odour. All three Dark Angels shared a glance with each other.

'What do you know of this world?' snapped Asmodai.

'It is where you will find Anovel,' said Astelan. The Fallen moved to the end of the bench and turned so that his legs were along it, resting with his back to the wall, entirely too confident for Sapphon's liking. 'When I did not send word of success from Tharsis, thanks to your untimely intercession, the others sought a fresh source of recruits. Anovel made a pact with the Death Guard, and was told to meet with them on the world of Ulthor. You know of it?'

'It lies on the fringes of the Eye of Terror,' said Sapphon. It seemed the ideal location for a trap and he looked to Ezekiel. The Librarian caught his glance and nodded.

'It is as he was told. If there is deception, it is by Methelas,' said Ezekiel.

'Now that we know where to pick up the trail, we should dispose of this renegade and begin the hunt,' said Asmodai.

'Not yet,' replied Sapphon. He stared at Astelan who

met his scrutiny with a blank expression, affecting innocence. 'You know that by divulging this to us you condemn yourself?'

'Most certainly.'

'What other truth do you possess to bargain?'

'Myself. I know of passwords and codes that are to be used in exchanges. It seems to me that Ulthor would be a dangerous place to attack, but with my help perhaps that will not be necessary. Why thrust your fist into the maw of a beast when I can bring forth what is within?'

'Absolutely not!' For one so often ignorant of subtext Asmodai had caught Astelan's meaning quickly enough. 'No prisoner leaves the Rock. You will die within these walls.'

'I concur,' said Sapphon, amazed that this was Astelan's gambit. Did he really hope that they would allow him out of his cell, offering him chance to escape?

'Ask yourself a simple question,' said the Fallen. 'What am I worth to you? More specifically, how many of your *brothers* will you sacrifice to keep me? A dozen? A score? A company?'

'Your threat is without basis,' said Asmodai.

'I can prevent their deaths,' Astelan continued, looking directly at Sapphon. There was no trace of amusement anymore; the Fallen had a hard stare and his jaw was set firm. 'Chain me, imprison me, do whatever you need to assure yourself that I cannot escape. Take me with you, or sacrifice the lives of your warriors to unfounded fear.'

Sapphon's hatred of Astelan returned with a vengeance. Asmodai ranted about knowing no fear but the Master of Sanctity did not listen. His thoughts were whirling, chasing themselves around his head. Astelan had to be planning to gain his freedom – *had* to be. And that could be made impossible. Nothing else made sense, unless the Fallen genuinely wanted to prove he was not in league with the Ruinous Powers.

Part of Sapphon wanted to let Asmodai have his way; to let his brother kill this manipulative bastard and be rid of him. He could not, with clear conscience. He was not Asmodai, who could argue away the death of a hundred battle-brothers with talk of purity and duty. Sapphon recognised the need for sacrifices; he was still a warrior first and foremost. But he had been chosen because he walked into the darkness, daring to consider the terrible, imagine the unimaginable. The whole Chapter would be needed for an all-out assault on Ulthor, and the fighting for Piscina was not yet done. Swift action would be impossible. Any lesser force risked annihilation against an enemy of unknown strength. Astelan was offering a third alternative.

'Brother Asmodai,' said Sapphon. The Chaplain ceased his raving. 'You swore an oath not so long ago. Do you remember it?'

'Of course. I do not present binding words lightly.'

'To what did you swear, by the shade of the Lion no less?'

'To support your methods to ascertain what we require, whatever that demanded of me.' Asmodai's face twisted with disbelief as he realised what Sapphon had asked. 'No! You swore there would be no trickery. You cannot use my honour against me like that.'

'I must,' Sapphon said with a sigh. He looked at Astelan sure in the knowledge that he was about to place his fate, partly at least, in the hands of a self-confessed genocidal megalomaniac. 'It is likely that one or the other, or possibly both of us, will be dead before this matter is finished.'

'Almost certainly,' the Fallen replied with an insincere smile. 'Do we have accord?'

Even as the Fallen uttered these words, Sapphon knew that the choice had already been made. The darkness, the unknown beckoned to him. Though he had not quite realised it, his choices for the past few days had been guiding him towards this moment with all the surety of a well-aimed bolt-round. What the Master of Sanctity could not know, however, was whether in reaching this point he would be hailed as one of the greatest heroes of the Chapter or forever reviled as a black-hearted traitor.

It surprised, relieved and then worried Sapphon that he did not really care which it was.

OATHS

Telemenus had no idea where he was. He had been led blindfolded to a chamber, his mnemonic sense of direction confused by the circuitous route, backtracking and, at one point, a period of weightlessness. He found himself in a circle of light, next to Menthius, Daellon on the other side of his battle-brother. A disembodied voice commanded them to pay respect to Grand Master Belial and they knelt as the Deathwing commander appeared from the shadow. There was no sound from his footfalls and nothing to hint of a door opening or what lay beyond in the utter darkness outside the circle of light.

Then the oath had begun, slowly spoken by Belial and repeated by the battle-brothers in hushed reply. Oaths of secrecy thrice-bound; oaths of fraternity until death; oaths mentioning names and places and ranks of which Telemenus knew nothing.

'Unto the Order, the Founder and the Lords of the Keep I shall oblige myself to all truth, secrecy and trust.'

Telemenus had sworn many oaths during his time as a Space Marine: when he had been taken as a novitiate; when he had been accepted into the Tenth Company Scouts; when he had received his black carapace; when he had first put on his power armour; before his first engagement as battle-brother. Twenty-seven oaths in total, not including pre-battle declarations, as he repeated the words intoned quietly by Belial. Of those, this being the twenty-eighth, only this latest recitation made no sense at all. He parroted the words as earnestly as Menthius and Daellon as they knelt in front of the Grand Master, but he could not help but feel that the others somehow drew a deeper meaning than he did.

He wondered if there was a teaching from the Chaplains that he had missed during his several recent incarcerations in the penitentium, or a book of vows he had forgotten to read.

'By the blood of my left hand I swear allegiance to Aldurukh and the Seven Signs of the Heavens. By the blood of the right hand I offer my life as penance to the fortunes of war. Unto the flat of the blade I place my honour, unto the edge of the blade I place my soul.'

Belial crouched and proffered the Sword of Silence, half of its dark blade exposed from the sheath. In turn, each of the Space Marines taking the oath laid their hands upon the sword for a moment. Belial then lifted the Sword of Silence, kissed the hilt and placed it on the floor beside him.

'With the Key of Caliban, to bear witness for my brothers-in-arms, I take up the mantle of the charitable, the wise and the strong. With the Key of Caliban, as my brothers-in-arms bear witness for me, I take up the burden of the hopeless, the ignorant and the weak. By such rites, under the stars of the Seventh Tower, I swear on the soul of my liege and my kin to speak nought of what passes in this circle.'

Belial took up the sword again, unsheathed it fully and stood up. With the point barely touching the ground he paced around the three oath-takers, slowly orbiting with the glowing blade. By the flicker of its light, Telemenus could see thousands of such circumferences inscribed in the grey stone of the floor, each a tiny, slightly wavering ring of varying width, dependent upon the number of brothers encircled at the time of the oath, he guessed. Some were at the very edge of the light, enough for a dozen brothers and more, and he wondered if there were larger circles still in which scores of newly elevated Deathwing had sworn their vows at one time. Belial dimmed the blade, lifted the hilt to his forehead and once more slipped it into its scabbard with solemn purpose.

'My honour is forfeit, my life sacrificed, my family disowned.'

Telemenus said the words, a little disturbed at their meaning. No Dark Angel owed allegiance to their family, not since that first oath at the beginning of their training. His life he had long considered in the hands of fate and his superiors. His honour, however, was something he thought solely his to protect and prize. Why would it be forfeit now?

'Unto the Order, the Founder and the Lords of the Keep I shall oblige myself to all truth, secrecy and trust.' Belial finished with a long bow, which the Space Marines returned. When Telemenus looked up again it was to see the Grand Master standing straight with arms folded across his chest.

'Embarkation aboard the *Penitent Warrior* begins in thirty minutes. Brother Daellon, Brother Menthius, you will report to Sergeant Arbalan. He will give you instruction.'

The other two battle-brothers departed without a word, though Telemenus caught a glance of concern from Daellon as they turned and left. Belial gestured for Telemenus to stand.

'Am I not to travel with the company?' Telemenus asked, horrified by the prospect. He cast his gaze at his bare feet. 'Have I shamed the Deathwing so greatly?'

'I am undecided,' Belial admitted. 'Look at me.'

Telemenus did so, and found himself the subject of an intense stare that bored into his soul.

'You lack commitment, Telemenus. Your brothers outstrip you in training and yet you continue to be distracted, losing focus at critical moments.'

Telemenus was about to defend himself, to point out moments of laxity from the others, but a twitch of an eyebrow and curl of a lip from Belial dissuaded him.

'Yes, Grand Master,' he said meekly.

'You are not without skill, that much is certain from your past achievements and battle record,' said Belial. 'Your recent excursion was less than exemplary.'

'Yes, Grand Master.'

There was a long intake of breath and the sound of Belial shifting from one foot to the other and back again as he considered what to do.

'Please, Grand Master, I implore you not to make rash judgement.'

'Rash? No judgement I make is rash, brother.'

'I am a worthy warrior. Give me leave to prove it and I will. If it is not to be, my life will be the price I pay.'

'And the lives of those that you fight alongside?' Belial said sharply. 'Do you offer up those as penance as well? Would you bargain the ruin of all we strive for on your ability to surpass expectation? Your life is worth much

– many decades of training and experience as a warrior of the Dark Angels. It is not to be thrown away lightly. Those of your battle-brothers are so much more valuable. But yet all warriors are ultimately expendable. Your armour? Your armour… Its service to the Emperor has outlasted yours tenfold, twentyfold. A relic of the great times of the Legion, that suit you would gladly allow to be damaged, perhaps destroyed.'

'I did not think, Grand Master.'

'You did not, and yet sometimes you think all too much. You second-guess the wisdom of those that have honed you into a warrior these many years. Doubt. It is like a stench that surrounds you, Telemenus. I caught its scent the first moment you came to me and it still cloys now, clinging to you no matter what you do to purge yourself of its presence.'

'I am not worthy, Grand Master. You are right, I should not endanger my battle-brothers with my presence, nor sully the honoured history of my armour. I will remain behind and continue to train.'

'That is not your decision to make.' Telemenus glanced up to see Belial regarding him not with anger, or pity, but a calculating look. 'A bolter can be fired a thousand times, a thousand-thousand times and never jam, and yet on the one occurrence it does misfire it could be fatal. There is no end to the test of battle, and no means to prove beforehand which bolt will misfire.'

Telemenus was not quite sure whether that boded well or ill for him. He chose a platitude that seemed to suit the situation.

'I am subject to your will, Grand Master.'

Belial thought some more, every passing second drawing out the agony, each moment a lifetime of uncertainty for Telemenus to endure.

'Your brothers still hold you in high regard, and Sergeant Arbalan informs me that you make progress with each passing day,' the Grand Master said eventually. He laid a hand on Telemenus's shoulder, surprising the Space Marine, who jolted upright and was met by a more kindly gaze than he had come to know. 'You will come with us, and you will continue to train. I will leave it to the reports of your brother-sergeant whether I consider you fit and ready for active duty amongst the Deathwing when we arrive at our destination. This is your only warning.'

'Thank you, Grand Master,' Telemenus said with a long exhalation of relief.

'Do not thank me. We leave for perhaps the most dangerous mission any of us will undertake during service to the Emperor. You may yet have cause to regret my indulgence.'

PART TWO

ULTHOR

PAINFUL DIVINATION

It seemed strange that such a ceremony should be conducted in the light, when so much of the Dark Angels inner mysteries took place in darkened chambers, but Harahel had been insistent in the manner in which the chamber aboard the *Implacable Justice* was arranged. He sat on a plain chair, a small throne almost, beneath a great wheel-like candelabrum, another dozen candles arranged around him at the apexes of a twelve-pointed star enclosed within a circle, in turn encompassing a hexagonal device marked with runes in dribbled lead. These were, Harahel had assured Sapphon, not part of any diabolic ritual, but a means to protect both the Librarian and those that would witness his delving into the warp.

With Asmodai, Belial and Sammael, Sapphon waited as Harahel readied himself, each of them dressed in their robes except for the Librarian who wore his power armour and the wire tracery of his psychic hood. Harahel's eyes were closed but there was a dull light glowing through the lids, briefly glimpsed more brightly as the eyelids flickered and his eyes moved from side to side.

It looked to the Master of Sanctity as though the Librarian was asleep, his hands tucked together in his lap, head resting back against the chair, legs slightly apart, mouth open just a fraction. There was no sign of the trepidation that had been evident when Harahel had entered; a trepidation Sapphon could easily understand because he felt a similar nervousness himself.

Like all Space Marines he feared no mortal threat; it was impossible for him to be afraid of death or injury or any horrifying creature of flesh and blood. Through psycho-hypnotic suggestion he could control that fear, crush it with iron discipline and drive it down into the depths of his mind where it could not affect his thoughts or actions.

The immortal was an entirely different matter.

As a Chaplain he knew intimately the workings of the Space Marine psyche, including his own, and for ten thousand years many had laboured to eliminate the fear of the supernatural and the uncanny, but no matter what therapies and mind-triggers were introduced there was always a residual reaction to the otherworldly. Sapphon had his own theories on the matter – that the daemonic and the Chaotic interfaced directly with the soul rather than through physical agency that could be barred – but whatever the cause, the fact remained that psykers and the corrupt always brought with them a feeling of unease.

'Do not fear for my soul, Brother Sapphon,' Harahel said quietly, sensing the Chaplain's thoughts. 'Every hour you spent reciting the hymnals and catechisms of the Chapter I spent hardening my spirit to temptation and possession.'

At the mention of such things Asmodai, standing to Sapphon's right, shifted his weight, perturbed. A smile crept onto Harahel's lips.

'Please, Brother Asmodai, draw your pistol if it would make you feel more comfortable. I assure you, the wards are intact. The only person at risk is me.' Regardless of the assurance offered by the Librarian Asmodai drew his bolt pistol and aimed at Harahel's head. 'Do not be too quick to use your weapon, brother, for there may be strange occurrences that are simply part of my delving into the warp.'

'You seek to send your soul to a world upon the edge of the Eye of Terror,' said Asmodai, aim unwavering, 'and I will take any precaution I feel necessary.'

'As you see fit, brother. Now I must crave silence and to assist me it would be beneficial if you all focused on a particular thing, to stop the turbulence caused by your disparate thoughts as I enter the immaterial.'

'The Canticles of Nazeus?' suggested Sapphon, and received a nod in reply.

He began the invocation, the others joining in after a few moments, their voices rising and falling as they chanted the verses, the acoustics of the chamber rebounding the words back at them in odd harmonies. Harahel was silent and still, though every few seconds a finger would twitch and his brow was deepening into a frown of effort.

The Librarian whispered something and the Space Marines ceased their chanting to listen. Around the Librarian's head a nimbus of power emerged, a faint glow of greens and blues that shimmered with the candlelight. It seemed to Sapphon that the area within the marked circle was darker than the chamber without, the light being drained away.

'Boundaries falling, walls breaking, the tumble of worlds and civilisations,' muttered Harahel, his lips barely moving though his eyes were flicking rapidly behind their lids. 'The barrier sweeps aside, revealing the light beyond, the silvery path.'

The Librarian straightened on the chair, his power armour whining with movement, limbs trembling slightly as his muscles became rigid for a moment. He relaxed again, frown softening, mouth opening with a gasp.

'On the border it stands, neither here nor there, real and yet unreal. Claimed but still free, the world of decay, a blossom in the dead garden. Upon the brink of hope and despair it stands. Death and rebirth, the spiral of decline, until nothingness...'

'He is losing his mind,' said Asmodai. 'Or something is taking it!'

'Hold fire and tongue,' said Sammael, laying a hand on the Chaplain's bolt pistol. Asmodai darted a look of annoyance at the Grand Master. Sammael glared back, eyes narrowed. 'Do not think reputation and rank greater than mine, Asmodai. Lower your weapon, *Brother-Chaplain.*'

With reluctance, Asmodai dropped the bolt pistol to his side. He glared at Sammael and returned his gaze to Harahel, who had been whispering throughout the exchange. The aura around the Librarian was growing, even as the hemisphere defined by the cabalistic ring continued to darken. The candles were tiny flames now, linked to Harahel with threads of light that danced and wavered as though stirred by a breeze.

'Look, in the light.' Belial pointed just above Harahel's head. In the nimbus of power shapes were coalescing, forming into recognisable features. A forest, drooping

leaves turned by autumn to russet and gold, mist streaming between the boles tinged with green and blackness,
a diseased smog. In the distance an immense edifice
soared above the woods, indistinct, giant and grotesque.

The view was ever-shifting, not a painting but more
like a vid-projection on a stream, constantly changing,
never quite becoming one thing or another. Sapphon
saw storm clouds and rockfalls, tides coming and going,
eating away at a towering cliff face of dark stone. He
glanced at the others, wondering if they saw the same
things: were these projections from Harahel or something else?

More movement caught Sapphon's eye and he looked
around the room. The shadows cast by the guttering light
seemed unnaturally sharp, jagged at the edges, not quite
corresponding to the people and objects that cast them.
The glimmer of the light caused the darkness to undu-
late in odd ways, ragged shapes hardening and softening
like a pic-capturing unit trying to attain focus. Various
grotesque silhouettes half-lurked in the shadows, always
on the edge of vision, disappearing when the Chaplain
turned his gaze upon them. Sapphon wanted to look
at the floor behind him, to see what had become of his
own shadow, but thought better of it.

'Ulthor, brother,' said Sammael, stepping closer to the
Librarian. The black of his robe seemed to suck in what
little light remained, leaving his face a pale mask floating in gloom. 'Cast your mind to the world of Ulthor. It
is close, brother.'

The two strike cruisers, the *Implacable Justice* of the
Ravenwing and the *Penitent Warrior* carrying seventy
warriors of the Deathwing, had braved a long journey
through the warp to rendezvous in wilderness space not
far from the last recorded location of Ulthor. On the very

edge of the immense tempest known as the Eye of Terror, Ulthor was an unknown quantity. Before making the final jump into the system, breaking into the immaterial fringe of the warp storm itself, the Dark Angels needed to know everything they could.

Harahel flinched and tensed again. His breathing came more quickly and his fingers moved from his lap to grip the arms of the chair.

'The black rose, a thousand flies crawling on the petals. The stem bends but does not break, swayed by foetid winds carrying pollen of despair to the bright flowers of hope. A choking presence, cloying.' The Librarian gasped loudly and flung a hand to his face, covering his eyes though they were still shut. The darkness around him was absolute, the vista of light-woven scenes playing about his head turning like a kaleidoscope, coming in and out of focus. 'A field of maggots, lain beneath the bosom of the world, full of vitality, waiting to burst forth. They hear me. The blind worms see me.'

Beads of sweat were running down the psyker's brow and the light leaking from beneath his eyelids took on a rusty hue.

'The warp is claiming him,' snarled Asmodai, shoving aside Sapphon to stand at the very edge of the psychic circle. 'Something is burrowing into his mind.'

'Do not break the field,' warned Sapphon, taking a step closer. 'We must trust to his assurances, brother.'

Asmodai darted a look at Sapphon that conveyed his contempt for the assurance of psykers more clearly than any words. Sammael moved up beside the Chaplain, eyes flashing with anger, but he did not lay a hand on Asmodai.

'The pods, all in a row, dangling from the tree of death like the hangman's fruit.' Harahel was feverish now, skin ashen, limbs twitching like a palsy victim. 'Little skins of metal, peeling back, revealing the maggot within the womb. The thorns drip with blood, coiling about the city, snaring all that would enter.'

'The city, Harahel, what of the city?' said Sammael, eyes flicking between Asmodai and the Librarian. 'Think of the city.'

'The majesty of decay, towering and fallen, standing solid upon the shifting sands.' Suddenly the Librarian stood up, knocking the chair to the ground. Sapphon felt a moment of dread as Harahel opened his eyes, revealing milky-white corpse eyes. A rope of saliva drooled from the corner of his mouth.

'No!' shouted Sammael, tackling Asmodai to the floor. Sapphon realised that his fellow Chaplain had been about to shoot.

'They are here!' snarled Harahel.

Sapphon looked at the way the Librarian's features contorted, inhuman, baring teeth, savage and unthinking. He drew his pistol while Asmodai wrestled himself free from the grip of Sammael. The Master of Sanctity aimed at the Librarian's left eye, knowing the shot would punch through into the pysker's brain and slay him in an instant, cutting off the conduit for whatever was trying to use his soul as a bridge into the mortal world.

He was about to pull the trigger when Harahel collapsed with a shriek.

The Librarian lay still, face down. The light flowed back from his body to the candles and the strange shadows faded back to normality. It was only now that Sapphon noticed the lead symbols of the floor had turned to indistinct blobs, sizzling, spitting and steaming as though on a hot plate.

Harahel pushed himself slowly to all fours and looked

at them. Trickles of blood marked him from ears, nostrils and eyes, quickly drying and clotting on pallid skin. Sapphon looked into the Librarian's eyes, dark brown with disappearing flecks of gold, and saw the warrior he knew looking back. Asmodai was not yet convinced, his pistol once again aimed at Harahel.

'What are the three Abjurations of Assiah?' demanded the Chaplain.

'Despise the mutant, abhor the heretic, loathe the alien,' Harahel replied, voice hoarse.

'And name the six principal Lords of the Keys,' Asmodai insisted, the muzzle of his pistol following Harahel's head as the Librarian righted the chair and, with much wincing and grunting, forced himself upright.

'Nessiad, Direstes, Thereoux, Mannael, Dubeus, and...' The Librarian hesitated, a twitch in his eye. For a moment Sapphon thought he saw something else, a dimming of the gold, a momentary stain of blackness flowing along a dilated blood vessel. 'And...'

Asmodai fired.

The bolt took off the side of Harahel's skull, ripping through the intricate wiring of the psychic hood, spattering gore across the rune circle.

'No!' Sammael's bellow rebounded around the chamber. 'A lapse of memory, that was all.'

Sapphon intercepted the Grand Master of the Ravenwing as he lunged at Asmodai. Dragging Sammael away, the Chaplain saw Harahel's corpse collapsing, his face, what remained of it, frozen in an expression of surprise.

'He was gone,' Asmodai said bluntly. He turned to Sammael and holstered his bolt pistol. 'It was a mercy.'

'You murdered him,' snarled Sammael.

'I think not,' said Belial, who had watched in silence for the last few moments. He gestured towards the protective ring. The lead symbols had vaporised completely. 'Something had come through.'

With an anguished moan, Sammael turned away, head in his hands. Asmodai watched him with impassive eyes.

'You were right to act, brother,' Sapphon said.

'I know,' Asmodai replied. He looked coldly at Sapphon, lips pursed for a moment in thought. 'I am always right.'

'Can we trust to the testimony?' asked Belial, ever practical. 'What hope can we wring from disaster?'

Sammael replied, voice breaking at the thought of the loss of a long-held companion.

'I know many… He shared many visions on the Hunt. I can see the signs, speak of their truth.' The Ravenwing commander composed himself and started to pace slowly about the ring, gaze down, not looking at the corpse in the middle of the chamber. 'Ulthor is trapped on the edge of the Eye, caught between the immaterial and material. There are denizens of the abyssal ones living there, sustained by the warp breach. A daemon world.'

'Nothing else?' asked Belial. 'Nothing of the Death Guard, perhaps?'

'Ah yes, the Death Guard are there, the "little skins of metal". At least, they have been there and might yet still be, or will be. The warp does not follow strict chronology. The birthing must be related to the gene-seed.'

'It is there already? The gene-seed?' Asmodai asked the question hastily, concerned and excited equally by the prospect.

'It is connected, but when and how I would not venture to say.'

'It follows that Anovel has been there, or is still there,' the Chaplain continued, invigorated by the idea. 'We cannot delay.'

'What of Astelan?' asked Sapphon. 'We will need him to broach contact with the denizens of Ulthor.'

'He is irrelevant,' snapped Asmodai. 'He has brought us this far but he will play us false and see us all doomed. We cannot expose ourselves to such risk.'

'But why collaborate to this point?' asked Sapphon.

'Spite?' suggested Belial. 'He has lured us here, the finest of the Chapter. A single misplaced word could warn the Death Guard of our presence and intent.'

'Brother Sammael, you must see that we cannot blindly attack,' Sapphon said, turning to the Master of the Ravenwing,

'I must concur with Asmodai and Belial.' Finally Sammael looked at Harahel's corpse. 'We have already sacrificed one brother to caution and circumspect. Further delay risks further danger. Better to strike fast and hard, as the Ravenwing and Deathwing have acted in concert for thousands of years. The Ravenwing will be the eye and the Deathwing the fist. Ulthor occupies a real space overlap. There is no need to translate from the warp and so we can arrive in orbit directly. The Ravenwing will recon in force and bring down the Deathwing against the concentration of the foe, else withdraw without overreaching our resources.'

'The Ravenwing will find the traitors and the Deathwing will crush them.' Belial pounded fist into palm to illustrate the sentiment.

'We are in accord,' said Asmodai.

'We are not!' said Sapphon, but his protests went unheeded.

Three hours later the two strike cruisers translated into the empyrean, destined for the warp-bordered world.

INTO THE EYE

From the *Implacable Justice* and *Penitent Warrior* Ulthor looked like many other worlds; a globe of swirling grey and green against a backdrop of stars. Looks were deceptive. As the Thunderhawks, heat-shielded Land Speeders, Nephilim fighters and Dark Talon interceptors of the Ravenwing dropped into what should have been the planet's upper atmosphere, everything started to change.

It began with altitude warnings blaring across the flotilla of incoming craft, warning of imminent impact. Pilots wrestled with their controls as hurricane strength gusts lifted and spun their craft where no air pressure should have existed. Instrumentation went haywire, crippled by the unreality of the daemon world's half-immaterial nature, unable to gauge massively contradictory measurements. Arcs of dark green lightning crackled across the hulls of gunships and earthed along the fuselages of the descending aircraft.

At least the Space Marines aboard hoped that they were

still descending, because it rapidly became impossible to tell. A thick murk of fog enveloped everything. Between the total lack of visibility and nonsensical instrumentation readings it seemed likely they would crash at any moment.

Like the other Black Knights, Annael had been virtually thrown from the saddle of his steed when the Thunderhawk carrying them had almost flipped over. Also like the others he was now dismounted, gripping a handrail and staring out through the armourglass of a viewport, trying to make sense of the miasma that churned past. So thick was the smog it felt that the Thunderhawk was stationary while eddies of dank mist curled past them, while logically Annael knew that they must be dropping down towards the surface of Ulthor at an incredible rate.

Moisture started building up on the outside pane of the viewing slit and he heard the pilot complaining over the vox of a mucus-like slick covering the canopy of the flight deck. Tybalain moved towards the cockpit, bent forward as though striding uphill, though Annael's senses told him the gunship was straight and level, as best he could judge.

'I would suggest we forget the whole endeavour as a bad idea, but I do not think we can return to the strike cruiser even if we desired,' said Sabrael. He tried to make his comments appear in jest but Annael detected the tenseness in his companion's voice that betrayed an uncharacteristic apprehension.

'A little late for regrets now, brother,' said Annael. The Thunderhawk lurched to the left. With a screech of metal the hand grip Annael was holding came away from the bulkhead, crumpling in his tightening grasp. He looked at it dumbly for a moment and then realised he had been holding on so tight he had pulled the five-centimetre-thick rail free from its bonding. He dropped the twisted piece of metal and forced a laugh. 'Let us agree not to tell the armourium how that occurred.'

The gunship was juddering now.

'In any other situation I would take that as a sign of a thickening atmosphere,' Annael said, hoping to dispel his unease with pointless chatter. It was a sign of poor discipline, but right at that moment that was the least of his many concerns. 'But here I think all wagers are void.'

His remark was greeted with silence, adding to the tension. Alone with just his thoughts for company, he started to mentally recite the Catechisms of Resolve to occupy himself.

'Look, the fog is thinning,' exclaimed Nerean, his helmeted face pressed up close to one of the larger windows. 'I think I can see movement. A Nephilim, maybe.'

Annael passed the empty bike clamps and benches arranged along the Thunderhawk's main bay to stand next to Nerean, mag-grips in his boots pulling his feet down onto the decking. Nerean swayed aside to let Annael see. There was a dark shape, he was sure, though how far away was impossible to judge. It was moving parallel to the Thunderhawk, wisps of cloud trailing from what must have been wingtips.

'Coming closer,' said Annael as the object started to resolve through the fog. He activated his vox to warn Brother Naethel, who was piloting their gunship. 'Possible collision, starboard side.'

'Affirma–'

Naethel's reply was cut short as a monstrous maw loomed out of the fog, lined with teeth as tall as men. The beast it belonged to was easily as large as the Thunderhawk, kept aloft on ragged wings, dark leathery skin pocked with sores and lesions. The creature slammed into the gunship, forcing Annael to take a step to avoid falling, the others grabbing hold of whatever they could to steady themselves.

'Where is it? Where did it go?' Tybalain demanded over the vox. Annael staggered back to the porthole and looked out but could see nothing.

'No sound,' said Sabrael. 'Not a screech or roar or anything.'

'Keep watch.' Tybalain clambered back down alongside the stowed bikes, looking out of the viewing slots to either side. 'Find it.'

'It disappeared,' said Annael. 'I am sure that it just disappeared.'

The fog was thinning rapidly. The streak of drop pods could be seen, alongside the resolving forms of other descending craft. Suddenly the cloud vanished altogether, revealing a landscape that looked like a diseased carcass: white, with thick hair-like structures forming patches of darkness, the whole vista bloated and torn with red valleys that looked like wounds. The pallid ground was rushing up to meet them and Naethel cursed over the vox as he pulled the Thunderhawk out of its steep dive.

Annael was sure he should have felt more G-force from the manoeuvre but instead he was getting moments of heaviness interspersed with periods of weightlessness.

'Nothing here is real,' he muttered.

'What was that?' demanded Tybalain.

'Nothing here is real,' Annael said, loudly and slowly. 'It is a warp dream.'

'A warp dream given form,' the Huntmaster growled back. 'Do not think for a moment that we can just wake up from this. We will be landing soon. Mount up!'

Landing on that fleshy surface seemed ridiculous but Annael did as he was commanded and sat astride the saddle of *Black Shadow*. Instantly he felt reassured; the solidity, the touch of the bike through his armour's tactile relays gave him a sense of purpose and reality.

From where he was sat Annael could see nothing of the ground, but the continuous bank of cloud above was visible through one of the ports. The whole sky was a sickly yellow and brown, churning with its own energy. Black patches with grotesque faces rippled across the bulging mass, extruding down after the descending drop craft with fanged maws and glaring red eyes, turning like sentient whirlwinds.

'There's some kind of city, the Grand Master is commanding that we rendezvous on the outskirts,' reported Naethel.

'City?' said Tybalain. 'Rendezvous where, brother? Coordinates? Distance? Bearing?'

'No geo-tracking devices functional, brother-sergeant. The Grand Master simply said to make all speed to the city. I can see a smudge of darkness to starboard, but there is a mass of storm clouds above. Black storm clouds, thick with activity.'

'Better to make groundfall outside of that,' said Tybalain. 'Set us down a kilometre from the storm's edge, as best as you can judge.'

'Affirmative. Making touchdown in approximately ninety seconds.'

Annael thumbed *Black Shadow*'s engine into life, feeling the mechanical steed shudder with power as he tested the throttle. The growl and smoke of the other bikes filled the interior of the Thunderhawk. The gunship banked heavily to starboard for a few seconds, affording a view of the ground. This close it looked even more like pallid flesh, though more ridged and humped than Annael had realised at higher altitude. There were undulations like folds of skin, smooth-edged crevasses and puckered orifices from which issued forth the noxious clouds that filled the sky.

'What is that?' asked Nerean, pointing ahead to a dark stain spreading across the bare ground. From the gunship it looked like columns of ants trekking out of their colony, but as the Thunderhawk closed the distance the insect-like creatures resolved into more humanoid forms, stocky and hunched, swathed in leper rags. The back of each splayed out into a hideous basket shape woven of bones and sinew, in which had been piled jagged pieces of rock the colour of raw meat. Their stumbling steps left faint imprints in the surface as they marched in files out of a maw-like opening beneath a bone-crested ridge.

'Where is the light coming from?' asked Sabrael. The Space Marine shifted in his saddle to look out of the windows on the other side of the gunship. 'I see no sun.'

Annael saw that this was true; no brighter patch in the clouds that might betray the presence of the star Ulthor had been orbiting.

'Do not expect the natural laws to apply here, brothers,' warned Calatus. 'I would say trust only your eyes and ears but I fear that even they may be misdirected in this cursed place.'

'Be sure of your target when you fire,' added Tybalain. 'Check armour transponders.'

They did as they were commanded, sending out bursts of data to each other to synchronise the friend-or-foe scanners built into their auto-senses. Four blips appeared on the tactical display of *Black Shadow*, Tybalain and Calatus in front of Annael, Nerean and Sabrael bringing up the rear.

The Thunderhawk shook violently and for an instant was plunged into darkness, every slit and window utterly black. The moment passed and putrid yellow light seeped in once more.

'What was that?' snapped Tybalain.

'Something out of the storm, brother-sergeant,' replied Naethel. 'I have located a level landing zone. Touching down in thirty seconds, combat deployment.'

The roar of the plasma jets became a whine as the pilot throttled back. More light filled the interior as the assault ramp beneath the cockpit opened, revealing pale soft ground speeding past a few dozen metres below.

'Braking for drop! Five... four... three...'

The Black Knights released the brakes on their machines while the clamps that held them in place on the deck snapped back into the bulkheads. As Naethel's count reached zero he hit the gunship's retro-thrusters, bleeding off their momentum in seconds. Inertia threw the squadron forwards along the deployment rails, gunning their engines as first Tybalain and then the others, one after the other, were flung forward onto the ramp.

The Thunderhawk had halted about two metres up and Annael felt as though he and *Black Shadow* were gently gliding through the air as Space Marine and steed left the end of the ramp at speed. The bike hit the ground harder than Annael expected, jarring his arms as his suit locked to compensate for the impact. Annael had imagined the surface of Ulthor to be soft like the flesh whose colour it shared, but the landing and squeal of tyres betrayed an unyielding, gritty substance.

'Over to the right,' said Tybalain. Annael looked up and saw the black roiling mass of the unnatural storm, tendril-like clouds flailing down towards the ground, swatting at drop pods and gunships, while Nephilim and Black Talons slalomed between descending columns of immaterial energy.

Beneath the tumult sprawled a dark conurbation that, on first look, resembled some immense carcass riddled with worm holes and gashes. It erupted from the flesh-coloured ground, a bizarre conglomeration of ribbed structures layered with tattered skin and gristle melded with huge brick-walled edifices with narrow windows. At the centre a termite mound-like structure rose up into the storm, its summit lost from view, immense flanks riddled with countless garrets and turrets. Frond-lined avenues radiated out from huge rusting gates, descending into the city, each teeming with movement that could not yet be identified.

Towering chimneys of brick belched forth what at first appeared to be smoke but upon closer inspection was revealed to be endless swarms of flies. Looking up again, Annael realised that the storm and its appendages were flies also, countless billions of fat black, bristled bodies and veiny wings. Closing the distance to the city brought a steady monotonous drone; an irritation that would have been deafening without the dampening effects of the auto-senses in Annael's armour.

Some distance to the right, perhaps half a kilometre away – Annael was starting to regain some sense of perspective now that they were on the surface – more of the stunted labourers shuffled and stumbled across bare rock, some carrying rusted saws, drills and axes; others had chains hooked into spinal growths on which were dragged sleds piled high with mouldering wood and timber thick with sprouting fungi. They paid no heed to the black vehicles sweeping past overhead and converging on the city all around them, staring ahead with wide, black eyes in flat noseless faces. Some had thick, matted hair and beards, others were devoid of all hair, their skin grey and blotched with pustules and boils.

'Servants of the Dark Powers,' hissed Calatus. 'Slavemasters.'

Annael had not noticed the slightly taller figures spread along the column. These creatures were more gangling, with bloated bellies and bony limbs. They were cyclopean, and each also had a single jutting horn on its forehead, some broken, others cracked; greenish-grey skin, yellowed in places like dying leaves, split with sores and tears that showed glistening organs and exposed sinew. They held rusted triangular blades and though Calatus had called them slavemasters there seemed to be no goading or lashing, no cajoling or threats.

'Listen,' said Sabrael. 'Adjust your audio scanners to lower range.'

Doing so, Annael heard a faint murmuring in the distance and realised it was chanting; the slow steady invocation of the daemons. There was no change in pitch or rhythm. Though he could not understand the words being spoken Annael was left in no doubt that the creatures were methodically counting, like children concentrating on the task.

'Shall we divert to kill them, brother-sergeant?' asked Nerean.

Tybalain considered the question for several seconds before replying, eying the distant column.

'Negative, unless they present a more obvious threat. We head for the city.'

Swathed with gloom, the great edifice of Ulthor squatted across the landscape like a brooding beast, spewing flies. Effluent and sludge oozed out between the ridges and undulations of the surrounding land in oily rivers. Yet for all its imposing size and disgusting appearance, the city seemed defenceless. Annael could see no towers or walls, no gun batteries or bunkers to protect the approaches. He pointed out this to his companions.

'That would be fortunate indeed,' said Sabrael. 'We can ride straight in and ask nicely if they have seen the one we seek.'

Looking at the hundred-metre high fungal fronds and quivering spires of vertebrae, twisted and heaped tiled roofs slicked with moss, and the ever-present fly swarm above, Annael knew that their mission would not be so easily accomplished.

CITY OF DECAY

The red bricks of the wall to Annael's left became a three-mouthed appendage that extruded itself towards the Black Knights, fangs of crumbling mortar dripping with ropes of dustlike saliva. He fired his pistol, smashing apart the bricks with three bolts, the constituent parts of the tentacle tumbling like a demolished tower.

Sabrael fired his bike weapon at a swelling bubble of veined stone bulging from the door of a building ahead; both Sabrael's steed and *Black Shadow* had been upgraded with devastating plasma talons instead of bolters whilst en route to Ulthor. The ball of plasma smashed into the uneven sphere, puncturing it like a gas-filled balloon, though instead of air the wound poured forth a torrent of vomit-like filth and maggots. This organic detritus immediately started congealing into another tentacle, growing lashes of worms with disturbing human faces that hissed and bared their teeth as Tybalain and his squadron roared past. Nerean struck with his corvus

hammer as he passed the apparition, smashing its glowing beaked head through the writhing pseudopod in an
explosion of milky fluid and fleshy matter.

The city itself had responded immediately to the presence of the Ravenwing. The first squadrons to enter the
low lying outskirts had been assailed by swarms of flies
and immense slug-like beasts creeping forth even as the
structures warped into flailing appendages and gnashing
maws. Sammael had ordered the company into three
spearheads, each driving into the heart of the city from
a different direction, aiming towards the mouldering
keep at its centre.

Gunships and fighter craft bombarded the writhing
streets ahead of the advance, trying to cut a way through
the ever-changing edifice with missile and shell. Where
bone and brick was shattered by lascannon and heavy
bolter it dissipated into sludge and mist, becoming the
formless ectoplasm of raw warpstuff. Such damage was
temporary; whatever conscious mind or mad whim
or base instinct that gave life to the city moulded the
warp-substance into fresh forms as quickly as they were
destroyed.

There were other problems. One Dark Talon pilot had
fired his aircraft's rift cannon only for the warp-powered
weapon to malfunction, engulfing his machine with a
hardening crust of filth that filled its jets and caused
it to plummet from the sky. Another had dropped a
stasis bomb; the resultant detonation spawned a towering monstrosity of rippling, barbed tentacles and
flame-spewing gullets rather than a time-dampening
field. From that moment the air support was restricted
to Thunderhawk attack and Nephilim strafing runs.

Similarly the Darkshroud Land Speeders that so often
accompanied the Ravenwing, shielding them with a

perpetual gloom, were forced to turn back from the city. When they activated their arcane engines instead of the usual swathe of shadow the Land Speeders had disgorged tides of ravening beetles and green-and-black-bodied wasps.

The city itself resisted them, but it was not without denizens to defend its streets. A giant that seemed to be an unholy blend of rotting tree and broken pillars lumbered into view a few dozen metres ahead, easily five metres tall. Its massive fists of gnarled wood lifted for the attack. There was no need for Tybalain to issue an order; the moment the beast appeared the Black Knights opened fire, concentrating their plasma talons on the monstrous conjuration.

Its wooden flesh sparked immediately into an inferno as the plasma blasts struck, while stone flesh ran in rivulets like blood. Still the colossus was not destroyed, taking a stride towards them, its root-like foot becoming one with the heaving, rippling ground, forcing the squadron to swerve hard around sweeping talon-tipped fingers. A fingernail shard of jagged marble slashed along the back of *Black Shadow*, leaving a ragged welt through the ceramite. Annael turned in the saddle and fired back with his bolt pistol, the shots doing little to the unnatural creature.

'Shall we go back for it?' said Sabrael, glancing over his shoulder. 'It seems a shame not to get better acquainted.'

'Negative,' replied Tybalain. 'Our only concern is to reach the inner district and place teleport homing beacons for the Deathwing. This is no place for us. The First Company can earn their honours today.'

The thought heartened Annael. There was probably less than two kilometres to go between them and the growth of gargantuan fungal fronds that surrounded the central keep as a curtain wall. If they pushed hard they would be there within minutes. Looking back past the burning figure of the giant, which was striding after the Black Knights, Annael could see the city animating itself even further, buildings pulling themselves up from the bedrock, reforming and changing into gangling colossi with hides of brick and bone armour.

'Signal the Grand Master, our air cover should concentrate on those behemoths,' said Annael. 'Reaching the fortress is not going to be the problem – getting out will be.'

Tybalain looked back and saw what Annael had seen. He nodded and there was a buzz across the vox of a coded channel opening. Annael did not have time to ponder what Sammael's response might be. A horde of the one-eyed daemons he had seen with the slave column was pouring out of grinning mouth archways at the far end of the street. Over the haphazardly slanted tiles of the surrounding roofs boiled millions of flies, an almost solid apparition that smashed into the Black Knights, thousands of bulbous insect bodies bouncing off their power armour, each impact negligible but together strong enough to knock Annael sideways and fling Nerean to the ground.

They had to stop, forming a circle around Nerean while he remounted, blinded and deafened by the mass of black bodies flying and crawling everywhere. The plague daemons burst through the tide of flies, serrated, rusted blades swinging. Annael reacted quickly, deflecting a triangular sword with his left arm while he drew forth his corvus hammer. He crushed the head of the creature that had attacked him, its body turning to slurry to seep into the ground.

His movement restricted astride the saddle, Annael

did his best to fend off the blows of the daemon-things trying to surround him. He swept his hammer left and right in broad arcs to knock them back and smashed off heads and limbs. He realised he was shouting, bellowing battle cries of the Chapter with every blow. He heard the sound of crunching and splitting bones, though he knew as sure as anything that the things he slew were not of true flesh and blood.

'We have lost the initiative!' snapped Tybalain. 'Break out and gain speed!'

Rusted blades shrieked across Annael's right shoulder pad and backpack as with another swing of his hammer he swept aside two daemons clambering over the front of *Black Shadow*. He gunned the throttle and slammed into the gathering crowd of creatures, using his steed as a battering ram. Nerean carved another path to his left, the rest of the squadron following, corvus hammers and bike guns blazing.

The buildings had warped around them, turning the roadway into a broad courtyard surrounded by bulging archways. Gates of fingerbones started closing across the exits. Annael accelerated even harder, ducking his head a moment before he crashed into one of the intertwining barriers. The force almost knocked him off the back of his bike but he clung on, front wheel rising as he powered through, splinters and chips of bone spraying in his wake. Moaning and shrieking, the plague daemons followed after the departing Black Knights, running after with awkward strides, joints twisted and cankered.

Spires of rock threaded with pulsing veins drilled up through the ground, rupturing like new teeth, cutting off the line of attack to the fortress, diverting the bikers along a colonnade of jutting ribs to their right. Slathering, frond-mouthed beasts lunged and flopped across the road ahead like basking seals. Plasma bolts seared through them, turning the hideous creatures into splashes of paste-like ichor and charred skin fragments. *Black Shadow*'s wheels slipped and slid as Annael passed over the remains, the tyres squealing for traction.

Another gigantic guardian loomed ahead, stepping over a fluttering barricade of feathery gills, its long arms contorted with extra joints, headless torso made up of a chimney still disgorging thousands of flies. A thick hide of encrusted filth slewed away like skin being sloughed off, revealing tarnished metal bars and crumbling brick-work. A furnace maw opened, spouting an arc of flame across the road, splashing onto the front of Sabrael's steed. His front tyre exploded, sending the bike into a cartwheel while Sabrael was tossed bodily into a lichen-covered wall.

Annael braked hard and spun his steed around, passing back between Tybalain and Nerean. He slewed the bike around another one hundred eighty degrees as he reached Sabrael. His battle-brother seemed reluctant to climb up behind Annael.

'Get on!'

Sabrael looked towards the smoking remnants of his bike. Many times he had boasted of coming through an engagement without his steed being hit and now he suffered the shame of a total loss. The Techmarines would not be coming here to reclaim the lost bike, not even in victory. Already the roadway was turning to mush beneath the machine, swallowing it like quicksand.

The crackle and heat of more flames from the giant washed over Annael.

'Sabrael! Do not be a fool!'

'One moment, brother.' Sabrael dashed back down the road, the black of his armour scuffed down the length of his left side where he had been thrown clear. He stopped beside the bike and did something to the controls before sprinting back and jumping onto the back of *Black Shadow*. He had the armoured casing that contained his bike's machine-spirit under one arm. 'A little gift for this vile place!'

Annael accelerated after the others, who were circling the daemon-giant, smashing away at its legs with their hammers, steering clear of its flame-filled mouth. A bang on the shoulder from Sabrael caused Annael to look back just at the moment his companion's steed exploded. The detonation was half-swallowed by the ground, but as the plasma chambers of the bike's main weapon overloaded a bright blue star engulfed the street, tossing burning gore and debris high into the air to leave a perfect half-sphere crater.

Sabrael laughed, but his joy was cut short as a fist wrapped in dying foliage smashed into the ground next to them, throwing up a fountain of dirt and pus. Stone shards and globules of fatty tissue pelted the Space Marines, slicking across the vid-display of Annael's bike and clogging one of his backpack's air intakes. The giant withdrew its hand, taking a step back as it swept a coiling tentacle at Tybalain. The Huntmaster ducked, the ser-rated edge of the vegetative pseudopod carving a furrow along the back of his bike.

'It is no good, we have to fall back,' said Nerean. 'It is too big for our weapons.'

'We can brook no delay,' said Tybalain. The behemoth was between them and one of the avenues leading up to the fortress. 'With the city mutating around us there is no guarantee we will find another route. We have to get past.'

Grand Master Sammael's calm voice cut across the vox. 'Stand by for support.'

A few seconds later the air ripped apart with the roar of an assault cannon, hundreds of impacts slicing along the body of the chimney-giant in a cloud of brick dust and pulverised mortar. Heavy bolter detonations tore into the mouth-furnace, turning corroded metal into flakes and slivers, spilling hot coals from ruptured innards.

The Grand Master's Land Speeder, *Sableclaw*, swept over the heads of his elite guard, still firing its heavy weapons into the giant. A stone knee exploded, toppling the creature sideways like a felled pillar, its parts separating as it crashed down. Smoke and flames swept over Annael and Sabrael as they raced through the billowing debris, bumping over pieces of molten flesh and shattered bricks.

Reaching the avenue, Annael could see that the curtain wall had suffered sustained bombardment; as he watched a Nephilim fighter swept towards a breach, its weapons systems chewing holes into the fleshy wall of fungus. *Sableclaw* swept around to come alongside Tybalain as they sped up the avenue rising towards the fortress, Sammael at the driver's controls.

'Smooth and swift, brothers.' The Grand Master spoke over the company vox, addressing all of the Ravenwing. 'Breach the curtain wall, activate teleport homers and leave the rest to our brothers in the Deathwing. Once your beacons have been set, fall back to the city edge by any means necessary. Air assets will continue support strikes under the command of Grand Master Belial.'

Affirmatives chorused back across the channel as the Ravenwing responded, bikes and Land Speeders converging on their target from across the corrupted city. Sammael stood up in his land speeder and held aloft the Raven Sword for his Black Knights to see. He looked down, meeting the gaze of each in turn as they raced up the avenue.

'For the Lion!' he shouted, pointing his blade at the citadel, and Annael shouted with him.

MANSION OF MADNESS

Telemenus thought it fortunate that his first teleportation incident had left him unscathed. His second most certainly did not.

He could not suppress a gurgling growl as his inner organs attempted to leave his body via his mouth. White-hot nails were driven into his eyes and ears. Hooks had burrowed into his brain and were ripping it apart piece by piece. All the while the telemetry from his sensorium spouted insanity, as it had done during the brief warp transition before, but this time it did not stop.

A wave of euphoria swept through Telemenus as his armour boosted the painkillers and anti-nausea stimms coursing through his modified circulatory system. Nausea turned to dizziness, which receded into a vague sense of displacement. Agony became pain, which resolved into a dull throbbing ache throughout every bone and muscle of his body.

The sensorium was still reeling wildly, unable to cope

with the warp overlap of the half-material world. With a spoken command Telemenus shut it down, keeping only basic auto-senses active so that he could see, hear and touch. That helped more than the stimms, removing the flood of data that threatened to send him spiralling back into semi-consciousness.

All of this had taken a handful of seconds; not long in itself but a lifetime of vulnerability in battle Telemenus realised. He took stock of his surroundings.

He was in some kind of semi-organic chamber, with walls of what looked like limestone deposits found in caves, stalagmites and stalactites forming pillars from bowled floor to arching ceiling. There were clusters of gristly nodules in places and softer, fluctuating panes of flesh between bone-like infrastructure. Around these seemingly natural formations were pipes, rusted and dripping. The smell was horrendous, of a cadaver left long to rot mixed with fresh faecal matter. Telemenus shut down his armour's olfactory filters immediately. What appeared to be tunnel mouths branched off at random angles.

Most importantly, Telemenus could see nothing of the rest of the squad.

Without the sensorium operating there was no way to detect their suit signals, and they were not within eyesight or earshot. In fact the surrounding area was disturbingly quiet, the silence broken by a distant, exterior humming and the occasional soft, wet pulse of fluid through the pipes around him. Light was emanating from scabrous growths, greenish and faint. He rubbed the grip of his storm bolter across one of the lesions and it flaked away like dry skin, revealing seeping veins beneath that trickled blood-like fluid from the wound.

Disgusted, Telemenus stepped away without looking.

He almost toppled as his back foot slipped on a slick of unidentifiable grey fluid bubbling up from a sphincter, dribbling down the slope of the floor into another orifice at the base of a wall.

'This is Telemenus,' he said, activating a company-wide vox-channel. 'Telemenus, seeking confirmation from anyone that can detect this signal.'

The walls pulsed inwards, several fleshy parts whistling like loosened valves. Yellow gas puffed from spiracles in the ceiling. It enveloped Telemenus and the paint on his armour started to fizz and bubble, eaten by the acid. The ceramite layer beneath was hardier, discolouring slightly but otherwise undamaged. Though his suit could survive inside a volcano or even withstand the massive pressures of gas giants and deep sea, it was not impregnable. Eventually a seal or weak point would give way. As another pulse of gas filled the chamber he decided he had better leave.

There was no means to tell which way would lead to the rest of the Deathwing. They were to teleport in two waves, but evidently despite the signals from the teleport homers planted by the Ravenwing the first wave had been scattered all across the target citadel. This was the situation they had hoped to avoid and it seemed the lost brothers of the Second Company had died in vain.

That was despondency talking. Without the effort and sacrifice of the Ravenwing perhaps the First Company might not have been able to teleport at all, or worse…

He focused on the positive aspects of his situation. He had arrived in one piece and was inside the enemy fortification. Somewhere here there were enemies to be killed, and their commander to be captured if possible. If he had survived then so too had others, he was sure. This place could not be so vast that they would never come together. Even now Belial was probably bringing squads together for a determined assault.

Telemenus thus saw that he had two mission objectives. His priority was to locate any enemy and slay them. The second mission was to join up with the other elements of the assault force. To achieve the second would require a degree of luck and starting out in any particular direction was as likely as any other to take him closer to allies. On the first, the slaying of the enemy, he knew that whichever way he went he would come across a foe sooner rather than later.

LEADERSHIP

It was obvious from the moment Sapphon recovered his senses that all was not well. Waiting with the second wave aboard the *Penitent Warrior* he had been horrified to learn that contact had been lost with the Ravenwing, only for hope to return when their teleport homers were detected. However, the moment Belial had teleported to the surface with the squads of the first assault the ships' scanners had fallen blank once more. He had ordered the second wave to teleport as soon as possible, using the coordinates fixed for the initial attack.

Of his five-man honour guard, only Fidellus with his thunder hammer and storm shield and Brother Satrael, armed with a heavy flamer, had arrived with the Master of Sanctity. Vox-checks showed that there was no comm-link between the squads and the First Company warriors were forced to shut down their sensoriums, which had been rendered useless by the warp-reality interface of Ulthor.

'Secure perimeter,' Sapphon ordered over the external vocalisers.

They had arrived in something like a furnace room, presumably somewhere near the base of the enemy stronghold. The air was dry and hot, a dozen open furnaces that burned with green-and-yellow flame spilled heat and light across crumbling bricks of floor and walls. The ceiling was thick with black soot, seemingly accreted over countless generations although Sapphon knew Ulthor had until a few years ago been an Imperial world and the construct they were now in had not existed then.

'Main doors secured,' reported Satrael. 'Corridor, thirty metres, no enemy.'

'No other exits,' confirmed Fidellus, rejoining Sapphon. The battle-brother looked around, storm bolter tracking the movement of his gaze. 'What is this place?'

Sapphon moved to a nearby pillar and drove his fist into it. Brick shattered, but underneath where one might have expected to find plasteel bars or ferrocrete was a bone-like substance along which ran dark veins. Sapphon punched again, breaking into another layer, this time of almost formless greyish slime, flecked with globules of gristle that started to coagulate, hardening into a new protective layer, turning red to match the brick.

'It is raw warp made into matter,' said the Chaplain, pulling his hand away with a shower of bloody droplets. He knew it was not blood at all but it was hard to think of the dark red fluid in any other way. He chose his next words carefully, for although many in the Deathwing had been initiated into the lore of the Dark Angels they were not all aware of the true nature of the warp and the daemons that inhabited it. 'A psychic construct, made possible only here at the edge of the Eye. No more real than the flame of a psychic blast.'

'Such flames can still burn and kill,' said Satrael.

'True,' conceded Sapphon. He motioned for Fidellus to follow and walked over to Satrael. 'Whatever may seem unreal here is certainly material enough to cause injury, even death. We must find the others quickly.'

With Satrael leading the way, the corridor only wide enough for them to advance in single file, the three Space Marines set out from the furnace room. The passageway took them to a junction, the route to the left staying level, on the right the corridor became a set of steps going up after a few metres, and it was upwards they headed. The tunnel-like stairwell was barely large enough for them to pass, backpacks and shoulders scraping furrows in the moss-covered brickwork as they forced their way up the steps.

At the top was another corridor, far wider, the brick-like skin giving way to a fleshy surface that undulated slightly as though rippled by a breeze. A slow, rhythmic thudding like a heartbeat could be heard reverberating along the walls and floor.

'Brothers!' Satrael called out as two ivory-armoured giants appeared through an archway ahead. Sapphon recognised their livery: Nemascus and Haerus. The two Terminators, part of the first assault, shouldered their way out into the corridor.

'A welcome sight,' said Haerus. 'The first we have seen since arriving.'

Sapphon noticed that there was thick ichor splashed across their armour, as well as cuts and cracks in the ceramite.

'You have encountered the foe?' asked the Chaplain.

'Aye, and they regretted it,' said Nemascus. He lifted a power fist, its disruption field crackling. 'Humanoid and others, not of mortal flesh.'

'Like this palace,' added Haerus. 'See?'

He kicked at the wall, which disintegrated at the blow. Another kick and a punch had opened up a hole into an adjoining chamber large enough for the Terminators to pass through.

'What of the warp-spawn, do they die as easily as the walls crumble?' asked Sapphon.

'They do, and a rare treat it is,' said Haerus.

'They fall as easily as living creatures here,' said Nemascus. 'No warp blessing to protect them. In this place, between material and immaterial, mortal and immortal are the same, it seems.'

'A good thing to know,' said Satrael.

'There is bad news also,' replied Haerus. He stepped through the hole and beckoned the others to follow. Sapphon ducked through and found himself in a long column-line gallery, though the columns appeared more like femurs, and the floor was awash with a shallow trickle of thick fluid. At the far end, the floor was bulging up in several places; horns and single-eyed faces were pushing out of the fabric of the palace.

'I see,' said the Chaplain. He opened fire, blasting apart the emerging daemons. Their burgeoning heads turned to black pools of filth, spreading out slowly through the mire. Moments later, half a dozen pillars started contorting, forming into pot-bellied figures, arms and swords lifting away as faces pushed out from the bone.

'Problematic,' said Fidellus.

'Indeed,' replied Satrael. 'We fight the whole building. It is all one mass: creatures, edifice, world. How can we kill such a thing?'

'We do not attempt to,' said Sapphon, heading up the gallery towards the manifesting daemons. Dangling polyps in the ceiling swayed towards him, growing eyes and barbs as he approached. 'We seek the Fallen, or news of his whereabouts. The nature of our location does not change this.'

'As you command, Brother-Chaplain,' said Satrael.

'Just so,' replied Fidellus.

Two of the daemons tore themselves free of the structure just in front of Sapphon. He smashed one aside with a single blow from his crozius arcanum. The daemon's flesh became a fog speckled with wet fragments that drifted to the ground like sodden leaves falling from a tree. Fidellus's power fist despatched the other, a blow to the midriff turning the otherworldly creature into a smear along the Terminator's arm.

'Unpleasant,' said Fidellus, trying to shake off the filth.

'Press on,' said Sapphon.

It was time-consuming to battle every apparition and half-formed assailant, and so the Deathwing warriors stopped only to fight those manifestations that were fully formed, or to clear away grasping, slashing appendages and other weapons of the palace itself. They headed steadily upwards when they could, Sapphon convinced that regardless of the strangeness of the stronghold, the normal hierarchy of the ruler wishing to be above his domain would hold true even here.

As they battled their way up through the citadel they encountered more of the First Company. Soon Sapphon's small force numbered eleven other warriors, and they advanced at speed, certain they would find more of their battle-brothers in the halls and chambers ahead. More confident than when he arrived, he despatched a squad of Terminators to look for other survivors, sending them away with the instruction that any warrior they encountered was to be sent up; in the higher reaches of the palace the Deathwing would come together again.

FURY

Mewls, whines, growls and howls added their harmony to the rhythmic thunder of storm bolter fire. The entire citadel rebelled at the presence of the intruders, ripping itself apart, reshaping stairways and columns, floors and balconies into grasping claws and cyclopean monstrosities. Walls fell away to become swarms of ravaging beetles, while sinewy roots erupted from doorways to ensnare anything that approached. Flies the size of bolt shells were vomited forth by lesion-marked maws torn out of window slits while giants made of brick and mould waded into the Deathwing with club fists and rusted iron teeth.

Asmodai did not register the strangeness around him, but saw the ongoing battle in a monochrome fashion: allies and targets. A tide of beetles crept over his black-painted armour, their carapaces shining like oil, turning him into a writhing statue of chitin and rage as he tried to sweep them away with the side of his combi-bolter and the butt of his crozius arcanum.

'Brother Allius!' The heavy flamer-armed Terminator turned as the Chaplain called his name. 'Cleanse me!'

The Space Marine hesitated a moment and then opened fire, washing burning promethium over the Terminator armour of his superior. Warning lights and sirens flashed at the temperature rise but Asmodai was unconcerned; his suit was designed to withstand far worse. After a few seconds, Allius ended the gout of flames, leaving a sticky, drying crust crackling across Asmodai's armour.

There was no sign of Belial. Asmodai had been standing right next to him on the teleporter pad, but a stomach-churning few seconds later and they had been deposited in completely different parts of the target area. A methodical search had ensued, in which Asmodai had gathered up twenty more of the Deathwing, but had revealed no sign of the First Company Grand Master.

There was a lull in the violence; colour and clarity started to return to the Chaplain as ire simmered down to dull anger. He noticed that two of his battle-brothers had been taken down during the fighting, though he could not recall how. Semmean had lost his right leg; Namnos had been punctured through the chest multiple times. Apothecary Temraen was attending to them both, his white armour splashed with blood as he attempted to examine Namnos's wounds.

'Brothers Tyronius, Vascaertes, protect the Brother-Apothecary and then follow when the casualties are secure.'

'Televacuation, Brother-Chaplain?' asked Tyronius.

'No,' said Asmodai with a shake of the head. 'No teleporter fix. The only way we leave this citadel is to fight our way out when the mission is complete.'

'Affirmative, Brother-Chaplain,' said Tyronius, moving

to stand guard at one of the corridors coming into the large hall. Vascaertes positioned himself to cover another entryway.

'Follow me, show the enemy no mercy,' said Asmodai striding towards a stairwell that had, a minute earlier, been a serpentine mass of barbs and suckers.

'I did not realise we had been,' muttered Sergeant Daeron.

'Enough flippancy!' snapped Asmodai, not turning to look at the wayward Space Marine. 'Ten days in the penitentium when we return to the ship. Concentrate on the task at hand, not on vacuous humour.'

'Apologies, Brother-Chaplain.'

Asmodai paid no regard to the sergeant's contrition. He was occupied using what auto-senses he had remaining to scan the stairwell ahead. It seemed dormant for the moment but he had no desire to march directly into the gullet of some daemonic conjuration.

The steps led upwards, splitting into two curving sets of steps. About twenty metres away each disappeared beyond two asymmetric archways before being lost in the gloom of fog and the buzzing remnants of the clouds of flies. Asmodai pressed on, turning right on a whim, for there was no means of knowing which flight would take him closer to the foe.

After another twenty metres, through which the stairs had curved through one hundred and eighty degrees, the Chaplain stepped through another misshaped opening onto a long ledge that ran alongside a wall on the right shaped like half a rib cage, arching overhead to link with vertebrae-like vaults. To the left the floor sheared away as though cut by an axe, ragged but steep. The ledge was four metres wide, narrowing and widening by a metre or so for stretches, angled slightly up and visible for several hundred metres before hanging fronds of red moss and ruffles of pale yellow fungus obscured the view.

Asmodai stepped out onto the ramp and looked down into the chasm. He stepped back in shock, taken aback for a moment before forcing himself to look once more.

The ledge seemed to be dizzyingly high – thousands of metres dropped away below the Chaplain. But it was not this vertiginous view that had surprised Asmodai. At the bottom of the shaft dwelled some immensely bloated creature; or several creatures, for it was possible that their flabby bodies were pressed so hard together in the confines that they could not be discerned as separate. Hundreds of eyes glared back at Asmodai, some of them clustered like an insect's, like the many-faceted crystal orbs of flies and spiders, scattered amongst bloodshot, disturbingly human orbs each easily a dozen metres across.

A gargantuan split rippled open along a portion of the creature – Asmodai was convinced now it was a single beast – revealing dark gums encrusted with wart-like growths each as big as the Chaplain, wrapped about broken and cracked fangs each as long as a gunship. Another maw gaped further alone the crevasse, a tongue slipped out languidly across bloated lips, forked and forked again, over and over again so that it became dozens of tendrils each about as thick as his arm, creeping and tasting its way up the slime-slicked sides of the canyon.

'Emperor protect us!' said Daeron. Asmodai had not noticed the sergeant come up beside him. 'Is that just another construct, or do you think it is the controller of the citadel itself?'

'It matters not. We lack sufficient firepower to inflict significant damage at this range.' Asmodai watched as a bubo the size of a shuttle craft erupted above an eye, the pop echoing up the chasm like a crack of thunder. From the pus that spilled forth emerged half a dozen shapes, floating like bubbles towards the Terminators as they headed out along the ledge.

As they rose higher Asmodai could see a darkness within the translucent skin of the bubbles, like larvae in an egg. The dark spots grew rapidly in size, other bubble-eggs boiling up after the first, spat forth by erupting boils and suppurating wounds in the creature's hide. The closest eggs burst, revealing monstrous fly-like beasts each as big as a Terminator, and on their backs clung more of the cyclopean daemons that had assailed the Deathwing since they had arrived.

'Open fire!' barked Asmodai, but the order was not needed; the Deathwing started to blaze away with storm bolters and heavy weapons the moment the first fly rider had erupted from its perverse cocoon. The cough of bolt-rounds cut across the thrum of insectile wings as the pestilent swarm rose out of the depths, hundreds-strong by the time the first wave reached the ledge.

Asmodai fired without relent, emptying the bolter component of his combi-weapon, the shots cutting through a trio of fly-riding daemons heading directly for the Chaplain. As he reloaded he switched to the plasma gun fixed by the artisans atop his modified bolter. One blast incinerated another daemonic attacker, its charred remnants fluttering back down the chasm like ash from a fire. To his right the Deathwing force had stretched out, advancing further along the ledge to ensure that their flank was protected. A barrage of bolt-rounds, assault cannon shells and cyclone missiles shrieked and roared down into the abyss, cutting swathes through the oncoming mass, though the daemons did not relent in their approach.

A flying creature with a lashing proboscis loomed up over the edge of the rock shelf, twice as big as Asmodai, its trailing legs tipped with claws, vestigial appendages in its thorax rippling and darting. Astride its back sat a canker-skinned daemon with a wide, fanged mouth, single red-pupiled eye and a curling horn in the centre of its forehead. Between the white nodules that broke its pale green skin were rents and tears, tatters of flesh turned back to reveal pulsating innards and flexing ligaments. Asmodai's revulsion increased as he saw something like a face leering at him out of the creature's spilling intestines.

'Foul spawn! Death to the impure!'

His first blow was met on the blade of a rusted sword as the plague creature buzzed past, its limbs lashing at the Chaplain's helmeted head, perhaps drawn to the skull into which it was fashioned. His next sweep dug the eagle-headed crozius arcanum deep into the belly of the creature, causing a ripple to flow across its flesh. The daemon rider's sword crashed down on Asmodai's shoulder, sending chips of ceramite flying. Where the blow had landed the ceramic coating started turning to dust, flaking away as though the bonds that held it together were breaking.

As the thing rose up, threatening to carry his weapon away, Asmodai wrenched the crozius arcanum free. The effect was like pulling open an effluent pipe as a streaming gush of maggots, half-solid blood and putrescence poured out onto the Chaplain. The sticky mess clogged the seals of his helm and dried in a crust over his left eye. He struck again before the creature flew out of range, once more the head of the power weapon sinking deep into the unnatural body. With a grunt he hauled back, pulling the flying beast toward him. He fired his combi-weapon, the plasma gun pressed up against the daemon-steed's lolling head, incinerating it in a moment.

Even as its mount ploughed into the ledge with a wet explosion of filth, the daemon lashed out again. Its entropic sword cracked against the casing of the Chaplain's combi-weapon. The plasteel cover bent unnaturally and then fell away, leaving the mechanical innards of the weapon exposed. Wires started to fray and metal parts coated with rust.

Tossing the useless weapon aside Asmodai seized the creature's wrist in his now-free hand as the decaying thing tried to stab him in the face. He pulled the daemon out from the foul wreckage of the flying creature and dashed it against the wall once, the rents in its body opening wider to spill out broken shards of bones and exploding organs. Utter disgust welled up inside the Chaplain as he smashed the daemon's head to a pulp with the flat of the crozius arcanum.

More daemonflies and their filthy riders appeared over the rim of the ledge. Asmodai knocked the first back with a punch and decapitated the second with a swing from his crozius arcanum. Something grabbed his right arm; a fly-thing had managed to punch one of its clawed feet through the seal at the elbow. More limbs closed around the Chaplain as he swung his blazing weapon back and forth. His blows cracked open daemonic chitinous hides and rent gory trails through immaterial flesh, but there were too many foes.

A rider slid low on the back of its mount and drove the broken point of its blade into Asmodai's chest. The rusted sword shattered, but where the oxide shards touched ceramite the armour crumbled like dust, exposing the secondary adamantium plates beneath. Mandibles lacerated gouges along his left thigh as another fly-beast latched on. Five of the creatures now had him. Asmodai felt the ground slipping away as they tried to lift him from the ledge.

For a moment he swung out over the chasm and was dangling right above the huge mass of the hive-like thing far below. Through a miasma of urine-coloured fog and the blots of flies crawling across his face he locked gazes with the immortal, enormous entity.

Its voice was in his head, he realised, and had been the whole time. It was a comforting feeling, not like the anger and despair he felt, but the warmth of paternal concern. It wondered why he fought so hard against the inevitable. Did he not realise that there was no triumph? All life ended in death. All civilisations fell to ruin. Even planets and stars, the galaxy itself, would one day be no more, claimed by the inevitable power of entropy. There could be no lasting victory against such fate.

Had not his own actions ushered in decay, in the bodies of the slain? He and his brothers were nothing more than hives for the billions of microscopic creatures that inhabited them, much like the citadel he had riled with his attack. Life was a temporary state of affairs, and filled with loss and pain. But death was an explosion of new life, fuelled by the fresh rush of mortal creatures.

He could enjoy that bounty too, if he but released himself from the pain that he craved so much. Life was torture, and for none more than Asmodai. He knew that every waking minute the thought of what had been taken from him, the innocence and purity he had known, gnawed at him, refusing to be forgotten. He might hunt for a hundred lifetimes and never bring Malvine Rhemell to account. What if he had that time? What if, rather than struggle futilely here and die in misery and solitude, he lived to fight on, not just for a hundred lifetimes but for a thousand, a million? Only the end of existence would end the Hunt. In his heart he knew no Dark Angel alive today would know peace; the true peace that would come when the last of the Fallen had been stricken from that long list. But if he ceased his struggles, allowed the destroyer hive to take him and be reborn, he would see that day, he would live long enough to bring freedom and honour back to the sons of the Lion.

Thinking of the Fallen normally brought rage, but now the appearance of the traitor's visage, the patronising sneer Malvine Rhemell had shown when he had seen the confusion written on Asmodai's face, the effect was of a cold waterfall washing over Asmodai like a cleansing balm. He could not die without knowing that his tormentor had been brought to justice.

But it was not in Asmodai's nature to surrender. The pain was his shield, the agony of shame and loss was the fire that burned in the furnace of his soul. It was a reminder that the universe was unfair, that good men could be brought low by their intentions, no matter how pure.

And this was the iron, the true armour of righteousness that protected him. Ceramite, plasteel and adamantium encased his body but his soul was layered with hatred, rage and disgust; more for himself and his own weakness than any other being, living or daemonic.

This would be a pathetic way to die, he thought. Swallowed by a daemon-beast on some Emperor-cursed world, unremembered and pointless.

And then it returned to him, the flame of anger.

Like a single spark in the whole firmament of his black soul, the rage shone bright, growing in strength as he fought back the influence of the daemonic fiend. The fact that it had considered him vulnerable to such an offer, the insult such belief brought to the Chaplain, fanned the flame. It had questioned his righteousness. Only he had that right, for there was no being purer in purpose than Asmodai. He would not be judged or swayed by a conjuration of fear and despair, born out of the self-loathing and blind hope of weak mortals.

He was the judge, not the judged. He was Asmodai, Master of Repentance.

'Die, filth of the abyss!'

Only a moment had passed though it seemed like an eternity to the Chaplain. Though his Terminator armour was not agile, it was strong. He flexed an arm, dragging himself back over the ledge even as he lashed out with his crozius. The flying creatures scattered from his rage, dropping him in their dread. He twisted his shoulder as he landed, ungainly but keeping enough impetus to turn the fall into a roll that gave him enough momentum to get to his feet again.

'Do not relent!' he roared to his battle-brothers, seeing them being pushed back along the ledge in places, surrendering the advantage of the chasm edge. 'With bolt and blade, with flame and fist, purge the unclean!'

He put into practice what he preached, stomping after the fly-creatures that had tried to capture him, his crozius making a red mess of the first, sweeping the rider from his perch on the second. A heavy flamer burst incinerated another. Storm bolter fire hammered into a fourth and fifth, turning them to shreds of flapping flesh and shattered cartilage that dropped back into the gorge. Asmodai saw Sergeant Daeron striding through the cloying flies and gore, reloading his weapon.

'Are you well, Brother Asmodai?'

'I am unhurt,' the Chaplain replied. For a moment memory of the encounter with the destroyer hive

threatened to overwhelm him, but recalling the daemonic entity's attempts to corrupt him only outraged
Asmodai even further. 'Burn and blast your way through.
Get the battle-brothers off this ledge, and find the creator
of this cursed place.'

'What of that?' Daeron gestured towards the beast at
the bottom of the chasm.

'It will wait, and we will be back for a reckoning.'
More daemon-things flopped into view, slug-beasts that
crawled down the wall and over the lip of the crevasse,
their fronded-ring mouths gnashing, emitting piercing,
almost joyful whistles as they slumped and slid their way
towards the Deathwing.

Asmodai thought of the Lion, and how the daemons
had thought to persuade him to betray the primarch. It
focused the Chaplain's mind on the Fallen; those detest-
able souls that had listened to such urgings ten thousand
years ago.

TRAITOR!

He thought of the Lion, dead at the hands of the traitors, of a world destroyed by hubris and a dream of
greatness and eternal deliverance quashed. He thought
of what the Fallen had done and looked at the daemons
clambering and flying out of the chasm.

TRAITOR! TRAITOR!

He would prove his worth. He was no coward. The
enemy would not escape this time.

TRAITOR! TRAITOR! TRAITOR!

What followed came easily.

CORRUPTION

'Can anybody hear me?' a non-stop succession of colour-ful phrases and curses followed, confirming to Telemenus the identity of his fellow Terminator.

'Daellon?'

'Emperor damn me! Telemenus?'

The citadel had become a labyrinth and Telemenus was sure that he had walked in circles for nearly an hour, except that the circle was changing every time he took a turn, so that even if he crossed his path a hundred times more he would never recognise the exact same layout of tunnels and chambers. He had quickly succumbed to the depressing thought that he would die alone in this awful place, until he had picked up the distant echo of a shout.

'Wait while I configure my audio pick-ups,' Telemenus called back. He stopped walking and adjusted the sensi-tivity of his auto-senses, hoping to detect the direction of Daellon's bellowing. 'Configuration complete. Call again!'

'Telemenus!' Daellon's shout almost deafened the Space Marine, erupting from the vox-link inside his helm. Feedback squealed close at hand, masking any location he might have picked up.

'Brother, your vox is on,' Telemenus replied quietly over the open channel.

'And working again, it would seem. A damn joyous moment for you to hear my voice again, I am sure.'

Both of them spent thirty seconds trying to contact anyone else, switching between squad, personal and company frequencies but with no success.

'It must be range interference,' said Daellon. 'At least that means we are close to each other. I'll use the external system again.'

Telemenus listened intently, the stereoscopic detectors of his auto-senses turned up to maximum sensitivity. He heard his name rebounding from a passageway behind and to his left. He backtracked and called down the oval-shaped corridor, which like much of the maze resembled nothing so much as an artery clogged with fatty tissue and rank black residue. He told Daellon to call again and by these means was able to navigate his way through two more turnings until he came up on his battle-brother from behind.

'A perturbing location,' admitted Telemenus as they raised their power fists to each other in salute. 'I assume you have seen nothing of our brothers?'

'You are the first,' said Daellon. 'I was right behind Sergeant Arbalan when we teleported, but the moment we arrived... nothing. Not that I would have noticed if he was right in front of me at that moment. I thought I was going to puke out my lungs and my brain would fall out of my arse.'

'Quite,' said Telemenus, who had never really come

to terms with Daellon's unique capability for colourful language. He skirted on blasphemy at times but, oddly enough, seemed perfectly capable of keeping his tongue in order whenever Chaplain Asmodai was within earshot.

'Not tried the sensorium since I switched it off, have you?' Daellon said. Without any spoken consent, the two of them started heading in the direction Daellon had been facing. 'I shot holes in the wall as a means of keeping track.'

'Good idea,' said Telemenus. 'And no, I have not reactivated my sensorium. I hate to think what would happen to it if we created a scanner net between us.'

'Damn good point. And do you see any holes here?' He waved a hand to encompass the gently flexing corridor walls.

'No,' said Telemenus. It took a moment for his companion's meaning to sink in. 'Oh. That would mean we are both lost.'

'So it damn well appears, brother. At least we have company now.'

As well as endlessly branching left and right, the corridors also went through dips and rises, so that the pair were never sure if they were still on the same level or not after a few minutes. Telemenus had a niggling feeling that they were making their way *somewhere* and though he had disabled his sensorium and did not have a perfectly accurate auspex-generated map to rely on he was also becoming more convinced that his surroundings had some kind of vaguely familiar pattern.

'Did you hear that?' Daellon's question snapped him from his thoughts.

'No, brother, what did you hear?'

'A moan, perhaps.' The two Terminators lifted their

weapons. Neither had seen any sign of enemy and it was easy to forget that they were in the heart of hostile territory. 'Or a groan.'

Daellon indicated the direction of the noise with his storm bolter, pointing down a narrower tunnel to their right. He led the way, power fist casting a blue glow across the organic walls, highlights shining from slivers of sinewy tissue that were expanding and contracting between ridged lines of cartilage.

'Is there a difference?' said Telemenus.

'A difference? What?'

'Between a moan and a groan?'

'No idea, now that you ask.' Daellon stopped. Without the whine of servos and the clump of their footfalls, Telemenus could hear the sound too now. It was a loud wheezing, rising and falling steadily. It seemed to be close.

They rounded the next corner side by side, storm bolters aimed, power fists raised. What confronted them was more disturbing than any foe they might have imagined.

There was something trapped within the tissue of the wall: a Terminator. The ivory of his armour was a stark contrast to the deep, fleshy red and the bluish veins that surrounded him. Tendrils of tissue-like creepers were already investigating, crawling into cracks between the plates, slowly but visibly expanding along limbs and torso. There seemed to be a dim haze surrounding the warrior. Magnifying his vision Telemenus saw thousands of tiny lice-like creatures covering the Space Marine like a fine film. The back of each tiny mite was marked with three overlapping pale green circles.

'Damn! Sergeant Arbalan!'

Catching up with Daellon, Telemenus could see the warrior's livery and heraldry clearly now and realised it was true. Arbalan had his power sword drawn but the upper part of his arm was melded with the stuff of the wall.

'Stay away from the walls, we could get drawn in too,' warned Telemenus.

The sergeant's helm was cracked down the front; the wheezing was his laboured breathing whistling out of the shattered ventilator grille. The back of his head was as stuck as the rest of him. Fingers flexed in the depth of a spider web of veins encasing his left arm.

'Helmet...' The sergeant sounded hoarse and weak. Daellon moved to comply, powering down his fist to twist free the sergeant's helm. It came loose with a sucking sound, the wall relenting its grip with a wet slurping noise. Daellon let the helmet clatter to the floor, preoccupied by what he had revealed. Arbalan's face was almost white, drained of all pigment. His hair was too and his eyes were pale with cataracts. As well as its pallor, his flesh was wrinkled and leathery like the hide of some large beast, gathered in folds around the eyes and under his chin. There was no fat between skin and muscles, leaving just bone at cheek and brow.

'Damn...' said Daellon.

'We will cut you free, brother-sergeant,' promised Telemenus, gauging the thickness of the fleshy folds encasing parts of the Space Marine. 'A few minutes work.'

'No point.' Arbalan coughed and then winced with pain. 'It is inside me as well.'

'How?' Telemenus was shocked. What sort of creature, what kind of attack could overcome a warrior of the Deathwing so completely? 'What did this to you, brother-sergeant?'

'Teleport misadventure, you idiot.' The sergeant moved his gaze to Daellon. 'Matter detection systems warped out by this place. Materialised inside this wall. I can feel those things, those bugs, burrowing into me, trying to make me part of the city. They are in my legs at the moment, and my stomach. I want to be dead before they reach my lungs or heart. I do not think they mean to kill me, but to pervert this physical form for their own ends.'

'There must be some way…' Telemenus looked around for some clue as to how they might rescue the Space Marine. There was nothing. However, inspiration came in a different form. 'Lungs! That is what this place reminds me of. Bronchial passageways. We must be in the fortress' lungs, or something similar.'

'How does that help?' snapped Daellon. He began pulling away chunks of flesh and gristle, freeing some of the sergeant's sword arm.

'Do not make me beg,' growled Arbalan, staring at Telemenus from his flesh cocoon.

'Perhaps if we found a Librarian, he could cleanse the taint from you,' Telemenus suggested, though he knew it was a hopeless situation.

'Telemenus, come closer.' The Space Marine complied with Arbalan's request as Daellon stepped away. When the sergeant spoke his voice was a whisper. 'There is more to being a great warrior than shooting straight. You have been a disappointment to me and to the Grand Master since you arrived. It is not patience or skill that you lack, it is humility, and that is why we have been scrutinising you so closely.'

'You think that I show promise?' Telemenus was confused, unsure whether Arbalan was praising him or criticising. 'The Grand Master pushes me harder than the others because he senses what I could offer?'

'No.' The sergeant's lips were almost non-existent and his skin all but a mask but he still managed a dissatisfied expression. 'With training and armaments like yours, any warrior can serve with distinction in the First Company. Remember, you are not special.'

Telemenus recoiled as if shot, stepping away from the sergeant. He shook his head.

'Now, which one of you is going to end it for me?' The sergeant grunted in pain, bared decaying teeth and blackened gums.

'I will, damn it,' said Daellon.

'No!' Telemenus stepped in front of his companion and raised his storm bolter, aiming at Arbalan's face. He met the sergeant's stare, knowing that Arbalan could see nothing of his expression past the helm of Telemenus's armour.

'At least I know you can hit me from that distance,' Arbalan snarled, unrepentant to the end.

'You deserve this,' said Telemenus. 'I owe it to you.'

He fired.

The pair of them turned away, the echoing retort of the single shot muffled by their fleshy surrounds.

'What did he say to you?' asked Daellon.

'Nothing of importance, I assure you.'

The answer hung in the silence, its falsity obvious to Telemenus, but there was no way of gauging his companion's reaction.

'Lungs, you say?' said Daellon after a moment.

'Yes, it seems to me that is the case.' Telemenus pointed to a branching corridor ahead. 'We follow the passages that are widening. It will bring us to the main airways, or whatever the equivalent is. Let us hope that some of our brothers are wise enough to do the same.'

A LOSING BATTLE

Blasting and hacking through the walls certainly made progress into the fortress swifter. Sapphon and his Terminators, swelled by other stray warriors picked up along the way to number thirteen Space Marines, found themselves embroiled time and again by daemonic assailants. There were recurring forms, of pot-bellied cyclopean daemons and bounding, slug-like beasts, and there was a myriad of unique and disturbing manifestations from the palace itself. There seemed to be no pattern or reason behind the waves of attacks; sometimes minutes passed without assault while on other occasions they were beset by seemingly endless hordes of creatures.

By the haphazard nature of the defence it was impossible to tell if they were any nearer their objective. Sapphon might have expected an organised defence force to layer itself in increasingly strong positions the closer he came to the commanders. Here there was no such rigidity. Sometimes a solitary daemon would pop into existence, easily cut down. Other times it appeared that the citadel was making every effort to reshape itself to bar their path only for their route to eventually lead to a dead end or in a circle.

After ninety minutes of near-constant fighting, Sapphon was aware that they were already thirty minutes over the planned operation time frame. Nobody had yet reported low ammunition – power fists, chainfists, thunder hammers and lightning claws were used to bear the brunt of the attacks – but it was obvious that the Dark Angels First Company could not fight on indefinitely. Worse still, there was yet no sign of Belial.

'We cannot know if the Grand Master survived teleportation,' Sapphon said, during a brief council with Sergeants Asarael and Caulderain. 'We must push on, to gather any remaining forces and, with luck, locate the enemy leaders.'

'Perhaps we need to draw back and think again, Brother-Chaplain,' said Asarael. 'We should secure a location and then send out sweeps and patrols to establish ourselves. Roving needlessly from one area to the next does our cause no good.'

Sapphon took the criticism without comment and looked at Caulderain. The sergeant did not reply for several seconds, evidently collecting his thoughts.

'I concur, in part.' Caulderain turned and looked back at the squad of Terminators guarding the rear. 'There is not a warrior here that would not gladly press forwards and take the fight to the enemy, but in doing so we may relinquish the true objective. Our deployment was compromised the moment the teleporting force was scattered. We have yet to recover from that setback.'

'So we should wait here and hope that others find us?' said Sapphon, unconvinced.

'They are as likely to locate us in one place as we are to run in to them by happenstance,' said Asarael. 'For the moment we fight without any clear sight of our objective. To be honest, with due respect, Brother-Chaplain, we are flailing like blind men here.'

'I appreciate your honesty, brother-sergeant.' Sapphon understood the logic of what he was being told but it strained against his instinct to remain in one place and simply allow the enemy to come at them when they pleased. He had always been taught that one should seize the initiative; that action was always preferable to inaction, daring and courage are at their highest when on the offensive. 'I must reject your assertion, however. I think that should the whole fortress be turned against us, as it surely would if we remain in one place for any length of time, we lack the resources to victoriously resolve such a situation.'

'But we cannot simply advance for the sake of advancing, Brother-Chaplain.'

'Brother Sapphon made his intent clear,' said Caulderain. 'We should turn thought as to how best to make mobility a successful strategy.'

Several more minutes of talking did not resolve the fundamental disagreement but Sapphon, Caulderain and Asarael did concur on a plan to widen the scope of their search. Having discovered there was limited vox-communication possible, up to about a hundred and fifty metres, they could divide into three or four forces, covering a wider area. If one prong of the advance encountered severe opposition there would be other squads on hand to quickly assist.

Another few minutes had passed when this new strategy bore results. Sapphon was called to Asarael's squad, out on the right flank of the attack. The Chaplain found them in a chamber that looked like the inside of an egg, the walls ridged and cracked rather than smooth, pale grey in colour. They had broken a hole into the wall, revealing a dark passage that spasmed intermittently like a gullet, the fleshy walls contracting several metres before expanding again.

'What have you found?' asked Sapphon, ducking his head through the ragged gap.

'The hole, Brother-Chaplain,' replied Asarael. 'It was already here.'

Sapphon stepped back and examined the breach. He could see marks where bolters had blown holes in the wall, these wounds then used as purchase for the fingers of a power glove to grip and tear.

'Already here, you say? Do you think we have come upon our own trail?'

'No, brother, I do not.' Asarael handed something to Sapphon; a storm bolter magazine. 'We found this.'

Examining the empty magazine, Sapphon recognised the marking from the armourium on its underside.

'This was issued by the Grand Master's artificer!' Sapphon looked at the wound in the wall again but it was impossible to tell how long since it had been made.

Redirecting the efforts of his squads Sapphon coordinated his search around the area where Belial had passed. Signs of intense combat, including heavy flamer and assault cannon fire, confirmed that the Grand Master had gathered another force with him. The trail they had left was clear to follow once it was located and Sapphon led his warriors on with some hope and expectation.

The Terminator squad forging ahead of the main body of warriors soon reported the sound of gunfire; the enemy had yet to use any kind of normal weapon. Sapphon ordered his squads to advance at speed and provide whatever support they could. They split along a number of brick-walled passageways, passing through yard-like spaces that opened out beneath a sky of tumourous growths hundreds of metres above.

It was in one such larger space that Sapphon found Belial. The Grand Master and a dozen Terminators blazed away with their weapons at a monstrous many-headed creature formed of mutated brick and twisted sinews of rusted iron and discoloured bronze. Blunt-nosed heads snapped forward with teeth of broken glass, kept at bay by the fusillade of the Terminators. More of the creature dragged its bulk from the far wall, a serpentine body growing out of the stone and mortar.

'Have your men flank left,' was the only acknowledgement Sapphon received from the Grand Master.

He complied, using the covering fire of the other Space Marines to close on the beast's body. The daemonic creature spied the Chaplain dashing towards its side and a blocky head swung down, smashing Sapphon from his feet in a crash of ceramite and bricks. Asarael stood over the Chaplain, firing intently, while Sapphon righted himself.

From an archway ahead another Deathwing squad emerged, assault cannon to the fore. They had been sent to come at the creature from behind, though their rear attack was now compromised by extra heads and limbs extruding from the daemon beast's back.

'Death to the xenos! Attack!' Sapphon charged to draw its attention. The Terminators around him responded in an instant, his battle cry delving deep into hypno-conditioned minds to override whatever they had been planning to do.

He slashed his crozius arcanum into a wide mouth, shattering brick and glass. Beside him Asarael buried his power sword hilt-deep in a sinuous neck. Power fists turned brick and metal to powder and shards.

The plot worked, distracting the daemon-thing from the squad coming up behind. The heavy weapons trooper aimed his assault cannon and let loose a sustained burst, hundreds of shells slamming into the creature, cutting away its lower half. Separated, the top part of the monster collapsed into its constituent parts, showering the Terminators with stone blocks, bricks, pieces of piping and twisted, rusted girders and support bars. As a bank of dust swept over the warriors, it seemed as though a roof had collapsed on the Dark Angels.

Sapphon picked his way across the mound of rubble, which shifted and broke beneath his heavy tread. He came across Belial snapping out orders to his warriors, sending them into the adjoining passages and chambers.

'Praise to the Emperor that you live, Grand Master,' said Sapphon.

'Thanks also for your safe delivery,' said Belial, out of politeness rather than conviction Sapphon presumed. The Grand Master looked past at the squads following the Chaplain. 'I see you have found some more of my warriors. Gratitude for keeping them occupied.'

'We endeavour for victory,' said Sapphon.

'A distant prospect, I must conclude,' said Belial. His voice lowered, a difficult trick with an external vocaliser. 'I do not think there is any target here for us to seize.'

'Someone must be in control of the fortress, even if the one we seek is not present in person.'

'Look around, brother,' Belial said, sweeping an arm to encompass the ruined chamber. He sounded bitter. 'There is nothing controlling this beast, for that is what we face. There are not mortal minds at work behind this conjuration. We have stepped into the body of a monster and it attempts to repel us, nothing more.'

This flat statement took Sapphon aback.

'We must be sure of that,' he said. 'To risk so many warriors, for the brothers we have already lost, we cannot take anything as certain. Though perhaps no mortal design controls this place it must have certainly been shaped by one. What point would exist in creating a palace in which nobody lives?'

'Do not think to get answer from me,' said Belial. 'I do not speculate on the workings of the abyssal foe, with good cause.'

'But one might seek shelter here even if not to be its ruler. Anovel came here, I am certain of it.'

'If your prisoner speaks truth, and there is no guarantee he does, then the one we hunt is no longer here. There is no mortal presence on this world, can you not feel it?'

'Supposition is not evidence, Grand Master.' Sapphon did not want to invoke his rank as Master of Sanctity – spiritual master even of Belial – but he felt he might have to. 'Until we have scoured every part of this citadel and whatever lies beyond there is no means to know what might be found.'

'A fool's errand.' Belial turned away and started to walk back down the pile of daemonic corpse-rubble but was stopped when Sapphon called his name. 'Yes, Brother-Chaplain?'

Sapphon bit back a word of command. If needed he could say the words that would make Belial compliant, for a time at least. Grand Master or not, he had been subjected to the same procedures and hypnotherapies as every other Dark Angel; it was this secret knowledge with which Sapphon had been entrusted.

But it was no way to conduct command of an ongoing

situation. Belial's loyalty and dedication were not in question and awkward inquiries would arise if Sapphon used the secret words in such a manner. Instead he limited himself to one last appeal; if not to reason then to vengeance.

'What of our brothers already slain in this duty?' the Chaplain asked. 'Are you willing to admit defeat so easily in their name?'

'We will recover their armour and take their gene-seed, as we would all that give their life to the Chapter.' Belial shook his head. 'We will not forget them.'

'I hope you remember that I advised against this course of action,' said Sapphon.

'It is noted that you wished to press on into an unknown situation for an indeterminate cause,' said Belial.

'No, not this immediate circumstance,' said Sapphon, approaching Belial so that he could speak quietly. 'I told you and our brothers that it was folly to commit our forces without more intelligence. I wanted to use the prisoner to gather information but you opposed my plan.'

'Does it make it easier to see this, knowing that you were right?' said Belial.

Sapphon looked around the chamber. Two Terminators had been killed in the recent fighting and he could see the war-plate of half a dozen more being carried in grav-nets slung on the backs of the survivors. He did not say as such, but their deaths were a vindication, not a condemnation. It irked Sapphon that their sacrifice would be doubly for nothing if they did not pursue the search for the Fallen, but he chose to hold his tongue, realising that Belial would not be swayed by argument.

'If the Hunt has faltered, let us consider how we might extricate ourselves from this predicament,' the Chaplain said, following Belial down the slope of broken brick and mangled joists.

'Do not be vexed on account of our exit, brother. I have a plan.'

'That sounds promising.'

'Do not be too enthusiastic, it will not be easy.'

AN UNEXPECTED ENCOUNTER

Something had changed.

Like a breeze rippling across grass, a shudder passed through the structure of the fortress. Bronchial tubes and arteries had given way some time ago to dank stone tunnels lined with mouldering timber supports and rafters. The wave was made evident by creaks of wood and stone grating on stone.

At first Telemenus could not tell if anything had happened. A few blocks had shifted and splits had appeared in some of the wood supports, but the hall they had been passing across remained the same. A constant dripping had echoed in the distance for several minutes. It had become a trickle and as Telemenus listened it grew into a steady stream.

'Look, there!' The beam of Daellon's suit lamp pierced the gloom, coming to rest on a fractured pipe off to their right in the depths of the grand hallway. The liquid pouring from the break was thickening, blobs of matter congealing in the spreading puddle. An eye blinked at the Space Marines, a small, rotund body forming around it. Razor-sharp teeth seemed to accrete from flakes drifting in the liquid.

'I think the fortress has found us,' said Telemenus.

'What?'

'It has noticed our presence at last.'

Daellon's storm bolter barked, turning the glistening pod-creature into a mush. Others were coming to life around it, popping into existence in the foam of the spilling liquid, which had now become a torrent bursting forth from several places along the rusted pipeline. The pool was rapidly spreading across the floor of the hall, sweeping the diminutive creatures towards the two Terminators. Dozens of eyes peered curiously at them out of the slime.

'I do not think it would be wise to remain here,' said Telemenus. He cast around, looking for an exit. There had been an archway about twenty metres ahead, but now the gap had been swallowed up, filled with root-like hangings intertwined with each other, each as thick as a man's arm. A dim luminescence still shone through the gaps from the corridor beyond. 'Up there. We will break our way through.'

Firing again at the emerging tide of bestial polyp-things, Daellon stepped sideways towards the opening. Telemenus strode more directly and started to tear at the root with his power fist, pulling away the thick strands in clumps. Something like a pained shudder pulsed through the tendrils and they suddenly sprouted dagger-like thorns. A chorus of snarls, whines and growls caused him to turn his head.

There were hundreds of the pustule beasts now, and the detached interest in their eyes had become outright malice. Frowns deepened and tiny fangs were bared. Clawed hands reached out of the ooze, forming from the rancid liquid, pointing accusingly as hisses of displeasure echoed around the hall. Wooden pillars bowed and twisted, splitting from the ceiling, knot holes opening into eyes rheumy with crusted sap.

A barbed tentacle from the archway lashed around Telemenus's storm bolter, trying to pull it from his grasp. He wrenched the weapon free, tearing more of the vine-like tentacle away from the opening.

'Save your ammunition,' he told Daellon, who was keeping up steady bursts of fire into the enlarging mass of bodies, detonating the growths like squeezed boils. 'Their numbers are too great.'

'Damn things do not stay dead,' said Daellon. He turned his back on the tide creeping towards them, flowing and glistening across the flagged floor like giant frogspawn on the surface of a pool, algal growths slicking ahead of the mass, becoming fungus and moss as it climbed the walls and wood beams. Where yellow and green pus stained the liquid, new clusters of claws and eyes formed.

More tendrils slapped and scraped against Telemenus's armour as he forced his way through them, tearing and pulling, the blue blaze of his power fist lighting the corridor beyond. Daellon punched his way through beside him, using his bulk to force his way into the passage ahead of Telemenus. Fang-like thorns clattered from their armour as they took several steps down the passageway.

Telemenus looked back. The polyp daemons were at the door, pudgy legs with clawed feet giving them mobility as they pulled themselves from the spreading ooze with slurping and sucking sounds. They chattered excitedly, making obscene gestures with tiny fingers as they waddled after the Terminators, propelling themselves with skinny arms as well as rolling and bouncing down the corridor.

The floor bucked beneath Daellon as a monstrous eye erupted from the flagstones, tossing the Terminator into a mutating wall. Remembering the fate of Arbalan, Telemenus powered down his glove and hauled his companion back to his feet, dragging him to the centre of the corridor. The tide of daemons behind was still growing in number, hundreds now piling in waves and mounds after them, their snarling and shrieking rebounding from the narrowing walls.

They opened fire, though Telemenus knew the casualties they inflicted were almost inconsequential. It was ingrained into them to fight, even on the retreat. Walking backwards, alternating salvos of fire, was slower progress than advancing, but they did not dare turn their backs on the wall of daemonic minions slinking, crawling and bouncing after them.

'Listen!' hissed Telemenus, his auto-senses detecting a different noise to the retort of the storm bolters and squeals of exploding daemons. It was the faint echo of a boom, the after-noise of a loud crack somewhere in the distance. Telemenus recognised it instantly, as did Daellon.

'Damn me, that sounded like a thunder hammer,' said the Space Marine. 'We should try to link up with whoever it is.'

'If we turn now they will be on us in moments.' Telemenus looked around the corridor. The stones were slewing away, revealing a strangely textured substance beneath, like hardened synth-gruel full of moving lumps. There was no way to bring down a roof or wall to block the path.

They fired together now, the combined fusillade of their storm bolters barely enough to hold back the burgeoning wall of vicious pustules. The fortress was trying to reform around them, splitting apart, showing inner sinews and bony structure. Stones and bricks were being shed behind them as the tunnel slowly constricted. Soon there would be no line of retreat.

This was not what Telemenus had expected at all; to perish swamped by a foul tide in the darkness of a warp-spawned nightmare, flailing futilely at his enemies. He had wanted a glorious death, gun in hand, slaying the foes of the Emperor. As a warrior of the Deathwing he had thought he would earn that honourable end. It seemed stupid, now that he thought about it. It was the lot of the Terminators to fight where others could not, in the shadowy places of the galaxy, far from witnesses, far from glory. It was not this that he had envisioned before the mission, when he had argued with Belial that he was ready for full battle.

The Grand Master's brow furrowed dangerously and Telemenus wondered if he had overstepped his mark, had been too insistent in his petition. Belial said nothing for several moments, his gaze on the deep grain of the wooden desk behind which he sat.

'Your right?' the Grand Master said quietly, looking up. 'You think it is your right to follow me into battle?'

'A poorly chosen word, plucked from my mind in haste,' said Telemenus. 'I have worked hard these past forty days, I am sure Sergeant Arbalan will agree.'

'I have the reports from Brother Arbalan.' Belial patted a pile of transparencies neatly arranged in the corner of the desk. 'He has been very thorough in his assessments of your readiness.'

'Nobody has spent longer in the firing range and in the drill hall than I, Grand Master. Give me a chance to prove myself.'

'A demand?' Belial's question was asked calmly, but it sent a thrill of nervousness through Telemenus. He would happily face a dozen orks, two dozen tyranid bio-constructs rather than endure this interrogation. Yet even this ordeal was nothing compared to the agony of potential shame should he be left behind whilst the other warriors of the Deathwing went into battle. It was an almost unheard-of dishonour, a fate that even the grievously wounded despised. Death would be preferable.

'A request, Grand Master,' Telemenus replied, trying to keep the worry from his voice. He needed to appear disciplined and competent. Better that than to plead, though if need be that was his last resort.

'Why do you think you are ready for battle as one of the First Company, Telemenus?'

It seemed a strange question, the answer obvious.

'I have shown consistent improvement in my training assessments, and I have attained the required proficiency with my Tactical Dreadnought armour. My scores out-rate those of Brother Daellon, and my disciplinary record has been exemplary since we translated into the warp. How could I not be ready?'

As soon as he asked the question, a turn of phrase that slipped out, he knew he had made a mistake. It was as though he was challenging his superior to justify himself, which had not been his intent. Telemenus wanted to explain the error, to apologise, but worried that this would show further vexation.

'Are you really ready, up here?' said Belial, tapping the side of his head with a finger. 'You were slow and clumsy in thought as well as body. There can be no indecision, no hesitation in battle. You know this.'

'Yes, Grand Master. And I have shown over many years'

service to the Chapter that I am capable in combat. Please do not take this as a boast, but to attain the Marksman's Honour is not simply a matter of shooting straight. It requires focus, clarity of purpose and dedication to the mission. These traits were not erased by my elevation to the First Company.'

Belial leaned back, his bulky chair creaking under the movement. The Grand Master tapped his fingers on the desk top, drumming out a short tattoo. He nodded.

'Points well made, brother.'

Telemenus sucked in a long breath, of excitement and relief.

'Is that permission to join my squad, Grand Master?'

'It is,' Belial replied. 'It is not only I that must trust you, Telemenus. Your battle-brothers will be depending upon your quickness of thought and accuracy of judgement. Let them down and dishonour is the least price we will pay.'

Telemenus saluted with a fist to his chest.

'I will bring honour to the First Company, Grand Master.'

'Do not be so concerned with reputation and legacy, Telemenus. Even the best of us will be forgotten by the long years to come. Act like the Space Marine I know you can be. That is the warrior I would want by my side. Look to your brothers and your battlegear, and let your honour take care of itself.'

Belial had as near as mattered warned Telemenus against this fate. Stubbornness and pride was holding him and Daellon here.

'We have to run,' said Telemenus, reloading his storm bolter.

'How? Where?' Daellon glanced across at his companion. 'We cannot outpace these creatures in this armour.'

'It is your choice, brother,' said Telemenus. 'In ten seconds I am going to turn and run as fast as I can. If you want to live, you should come with me.'

'What life is worth running away for?'

'To continue the battle, brother. Others are close at hand. We can still try to achieve the mission.'

'Damn.' Daellon fired a long stream of bolts into their foes. 'Damn you, damn this Emperor-cursed pit, and damn these stupid balls of shit!'

They turned together. Telemenus tried not to think about what he was doing – his armour would interpret his intent without his conscious effort. He broke into a run, not exactly a sprint but after a few paces he had gathered speed, as had Daellon just behind him. Feeling more confident he stretched his strides a little, bounding from one foot to the other, the top of his backpack carving a furrow through the descending flesh of the ceiling.

He did not look back, but concentrated on the winding, undulating passage ahead. Settling into a steady rhythm, aware of the thudding of Daellon's boots and wheeze of actuators still close at hand, he listened for the sound of combat – the noise of a thunder hammer impact, the crackle of power fists and lightning claws, the staccato detonations of storm bolter-rounds.

A brighter, bluer light illuminated the tunnel a few dozen metres ahead and Telemenus could see the passage widening into a larger chamber. He saw the telltale flicker of bolt propellant as rounds flashed past the opening. Daellon laughed.

'Emperor-damned miracle, it is. A damned miracle!'

The two Terminators burst into a cavernous space easily a hundred metres high, veined and vaulted like some immense pulmonary chamber. Droplets of spattering fluid fell from open sores above and the uneven floor forced them to slow, lest they tripped on one of the cartilaginous ridges and masses that protruded through the skin-like surface.

Telemenus's eye was immediately drawn to a figure in

black Terminator armour and he recognised the markings of Brother Sapphon. With the Chaplain were eight other Terminators, almost surrounded by a crowd of humanoid, single-eyed daemons that crashed rusted blades against the Space Marines armour, their bodies twisted and rotting. The Terminators blasted and punched their way through the group, lightning claws carving ruinous tatters in immaterial flesh, while Sapphon bludgeoned and decapitated with his crozius arcanum.

'Praise the Lion!' Telemenus called out over the short-range vox. 'A happy moment this is.'

Sapphon turned in their direction, skull helm half-covered with sickly ichor. He pointed at them with his crozius.

'Beware!'

Daellon and Telemenus pivoted at the Chaplain's warning. Dozens of the pustule-beasts boiled through the widening archway behind them, bursting out under the pressure of their numbers. Yet it was not these that had so concerned Sapphon. Behind them loomed something enormous, a bloated shadow that lumbered after its diminutive children.

Squeezing its bulk into the cathedral-like hall with surprising swiftness, the immense daemon was a hill of a beast, a mound of pestilent, torn flesh bloated with gas and fluids that bubbled from weeping sores in its green hide. It was nearly five times the height of Telemenus and Daellon, its broad shadow eclipsing both Terminators. Its wide, flat face was split by a slash of a grin, dagger-teeth discoloured and fractured. Broken horns jutted from either side of its head, dangling with streamers of entrails and foetid matter.

'Get back!' Daellon stepped in front of Telemenus

and opened fire, stitching bolter detonations across the beast's chest.

The daemon swung its right arm, flab bulging and rippling, a flail of rusted chain in its fist, each of the three massive lengths ending with a clutch of monstrous skulls. The flail slammed into Daellon. The whip-crack speed of the heads hit with a deafening crash, sending the Space Marine clattering a dozen metres across the floor, bouncing and twisting awkwardly over the uneven surface.

Telemenus raised his storm bolter and fired but it was pointless. A rusty pick whose head was as big as his torso plunged down, its tip punching through the left side of his plastron. A thousand crooked nails dragged through his ribs and innards where the pick cut deep into flesh to erupt from the base of his back. Telemenus could not swallow the screech of utter agony ripped from deep within his soul as the daemon dragged free the weapon, the rusted pick chewing at his wounds like a million insects gnawing in his flesh.

He met the gaze of the daemon and tried to fire again, but the storm bolter had fallen from his hand without him realising it. The daemon pouted, brow furrowed, a look of sympathy more than anything else. Telemenus collapsed to his knees, looking as though he had fallen in supplication to its mighty form. Blood frothed from the wound and smaller daemons poured around him, forked tongues lapping at the spilt life-fluid. Telemenus mustered enough strength to swipe them away with his power fist, leaving them as burst smears across his broken armour.

Telemenus fell forwards and was unconscious before his masked face slammed into the floor.

REALITY DAWNS

'Destroy it! Purge the unclean beast!'

Sapphon's command was fuelled by the horror he felt as he watched two Terminators laid low by the creature's attack. The Deathwing gathered about him, pouring fire from all directions into the hulking monstrosity. The gigantic daemon let out a long, gurgling laugh and pointed its pick at the Terminators.

'Slay them, my pretties!' Its voice rumbled at the lowest depth of hearing, guttural and churning. The bass vibrations caused splinters of bone to fall from the ceiling, bringing showers of ichor and waste. The sea of daemon-mites that had preceded it into the chamber flowed towards the Deathwing. Storm bolter-rounds exploded within its flesh, leaving pocks of blood and pus, but it seemed unmoved by the wounds. 'Make nests of their gizzards. Lay the eggs of decay in their eyes. Let free the pleasing snap of bone and splash of bile.'

It laughed again, hauling its bulk further into the

cavernous space, folds of rotted flesh leaving skin scrapings along the sides of the archway. Tatters of thick hide flapped like banners from these new wounds.

'Heavy flamers, keep back that swarm,' ordered Sapphon. 'Cadmael, fragmentation rounds. Thin their numbers.'

The cyclone-armed Terminator sounded an affirmative and a second later a flurry of rockets spread across the hall, falling amongst the tide of deamonspawn in blossoms of fire and shrapnel. Burning promethium from the weapons of Satrael and Nadraeus incinerated the small daemons by the score, leaving a slick of burning, deflating bodies.

'No!' The great daemon seemed genuinely upset by the loss of its minions. Its guffaws became stentorian grunts and moans of anguish. 'My pretties! All crisp and shattering! No!'

Several close combat Terminators, two with thunder hammers and storm shields and another with gleaming lightning claws, advanced to stand guard over the inert forms of Daellon and Telemenus. The daemon turned on them, eyes blazing with yellowish warplight. 'Make them pay, my pretties. Build the maggot-pile with their guts and sow the spores of entropy in their brains. Trample the blood mulch and sprinkle the enriching pus of nourishment upon their flesh!'

The gigantic apparition started to cough, its stomach heaving. Opening its mouth wide it spewed out a thick gout of blood, worms and filth at Brother Galain. The Terminator's raised storm shield blazed with energy, deflecting much of the disgusting torrent, but thick globules of filth spattered his armour, hissing like acid as they burned into the ceramite.

'Storm bolters are not having any affect,' said

Caulderain, reloading his weapon. He brandished his sword. 'We must seek other means of slaying.'

The sergeant was right. The volleys of fire from the Terminators either bounced off the creature's immaterial hide or else left small welts and wounds that caused it no grief at all. Though its chest and belly were riddled with holes, they were insignificant next to the long gashes and open sores that already split its flesh allowing glistening intestines and bulbous organs to bulge out.

'Close order, assault weapons to the fore,' barked Sapphon, breaking into a run with his crozius arcanum held ready.

The thunder hammer-armed warriors were closest and ploughed forward into the attack within moments. The heads of their weapons crackled with building energy, which exploded with streaks of power and the distinctive crash of sound that gave them their name. The daemon's flesh wobbled and recoiled from blows that would have slain lesser creatures outright.

'No, that will not do at all!' bellowed the creature. Brother Galain brought up his storm shield again, warding away the swinging daemon-axe with a detonation of power. Brother Vestes beside him tried his best to parry the skull-headed flail, but was caught on the shoulder and sent spinning away. His lightning claws throwing sparks, Brother Zameus took his place, slashing and hacking, his relentless attack throwing gobbets of daemon flesh high into the air.

Sapphon charged across the field of daemonspawn, ignoring the sensation of them bursting underfoot. Caulderain was at his right shoulder, another Terminator to the left. They fell upon the daemon's exposed right flank as it drew its pick back for another swing. Caulderain's sword pierced its armpit. Sapphon leaped up and grabbed a fold of flesh in his fist, putting his momentum into his crozius to smash the power weapon deep into an exposed gut. Below him power fists punched and tore at the daemon's bulk.

Chins and jowls wobbling with rage, the daemon swung towards this fresh attack. Its pick slammed into a Deathwing warrior and crushed his helm down to his breastplate. Using his crozius as a lever, feet pushing through leathery skin for purchase, Sapphon hauled himself up another metre towards the daemon's head. It glared down at him, eyes with veins as thick as ropes swivelling madly in their sockets as they tried to focus.

Zameus buried his lightning claws fist-deep into the daemon's thigh and stretched outwards, tearing apart skin, sinew and flesh. The daemon howled in pain, Sapphon suddenly forgotten. Shuffling its bulk, toppling three Space Marines as it did so, it heaved itself forward, burying Zameus under its massively swollen gut.

Sapphon used this opening to drag himself up to the monster's chest, free hand plunged into fatty tissue to maintain his position while he swung his crozius arcanum with all the considerable strength of his Tactical Dreadnought armour. The blazing eagle head of the weapon crashed into broken teeth, shattering them further, ripping out of the beast's cheek with a spray of thick blood and mucus-laced saliva.

'Suffer... Not...' Sapphon panted as he rained blow after blow against the skull of the daemon. It flopped backwards under the weight of the Terminators raining blows upon its unnatural body. 'The... Unclean... To... Live!'

With a last spasm of belligerence, the daemon scattered a handful of Terminators with a swing of its flail, shattering pauldrons and cracking plastrons. Sapphon knew the thing was not of flesh and blood but an accumulation of warp-matter and psychic energy; it had no brain or nervous system that might control a mortal. Despite this, he pounded his crozius arcanum into the thing's head until nothing was left except for a bloody, pus-ridden mush.

Gas erupted from the daemon's deflating body, spraying a cloud of yellow filth into the air like a fountain. Sapphon rolled off its bulk to his feet, slicked head to foot in grime and gore.

'Immolate it!' he called, signalling for the other warriors to step away and allow the heavy flamers to do their work.

With white hot flames licking across its corpse, the daemon started to sink into the material of the palace, spreading out like melting fat, discolouring the floor and running in rivulets around bony growths.

'It is not truly dead,' Sapphon told the others. 'It, or other things like it, will manifest again.'

'What of the casualties?' asked Caulderain.

'Both alive,' reported Apothecary Cassaen. He pointed at Daellon. 'Unconscious but the armour took the brunt of the hit. Telemenus does not fare so well. The wound is grievous but not fatal, but the injury is already infected by the pestilence of this place.'

Sapphon joined the Apothecary and saw what he meant; black lesions were blistering the wound in Telemenus's chest while a thin drizzle of milky fluid seeped from the fresh scab of Larraman cells closing off the injury.

'Can you treat it?'

'I can boost the armour's conventional anti-disease systems but this is no natural malady. The skills of the Librarius would be more use here.'

'Wake up Daellon. Carry Telemenus. I have an idea that may be beneficial to him and us.'

The last of the daemonspawn had been purged from the room. Galain and Temraen half-lifted Telemenus between them, while Caulderain marshalled the other Deathwing into formation. The sergeant signalled when they were ready to proceed and fell in beside Sapphon.

'As much as I would not abandon a brother here, the lives of many more than Telemenus depend upon our swift success,' said the sergeant.

'That may be so, but Belial's plan is not without significant risks,' replied Sapphon. 'Once we have broken free and located one of the Ravenwing teleport homers, one of us will have to recalibrate the signal and force-teleport back to the *Penitent Warrior* with the targeting information we have gathered. Such a manoeuvre is highly unpredictable, and in that regard Telemenus is as likely as any of us to succeed. And if the reverse teleportation succeeds he will be aboard the strike cruiser where Brother Ezekiel can attend to him.'

They advanced in silence for a few minutes, steered by the gentle pulse of a nearby teleport homer on their specially-tuned sensorium. For the moment it seemed the fortress had expended itself conjuring the massive plague daemon and their progress went unopposed.

'If not for Telemenus, who would be making the force-teleport?' Caulderain asked as they stopped at a junction with a ribbed tunnelway to get their bearings.

'I would ask for a volunteer, of course,' said Sapphon. 'Does it matter?'

The sergeant paused before replying.

'It is tantamount to a terminus mission. Tradition dictates that we should draw lots. Would you have entered yourself into the draw?'

'What sort of question is that to ask of me?' said Sapphon. 'I do not understand what you think you are implying.'

'The warriors grumble and talk, Brother-Chaplain, and I chastise them for it. But I have to know whether you consider yourself above such sacrifice.'

Sapphon drew in a sharp breath, astounded by the insolence of the question. He tempered his response, knowing that there was no malice intended by Caulderain's inquiry.

'My bravery is beyond question, brother-sergeant. Why would the battle-brothers doubt that?'

'Not your courage, Brother Sapphon, but your dedication to them. The Hunt consumes Brother Asmodai and we understand why he is so harsh in his discipline. You are our spiritual leader, the head of the Chaplains, but rarely do you walk amongst us and hear our woes or give us praise. Since your ascension there are those that think you have abandoned us.'

The observation bit deeply but Sapphon could not argue against such concerns. His duties as Master of Sanctity – his real duties to the Inner Circle – did not allow him the time needed to perform the usual ministrations of a Chaplain. It was not until that moment that he realised how much the Deathwing looked to him for guidance; Belial was almost as uncompromising as Asmodai in his treatment of his warriors.

The truth was that the Hunt for the Fallen overtook any other consideration, and his role in the Hunt was of paramount importance to the Supreme Grand Master and the Chapter. However, this mission to Ulthor was going poorly, and it was likely they would leave in defeat. The Deathwing would need to believe in their leaders in the coming days and weeks.

'Yes, brother-sergeant, I would draw my lot with the others,' Sapphon lied.

FAITH

A susurrant scrabbling woke Telemenus. Everything was dark, save for a single patch of light that surrounded him but lit nothing else. He was out of his armour, kneeling on a hard floor, though all he could see of the ground in the circle of light was a flat white surface. He laid a hand upon it, feeling neither warmth nor cold.

'Is this death?' he asked, quickly realising that he was in no mortal space. 'Is this all that awaits us? Oblivion?'

His voice disappeared into emptiness.

Another light appeared, a glowing shape that grew larger and larger. It was a skull, thrice the size of Telemenus. It hovered just out of reach. Telemenus thought he could hear the beating of massive wings and something moved in the darkness beyond. An eagle settled upon the top of the skull and regarded the Space Marine with a single eye; the other was an empty socket fitted with a blood-red gem.

'What are you?' asked Telemenus.

'You know me.' The voice was incredibly powerful, but not loud. It filled Telemenus, far more than sound. 'I am the beginning and the end. I am the harbinger and the resolution. I am the creator and the destroyer.'

'Forgive me, Lord Emperor!' Telemenus cried, abasing himself, forehead to the ground, palms laid on either side. 'I am not worthy.'

'Not yet. Look at me, Telemenus.'

The Space Marine forced himself to look up but did not straighten. He trembled, every fibre of his body awash with fervent energy. The eagle was unmoving, claws digging into the bone of the giant skull. Distant flames burned in the eye sockets of the apparition, and in that flame Telemenus saw himself reflected, a tiny silhouette consumed by the fires.

'I serve your will.'

'And I receive your service.' Warmth washed through Telemenus; a sensation he had not felt for many decades, repressed by training, suppressed by hypnotic suggestion. It was the feeling of being loved. From his childhood he had never known such a feeling, washed away with an infancy of bloodshed and hardship, but his body remembered. In the womb and in the cradle, a pure, unconditional love, and it was this that he felt from the Emperor.

'I died?' Telemenus was afraid to ask the question. It was strange that in life he had not been fearful of death.

He was shaken by the terror of the thought. It felt odd to be afraid, and the fear in itself added to the sensation, feeding back into itself to raise his dreads to a terrifying level. Now that he was divorced from his mortal shell emotion was raw, unchecked by artificial stimulants and hormonal therapies. The fear that gripped him was primal, unstoppable. He realised that this must be how every battle-brother felt when they died. They lived and fought without fear, but in the end they all died suffused with dread and utterly alone.

'Never alone,' declared the Emperor. 'Those that die in my service are never alone. What lord you think I am, to demand such sacrifice and offer no succour in its delivery? Fear no more, Telemenus. Be strong in the knowledge that you do my work.'

'I have faltered of late,' said Telemenus. 'My faith is tested.'

'All faith is tested – it is the nature of the faithful to endure hardship. If doubt did not exist, there would be no triumph over it. How can victory be achieved without battle?'

'I did not die well.' Telemenus had a brief flash, of a rusted shaft penetrating his flesh. The memory brought a spasm of pain from waist to shoulder.

'That has not yet been decided.'

'My fall will be remembered with honour?'

'Whether you have died.'

'Oh.' Telemenus sat up and linked his hands in his lap. He kept his gaze down, only occasionally glancing up at the divine spectre before him. 'It seems unlikely that I will survive such a blow.'

'I made you well, and you are strong enough to withstand such injuries. Fortune plays its part and only one lung was crippled. Your hearts still beat and that is enough for the moment.'

'But my life still hangs in the balance? Do you suspend your judgement?'

'Life and death are not mine to grant, not in this way. I breathed life into the gene-seed that created you. I gave life to your primarch. But death, death comes from many places and it has nothing to do with my judgement. The unjust sometimes live and the worthy perish. There is not a force in the universe that can overcome that primal truth.'

Telemenus pondered this revelation for a while. He could feel a scratching inside him, like a fingernail picking at the interior of his body.

'That is a disease trying to ravage your inner organs. The blade brought a daemon-curse and it is trying to devour you.'

'Will you protect me?' said Telemenus.

'I always protect you, Telemenus. Do you not feel my hand at your side in battle? Do you not feel my breath upon you when the rage sustains you? Have I not given you this fine body and the greatest weapons and armour of my followers? What else do you require?'

'Purpose.' Telemenus mumbled the word, knowing that he had to tell the truth but horrified by the admission. He could feel his strength ebbing away. He sagged, limbs weak, heart beating feebly in his chest. He knew he was losing the battle with the infection. It was leeching away his life, and he had not the will to fight it. He did not know whether he deserved to live. 'I no more see the cause for which I fight. The Marksman's Honour was but a temporal goal, an easement of my pride in place of true calling, but it is no substitute for conviction. Even before I knew of the Fallen, before the lies and secrets were laid bare, I had doubts. I was jealous of my brothers and suspicious of my superiors. I relinquished my honour in pursuit of vainglory. Forgive me, Lord Emperor, but I have brought shame to you and the Chapter.'

'You are not in a position to make such judgement, Telemenus, but your confession is heard. Do you wish forgiveness, or to make atonement?'

'I do not understand, Lord Emperor.'

'If you die now you surrender to my will, burdened by this despair and loss. Live and you are granted fresh means to fight in my name. If you are delivered back to the mortal world, will you transcend the distractions that have plagued you? Will you make amends for your transgressions?'

'I will!' Telemenus forced himself to his feet, legs trembling. He clenched his fists to his chest, feeling his hearts strengthening as they were spurred by purpose. The thought of a fresh start, of returning to his body with honour and duty and vigour meant more to him than anything else; not for the sake of life but for the sake of the Emperor.

He looked at the dead visage before him.

'This is a fever-dream, made real by the Eye of Terror,' said the Space Marine. 'I see that now.'

'Are you so certain?' said the giant skull. 'Here there is no definition of real and unreal, all things are possible. Does not the light of my Astronomican stretch across the warp to the far corners of the galaxy? Do you think me incapable of reaching out to my dying servants?'

'I… I am not sure…'

'Do you seek proof, Telemenus?'

'No.' The Dark Angel's body was clad in armour now, the white of the Deathwing. He felt power surging through him. 'Belief is enough.'

He opened his eyes and found himself staring into the bottomless pits of Chief Librarian Ezekiel's gaze; one real eye and one bionic. Telemenus could not move his head but he felt Ezekiel's bare hand upon his chest; a suffusion of warmth coming from the fingertips pressing into his flesh.

'Where…?'

'Aboard the *Penitent Warrior*, brother.' Ezekiel removed

his hand and stepped back. Sensation started flowing back into Telemenus and he blinked to clear his eyes.

'I do not understand.'

'Nor I, not fully. You force-teleported back to the ship and your vox-system contained a recording from Brother Sapphon.'

'We lost all comms on the surface. The sensorium went haywire.'

'So we gathered. Sapphon's message contained a detailed firing solution, based on a triangulation of the teleporter homing beacons. We will commence bombardment shortly.'

'Not everybody was in vox-contact,' said Telemenus. He tried to sit but could not. He was still paralysed below the neck. Sensation had not yet returned to his arms or legs. 'If they do not know of the orbital strike...'

'An unavoidable situation. We are broadcasting data across the teleport signal, we hope that will be sufficient warning for those unaware of the plan.'

Telemenus's thoughts turned to himself and his recent experience.

'The infection? The daemon-curse?'

'Cleansed, both physically and psychically.' There was something in Ezekiel's demeanour that suggested he was not being fully truthful. Telemenus was tired of secrets and falsehoods.

'Were you... Were you the Emperor?' Ezekiel looked genuinely confused by the question. 'Never mind.'

'The infection was deep, its corrupting influence spreading. Drastic measures were required to excise it.'

'Drastic? How drastic?' It was no shame to be fitted with a bionic or augmetic; to some Dark Angels such alterations were considered a badge of honour. To fight on for the Chapter was the only concern that filled

Telemenus at the moment. 'How much was excised?

Ezekiel stepped away and a Chapter serf in the robes of an apothecarion orderly wheeled a lighted mirror into place with a screech of poorly oiled bearings. Telemenus moved his eyes to the right and looked down at his body.

Very little remained. Everything below his ribs was gone, as was his left arm.

The wounds were stitched and heavily cauterised and a splay of cables and pipes connected him to a life system building into the bottom of the bunk. His skin had a dark cast to it, evidence of the canker that had tried to overwhelm his Space Marine physiology. His veins and arteries stood out like cords.

He was just a head, torso and arm. For a moment it didn't register that he was looking at himself. Yet he felt very little pain and he certainly was not upset by the discovery; perhaps the sustaining elixirs pumping through his body were suppressing the natural horror he thought he should feel. He looked at Ezekiel, who watched with soul-searching eyes.

'Yes,' said Telemenus. The anti-pain stimms were flooding his system and it was hard to form any coherent thought. 'That certainly was drastic.'

DIVISION

Asmodai felled another cyclopean daemon with a punch that turned its face to a pulped mess. The remains of its body collapsed into a pile, strands of mould quickly covering the unnatural corpse.

'Brother-Chaplain!' Sergeant Daeron's call did not distract the Chaplain as he caved in a daemon's chest with his crozius. 'Brother Vascaertes reports detecting a signal anomaly, four hundred metres ahead.'

'Signal anomaly? Be more specific, brother-sergeant.' Asmodai presented his left shoulder to deflect a serrated daemonblade away from his chest. He turned back sharply, smashing the back of his hand across the creature's face before driving the head of his crozius arcanum into the side of its neck. Thick sludge spewed from the wound as the plague-creature fell back, an anguished moan escaping tattered lips.

'Apologies, Brother-Chaplain, that is all I know.'

'Brothers, rally to me! Push on to Vascaertes's location.'

Progress had been tortuously slow, opposed every step of the way by daemons of all shapes and sizes. Materialising out of the warpstuff that formed the structure of the citadel, there was no end to their attacks. Ulthor was partially submerged within the warp itself, the abode of the daemons. Every time a physical vessel was destroyed the essence of the daemon entity simply formed another. Vascaertes and several others had been sent ahead to scout the surest path to the centre of the palace but it seemed they had discovered something else.

Asmodai and the others came upon the lead squad, who had formed a wall of storm bolter fire and armour across a bridge that spanned a seething river of blackness fifty metres below. The surface of the fluid roiled with a life of its own, forming transient shapes that looked like half-formed faces. Vascaertes and his companions kept up a steady stream of fire, keeping back several enormous slug-beasts and a tide of spiderlike, gangling creatures with mandible faces and eerily human hands.

The Space Marines with Asmodai moved up to lend further support, assault cannons and storm bolters adding to the barrage of fire, tearing apart the oncoming horde of misshapen daemons.

'Vox-channel kappa,' said Tyronius. 'Automated signal coming through.'

Asmodai used a sub-vocal command to activate his vox-receiver on the frequency. At first the Chaplain heard a stream of numbers, voiced by a servitor. After that followed a message which he immediately recognised came from Brother Ezekiel. The Librarian had remained in orbit, removed from direct contact with the warp space overlap. The psyker had been unsure whether even Space Marine training and centuries of experience were enough to shield against psychic possession on a daemon world.

Now he was somehow sending a message down to the surface.

+Orbital support has been ordered. Placed bombardment will commence at five-oh-eight-oh-seven-alpha. Target coordinates attached.+

Asmodai listened as the numbers were reeled off again and then cut the link.

'A bombardment? We cannot even maintain vox-contact over two hundred metres, how are they targeting the palace?' said Sergeant Daeron.

'The vox-channel is on the same register as the teleport homers,' said Vascaertes. 'They must be riding the carrier wave to triangulate a targeting pattern.'

'For us to pick up the signal there has to be a homing beacon within two hundred metres of us,' said Daeron. 'But the Ravenwing could not have penetrated very far into the interior of the fortress. We must be moving towards the outside, not the centre!'

'That time-code gives us less than five minutes, brothers,' said Apothecary Temraen. 'Can we calculate the positions of the bombardments?'

'Better that we head for the beacon and exit the citadel,' said Daeron. 'We are almost out of ammunition and we cannot hope to achieve anything but a successful evacuation.'

The din from the weapons of the Terminators intensified as several of the Deathwing moved to the edge of the bridge and started firing down at the amorphous shapes growing up towards them. Black liquid solidified into hard edges that glinted with warp energy, shattering under the impacts of bolts and shells.

'Defeatist nonsense,' snapped Asmodai. He recalled the subversive influence of the destroyer hive trying to possess him. 'With orbital support we will be able to

255

breach the inner sanctum of this place and destroy the consciousness at its heart. If we have reached the edge of the fortress we need to turn back. Calculate those target coordinates and retro-plot a new course.'

'To what end, brother?' said Daeron. 'There is no mission to carry out. We withdraw while we can.'

'Do not countermand my orders, brother-sergeant,' said Asmodai. He joined the line of warriors guarding the bridge. The fusillade had almost died out as quivering stains and bubbling smears were all that remained of the most recent wave of daemons. 'Daeron, Navaesus, Vascaertes and Manneus will form rearguard. We advance by threes, one hundred metre dispersion, maintain vox-contact.'

'No,' said Daeron. 'We cannot sustain further losses, Brother-Chaplain. We have failed. We have to withdraw and regroup under cover of the bombardment.

'Do not defy me!' roared Asmodai. 'I am your superior and you will obey me. When y–'

The Chaplain's words were lost in a thunderous crash from above. The bridge shook and the sluggish river spasmed, a wave of viscous darkness splashing up the supports. Pieces of jagged masonry and shards of bone broke away from the ceiling, raining down equally on the dark river and the armour of the Terminators.

'The bombardment has started!' said Vascaertes.

'It seems our chronometers have been affected as well as the sensorium,' said Temraen.

'Brother-Chaplain!' Daeron spoke sharply but quietly. 'We are as likely to be obliterated by our own ships as we are to fight through. Give the order to withdraw!'

It tore at Asmodai's soul to order a retreat. Even if the Fallen was not here, this was a stronghold of the enemy, taken from the Imperium. It was his duty to avenge that loss and punish those that had attacked the realm of the Emperor.

Another impact ripped open the ceiling above, sending a shower of debris crashing down on the far side of the warp-river. Through the ragged hole the Chaplain could see yellowish clouds, formed into scowling faces and snarling mouths. Dark blurs descended from the cloud layer, shells descending at supersonic speed to smash into other parts of the fortress. He could feel further impacts shaking the whole citadel. A beam of bright white burned through the cloud for an instant as a laser lance opened fire from orbit, carving a furrow of destruction across the surrounding city.

'We cross the bridge and break out under the breach,' Asmodai told Daeron. 'There will be a reckoning later, brother-sergeant.'

'A fate I am happy to endure, brother, if we survive this,' said the sergeant.

RETREAT

The flash of detonation reached Annael a few moments before the shriek of the descending ordnance and the boom of impact. The city convulsed. Chimneys and towers and spires trembled, the roadway and buildings heaved, ascending hundreds of metres as though all of Ulthor had drawn in a gargantuan breath. Flames blossomed along the flank of the central edifice, scattering debris and chunks of burning flesh.

Along with the rest of the Ravenwing, Tybalain and his squadron had been patrolling a perimeter around the central fortification, keeping back daemon-giants and lesser beasts with hit-and-run attacks, drawing the wrath of the city away from the Deathwing within. There had been no communication from the First Company but bike auspexes and Land Speeder passes had identified fierce fighting within the confines of the palace structure. Annael observed the destruction being rained down from the heavens from about a kilometre away, as the squadron took a pass along a bucking plaza between three domed buildings with faces screaming from their walls. Bells pealed a deafening clamour from swaying towers around them.

They brought their bikes skidding to a halt as Tybalain braked hard and turned to watch the ongoing destruction. A lance-beam scored an arc around the base of the pallid structure, steam and smoke rising in billows where the laser seared through warpflesh.

'Does that bode well or ill?' asked Nerean.

'Ill for any enemy beneath such fury,' said Sabrael, sitting behind Annael. They had stowed the machine spirit of his bike in one of *Black Shadow*'s panniers and he carried both his own bolt pistol and Annael's.

'And the Deathwing?' said Annael. 'Have they left targeting beacons, perhaps?'

'Surely they would not bring down a bombardment onto themselves,' said Nerean. 'And the ships would not open fire without a direct command, would they?'

The question hung in the air, none of the Black Knights willing to answer it. It was possible that the assault had gone so badly wrong orbital attack was the only option left. If that was the case, Annael realised, it was a sure sign that there was no Fallen Angel inside. The others seemed to have reached the same conclusion.

'The whole mission has been a waste of time,' said Sabrael. 'Whatever, whoever brought us here has made a sore mistake.'

'Vital intelligence may have been gathered,' argued Annael. 'We cannot say for sure that our journey here has been in vain.'

'Vain or not, we cannot remain here,' said Tybalain.

'You have received word from Sammael?' asked Calatus. 'Fresh orders?'

'No, vox-traffic is still intermittent,' admitted the Hunt-master. 'The bombardment must be the culmination of the assault, either for the final push or to assist retreat. We should ride back to the citadel outer reaches and provide assistance and support.'

'What if the entire area is to be vaporised?' Sabrael asked. 'It would be unwise to remain within the city limits for long.'

'The Grand Master will be at the heart of the city, so we will attend,' said Tybalain, his tone indicating that this was the final opinion on the matter. 'Keep comms open for any transmission.'

As they cruised back towards the spasming towers and spires of the palace the city was in full revolt. Build-ings collapsed into fragments around them, spraying shards of stone and glass and metal splinters. The hard substance of the road melted away, creating a mire that sucked at the tyres of their bikes, the filthy slew riddled with breaking rocks that threatened to unseat the riders with every bump and turned wheel.

'Pick a kinder path, brother,' Sabrael complained. He had holstered one pistol and was holding on to Annael's backpack with his free hand. 'Your riding has not improved since our first encounter.'

'And your tongue has not stopped since,' Annael snapped back, trying to discern the safest route ahead, pillars toppling on both sides, sinkholes opening up in the ground without warning. Other dangers were mate-rialising: tendrils weighted with chunks of masonry like immense flails and bladed appendages that spun with maddening speed, the air alive with shrieks and whines.

They were about half a kilometre from the citadel, a pinnacle wreathed in smoke and flames towering above them. Larger shapes cut through the gloom, leaving contrails from their wings.

'Thunderhawks!' exclaimed Calatus.

The gunships were dropping quickly through the haze and smog, disappearing behind the spasming buildings while fighters and interceptors cut tight circles above, their weapons directed against extrusions and tentacles streaming from the palace walls.

'The Deathwing are evacuating,' said Tybalain.

Distracted, Annael did not see a tooth-like rock erupting from the ground just in front of *Black Shadow*. Sabrael's cry of warning did not come in time and the front wheel rode up wildly as the bike hit the protrusion at speed.

Annael wrestled to keep his steed straight as the back wheel dragged through the mud, the weight of the bike slipping to one side, threatening to tip over completely. Sabrael reacted in an instant, leaning out to his left to put his weight behind Annael's effort, his momentum hauling the bike back onto course. Annael compensated, dipping to the other side as *Black Shadow* crashed level again, churning a spray behind them.

'Stop your wriggling,' snapped Annael. 'You almost tipped us over.'

'Wriggling?' Sabrael's voice rose in pitch. 'I just saved us!'

'Quiet!' Tybalain's curt command silenced them both. Sammael was transmitting over the company vox-channel, ordering the Ravenwing to pull out of the city and await extraction on the surrounding plains.

There was no debate as the Huntmaster led them around in a tight turn, engines roaring at full power as they ploughed through the thickening mud and slime gripping at wheels and feet. The filth squirmed and swelled ahead, forming hummocks and barricades; the first they avoided, the second they plunged through heedlessly, doused in grime and bloody fragments.

Annael risked a glance back, past Sabrael who was holding on now with both hands.

'What do you see?' Sabrael asked.

'The city is tearing itself apart.' Annael swerved past a giant, stubby fingered hand that thrust out of the mire. 'Something monstrous, manifesting from the citadel.'

Annael felt Sabrael's weight shift as he turned to see.

'Emperor save us,' exclaimed the Dark Angel.

'What is it?'

'Best not to look. Just ride!'

Annael turned his head for a fraction of a second. In that moment he saw three things. Firstly, the fly cloud was descending, a pall of absolute blackness falling from the sky. Secondly, the city just a few hundred metres behind them was no more. Spires, roads, alleys and chimneys had been replaced by a landscape of monstrous jutting bones, immense tentacles and blisters exploding with swarms of daemon-things. Lastly, the central palace had mutated into a single impossibly-large apparition. He had seen a Thunderhawk passing in front of an eye half a kilometre across, its heavy bolters and lascannons spitting fire ineffectually at the unholy monster.

'Lion's oath,' he cursed, almost losing control of his steed in the moment of shock.

'I said best not to look! Eyes ahead, brother. Keep your eyes ahead!'

The road, more like the sodden bottom of a river, was sloping away ever more steeply. The city was still rising up, Annael realised, swelling like a bubble about to burst. As soon as he thought of the analogy he regretted it, fearing what was to come.

'Hold on!' he told Sabrael, leaning hard to the right. The bikes ahead of him were churning up the ground too badly to follow; better to cut his own way through the mud. The ground looked firmer over to their right and he angled the bike towards it, opening up the throttle to full. As the wheels hit the patch of hardened dirt *Black Shadow* lurched forward.

Annael stood up, leaning all his weight forward as the front of the bike threatened to upend them again. The slope was almost at forty-five degrees now but there was no chance Annael was going to slow down. Carving a furrow through the grime, speed breaking the hundred and fifty kilometres an hour mark, they arrowed straight towards the open plains ahead.

Land Speeders screamed past to either side while the shadows of gunships above overtook the speeding bikers. Monstrous bellowing and enraged howls followed the Ravenwing as they burst out onto the plain.

'Where are you going?' Sabrael asked over the vox, the rush of the wind too loud to hear anything else now.

'Does it matter?' Annael replied, unable to shake the feeling that something horrific was only metres behind them, ready to swallow them up the moment he slowed down. He could not risk looking back – and dared not even if he could – but fixed in his mind was the image of uncoiling swarm-tentacles and grasping clawed hands and sentient tar-pits, clawing and buzzing and sucking, desperate to drag them back and sink them down into oblivion.

'No,' said Sabrael. 'Far away from here is good enough for me.'

Annael carried on at full speed for another ten kilometres, far beyond the outer reaches of the city, before he started to ease up on the throttle. He eased the bike in a gentle arc to the left, still travelling at a hundred kilometres an hour, giving them the chance to see what was happening. Squadrons and individual bikes were scattered across the pale ground of the flats, banks of dust kicked up in their wake. The horizon was black with the swarm cloud, the flare of plasma jets bright against the darkness as gunships and fighters climbed up to orbit.

It was clear in that moment, as the Ravenwing retreated in disarray, that the Dark Angels were quitting Ulthor, and not with the honour of victory.

'Do you think we will be coming back?' Annael asked.

'By the Lion, I hope not,' said Sabrael. Annael did not disagree.

DESPERATE TIMES

'Grand Master Belial requested that I send news back to the Chapter within the hour,' said Ezekiel. 'I cannot do what you ask.'

Sapphon sat down opposite the Chief Librarian and laid his hands on the table, fingers splayed. The Chaplain took a deep breath and sighed.

'I understand,' said Sapphon. 'The Supreme Grand Master should be prepared for our return. This shameful loss will not be forgotten swiftly.'

'Nor should it,' said Ezekiel.

The Librarian's chamber was almost pitch black, lit only by the radiance of a comms monitor and a single glowglobe in the ceiling rose above the small table. It was a cramped space, the cell made all the more claustrophobic by the lead-filled grooves in the walls that served to break up psychic connections. It felt as if they drained the life from Sapphon as much as they guarded Ezekiel against daemonic intrusion.

A large writing pad, ruled like a ledger, was open on the small desk beside the Librarian, an autoquill beside it. The pad was filled with strange symbols Sapphon did not recognise. Ezekiel noticed the object of his attention and turned, pulling the hefty tome onto the table for the Chaplain to see. He looked at the rows of neatly formed runes but could make no sense of them.

'Messages, warp dreams, divinations,' explained Ezekiel. 'The code is unique to the Librarius, with my own interpretations, of course.'

'Everything you see, it is recorded in here?' Sapphon was surprised by just how slender the volume was. 'Is this the only one?'

'It is mine alone, yes,' said Ezekiel. 'The rune system is pleasingly efficient. It is almost impossible for me to explain to you, a mundane, but another Librarian with the same training as me would know many of the symbols used without need of any further information. They convey a... a sense of an image, a sound, scent or feeling. All psychic contact is merely extrasensory perception rendered into physical form. Foreboding, hope, despair, a tower or key, or perhaps even life and death. Combined together a few simple concepts convey a lot of meaning.'

'And what entry were you completing when I arrived? A dream?'

'The transmission I am about to make on behalf of Grand Master Belial,' said Ezekiel. He shut the book with a heavy thud. 'What has been recorded must be carried out.'

'And what do those symbols mean, brother?' said Sapphon. 'Loss? Shame? *Failure*? Does it not tear your heart to contemplate that message? In the centuries to come when your successors study your life, the prophecies and communications that will be all that remain of our deeds, what will they think of today?'

'The Dark Angels have suffered defeat before,' said the Librarian. 'Our history is glorious, but not perfect.'

'Oh, it is far from perfect, brother, as we both know well.' The Librarian's eyes narrowed as he took Sapphon's meaning. The Chaplain shook his head ruefully and continued. 'We still have a chance to rectify part of that failure, both in the distant past and more recent setbacks. Ulthor was a misstep, an avoidable loss. To return in shame, to not learn the lesson of defeat would only increase the dishonour.'

'We cannot undo what had passed,' said Ezekiel. He lifted the book back to the desk, placing it inside a roller shutter. He pulled down the linked slats of wood, revealing a Dark Angels icon branded into its surface. There was a click of a lock catching. 'The past is done.'

The Chaplain thought this a dismissive conclusion; one easily reached by someone that had not been in the plague stronghold and seen the corruption within. Too many warriors had died in folly for the misadventure to simply be relegated to history. But what was the point in trying to make Ezekiel see thus? He had gazed into the nature of the warp countless times and the horrors of Ulthor would seem trivial in comparison. It mattered not that between the two companies sent down to the planet seventeen Deathwing and eight warriors of the Ravenwing would not be returning, not to mention the loss of armour and bikes almost as damaging. In recent history it was a loss without precedent.

'The past is indeed done,' said Sapphon. 'We can only shape what is yet to come. I ask only for a little time, brother. An hour, if that is what you promised the Grand Master. All I say is do not send that message yet. Grant me this favour, brother.'

'And what do you intend to do with such a gift? The

trail is lost, Sapphon, as cold as the bodies of those that died following it into the plague palace.'

'And that is where we went wrong. It was never my intent to assault Ulthor, but that was forgotten. Worse than forgotten, wilfully overlooked. Even you, brother, argued against me.'

'And now I owe you this favour?'

'We are brothers, we owe nothing to each other except loyalty and protection.' Sapphon smiled. 'But would not the message to the Rock be just a little more bearable if we could still give cause for hope. The shame will not be lessened, but might we promise just a sliver of light for the future?'

The Librarian stood up and turned away, disappearing into the gloom. Sapphon could see Ezekiel, hunched shoulders, head bowed, hands gripping the edge of the shelf above his ward-inscribed bunk.

'I have looked into the mind of Astelan, remember. There are doors in there locked by a power greater than mine, but I think that is for the best. We do not want to open such portals – not now, not ever.'

'I seek no magic portal, only cooperation already offered. Delay your astrotelepathy for an hour, no more, and grant me the chance to seek confirmation of Astelan's continued intent to aid us. If it was his aim to have us bloodied at Ulthor he has succeeded. If he thought we might be destroyed, he has failed. There is nothing further he can do.'

'We both know that is not true,' said Ezekiel, turning around. His good eye was a spark in the darkness, reflecting a silver gleam from the anti-psychic wards around him. 'In this place my talent is suppressed, but it is not gone. We both know what it is you seek.'

'I seek the truth, and victory, like every member of

the Inner Circle,' Sapphon said. His heart quickened at the thought of the Librarian peering into his mind, but he knew that the wards and the oath of the Librarius prevented such intrusion. Only exceptionally strong emotions and projected thoughts could be detected. 'We crave redemption, brother, I will not deny it. It was my idea to come to this place, even if we did not follow through on my strategy. When we return, my disgrace will be complete.'

'And you think to appease those of the Inner Circle that wish you removed with further involvement in the machinations of a Fallen Angel?'

'I have no other choice. I must follow through this cause and course to its conclusion, for good or bad.' Sapphon went over to the Librarian and stood in front of him, fist clenched over heart as though making an oath. 'This defeat is not final, but I am ruined by it, brother. You have never been amongst those who opposed my elevation. Exercise a modicum of choice now, brother, and allow me this last attempt to save not only myself but perhaps secure a great prize for us all.'

Ezekiel stared long and hard at the Chaplain. His gaze was dead for a moment, looking through Sapphon, seeing sights that no normal man would see. There was a hint of pain and resignation in the ancient look. Sapphon was strong-willed but he had never felt his body being stripped away, his soul exposed in such detail before. Even though Ezekiel had no access to his psychic powers it was an intimidating feeling to be scrutinised in such a fashion; Sapphon wondered how the Fallen could resist such attention backed by the full psychic might of the Chief Librarian.

Eventually Ezekiel offered a hand. Sapphon took it and gripped it tight, reassured by the gesture.

'Two hours,' said the Librarian. 'I give you an extra hour for the sake of all our souls.'

Sapphon thanked the Librarian and left. He headed to the part of the penitentium that had been cordoned off from the rest of the ship's complement. Two Death-wing Knights in full armour and wielding large maces, Hastfed and Molochai, stood guard at the door to Astelan's cell. They stepped aside at the Chaplain's approach.

'He has been singing,' reported Molochai, obviously disapproving of such behaviour. 'I would have told him to shut up but your instructions were to exchange no word with the prisoner.'

'You judged right, brother,' said Sapphon, producing a key from a pouch at his belt. Normally the cells were not barred – to leave before penance was complete was unthinkable for a Dark Angel – but it had been a wise precaution to install a lock on this particular chamber. The key was gene-coded to Sapphon – Asmodai had another – and as well as physically fitting the complex lock it transmitted a unique sonic code.

Sapphon unbolted the door and lay a hand on it but did not push it open. He turned to Molochai.

'Singing what, brother?'

'I did not recognise it as any battle hymn or prayer, brother,' replied the knight. 'I could not even tell you what language it was.'

'Very well. Remain at your posts.'

Sapphon stepped inside the cell and closed the door behind him. Astelan was clothed in a grey smock and ankle-high boots and had regained a lot of his lost weight. He was shackled by the ankle to the bench at Asmodai's insistence. Several books were piled beside the Fallen and he sat reading another. Every penitentium cell contained volumes of Chapter teachings as well as treatises on Guilliman's famed Codex Astartes. Sapphon quickly scanned the titles of the books that had attracted Astelan's attention. Unsurprisingly they were those that concerned battle doctrine and organisation.

'It was very different, when I first joined the Legion.'

'I am not interested in your reminiscing, Astelan. I need assurances from you.'

'Then you will have to indulge me,' said the Fallen, lifting the book so that his face was concealed.

Sapphon slapped the book away, in no mood for Astelan's theatrics and posturing. Asmodai was not the only one capable of inflicting pain when necessary. The Chaplain grabbed one of Astelan's wrists and twisted, forcing him to turn, face against the wall. The Fallen did not resist but waited meekly, cheek pressed against the plasteel of the bulkhead.

'I told you that if you played me false you would die in agony,' snarled the Master of Sanctity. 'The next words to pass your lips will stand testament to the choice you have made.'

Astelan wisely remained silent, his flippant remarks and insults gone for the moment.

'I see that I am understood,' said Sapphon, still keeping his grip tight. 'Admit that you lied to me. Confess and death will be swift but without pain.'

The Fallen remained still, breathing quick and shallow, open hand and face pressed against the wall.

'Blessed is the mind too small for doubt,' he whispered. 'Do you claim that as your greatest teaching, or do you possess a more open and analytical mind, Sapphon?'

It was not the reply the Chaplain had been expecting. He relinquished his hold and stepped back, trying to work out what Astelan meant. The Fallen stretched and rolled out a kink in his neck, eyeing Sapphon with suspicion. The distrust was mutual, but despite everything that had passed in the last few hours Astelan could still prove useful.

The Chaplain wished he could be rid of the burden of this traitor, to release him into Asmodai's unkind care once more, but there was more than simply Sapphon's reputation and position to consider. The threat posed by Anovel, allied with the Death Guard perhaps, was very real. The attack on Piscina was no phantom of potential dishonour, it had actually happened. He had listened to Boreas's testimony many times since it had been unearthed by Malcifer and Sammael, and it told a tale of deliberate assault and provocation against the Chapter.

'You claim doubt is not a weakness? It was doubt that corrupted you and turned you from the true path of loyalty. That is why your protestations of honour and allegiance to the Emperor ring so hollow, Astelan.'

'If you did not have doubts, I would be having this conversation with Asmodai.' The Fallen shook his head. 'No, I would be bleeding at the hands of Asmodai, no conversation involved. It is doubt that keeps you here – the doubt that I lied to you. Your brothers, the other ones that know about me, they are convinced that I have misled you. It is clear that something has gone wrong. You attacked Ulthor, I assume? You may have me here in the bowels of the ship but even so I can remember the noise and feel of a warship emptying its launch bays. I heard the battle-sirens.'

Sapphon hated that Astelan could glean such insights from the scantest clue. In moments the Fallen had turned hesitation to his advantage, challenging the Chaplain to dispute these claims, any failure to do so confirming them.

He was moments from turning and leaving; calling on Asmodai to make the Fallen pay for his treachery with torment. They would return to the Rock and Sapphon would face dishonour. No penance for the Chaplain, no humiliation in front of the Chapter. Such matters had to be dealt with in circumspect manner. The Inner Circle would let its displeasure be known only amongst themselves. To the rest of the Dark Angels, it would seem that Sapphon was Master of Sanctity, spiritual leader. To Sapphon it would be the silent judgement, a tacit sentence of death. Every drop assault, every forlorn hope, every last-ditch defence and terminus mission he would be expected to lead from the front until Sapphon had offered the only reparation left to him: his death.

'Let me make a further guess,' Astelan continued. Sapphon wanted the Fallen to be quiet but knew that another outburst would only encourage the traitor. 'You did not find what you seek. If you had suffered defeat that would not be enough to bring you here, you would be preparing fresh assault to secure Anovel.'

'You seem sure of your deductions, Astelan. What makes you think you read the situation correctly? You were a war-leader, a fighter, when did you gain such illuminating insight into the minds of others?'

'I learned such things as you and your brothers applied brand to my flesh and parted skin with rasp and knife,' snarled Astelan. 'When your witches tried to prise open your mind they opened to me for an instant and I stared back. Boreas was a fine torturer, though Asmodai was more efficient. He was also nearly your equal in manipulation. I almost fell for his tricks and lies, but I did not give up. I learned your ways, the means by which you pull secrets from the heads of others and cloak yourself with false faith and misdirection.'

The Fallen swept the pile of books from the bench, quivering with anger.

'Deceit and treachery, hidden behind superstition and dogma!' Astelan's hands formed fists. He did not turn them on the Chaplain but controlled himself with visible effort. 'Nothing you represent stands for the ideals of the Emperor any more. I am done with helping you.'

Sapphon smiled. He slowly picked up the books and returned them to the gaps on the shelf on the wall of the chamber. He did not turn around.

'No, Astelan, you are not done with helping me. The fact remains that you stand accused of consorting with the Ruinous Powers. Save your fake rage. Nothing you have said or any act you have performed supports your professed innocence of this crime. It was a foolish hope of mine that you might be telling the truth. A doubt, you would call it. Now you accuse me of disloyalty, as deflection from your own guilt.' Sapphon turned to face the Fallen, who was sitting on the bench once more, arms folded, expression set defiantly. 'Petty games. You lie to yourself even more than you lie to us. I do not think you were as pivotal in the rebellion as you claim to be. You were a pawn of Luther as much as anybody else. He fell to the Dark Powers and you fell with him. You were nothing – a failed commander sent back by the Lion to where you could do no more harm. A spoilt child, believing you were special because the Emperor called you a warrior in his First Legion.'

'I know that you do not believe that,' replied Astelan. 'Boreas told me that my name was at the top of a list of Fallen, the list of those you hunted.'

'That much is true,' said Sapphon. He saw a glint of triumph in the Fallen's eyes; triumph that was soon

crushed by the Chaplain's next words. 'That list was simply alphabetical, Merir *Astelan*.'

The Fallen said nothing, resentful and petulant at this
declaration. Sapphon did not allow himself to become
too confident. He had wrested control back from his
adversary but he had not gained what he needed.

'You refuse to confess and you refuse to repent,' said
the Chaplain. 'You have nothing of worth to us in
terms of information. We have wasted many hours with
you, Astelan, and I will waste no more. You were no
architect of the schism. I do not even think you were a
co-conspirator with the other Fallen. Perhaps you were
a lackey, but nothing more than that. My time is better
spent with Methelas. We can still extract what we need
to know from him.'

The two locked stares, testing each other's will. Each
knew that they were entwined through bluff and double-
bluff, half-truth and pretence. And despite the elaborate
vocal and mental dance they had enacted, the simple
matter remained that they were bound together by
something far more potent: mutual need.

Astelan relented first, his grim expression breaking into
a smile. He thought for a moment, chewing his lip.

'You are far more testing than Asmodai,' the Fallen
confessed. 'Even the Librarians have nothing on you,
Brother Sapphon. I am a devious bastard, but I do not
understand how you can keep straight all of the lies
you tell, how you can be so flexible to accommodate all
of the cerebral and moral contortions. I would like to
promise that the lies stop here, but you would not accept
that and I cannot offer it. You are right, though, that my
only usefulness to you is in aiding with the capture of
Anovel.'

'We have accord, once again. I think you brought us to

Ulthor in good faith. Do you think Methelas knew your intent when he divulged the plan to you?'

'It would be unlikely, but not impossible,' admitted Astelan. He shrugged. 'I do not think Methelas was in a state of mind to devise such an elaborate counter-ruse on the spur of the moment. Although his flesh has been transformed by his dark allegiance, so that pain will not rip from him what you seek, he was still shocked by the recent turn of events.'

'And even if he thought to deceive us, he must have known what awaited us on Ulthor by some fashion. Such news is not common rumour.'

'True, the place was not plucked at random from the air. The name meant nothing to me. It was certainly not one of the systems we conquered as a Legion. Methelas's knowledge of it must have come from a more contemporary source. I think he spoke in earnest, boasting it seemed, assuring me that his capture had not halted the great scheme.'

Sapphon let out a sigh of exasperation and rubbed a hand across his forehead.

'We still have not made any progress towards apprehending Anovel or thwarting his schemes.'

'But you have inflicted setbacks,' said Astelan. 'My capture, the taking of Methelas, these may yet prove irrecoverable intercessions. It depends whether his new allies have the resources Anovel claimed they possessed.'

'New allies?'

'The Lord Cypher and several other Fallen.'

Immediately alert to subterfuge at the mention of the name of the thrice-cursed one, Sapphon loomed over Astelan, fists balled.

'You denied any knowledge of Cypher! Another lie?'

'I knew nothing when you asked,' said Astelan, holding

up his hands. 'Methelas mentioned him in passing.'

'And you kept this information from me until now.'

Frustration became anger. Sapphon resisted the urge to strike the Fallen, knowing it would take them right back to where they had been when he had first entered the prayer cell. Astelan had learned much in the past few minutes but the Chaplain was no closer to his objective and had no desire to start again with that disadvantage. A part of Sapphon found Astelan's deft manipulation amazing, but it was swamped by the far larger part that hated the Fallen for turning such talent against the Lion and the Emperor.

He had lied about Astelan being unimportant. Time and again the former Chapter Master's name had occurred in testimony wrought from other Fallen, naming him as one of Luther's chief lieutenants and a prime architect of the rebellion. Luther had found it easy to sway the native Calibanites to his cause, but it had been Astelan's influence that had brought the Terran-born Dark Angels under the arch-traitor's cause.

'You did not ask,' said Astelan. 'I do not understand this preoccupation with a defunct honorific of a knightly order that was disbanded ten thousand years ago. I see the mere mention of his name causes you great vexation. What did he do to earn such hate and dedication?'

'Do not concern yourself with the exploits of Cypher,' Sapphon said hurriedly. He stepped away, trying to think. 'Focus on keeping yourself out of the clutches of Asmodai. Tell me about Anovel. Tell me where we might find him. Port Imperial is no more. Ulthor is beyond our limits. Where else will we pick up the trail?'

'You have become a parody of yourselves.' Astelan laughed, with bitter humour. 'You have shaped your existence for the Hunt, and blinded yourselves to other opportunity. It is sad to see what has become of the Dark Angels.'

'You have a point to make? Make it!' snapped Sapphon.

'We were the First Legion, Brother Sapphon. Consider for a moment what that means. We had to do everything. We fought fleet actions and planetary assaults, razed fortresses and captured whole worlds. We were both the hammer and the anvil, the bait and the trap. We brought death from afar and slaughter at close hand. We acted and others followed.'

'I fail to see any relevance to the current task.'

'The Lion learned a simple lesson in the forests of Caliban: hunt or be hunted. Do you not think that remarkable?'

'The primarch learned how to be strong. His perseverance is an example to us that we shall never forget.'

'Not until the last Fallen has been hunted down?' It sounded peculiar to hear the refrain from the lips of a traitor. Sapphon did not like it, and suspected some hidden insult or taunt in Astelan's choice of words. The Fallen looked serious, watching his captor intently. 'Even when the Lion was found and raised within the Order, always he was the hunter. From Aldurukh the knights rode out and slew the great beasts of the forest.'

'I know the history of our primogenitor,' said Sapphon, irritated by the Fallen's meandering.

Though Ezekiel had granted him two hours, he was fully aware of the time slipping past. He needed a fresh plan of action, some new insight or scrap of information to present to the other commanders before they set course back to the Rock. As soon as the journey began he would be damned. Asmodai would ascend unopposed to the rank of Master of Sanctity and sooner or later his lack of subtlety, his bull-headed stubbornness would go too far and bring the Chapter into outright disrepute or conflict with the Inquisition. It was all Azrael could do to limit the damage done by the Master of Repentance at the moment; if there was no balance to Asmodai's blind zealotry the Dark Angels would become their own worst enemies. The thought spurred Sapphon and leant harshness to his mood.

'I am not interested in your warped version of past events. I tire of your sly asides and furtive trickery. The Lion destroyed the great beasts with the last hunt, and Caliban was delivered from the grip of darkness. What bearing has that on matters at hand?'

Astelan shook his head with an expression of incredulity. He waited for several seconds, expecting some further remark perhaps. Sapphon glared back.

'You really do not see the similarity, do you?' Astelan crossed his arms, refusing to concede to Sapphon's desire for haste. 'The hunt for the great beasts? The hunt for the Fallen?'

The Chaplain said nothing.

'When the last Fallen has been found, what then, *Interrogator-Chaplain* Sapphon? What will you hunt next? Who will you interrogate?'

Sapphon denied Astelan any satisfaction of an answer. The Fallen had no genuine point to make and was simply hoping for some kind of offended response. Sapphon would play this game no longer.

'Have you ever considered *not* hunting the Fallen?' Astelan asked, unfolding his arms, leaning forward with elbows on knees.

The Chaplain allowed his silent stare to be answer enough.

'My point is proven by your reticence to envision any alternative to the current situation. You track, follow and hunt. You are the Lion in the great forest. You are the Order sweeping away the beasts. Do you know what the ordinary people of Caliban did to protect themselves from the ferocious creatures that preyed on them in the night?'

'I am sure you are going to tell me, even if I do not desire to know.'

'They set traps, Brother Sapphon. Pits and deadfalls, snares and spikes.'

'How completely uninteresting.'

'They used themselves as bait, more often than not. A very dangerous vocation, but one that was held in high regard. Not the weak and the expendable, they were not left out for the great beasts. The monsters of the forest preyed upon the strongest. They had a sense for it, I am told. It is why they came for the primarch again and again, drawn to his puissance and energy.'

'Must I fetch Asmodai?' said Sapphon, turning away. 'Perhaps he is right. I indulge you too much, traitor.'

'The best bait was another great beast,' Astelan said sharply as Sapphon reached the cell door. 'If you could capture one alive it would draw others from all across the forest.'

Sapphon stopped. He had allowed the debacle on Ulthor to cloud his thinking, desperately seeking some clue or spoor to follow in the absence of Anovel himself. That had not been the intent. Astelan had not been brought along simply to ascertain whether the Fallen was on Ulthor, but to draw him forth.

'A great beast? Are you suggesting we use *you* as bait to catch Anovel? Where would we set such a trap?'

Astelan smiled.

THE GAMBIT

Disbelief struck Asmodai dumb. He stared at Sapphon, torn between incredulity and despair. Sammael rose from his chair on the opposite side of the council table. Power armour whined as the others turned to look at him. They were still in the Ulthor system and everybody was at combat readiness but the necessities of ship life and the needs of maintenance meant that the company's Terminator suits were being tended by the Techmarines.

'Tharsis? The world Astelan enslaved?' said the Grand Master of the Ravenwing.

'You must know that he may still have sympathisers there, even after all of these years,' said Belial.

'Idiocy!' Asmodai finally found his voice. Sapphon opened his mouth to reject the accusation but Asmodai did not grant him the time. 'Have you learned nothing from the disaster at Ulthor? How many more of our brothers would you sacrifice for these insane ideas?'

'Any brother that died on Ulthor can be laid before

you, Asmodai!' Sapphon snarled back. He thumped a hand on the table. 'I told you, all of you, that we had to be sure of our target first, but you overruled me.'

'Because you wanted to allow a known traitor to make contact.' Asmodai was so outraged he could barely speak. 'Do you think we are fools, Sapphon? To repeat a past mistake is regrettable and to do so immediately borders on treacherous incompetence.'

'If we had stayed with my plan, and allowed Astelan to make representation in the correct manner, we would have known that Anovel was not on Ulthor.'

'How?' said Belial. 'There is no surety when dealing with this serpent-tongued Fallen. He may have conveyed warning or message from Methelas without us knowing. Any information from him is deeply suspect and only the evidence of our eyes can be trusted. No matter what Astelan told us, we would have had to go down to Ulthor.'

Sapphon brooded, silenced by the Deathwing commander's logic. Asmodai was not content to let his fellow Chaplain simply stew in his own anger.

'You go too far, and this time there must be consequence.'

'*I* go too far?' Sapphon seemed incandescent with anger, enough to match Asmodai's own. 'I have lost count of the number of times your reckless actions have brought suspicion upon the Chapter. How many times has the Supreme Grand Master been forced to dissemble and lie and grovel because of your constant mistakes, Asmodai?'

'This is no time or place for such argument,' said Sammael, looking back and forth between the two Chaplains.

'You are wrong,' said Sapphon. He stood up and started to pace, backwards and forwards in front of a large comms-screen set into the dark wood panels of the wall. The flickering light of the ceiling strips caused his shadow to flutter like wings across the matt grey surface. 'This is exactly the time and the place, Brother Sammael. If we return to the Supreme Grand Master now, without further effort, we have achieved nil. Nothing. Shame will be upon this campaign and those who took part in it will bear that dishonour, living and dead. Should we not bend every sinew to the effort of rectifying the deficit?'

Asmodai could not believe that Belial and Sammael appeared to be considering this argument. The Chaplain turned to Ezekiel, who had been sitting silently at the foot of the table during these exchanges.

'Brother-Librarian, do not hold tongue on fresh opinion. What think you on this matter?'

Ezekiel laid his hands upon the table with precise, deliberate slowness. He looked at Asmodai and then Sapphon, expression impassive. Without a word he shook his head.

'I will interpret that as an abstention,' said Sapphon.

'No vote has been called,' said Belial. 'No motion raised.'

'Did I not speak clearly and at length concerning my newest proposal, brother?' Sapphon threw up his hands in exasperation.

'That was meant to be considered a course of action?' Belial frowned with bemusement. 'I thought you were spilling forth addled contents of mind, not making serious entreaty. We cannot take Astelan to Tharsis.'

'Why not?'

'He is a traitor and a danger to the whole Chapter,' said Belial.

'More specifically? What risk is there in taking him to Tharsis? He has made no attempt to escape thus far. The world is firmly under the rule of the Emperor once more. There is no mischief he can undertake.'

GAV THORPE

'I am inclined to the Brother-Chaplain's plan,' said Sammael. 'We purged all remnants of Astelan's sacred bands when we retook the planet. He is despised there, even if his name resonates still with a few scattered anti-Imperialist voices.'

'Think on it, brothers,' Sapphon said, dividing his attention between Belial and Ezekiel, knowing well that Asmodai would not be swayed by any argument. 'I do not promise that we will return to the Rock in triumph, but we will be reunited with our Chapter-brothers knowing that we spared no exertion. How many times must we regret a lead not followed? How many times do we lament the trail left to grow cold by other endeavour?'

'Do not discuss this heresy any further,' snapped Asmodai, his thin patience worn through already by Sapphon's bleating. 'We will return to the Tower of Angels and seek fresh endorsement from the Inner Circle. Brother Sapphon is free to present his case before the Supreme Grand Master and others, and I will abide by their judgement. Again.'

'To delay is to court failure, brother.' Sapphon spoke quietly now. It annoyed Asmodai when his Brother-Chaplain did so, because it always seemed patronising.

'I see no need for haste.'

'Let me remind you all that Anovel is not our goal here.' Sapphon stared at Asmodai, sincere and intent. 'There is another who is still close at hand, his purpose not yet complete.'

Asmodai could not stop the flutter of excitement he felt whenever the prospect was raised. Even now, burning with anger, the thought of apprehending the arch-Fallen and subjecting him to the torments of repentance warmed his soul.

'Methelas confirmed to Astelan that Anovel

communicated with Cypher, perhaps even met him,' Sapphon continued. 'The incident on Piscina, the loss of our Chapter fort, is still hot in our minds. While the Chapter is distracted suppressing the rebellion and ork attacks brought forth by this interference, Cypher is free to enact whatever plan he wishes. If we allow ourselves to be turned from the pursuit, we grant the thrice-cursed one free charter.'

'Do you really think we are that close to capturing him?' Belial seemed to be softening in his opinion.

'Conjecture and pretty tales,' snarled Asmodai, disappointed with himself that he had entertained Sapphon's wild scheme even for a moment. 'Cypher will not be found on Tharsis. You create tenuous link to obscure poor reasoning.'

'Anovel still waits for confirmation from Astelan that he has found a recruiting world fit for their purpose.'

'After fifteen years it seems doubtful Anovel much cares what has happened to Astelan,' said Belial.

'But curiosity alone may pull in our favour,' countered Sammael. 'Can Anovel afford not to respond? Ulthor is no place to start a new Chapter. That much we have confirmed.'

'Why do you entertain these notions with such conduct?' Asmodai could not comprehend what purpose his brothers thought was served by this idle talk. 'Brother Sapphon, recuse yourself to the penitentium and spare us further madness. Brother Belial, Brother Sammael, do not exacerbate Sapphon's vexed condition with pointless curiosity.'

'Do you not want to catch Cypher?' Sammael's question surprised Asmodai. It took him a moment to formulate a reply that adequately summarised his feelings on the matter.

'I want every dark-spawned Fallen to feel the touch of judgement, brothers, but wanting it does not make it happen.'

'Exactly!' declared Sapphon. 'Only by action will we achieve that victory. We do not need permission from the Supreme Grand Master. The highest members of the Inner Circle are in this chamber. We form a quorum with enough experience and judgement to decide this matter alone.'

'Such talk borders on mutiny,' said Asmodai, horrified by what he was hearing. He pulled his pistol free. 'I will not allow such sedition to continue.'

'Put away your sidearm, Asmodai.' Belial spoke calmly and slowly, and a glance at the Grand Master of the Deathwing showed he was resolute. Asmodai slid his weapon back into its holster.

'One does not free the caged bird to catch another,' said the Chaplain. He could not remember where he had heard the phrase but it seemed appropriate now. 'If we are to vote on this, then so be it, but I tell you now it is further folly.'

'The vote is called,' said Sapphon. 'A show of hands should suffice.'

The others nodded, including Ezekiel.

'Those that wish to travel to Tharsis and attempt to draw out Anovel, raise your hands.'

Sapphon put his hand in the air, and likewise Sammael.

'The vote fails,' said Asmodai, trying not to sound triumphant but knowing he had failed. 'Two votes do not carry the motion.'

'Brother Ezekiel has already hinted at abstention,' complained Sapphon. 'Raise hands now those that oppose the plan as I have set it forth.'

Belial and Asmodai showed their disapproval. Ezekiel sat unmoving.

'We are at an impasse, it seems,' said Belial.

'This is ridiculous,' Asmodai said with a snort of derision. 'Such behaviour is unbecoming of the Inner Circle.'

'The white or the black, brother?' Sapphon said, looking at Ezekiel. 'In the Inner Circle there are no abstentions. Make your will plain for all.'

'This is not the Inner Circle. I will not cast a deciding vote. Though two each stand to either side, I will not be held alone responsible for one course of action over another. Neither argument has convinced me – I see merit in both views.'

'The motion does not carry,' said Asmodai. 'A majority is needed. We return to the Rock.'

Belial stepped away from the table, ready to leave. Sammael looked disappointed, sighing heavily.

'Wait! Perhaps there is another means to decide,' said Sapphon.

'Trial by combat?' suggested Asmodai eagerly, relishing the prospect of legitimately unleashing much frustration and rage on his fellow Chaplain.

'Let fate, or the hand of the Emperor, decide,' said Sapphon. He plucked a bolt pistol cartridge from his belt and thumbed a round from the top onto the wooden tabletop. Placing the magazine back in his belt, he took up two goblets and upturned them, either side of the bolt. He looked at Asmodai with an eyebrow raised.

'A child's game?' Asmodai shook his head. 'When reasoned argument fails, you resort to trickery.'

Sapphon stepped back from the table. He looked at Ezekiel and waved a hand towards the goblets and bolt. Ezekiel nodded and took Sapphon's place, resting a finger on each upturned cup.

'I am willing to allow providence, the fortune of the Emperor, to let itself be known,' said Sapphon, manner serious, speaking softly. 'I am willing to surrender my fate to a greater fate. Are you so invested in your desires to refuse the same, Brother Asmodai?'

'Is this the will of those gathered?' said the Master of Repentance. 'Do you endorse this charade?'

Sammael nodded with a half-smile. 'Better this than another hour of endless discussion,' said the Ravenwing leader.

'If you both swear to abide by the result, I see no better resolution,' Belial conceded.

'I swear,' said Sapphon, a little too quickly for Asmodai's liking.

'I swear also,' said Asmodai, grimacing as he forced the words from his mouth. 'In the Emperor's will we trust.'

'The challenge was set by Brother Sapphon,' announced Ezekiel. 'The choice is yours, Brother Asmodai. Turn away.'

The Chaplain did as ordered. He heard the scrape of the goblets on wood, moving three times.

'When you are ready, brother. If you reveal the bolt, your will shall be done. If not, Brother Sapphon wins the vote.'

Turning back, Asmodai looked at the two cups. They were impossible to tell apart, save for small scratches and dents. He did not know under which the bolt had been placed and there was no obvious means of deduction. He reached his hand towards the goblet on the left and then glanced at Sapphon. The Chaplain's features were set, showing no hint of his thoughts. Asmodai stared at the cups as though trying to bore through them with pure hate.

In a quick movement he changed his mind and lifted the right-hand cup. There was empty table beneath. The metal of the goblet crumpled as Asmodai clenched his fist in anger. He tossed the mutilated vessel aside and glared at Sapphon. The other Chaplain looked relieved rather than triumphant.

Asmodai was about to turn away when a thought occurred to him. He snatched up the other cup. The bolter-round sat underneath, glinting in the erratic light. With nothing to say, he stormed to the chamber door. He stopped at the threshold and turned back, his gaze sweeping across all of them.

'Upon your heads and souls be it, brothers,' warned the Chaplain. He focused his stare on Sapphon. 'If this plan turns to misadventure, I will name you traitor. Your life and your honour now weigh in the balance. Are you sure this is your wish, Brother Sapphon?'

The other Chaplain replied without hesitation.

'What will be, will be, brother. I regret nothing.'

'You will,' said Asmodai. 'When you are taken down the long stair to the cells and my blades part your flesh. When your cries merge with the other traitors', you will know a very deep, very personal regret. I guarantee it.'

Asmodai left, leaving the others secure in the knowledge that he did not make idle threats.

CONTEMPLATION

The clamour of rivet-binders, molecular drills and lascutters had passed. The Techmarines and servitors had left. Armoury bay seven of the *Implacable Justice* was almost completely silent. Almost.

There was the ever-present thrum of plasma drives and the almost imperceptible hiss of gases and liquids passing through the pipes overhead. The quiet scrape of a slightly misaligned fan in one of the overhead air circulators broke the still. Muffled by bulkheads came the clatter of machinery from the servants of the armoury continuing their labours in bay six.

Annael knelt beside *Black Shadow*, alone with his steed. Seven days out from Ulthor and it was the first time he had an opportunity to offer thanks to the bike for saving his life – and the life of Sabrael. He whispered devotions to the machine-spirit of the bike. Arranged on the deck in front of him were four jars, each containing a different sacred libation. The Techmarines had taken some convincing to part with them, but Annael's impassioned pleas to make dedication to his steed had proven enough.

He had already flushed the engine with the Oils of Vitality and polished the metalwork with the Unguent of Readiness. He had applied the Lubricant of Swiftness with a square of soft material stitched with four sacred runes, the meaning of which remained a mystery to him. The last, the Tonic of Cleansing, remained stoppered for the moment.

In his right hand Annael held the litanies he had hastily scribbled as they had been recited on the other bikes, and he was sure he had misheard. It was impossible though, his hearing was pitch perfect. He spoke the words, knowing that he lacked understanding of their deeper meaning, in the hope that *Black Shadow*'s machine-spirit would be pleased.

Finishing the chant, he pulled the stopper from the bottle, his gauntlets making the task a little awkward. He poured a little of the contents onto the bristles of a small brush in his left hand. He stood upon and started to clean around the runepad and dial controls of the bike's main display. A gentle froth built up, which he delicately wiped away with the blessed cloth.

Sharing this moment with his steed allowed Annael to think about what had happened on Ulthor free from guilt or concern. Away from his battle-brothers he could look back at the memory and glean what he could from the experience. He found it hard to imagine that Sammael had led them into such a debacle. From the moment they had entered the city the Ravenwing had been at a disadvantage.

Annael told himself that whatever had been on the planet – whoever this Fallen Angel was they had been seeking – it must have been important. It was hard though, to have faith without question. Since the Seventh Rite, since learning the truth about what had happened during the Horus Heresy – the deeper truth not shared even with the rest of the Second Company – he had felt tainted by the knowledge. He understood why it had to remain secret, on an intellectual level. It was a dangerous thing to know, that even a Dark Angel could be flawed. It was one of the seeds of doubt the Chaplains had repeatedly warned against during Annael's centuries of service. The seed of doubt was nurtured by selfishness, secrecy and unbrotherly thoughts. But the same Chaplains that had taught him this now demanded that he keep silent what he had learned.

In the fraternal prayers and briefings he had felt uneasy amongst his battle-brothers. He was worried that a strange mania would seize him; cause him to blurt out to everybody the truth of what he had been told.

He sought reassurance, applying himself to the cleansing of *Black Shadow* with focus and vigour. He wanted to talk about the changes he was undergoing, but it felt foolish to speak of them with the other Black Knights. Tybalain and the rest seemed untroubled by their burden. They were made from much sterner stuff, Annael recognised. He had thought to broach the subject with Chaplain Malcifer but when opportunity presented itself each day after massed benediction he would find himself leaving with the others, his concerns bottled up.

He needed a confidant that would not judge him, or pity him; someone that he could share his secrets with and so aid in the carrying of the burden.

'Would that you could carry it too,' he said to *Black Shadow*. He ran the brush down the side of the vidscreen, picking out flecks of dirt. It occurred to Annael that perhaps it was not such a strange notion. His steed bore him into battle, and through its strength *Black Shadow* carried him to victory and brought him back to safety. Perhaps it could offer more. Certainly it would not speak to any other of Annael's confessions.

'If you could speak, what tales would you tell,' Annael said, feeling foolish but pressing on with hope that he had found an answer to his problem. 'A spirit seven thousand years old, given new body after new body. There is little you have not seen, faithful steed. Traitors and allies, victory and defeat, honour and shame. I wonder how I compare to those that rode before me. Am I worthy? Have I proven my courage and dedication as well as they did?'

He applied the brush with determination, sharing in the action of cleansing.

'Many brothers died on Ulthor. Some of yours too will not return to the armoury. Do you feel their loss? I used to think that not a battle-brother died without purpose. I am not sure that is true. What will be said of their deaths when we return to the Tower of Angels? What will they put in the Roll of Heroes? "They died in battle". We all die in battle, it is the fate every Space Marine shares. Even you, *Black Shadow*, perpetual mount, will die some day. Not while I can prevent it, of course. You have saved me and I will repay the debt a thousand times if necessary.'

Annael placed the bottle and brush on the deck and swung a leg over his bike to sit in the saddle. He gripped the handlebars, feet still on the floor, and felt welcome.

'What goal did we serve, coming here?' There was no plan behind his words, just a flow of thoughts that needed to be set free from the confines of his mind. 'Will they ever tell us? It troubles, and perhaps it should not, that I might be killed and not know the reason why my life was laid upon the altar of battle. Is that selfish? Probably. It is not my place to reason the manner of how or where I fight. I am a weapon, made by the Emperor for the protection of His domains. I am a Dark Angel, a son of the Lion, and to serve the Supreme Grand Master is my only purpose.'

He fell silent and listened for a moment, thinking he had heard a sound of someone entering the armoury bay. Nothing disturbed the usual noises.

'Of course, I know these thoughts are wrong. I should share them with Brother Malcifer so that he may set mind at rest and renew attention to duty. Is it a disobedience not to confess my failings, surely it is, but I cannot bring myself to air these doubts, knowing it should bring shame upon me. Cleansing and penance have their place, but why should I not ask these questions? I am a Black Knight, favoured of the Ravenwing, holder of the secrets of the Seventh Rite.'

Even uttering this fact felt like an act of betrayal to the Chapter. More than that, it felt as though he made a mockery of the deaths of Zarall and Araton. He had not spoken to Malcifer or his squadron-brothers of the guilt that still surrounded events on Thyestes. Disobedience had brought him here, through the sacrifice of his battle-brothers' lives, and to squander that on the fear of punishment was itself a terrible crime. It might have been better had he stayed true to duty and ignored Sabrael on that cold night. He would likely be dead, but perhaps that would be preferable to the angst that plagued him.

'It is unseemly to prefer the company of machines to flesh.' Sabrael's voice shocked Annael out of his contemplative mood. He turned in the saddle to see his battle-brother approaching across the bay, pistol on one hip, the Blade of Corswain scabbarded at the other. Annael wondered if Sabrael ever had a moment's doubt; if his vainglorious facade hid something more sinister. 'Unless you would prefer the red of the Techmarine to being a Black Knight.'

'I pay homage to the machine-spirit,' Annael said quickly, waving a hand towards the unguents as explanation.

'You provide further evidence of your guilt.' Sabrael stopped a couple of metres away, a smirk on his lips.

'Guilt?' said Annael. 'What guilt?'

'I spoke in jest, but perhaps without thought,' said Sabrael, growing serious. 'A man who seeks solace in the company of his machine might perhaps prefer it to pass unremarked.'

'No, not at all,' said Annael. He forced a smile and good humour. 'I felt it worthwhile to appease my steed after the iniquitous deed of saving your worthless hide.'

'Saving my...?' Sabrael grinned and shook his head. 'Had it not been for my swift action on the retreat we would have both been swallowed by that wall of filth!'

'Had you not been hanging from the back of my steed like a drunken jokaero I would have been out of the city with time to spare.'

'I think you will find that had I not intercepted that incendiary attack on your behalf, you would currently be a crispy stain on the roads of Ulthor.'

The outrageousness of Sabrael's claim left Annael speechless, first with indignation and then with the absurdity of the debate. Annael's smile was genuine now, darker thoughts forgotten, spirit lifted by the simple camaraderie.

'Come with me, brother,' said Sabrael turning away.

'Where to?' Annael asked. Sabrael did not reply, so he

dismounted and followed the other Space Marine.

They cut between the other bikes of the Black Knights, including Sabrael's new steed. It was a standard Raven-wing mount, with bolters not plasma talon, freshly painted and polished, the old machine-spirit installed into its cogitating banks. Sabrael stopped beside it for a moment, laid a hand on the saddle and moved on.

At the back of the bay, under the shadow of dormant cranes and running gear, Sabrael stopped beside a door barred by a wheel lock. He spun the lock, which opened without a sound, and pulled the door. Beyond was a narrow passageway, just wide enough for a Space Marine to pass in armour. Sabrael stepped through the doorway and turned left.

'Where are we going?' whispered Annael, standing at the doorway. The corridor was lined with pipes, a faint steam in the air; a maintenance conduit. There was no answer from Sabrael. Annael hesitated for a few more seconds, remembering what had transpired the last time he had followed Sabrael against his better judgement. His companion's natural confidence was infectious though, and Annael's curiosity had been piqued. He stepped into the corridor and followed, the other Space Marine silhouetted against dull orange lamps twenty metres ahead.

The access space ran along the armoury bays, parallel to the main thoroughfare of the deck that ran half the length of the ship. He had to stop to turn and look back, the cramped confines restricting his movement. As far as he could see the conduit ran aft, buried within the armoured skin of the strike cruiser.

'Come on, you laggard,' Sabrael called back. He had opened another door and was lit by pale yellow light from another armoury bay. 'You walk as slowly as you ride.'

Sabrael waited until Annael had caught up with him before stepping through the opened hatch.

'Welcome,' said the Space Marine as Annael followed, 'to Armoury Bay One.'

'Bay One? Is that not the personal armoury of Grand Master Sammael?'

His question needed no spoken answer. The bay itself was half the size of the others, about fifty metres by one hundred. There was loading and maintenance equipment stored along the walls, and at the centre of the deck waited *Corvex* and *Sableclaw* – the Grand Master's jetbike and Land Speeder. Annael had seen Sammael's famous steeds in battle, but never so close, never able to examine them in detail.

Both anti-grav machines were locked to the deck in broad clamps, pistons and hydraulics holding the skimmers in place. Annael went first to *Sableclaw* while Sabrael inspected *Corvex*. The Land Speeder's gun mounts were empty at the moment, the ammunition feeds and hoppers opened for maintenance and cleaning. Annael had training on a Land Speeder – all Ravenwing warriors could pilot skimmers as well as the aircraft used by the Second Company – and the controls were mostly familiar. There was a complex suite of scanner arrays and communications screens that he assumed were for commanding the company.

He wanted to run a hand over the jet-black paint; to climb up into the driver's chair or the gunner's cupola. The urge was almost overwhelming but he fought it, knowing that it would be an act of disrespect.

He turned around and found that his companion shared no such constraint; Sabrael sat astride *Corvex*, turning the handlebars and leaning left and right as though slaloming through an enemy battleline.

'Sabrael!' snapped Annael.

'Does it suit?' asked the other Space Marine. 'Do you think I will be a fine Grand Master?'

'I think you a fool if you aspire so highly,' laughed Annael. 'Who would give you command of a company? You can barely control yourself.'

'Is that not to my advantage?' said Sabrael. Annael realised he was being serious. 'The unexpected, the daring, they are the greatest weapons of the Ravenwing. I am sword master, bearer of the Blade of Corswain, Black Knight of the Dark Angels. Why should I not be a Grand Master one day?'

'Tybalain may have greater claim before you.' Annael did not want to tell his battle-brother, but the thought of Sabrael leading the Second Company was nearly more dread-inspiring than the denizens of Ulthor. 'It is unseemly to harbour such ambitions. Be content with your current station.'

'I do not seek to usurp any other's rightful claim, nor ignore the chain of command. I merely dream of serving with even greater glory. Is that so wrong?'

Annael did not reply, perturbed by the topic. He took several steps towards the other Space Marine, intending to pull him off the jetbike. A thrum of electricity and the flicker of overhead lights filled the chamber before he had the chance. One of the bay's main doors rumbled open, revealing a solitary figure standing on the ramp down to the central corridor. He was short and young, a serf dressed in the red robes of the armoury. He had a digi-slate in his hands and seemed preoccupied as he stepped into the chamber. He looked up, stopped, eyes widening as he saw the two Space Marines.

'You... You're not supposed to be here,' he said, hands trembling.

'We are Black Knights, the right hand of the Grand Master,' said Annael, stepping away from the two machines. Sabrael dismounted and gave *Corvex* a parting pat on the handlebars.

'That is right, we pass where Sammael passes. Who are you to question our right to be here?'

'You misunderstand me, masters,' said the serf. He bowed in apology. 'I merely meant that Lord Sammael has issued order for the company warriors to assemble for briefing. It sounded important.'

'Damn,' muttered Sabrael. He looked at Annael. 'I knew I came to tell you something. It slipped my mind.'

'Idiot!' snapped Annael. 'Selfish, vain, pompous idiot!'

Sabrael was already heading towards the open door, breaking into a run.

'If you had not been cleaning your bike,' Sabrael called back, 'none of this would have happened.'

Annael glared at the serf, who stepped back, holding up the digi-slate like a shield.

'I do not have time for this,' said Annael, shaking his head. He followed after Sabrael, realising that whoever arrived at the briefing last would have the most penance to complete.

PART THREE
THARSIS

OLD WOUNDS

With Asmodai and a squad of Deathwing as escort, Sapphon opened the door to the cell. Astelan looked up, closed the book slowly and stood. He was pensive.

'We have arrived?' asked the Fallen.

'Yes, we will make low orbit over Tharsis in twelve minutes,' replied Sapphon.

'Come with us,' said Asmodai, beckoning to the Fallen with a brusque wave.

'My guard dog, I presume?' Astelan smiled insincerely at Asmodai, who said nothing, jaw clenched with anger.

'If you attempt to escape or if you attempt to mislead us, if you attempt to make unauthorised communication with anyone or attempt to contact the enemy you will be executed immediately.' Sapphon emphasised each point slowly, gauging the Fallen's reaction. Astelan nodded his consent but stopped as they turned down the corridor.

'I am under-dressed for the occasion,' said the Fallen,

holding out his arms and looking down at the plain grey robe of a prisoner.

'What do you mean?' said Sapphon.

'If you attempt to delay or hinder us, you will be executed,' said Asmodai. His gauntleted fingers flexed on the haft of his crozius arcanum. 'Do you wish to make further objection or would you prefer to be returned to the Rock where your just punishment awaits?'

'Justice will come to each of us, I assure you,' said Astelan. He turned his attention to Sapphon. 'I am serious. You cannot expect me to proceed without war-plate.'

'Out of the question!' said Asmodai.

'I am inclined to agree,' said Sapphon.

Astelan folded his arms defiantly.

'Anovel will be expecting communication from Astelan, Lord Commander of Tharsis. The astropaths will need to send images to confirm my identity. If I am not garbed in battle-plate it will arouse suspicion.'

'I warned that he would push us further,' Asmodai said to Sapphon. He looked at the Deathwing. 'Return him to his cell.'

The Terminators stepped forward but were stopped by a word and a raised hand from Sapphon.

'Not yet,' said the Master of Sanctity. 'He makes valid argument.'

Asmodai looked at Sapphon for several seconds without blinking.

'I argued against taking him from the confines of the Rock. Under protest only do I allow this prisoner to leave this ship. Do not expect me to allow him to do so in full armour! I think you underestimate his abilities. He is a Space Marine, and furnished with power armour could cause significantly more damage than I am prepared to accept.'

'It is not your decision, brother,' said Sapphon. He looked at Astelan. 'There is also another benefit to this course of action. Our prisoner's face is well known on Tharsis, and though there are few that survived his purges still alive there will be those amongst the new Imperial commander's staff that will recognise his features. Concealment of helm negates such risk.'

'Throwing his corpse into a hole with a bolt in his head negates all risk, brother, should I pursue that option?'

'Also, power armour will transmit location signals at all times, so he will be even harder to misplace.'

'I have no intention of wandering off,' said Astelan.

'I would not recommend it,' said Sapphon. 'If the people of Tharsis find out who you are, they will try to kill you.'

'And will you protect me?' Astelan looked at Asmodai, smiling at the prospect.

'No,' replied the Chaplain. 'I will kill you myself.'

'Such perseverance, Asmodai. I can see why they made you a Chaplain, after all.'

Asmodai stepped up to the prisoner, and though the Chaplain was armoured Astelan was almost the same height, having regained his full build and strength. The Fallen's face was reflected in the ruby lens eyes of Asmodai's skull-mask, equally impassive.

'I will see you dead by my hand, traitor. Boreas should have executed you. Do not think I will repeat his mistake.'

Astelan stared back at the Chaplain. Sapphon could see murderous intent behind the Fallen's eyes and was taken aback for a moment. He had become used to the conversational, urbane aspect Astelan had presented in recent weeks, but was now reminded that this was an individual who had opened fire on his own primarch in cold blood and later enslaved a world and slaughtered billions in an insane cause; a world to which he was about to be returned.

It was not possible that this was the intent of Astelan. It was too happenstance that they had ended up in this situation. Whatever the Fallen was capable of, no matter how well he might have hoped to manipulate the Master of Sanctity, Sapphon could not see any way in which Astelan had planned for a return to Tharsis. However, even if it was not by Astelan's design that they had come here, the Fallen was certainly capable of taking advantage if presented with the opportunity.

'If you wrong me, I will kill you first,' Sapphon reminded his prisoner. 'I guarantee it.'

Astelan smiled and stepped back from Asmodai. He moved back to the cell door and looked over his shoulder at them.

'I think it may take you some time to prepare my armour,' said the Fallen. 'You possess only later marks of war-plate, which will require some modification as well as the application of older symbols and my personal heraldry for it to be fitting. I can wait.'

Sapphon left, taking Asmodai with him in case the Fallen provoked the Chaplain to a lethal response. Ever since the council had gone against his wishes eighteen days earlier, the Master of Repentance had been in a state of near-murderous rage. The First Company warriors on board the *Penitent Warrior* had learned to give him a wide berth when possible, lest they incur his wrath and days in the penitentium for the slightest infraction. Sapphon had not attempted to speak with this battle-brother until the time had come for them to fetch Astelan from his cell.

Asmodai excused himself and headed in the direction of the Reclusiam while Sapphon made his way to the armoury. He made known his needs – met with quizzical looks but no spoken questions – and was told it would take several hours for the battleplate to be made ready to his specifications.

It was a delay Sapphon had not wanted, and while Asmodai cloistered himself in solitary contemplation, the Master of Sanctity felt the need to spend some time with the battle-brothers. Although his duty was to the Hunt above all other considerations, it would be good to share words with the Deathwing after recent setbacks; not only for their spirits but for Sapphon's also. It seemed long ago that they had been faced with the simple task of eradicating the orks in Kadillus Harbour. How quickly news of the Fallen could change the fate of the whole Chapter.

He went around the dorters of the squads where they tended their battlegear, ready to fight at a moment's notice, making small talk and offering such advice and benedictions as were required of him. The distraction was useful, allowing Sapphon to lose himself in the minutiae of personal contact again. It was too easy to become distant from this, the fighting heart of the Chapter. It reassured the Master of Sanctity to know that whatever lies he had told, whatever misdeeds he had perpetrated in the cause of the Dark Angels, it was to protect something pure. The warriors of the Chapter, even the Deathwing who had been taught of some of the ancient shame, were protected by his sacrifice. As they had all sworn, their honour was forfeit, surrendered to protect the honour of others.

Whenever he had doubts, and Sapphon was certainly not above doubts unlike Asmodai, it was from the battle-brothers that he drew strength, even as he bolstered their fortitude. Many foes had been vanquished, worlds protected, billions of lives saved by the efforts of the Dark Angels. That was a worthy cause. That was something for which he felt no shame at all.

Just before the appointed hour arranged with the Techmarines, Sapphon found himself alone in his chamber, preparing himself for the trip down to Tharsis. He asked himself again if he was doing the right thing. As when he had asked himself a dozen times before, the answer was yes. Asmodai's road was the easy route, but it was the slow path. Sapphon had a chance here and now – a chance he had engineered with his own will and desire – to take a massive step forward in the Hunt. It was this type of insight, the crossing of lines to seek new paths, which had been the cause of his elevation to Master of Sanctity.

With a Deathwing escort he took Astelan to the armoury, which had been cleared of all but the highest ranking Techmarines. When the arming process was complete, Sapphon's doubts returned with a vengeance.

Clad in full war-plate, Astelan was the very image of the ancient Dark Angels. His armour was black, like the Chaplains', the sword-and-wings insignia picked out in dark red on his left shoulder. His right carried insignia not used for ten thousand years; a heraldry comprised of personal symbols indicating his origins on Holy Terra itself, along with markings for the Chapter he led and the Order to which it had belonged.

It was incredible to Sapphon that when Astelan had first donned power armour the Emperor still walked abroad, and had personally led the Dark Angels into battle. Astelan's command had numbered more warriors than the entire Dark Angels could now muster, and in turn was only one of dozens of such commanders. Terra had been reconquered and the Dark Angels had been the spearpoint of the Emperor's armies to retake the whole galaxy.

The sight of Astelan and the thought of what he had once represented took Sapphon's breath away, leaving him humbled before the magnitude of duty and ten thousand years of history. Astelan's right greave and down the right forearm were filled with names painted in small, white letters. Sapphon recognised them from the ancient annals: each a battle honour of the Legion. There was a lump in his throat as he looked at Astelan and was reminded that this warrior fought at Caerthorn, Betel Nineteen, Sathathorix and Greiman's World. He had liberated hundreds of systems from the darkness of the Long Night, decades before even the Lion had been found.

What pride would that create? Sapphon wondered if any Dark Angel of the present day could ever emulate such courage, dedication and spirit. To venture into the shadows between stars seeking the last remnants of humanity, bringing retribution and hope in equal measure. Was it a wonder that some of them had started to think of themselves as better than the humans they saved? Time and again the testimonies of captured Fallen had told the same sorry tale, of humility falling to arrogance, duty to ambition. Even those that repented, who had seen the error of their decisions before the touch of a Chaplain's blades, could not be pardoned for those transgressions, even if they could be forgiven.

He had always known what the Fallen were, but it had been so easy to think of them only as traitors, as debased servants of Dark Powers who had willingly turned aside the grace of the Emperor's service to pursue their own ends. They had been objects, even Astelan; things to be hunted and turned to the Dark Angels purpose.

Now Astelan was revealed again as what he once was: a Space Marine of the First.

The Emperor's Finest.

Dark Angel.

'A thuggish child dressing up in the armour of his betters.' Asmodai's contemptuous declaration broke Sapphon's trance. Astelan replied with a condescending smile and any semblance to the noble and honourable warriors that had led the Great Crusade from Terra was shattered. Sapphon saw only a selfish, immoral murderer again.

'Follow us,' said the Master of Sanctity, his tone made harsh by the regret of his earlier sentiment. Asmodai had not been enamoured for a moment, and it shamed Sapphon to think of such a moment of weakness.

'By your command,' said Astelan. He fastened his helm in place.

A Thunderhawk waited for them in one of the launch bays. Clearance had already been confirmed by orbital command of Tharsis, though Belial had noted that the system's authorities had received the arrival of the Dark Angels with a less than enthusiastic response. Sapphon could not blame them. Like Piscina the actions of the Fallen – of Astelan – had sullied the name of the Chapter for generations.

'What web of lies did you spin for my usurper?' asked the Fallen as they sat down in the main compartment of the gunship. Through the modulation of his helm his voice was even deeper, so reminiscent of Sapphon's battle-brothers. The Master of Sanctity forced himself to remember that it was the same voice that had issued the order for Caliban's defence systems to open fire on the Lion's fleet.

'Be silent or be silenced,' said Asmodai.

'Too late for threats,' replied the Fallen.

An instant later Asmodai was next to Astelan, the muzzle of a bolt pistol pressed against the eye lens of the Fallen's helm.

'I have a habit of vexing my superiors with rash action,' growled the Chaplain. 'It is a fault, I admit. Ask Brother Sapphon whether he thinks I will pull the trigger.'

'He will,' said Sapphon. 'He has been guilty of far more counter-productive acts and has yet to show any remorse for them. Believe me, if you value your life you will not push my brother any further. His temper is raw at the moment and I would not agitate him further.'

'You draw no weapon in my defence, Sapphon?' said Astelan. 'I am essential to the success of your plan. I would think you value me more highly.'

'Whatever you think, regardless of our differences of method, Brother Asmodai is worth a thousand of you,' said Sapphon. 'Especially now.'

The Fallen was subdued by this and said nothing more. Asmodai sat down but kept his weapon free as he fastened the security harness. A few moments later the last of the small group joined them: Ezekiel. The Librarian sat a little way from them, eyes fixed on Astelan.

'That completes our landing party,' announced Sapphon. He gave the order to the pilot to lift off.

It took nearly an hour for the descent to the surface, which passed without any comment from Astelan. The Fallen appeared to have accepted the gravity of the situation – and his tenuous part in future events – and sat immobile for the entire journey.

Sapphon spent the time trying to conceive of every possible way in which the Fallen would try to escape or otherwise betray his captors. Under close guard, unarmed, the former was impossible. Even if Astelan somehow overpowered one of the Chaplains, the other, with the Deathwing and Ezekiel for support, would kill him in moments. The second was trickier in prospect, but Sapphon believed he had those eventualities covered as well. It made no sense for Astelan to reveal his identity to anyone on Tharsis – unless he believed that the Dark Angels would protect him from retribution. He was being granted access to the world's astropathic choir to send his message to Anovel, which came with its own dangers.

The content of the message would be scrutinised but it was the nature of such psychic communication that codes and passwords, cipher images and innuendo were used. What possible damage could he do with a simple message? Warn Anovel? That only made sense if the Fallen was already at or heading to Tharsis. Send for reinforcements? It was a possibility, but with the loss of Port Imperial such forces as Anovel might have had access to were much diminished. The Deathwing and Ravenwing, despite their casualties at Ulthor, were a match for almost anything the traitor could call upon at short notice.

Above it all, as long as Astelan believed his life hung in the balance he would remain compliant. With Asmodai only a trigger's breadth away from ending the Fallen's life, Astelan had to know any treachery would be rewarded with death the moment it was uncovered. Survival instinct was the surest guarantee Sapphon could depend upon.

After making planetfall at the Imperial commander's personal star port they were met by a small delegation of functionaries dressed in elaborately patterned togas, wooden sandals, shaven heads and long beards. Each carried a dataslab and quill, save for their leader, who introduced himself as Comptroller Farius Contrateus Danageo. He held a communications sceptre shaped as an eagle's claw gripping a green glass orb, and over his bare scalp and right ear was arranged a receiver of some kind, two long aerials jutting up like the antenna of an insect.

He did not look pleased to see his visitors.

'Felicitations from Imperial Commander Gastrex, honoured lords of the Dark Angels.' Danageo's bow was perfunctory, his eyes roaming from one super-warrior to the next in the few moments it took to dip and rise. He blinked rapidly as his roving gaze returned to the skull masks of Sapphon and Asmodai and then his eyes seemed to fade and his expression slackened.

'And such to the Imperial commander,' said Sapphon. 'All is in order as we requested, I hope.'

'Hmm, requested, yes,' said Danageo, and Sapphon could easily imagine that Belial's requests might sound much the same as his commands. 'If I could just have your titles and names, for our records.'

There was a moment's pause. Sapphon wondered why he had not considered this possibility. Astelan stepped forward, causing Asmodai to stiffen, hand on pistol.

'Brother... Belath,' said the Fallen, inclining his head slightly.

'I am Brother Sapphon, Master of Sanctity,' the Chaplain said, trying not to appear unduly hurried. The others gave their names and the scribes noted them down on their data-slates. Danageo lifted the orb of his sceptre to his lips and said something. The glass globe lit up with each word. A few seconds later the gates behind the group rumbled open, revealing a gaping tunnel leading into the lower levels of the Imperial commander's administration complex. A company of soldiers, roughly one hundred and fifty strong, waited inside the gates. Heavy weapons on tall tripods were trained on the Space Marines.

'You were told to bear no arms in our presence,' said Sapphon. It was unlikely the Tharsis defence forces had many weapons to threaten a Space Marine, but it had been decided not to risk giving Astelan any opportunity to arm himself from an inferior foe.

'And we were told that you came with peaceful intent also,' replied Danageo, unfazed. The comptroller looked pointedly at the weapons of the Space Marines. Sapphon decided the device on his head, which in places pierced the skull, had some kind of emotional dampening effect because he had never seen a normal man so coolly face up to the warriors of the Adeptus Astartes.

'We will not disarm,' said Asmodai. He looked around as though expecting ambushing forces to appear from the surrounding landers and buildings.

'We do not expect you to,' said Danageo. He whispered something else into the comm-sceptre and the defence force soldiers turned and filed away into the palaces. 'You cannot expect us not to take precaution, however. Past encounters with the Dark Angels have been less than favourable for our people.'

Astelan was looking directly at the comptroller, head slightly tilted to one side in thought. The sooner the Fallen was back on the gunship and returning to the *Penitent Warrior*, the easier Sapphon could breathe.

'Understandable,' said the Master of Sanctity, stepping past Asmodai and the Fallen to lead the Dark Angels group. 'Please convey us to your astropaths and we will disturb you for no longer than necessary.'

REASONS TO HATE

The chamber of the astropaths was a hemispherical arena with a floor gently sloping down to the sarcophagi where the psykers performed their work. Crystal arrays hung from the ceiling like chandeliers, connected to each other with bare, sagging cables that flickered with multicoloured energy. Every astropath was capable of sending signals out into the aether, and receiving the communications of others; the amplifying machinery of the choir-hall served to increase that ability a thousandfold.

Simply stepping into the chamber sent a frisson of unease through Asmodai. The warp was essential, this much he knew. It allowed the ships of the Emperor to travel from world to world within weeks rather than lifetimes. Without astrotelepathy those worlds would be even more isolated, tiny enclaves of humanity, each a besieged gem in the darkness of the galaxy. Warp communication was erratic but it was all that held the

Imperium together. Without it the Dark Angels and
the other Space Marine Chapters would be next to useless. A whole wing of the Rock was given over to the
Librarium of the Chapter to sift through the overlapping, contradictory signals of the warp, seeking telltale
signs of alien invasion, listening for muffled cries for
aid, interpreting dream-prophecies for hints of calami-
ties yet to pass.

All the same, it was the warp that had corrupted the
Fallen. Asmodai did not know the details of how, only
that the warp was home to daemons and the infernal
powers that spawn them. Contact with the warp was ever
a danger, a temptation.

There was more to Asmodai's distaste for the empyrean than simple intellectual distrust. His was a primal,
personal antipathy. At times like these the Interrogator-
Chaplain felt his most vulnerable – in the company
of psykers, at the moment of transition when a starship breached unreality, on the edge of sleep whilst in
the warp. At those junctures when his soul was most
exposed he would have glimpses of Malvine Rhemell.

It would come with a moment of paralysis, just like
now. A shock to the nervous system as an ever-present
threat and a half-glimpsed face leering in insane triumph. A billion voices shrieking. And then, a flicker
within a flicker, a terrible microsecond of absolute horror as Asmodai saw not the face of the Fallen but his
own, reflected back at him, distorted and terrible.

TRAITOR!

Always the accusations of the dead, an after-echo ringing in the ears of the Chaplain.

He had told no one about these experiences. Instead,
as now, he raised up steel walls of pure will, erecting
a fortress of hate and fury to defend himself against

encroaching doubt. It lasted perhaps a second, nothing more, yet it felt like an hour of torment.

Traitor!

His purpose was just, his cause pure, his duty unsullied.

Traitor.

And the voices died away, the face of the traitor faded, and all that remained were the rage and the revulsion that kept him sane.

Asmodai blinked once, dismissing the last of the phantasm that had assailed him, and watched the others descending the steps towards the astropaths, led by the comptroller.

There were seven astropaths in the hall, each held upright in the open meshwork of a psi-booster. They were arranged about the edge of a circle inscribed at the heart of the hall's dark stone floor, marked much like the wardings Harahel had created for his ritual, though more substantial. The psykers looked asleep with their eyes open; blind orbs, clouded with white from the soul-binding ritual that protected them from daemonic interference. Their lips moved, some in synchrony, some speaking at odds, their murmuring creating an overlapping chatter.

Each astropath was attended by a servitor-scribe, haggard half-machines that noted down everything that passed the lips of their appointed psyker. Sheaves of these transcripts were taken away by messenger serfs, who wore blinkered, heavy helms to protect against repeated exposure to the crawling warp power that caused the sigils on the walls and floor to gleam.

Asmodai followed a few steps behind, his eyes never leaving Astelan. The Chaplain's instincts screamed that this was a terrible idea, but he refrained from taking action. Sapphon called him uncompromising and dogmatic, as though that was some kind of insult. Asmodai did not take it as such. Ten thousand years was a long time to perfect an art and he would not be so disparaging of so many lessons hard-learned. Allowing a Fallen access to astrotelepathy was an error of potentially calamitous proportions, and not to stop this imprudence took every fibre of Asmodai's self-control – though his brothers doubted such a thing existed.

Sapphon spoke to the comptroller, who called forth a group of attendants who had been waiting in a small shielded enclosure beyond the astropaths. They disengaged one of the psykers from her transmission rig and brought her to the group. To Asmodai she had a curious look of youth and age at the same time. She stood straight and strong, and her hands were smooth and supple. Her face, though, was lined and her eye sockets grey and sunken, the vitality leeched from her by close exposure to the psychic magnificence of the Emperor.

'This is Lady Nadia Mischenko, one of our finest astropaths,' said Danageo. 'She is choir-mistress of this facility.'

'Our gratitude,' said Sapphon. 'This will not take too long.'

The comptroller did not catch the implication of the Chaplain's words and remained with the group.

'Not for your ears,' said Astelan.

'You may wait outside,' added Sapphon.

Danageo frowned at this but did not argue. When he had departed, Sapphon sent the Deathwing escort to guard the doors and watch over the attendants. Ezekiel also moved away to one side of the chamber, where he stood with hands clasped and eyes closed. Sapphon asked Lady Mischenko to give them a moment and when she had withdrawn he turned to the Fallen.

'Our Chief Librarian will be monitoring the broadcast,'

said Sapphon. 'If he detects anything untoward he will block the transmission and you will be executed.'

'In front of so many witnesses?' replied Astelan. 'A difficult event to explain away.'

'A concern you will not share,' said Asmodai. 'We have ways of turning aside scrutiny.'

'I see.' The Fallen looked over at Ezekiel. 'How am I to know what your witch deems improper?'

'Do not burden yourself with such worries,' said Sapphon. 'Simply send your message and the task will be complete.'

'And once my part in the bargain is done, what will you do with me? How can you assure me that you will not simply kill me out of hand once the deed is finished?'

'If your end comes so quickly, be thankful,' said Asmodai. 'I would have it last far longer.'

'Your just fate will not come so soon,' said Sapphon. 'Your usefulness does not end with the simple broadcast of message. If we receive reply we will need you to decode it. If Anovel actually comes to Tharsis, and I am not convinced that he will, we require you to make representation that will lure him fully into the trap. You are an experienced starship captain, Astelan. You know that until we have Anovel's ship approaching orbit he will be free to slip away again. Your function as bait gives you a stay of execution at least until the other traitor has been delivered into our hands.'

'Convincing arguments,' said Astelan. He raised his hands to his helm, and Asmodai reacted quickly.

'You were told to leave your helmet in place,' said the Chaplain, bolt pistol raised.

'Anovel will want to see my face,' said Astelan, moving his hands away from his head. 'None of the astropaths will recognise me, I promise you.'

'Such promises are empty,' said Asmodai, but the Fallen was probably correct in his assertion. The Chaplain lowered his pistol. 'You may proceed.'

The Fallen unclamped his helm with a hiss of escaping air and hung it onto his belt. Receiving a nod of approval from Sapphon, he approached Lady Mischenko. The astropath nodded her understanding several times as Astelan quietly explained his message. She beckoned for the Fallen to accompany her and returned to the cradle of her psi-booster. As she stepped back into the machine a web of crystal wires embraced her thin form, creating a glittering cocoon from waist to neck.

Asmodai watched the proceedings carefully, looking for any sign of deceit from Astelan. As Mischenko stared with dead eyes the Fallen spoke at length, gesturing on occasion to emphasise some point or other. The Chaplain could see Mischenko's lips moving, keeping pace with Astelan's voice so that it seemed she spoke with his deep tones. Light glimmered along the psychic network, disappearing into the amplifiers. Asmodai imagined the coded message being flung out from Tharsis into the void, settling in the warp like scraps of paper dumped onto the torrent of a fast-flowing river. At the heart of the chamber they could feel the pulse of barely-controlled psychic power, although he did not suffer his usual nightmarish intrusion. Instead he was dimly aware of signs and shapes, of symbols and figures plucked from the thoughts of Astelan and dispersed through the mind of Lady Mischenko.

'It is done,' she said huskily, her complexion more pallid than before as she stepped out of the psychic meshwork. 'I have shared the signal-marks with the others so that should we receive reply we will recognise the intended recipient.'

'What of the message?' said Sapphon. 'Did it mean anything to you?'

'Nothing,' the astropath said with a shake of the head. She pulled up the hood of her robe and beckoned to her attendants. 'Please excuse me, but it was a long and complex broadcast. I need to rest.'

'We are done here,' said Sapphon.

'A moment,' said Asmodai. He walked over to the servitor-scribe attending Mischenko's position and snatched up the last few pages the half-man had written.

'A wise precaution,' said Sapphon. He looked at Astelan and pointed to the helm at his belt. 'Time for you to become Brother... Belath, was it not? From where did you pluck such a name?'

The Fallen's expression became a twisted smile.

'A battle-brother from long ago,' said the Fallen. 'It seemed apt for the occasion.'

Ezekiel joined them as Astelan replaced his helmet. The Librarian gave a slight shake of the head.

'I detected no treachery, and what I received of the message seemed genuine,' the Librarian reported. His eyes blazed for a moment as he stared at Astelan, who jerked suddenly and stumbled. The glow of Ezekiel's eyes intensified and the Fallen dropped to one knee, hands clutching the sides of his head. The psychic fire dimmed and the Librarian looked away. 'Yes, I am sure that nothing was concealed that would warn of our presence or intent.'

'Damn you, witch,' Astelan moaned, slowly straightening. 'Was that necessary?'

'We will return to the *Penitent Warrior*,' announced Sapphon. 'I am sure the comptroller will inform us of any developments.'

'How long do we remain here?' said Asmodai. Enough

time had been wasted on this distraction and he was eager to return to the Rock.

'I do not know,' admitted Sapphon. The Chaplain looked at Astelan. 'How long do you think we should grant you before we declare the attempt failed?'

'Thirty days,' said the Fallen. 'If I am right, Anovel will have stayed within a few hundred light years of this system and Port Imperial, especially if he has been to Ulthor. Thirty days is plenty enough time for a message to be heard and reply sent.'

'An honest assessment,' said Sapphon, sounding surprised. 'Thirty days for your vindication.'

'*If* Anovel is alive, *and* listening, *and* believes me,' the Fallen added. He turned his gaze on Asmodai. There was no way to know his expression beneath the mask of his black helm. 'I do not hold out much hope.'

Asmodai said nothing. For fifteen years Astelan had evaded his just punishment, waiting upon the return of Boreas. Now Boreas had succumbed to the lies of the Fallen and it was only a matter of time before Asmodai was granted his desire. When this nonsense was finished Sapphon would have no choice but to hand control of Astelan's interrogation to Asmodai. Not only would he earn a third black pearl for his crozius arcanum – one for each Fallen that repented by his hand – but he would derive a large amount of personal satisfaction from the inevitable conclusion to this affair. Astelan begging for forgiveness, denouncing his falsehoods and admitting his treacheries would be ample reward for the frustrations inflicted upon Asmodai in recent weeks. He would prove wrong the critics within the Inner Circle and show that uncompromising attention to duty and tradition would see the Dark Angels returned to their full glory.

He could wait thirty days.

SUSPENSION

Time ceased to have meaning for Telemenus. Like all Space Marines his enhanced physiology had many means to combat the physical trauma he had suffered during the confrontation with the daemon. Chief amongst these was the sus-an membrane that allowed his body to fall into a biostasis, reducing vital functions to an almost zero-state. During those times he was utterly unaware of his surroundings or the passage of time.

He woke to find himself hooked up to a life support system similar to the one found in his armour. The sprawling pipework and coiled cables of the machine interfaced with the nodes and sockets fitted into the sub-dermal black carapace that had been installed as the last transition from Scout to full battle-brother. Rather than auto-senses and stabilising systems, the implants instead allowed a cogitator to regulate his breathing, blood flow and nervous system – functions that had been seriously impaired by the daemon's attack.

Apothecary Temraen was adjusting something on the machine, his white robes sullied with flecks of blood and a yellowish stain from some other vital fluid. He turned as he noticed Telemenus stir.

'Adrenal boost to snap you out of the suspended state, brother,' explained the Apothecary. 'Emergency surgery is complete but there are some extra procedures I need to perform and prolonged sus-an operation would be detrimental at this stage.'

Telemenus murmured something in reply. He was not quite sure what. It seemed to satisfy Temraen, who nodded thoughtfully.

'It is unlikely, but once you have been returned to the Rock the full facilities of the armoury and apothecarion will be turned towards your physical rehabilitation. Extensive augmetics and bionics are still a possibility. Even with every effort it is unlikely that you will regain full combat status.'

A dense fog permeated Telemenus's thoughts making it impossible to concentrate for more than a few seconds. He nodded as the Apothecary told him he would be applying a sedative in preparation for the coming surgery.

After that Telemenus drifted in and out of various states of consciousness. Sometimes Brother Sapphon came to talk to him, on other occasions it was Brother Ezekiel. Brother Temraen was a frequent visitor.

More often, Telemenus spent his time in the company of the Emperor, who had become a suffused golden glow that lingered on the edges of the chamber.

'They will not let me fight again,' Telemenus said during one such encounter.

'You are too broken,' the Emperor replied.

'If I cannot fight, what is the point of my existence?'

'You might yet go into battle. Mechanical restoration

will allow you to be a pilot or a driver, or perhaps a gunner in a Predator or Land Raider. Only in death does duty end.'

Telemenus laughed. It seemed strange to hear the mantra from the Emperor Himself.

'I am the embodiment of that principle, Telemenus,' the Emperor said sternly. His essence moved from the corner of the ceiling to settle upon the pulmonary monitor beside the bunk, making the ticking box glow with a golden aura. 'Grievous were my wounds but my duty to mankind would not allow me to relinquish this mortal vessel. Ten thousand years I have endured, persisting in this realm to guide my people to their destiny.'

'You are far greater than I,' said Telemenus, humbled by this revelation. 'But I will aspire to honour your sacrifice.'

'You more than any shall come to know me,' the Emperor continued. 'This half-waking life, sustained by the Golden Throne, every moment a struggle along the precipice of oblivion. Do you feel my grief, Telemenus?'

'I feel it,' whispered the Space Marine, as the sense of loss the Emperor had suffered welled up within him.

'Feel what?' asked Brother Sapphon. 'What are you looking at?'

Telemenus turned his eyes from the metal box of the monitor and focused on the Chaplain standing at the foot of the bed. It seemed odd every time Telemenus looked that way, to see the sheet laying flat where his hips and legs should be. He wanted to wriggle his toes to make the sheet move, perplexed by the lack of response.

'The Emperor's sacrifice,' he whispered. 'I share it.'

Sapphon smiled but there was more sadness than joy in the expression.

'Of course you do,' said the Chaplain, without hint of condescension.

'What will become of me?' Telemenus asked.

'I do not know, brother,' Sapphon admitted. 'Much depends on what happens here.'

'Where are we? Are we returning to the Rock?'

'Not yet, we still have a mission to perform.'

'The longer we stay here, the more my body will deteriorate. I think I remember Brother Temraen telling me that.'

'Yes, I am sorry, but that is unavoidable.' Sapphon sighed and stepped closer, moving along the right side of the bed to lay a hand on Telemenus's chest. 'We must be here at least another fifteen days. You remember how I told you of the Fallen?'

'How could I forget?' Telemenus grimaced at the memory of the traitors.

'One is coming here, to Tharsis. When we have captured him, we will return to the Chapter and you will receive the attention you require. The treatment you deserve.'

'That is good. It will be worth returning with a victory.'

'The best kind,' said Sapphon, withdrawing his hand. He looked away for a moment, towards the chamber door.

'I am sorry for causing you distraction at this important time,' said Telemenus.

'No, it is I that am sorry, that my duties elsewhere limit the time I can spend with you. It is a noble sacrifice you made, fighting for your brothers.'

'It was stupid!' Telemenus's anger at himself came in a rush as he recalled the circumstances of his injury. 'I should not have been so ignorant of the danger. And Daellon... How is my battle-brother? Did he survive?'

'Yes, he did,' said Sapphon, brow creased with concern. 'He has visited you several times, as have others of the company. Do you not remember?'

Telemenus tried, but he could not picture his brother's face at all, nor recollect seeing anybody else. He shook his head in frustration. His memory was meant to be perfect.

'Calm yourself, brother, such agitation will vex your wounds,' said Sapphon.

'My head was uninjured yet my mind is so addled,' Telemenus said with a snarl. 'My body can be repaired, but…'

'A side effect of the contagion that tried to infect you, that is all,' Sapphon spoke quietly and calmly, and placed a hand on each of Telemenus's shoulders, holding him still as he tried to sit up. 'It will pass.'

'He is lying, of course,' said the Emperor. The auric light was filling the room. Sapphon had disappeared, though how long ago was uncertain.

'How do you know?' Telemenus asked, before he realised how redundant the question was. 'You are the Emperor, of course you would know. Why would he lie to me?'

'To protect you. The same reason he and others like him have been lying to you since you were first chosen to become an aspirant.'

'That has troubled me. If we had not disobeyed orders and encountered the Fallen warlock, would I have ever known?'

'Did you ever ask the right questions?' The Emperor had always brought warmth with Him before but now a strange chill pervaded the medicae cell.

'They would have lied to me regardless. Would it be so disastrous if the battle-brothers knew?'

'Only you can answer that question, Telemenus. You were a battle-brother once. You had doubts and suspicions. What would have happened if you had been told?'

'If the cause is just I do not understand why such a thing must be kept secret. I would have fought just as hard and with as much conviction and courage as before. The Deathwing know the truth and they are counted amongst the bravest and most loyal warriors of the Chapter.'

'Perhaps, like them, you are special. Your strength of mind means that you are capable of knowing the truth of what happened ten thousand years ago.'

'Sergeant Arbalan told me that I was unremarkable.'

'Do you really believe him?'

'No.'

'Who do you address?' Telemenus wondered why the Emperor's voice had changed, and then realised he had been spoken to not by the Master of Mankind but by Brother Ezekiel. The Librarian was accompanied by Apothecary Temraen. Both looked concerned.

Ezekiel repeated the question. It was obvious that the ghostly golden aura hovering around the light fittings was not visible to the others. Telemenus thought about his answer for a moment. It occurred to him that it was not every Space Marine who received direct audience with the Emperor. It marked him out as having a greater fate, confirming what he had suspected for some time. Were they ready for the truth? He decided that they would not understand, not yet.

'Myself,' said Telemenus. Ezekiel was one of the worst. He could look into the souls of others and must know what deception lay in the hearts of the Chaplains. 'It helps to keep my mind active.'

'I see,' said Ezekiel, though his body language expressed dissatisfaction with this answer. 'I am going to probe your mind to ensure no... remnant of the infection remains.'

'Physically you are stable,' Temraen added. Telemenus thought the clarification unnecessary until he realised what the Apothecary had not said. If Telemenus was physically stable, they judged him mentally unstable? He had been wise not to reveal the Emperor's presence; such a thing would have been interpreted badly.

'I feel good in myself,' said Telemenus. The door opened and Sapphon entered. To have all three of his guardians – medical, spiritual and psychic – in the room at the same time unsettled Telemenus. 'I am coming to terms with what happened to me and what service I might perform in the future.'

'Is he cogent?' the Chaplain asked, looking between Telemenus and Temraen.

'Fully aware,' replied the Apothecary.

'Good.' Sapphon approached and the other two Space Marines gave him room to stand beside the bunk. He glanced at Ezekiel and received a nod in return. 'Telemenus, it is very important that you are honest with me. I need you to answer some questions. Brother Ezekiel is going to scan the surface of your mind to make sure that you have brought nothing of Ulthor with you.'

'Of Ulthor?' Telemenus thought about this for a moment before realisation dawned. 'Something daemonic?'

'Yes.' Sapphon was being very earnest, almost too sincere. 'You have been saying some strange things while you are asleep.'

'It is not uncommon whilst the catalepsean node is in effect following physical trauma,' Temraen said hurriedly. Telemenus realised he had been the subject of debate between the Apothecary and Chaplain. Evidently Sapphon had won his argument. 'Coupled with intermittent use of the sus-an membrane, periods of non-lucidity whilst appearing competent are not without precedent.'

'I am not afraid, brother,' said Telemenus, giving Temraen what he hoped was a reassuring smile. 'There is nothing inside me, but it would be better to allay Brother Sapphon's fears.'

'Good, then we are ready to begin.' The Chaplain checked once more with Ezekiel. The Librarian stared intently at Telemenus with his dark eye, motes of psychic energy flickering in his irises. The Space Marine felt the psychic touch just behind his eyes, and for a moment it was as though someone else was looking out through them. The thought alarmed him.

'That is my presence,' Ezekiel said softly, 'do not be alarmed.'

Swallowing hard, Telemenus tried to relax.

'What do you remember of Ulthor?'

'Everything,' Telemenus answered. He closed his eyes and brought forth the memory; shared it with Ezekiel, every aspect and feeling. The blade of the daemon's pick drove into his shoulder and unleashed its deadly contagion. He felt the rust peeling off against his innards even as organs burst and bones shattered. In minute, agonising detail he relived the blood welling up through into punctured gullet and the sensation of flesh and armour exploding outwards as the point of the pick head ruptured through his back.

'Enough,' muttered Ezekiel through gritted teeth. 'Afterwards. Think of afterwards.'

There was very little to recall. Snippets of scenes, brief glimpses of being carried alongside Brother Sapphon by his fellow Terminators. More had come back to him since, processed and neatly packaged by his subconscious while his body and conscious mind had rested. The feeling of the force-teleportation, not quite understanding what was happening. And then he waking up with Ezekiel again. The memory came full circle, uniting the Librarian he remembered with the one meshed with his mind at that moment.

'What is your name?'

Sapphon's question came as a surprise, so caught up had Telemenus been with the reconstruction of his near-death. The Chaplain's tone was curt, official.

'Brother Telemenus, First Company, the Dark Angels of the Adeptus Astartes.'

'Where are you?'

'Aboard the strike cruiser *Penitent Warrior*, in the Tharsis system.'

'Who is in the room with you?' Sapphon dropped his voice and Telemenus could feel Ezekiel's othersense tentatively moving through his thoughts.

'Brother Sapphon, Brother Ezekiel and Brother Temraen.' Telemenus kept his gaze fixed on the Librarian, focusing on the sense of connection rather than the flicker of gold that shone like a halo around the psyker's head.

'Recite the fifteenth verse of the Catechism of Fortitude.'

'There are only twelve verses,' Telemenus replied without hesitation. The Space Marine glanced at Sapphon who had been leaning forward, hands on the side of the bed, and half-smiled. 'You should know that, Brother-Chaplain.'

'I should, and I do,' the Chaplain said, standing straight. He did not smile back but his face was more relaxed.

'I detect no further taint,' Ezekiel declared. Telemenus let out a gasp as the psyker pulled back his presence. 'Thank you, Telemenus, for allaying our fears.'

'The gratitude is mine,' he said. The golden shimmer of the Emperor's manifestation slid across the room to illuminate a shelf of surgical implements. Telemenus kept his gaze on Sapphon. 'Your concern for my well-being is heartening.'

'With your permission, I will continue,' said Temraen, reaching for a syringe filled with a thick red liquid.

'Of course,' said Sapphon.

The Apothecary fitted the needle of the injector to an intravenous feed on the side of the life support machine.

'Neuron degeneration is a distinct possibility,' said Temraen, checking some of the readings of the machine's output screens. 'This elixir will suppress your normal brain activity and boost the effect of the sus-an membrane. All cellular function will become virtually static. The next time you are awake you will be at the Tower of Angels.'

'You are putting me into a coma?' said Telemenus, forcing himself to keep the alarm from his demeanour. He knew that in such a state he would not be graced with the Emperor's presence. He could see the golden shine hovering over the bed where his knees would have been had he still possessed legs.

The Apothecary was already pushing the plunger on the syringe as he replied and Telemenus did not hear what was said.

'Peace, Telemenus,' the Emperor told him, the golden aura enveloping everything that remained of the Space Marine's body, flooding him with warmth.

'Only in death…' Telemenus began, and then he knew no more.

EXPECTATION

Every hour that passed seemed to drag but all too soon for Sapphon twenty days had gone by without any sign of Astelan's message reaching its intended target. The curious matter with Brother Telemenus had been a welcome distraction to Sapphon, and the Chaplain had spent much time in the Reclusiam forcing himself to remain calm and alert, chanting hymnals and reciting litanies as a means of staving off the moments of regret and worry.

Both strike cruisers and their companies were kept at full alert, in case Anovel responded in person without first sending word of his impending arrival, and there was a tension felt by everybody aboard. Discipline remained high despite the inaction and tedium; the battle-brothers were able to lose themselves in the daily routine of drills and rituals. Sapphon trained and prayed with them when he could, but often Asmodai was in attendance and the flagrant hostility from his fellow Chaplain was threatening discord.

For many warriors the time before battle was spent in contemplation of mortality but it was not impending injury or death that occupied Sapphon's thoughts. He welcomed the prospect of battle, for that would mean his ruse had been successful. What kept a cold knuckle of dread in his gut was the very likely event that thirty days would pass without anything untoward happening at all.

As much as he tried not to linger on the prospect, time and again the Chaplain's thoughts returned to the dire consequences of failure. Sapphon decided to share his concerns with Sammael, intercepting the Ravenwing commander as he arrived on the *Penitent Warrior* for the daily command council. As Sammael left the landing bay where his gunship had landed Sapphon joined the Second Company's Grand Master.

'Little to report, I fear,' said Sapphon after the customary exchange of greeting. 'Asmodai may yet prove the wiser head.'

'Never that, whatever happens,' said Sammael. They started walking towards the closest conveyor, boots ringing along the deck in the otherwise empty bowels of the ship. 'Being righteous does not make one wise.'

'I would expect no other attitude from the Grand Master of the Ravenwing. We both desire the end of the Hunt, not merely its prosecution.'

'It was not always so,' confessed Sammael, glancing at the Chaplain. 'It used to concern me, the idea that one day the Hunt might end. What would be the purpose of the Ravenwing with no more prey to chase? What would become of me?'

'But that does not bother you now?'

They came to the doors of a broad conveyor carriage. Sammael activated the call rune and a distant clatter of chains and gears sounded from the shaft beyond.

'I have achieved a spiritual equilibrium, I would say. My whole concern is to capture the Fallen. To think past that duty is a distraction, and risks moving aim from the present target.'

'You think we have approached the situation with Anovel in the wrong fashion?' Sapphon had hoped Sammael would be an ally on this matter but it seemed he had been wrong. 'Have I wasted the time of all of us in this false errand?'

'Not at all,' said Sammael. He removed his helm with a hiss of escaping air and smiled at Sapphon. 'It is secure in the knowledge that there are minds such as yours working towards an end that brings me peace. Sometimes we become too caught up in the Hunt, in the moment of running the quarry to ground, that we forget that this was not our first purpose.'

With a loud squeal of brakes and a thump the conveyor car arrived. Sammael prodded the keypad to open the doors, which whined apart. Sapphon put his hand in front of the Master of the Ravenwing, preventing him from entering.

'You should not be so quick to speak such sentiment in front of Asmodai,' Sapphon warned.

'It is a thought I have kept to myself,' Sammael assured him. 'But it is one that was placed in my mind by a Chaplain, even so.'

Sapphon took his arm away as Sammael stepped forwards, allowing the Space Marine into the plasteel-lined box of the conveyor.

'A Chaplain? Malcifer, you mean,' said the Master of Sanctity, following Sammael. The door closed with more grinding of gears and a clang.

'No, not Malcifer. He is freer of spirit than many of your

calling on matters of discipline, a necessity amongst the Ravenwing, but he is as orthodox as Asmodai in other beliefs.'

Sapphon absorbed this, trying to think of who amongst the Chaplaincy might have seeded such thoughts with Sammael.

'It was the last testimony of Boreas,' Sammael said. He keyed in the code for the upper command deck where the ship's counsel chamber was located. 'The exact words escape me, but I remember listening to his final recording, in that place where he and the others had died, and they set in me chains of thought I had not before considered.'

'As was his intent, I suspect,' said Sapphon. He had listened to Boreas's account of the demise of the Piscina garrison many times and was still undecided whether Boreas had remained true to his position as Chaplain or had turned renegade. 'It would be easier to take Boreas's enlightenment with more favour if one could eliminate the suspicion of Astelan's involvement.'

'And that same suspicion falls upon you now, brother,' Sammael reminded Sapphon. 'Are you sure this is our plan and not the machinations of the Fallen?'

'Yes,' Sapphon lied. Sammael was known for initiative and innovation but it would serve no purpose to have the Grand Master of the Ravenwing doubting the validity of their current strategy.

'Boreas claimed that we had come to define ourselves by the Hunt, and I refuse to allow that to be true.' Sammael looked directly at the Chaplain. 'The Fallen do not define the Dark Angels. Many are our accomplishments and victories across the Imperium. The Hunt does not diminish the value of those campaigns and achievements.'

'You are right.' The conveyor shuddered to a halt. 'Keep faith with our purpose and we shall be absolved in time.'

Sapphon stepped out into the corridor, but this time it was Sammael that checked him, placing a hand on his arm.

'There was something else that Boreas claimed,' the Grand Master said quietly. 'He told us "There is no light and dark, only the shades of twilight in between." It is a revelation to me that a Master of Sanctity would be the one not of light but of grey uncertainty.'

'What would you prefer? That all of the Chapter walk the precipice between truth and doubt?'

Sammael did not answer and they continued to the council chamber without further comment. Belial and Asmodai were already waiting for them. The other Chaplain looked at Sapphon with suspicion as he entered a step behind Sammael, but said nothing.

'There has been a development,' said the Grand Master of the Deathwing.

Unnoticed before, Ezekiel stepped forward to the table as Sapphon seated himself.

'I have detected a ship exiting the warp,' announced the Librarian.

'When?' demanded Sapphon. 'Why do you tell me this only now?'

'It is not my role to act as your personal informant, brother.' Ezekiel rarely raised his voice or spoke harshly, but this simple statement was enough remonstration to cause Sapphon to bow his head in apology. 'I address this command council as one. As it is, not more than an hour ago was I able to confirm the tremors in the warp that herald a translation into real space. A large one, my experience tells me, though not quite as significant as a battleship.'

'Alone?' said Sammael.

'For the moment. There are other bow waves approaching, ripples of arrivals yet to come I think.'

'We did not expect Anovel to arrive alone,' said Belial. 'It is not so strange that he had a small flotilla with him.'

'What is strange is his lack of communication warning of his impending arrival,' said Asmodai. 'He approaches with stealth.'

'Or has made good speed and outpaced his astropathic reply,' countered Sapphon. 'To arrive so soon indicates that he was not so far away.'

'And that does not give you concern, brother?' said Asmodai. 'This entire situation reeks of complicity between Astelan and Anovel.'

'We must confirm that this is indeed the Fallen,' said Belial. 'If so, we will strike as swiftly as we can and take him captive.'

'And how do we enact such a miracle?' said Sapphon. 'The moment he detects any intent against him he will flee. We have to lure him further in-system and then he will be vulnerable. Until then we must hide the presence of two strike cruisers and bring him to orbit over Tharsis.'

'It is you that expects a miracle,' said Asmodai. 'I do not think our prey will blindly wander in to such unknown territory.'

'Which is why we must use Astelan again,' said Sapphon. He waited for the inevitable outburst from Asmodai, but none was forthcoming. The Chaplain was frowning deeply, as was Belial, but voiced no objection. Surprised, it was a moment before Sapphon could continue. 'Astelan must send word from the surface that all is ready for Anovel's arrival. The traitor must be welcomed with open arms and given safe passage to the inner system.'

He looked at Asmodai, expecting the derision to begin. Instead the Master of Repentance nodded.

'That would seem prudent,' said Asmodai. 'I will travel with the prisoner to the surface and the strike cruisers should withdraw into the blind spot behind one of Tharsis's moons.'

'I am not leaving you alone with Astelan,' said Sapphon.

'Then I will go,' said Belial. He shot Sapphon a challenging look. 'We will take a force of Terminators as additional security. Unless you think I harbour some agenda also?'

'No,' Sapphon conceded. 'I believe that what you propose is adequate.'

'I concur, with a caveat,' said Sammael. 'We will withdraw to orbit on the opposite side of Tharsis for the moment, but remain on station to respond if needed. The *Implacable Justice* can outpace any other ship in the sector, as long as Anovel does not have too far a head start. Bring him a half a dozen days away from the safe translation belt and we'll be able to catch him.'

'Consensus?' said Belial, looking at each of the officers in turn. They nodded their agreement. 'So be it. Sapphon will speak to Astelan. We will lay our trap.'

COMPLICATIONS

Another four days passed during which Astelan was escorted to quarters within the Imperial commander's palace on Tharsis. From there the Fallen sent transmission to the newly arrived ship, an ex-Imperial Navy heavy cruiser it seemed, requesting identification. It took another two days for the reply to come back, confirming by vox-channel that the commander of the ship was indeed Anovel.

Astelan granted the ship safe passage to orbit, but twelve hours later Anovel's ship was still in the outer reaches of the system and had come to a halt. Astelan's representations to Anovel went unheeded until a short message was received announcing that Anovel was awaiting the remainder of an accompanying flotilla.

Over the course of the next six days Ezekiel reported the ships he had felt approaching the warp breaking through into the Tharsis system. Many were small warships and transports, barely large enough for warp travel. Some were cruiser-class, reminiscent of the ships the

Ravenwing had encountered at Port Imperial. Every few hours it seemed that another enemy vessel arrived until there were fourteen in total assembling in small groups around the edges of the star system.

Belial convened a vid-council; Sapphon joined from the *Penitent Warrior* and Sammael took part aboard the *Implacable Justice*. Asmodai's absence was explained by Belial's opening address.

'Brother Asmodai believes Astelan knew of the size of Anovel's force and deliberately brought us here as part of an ambush.'

'Where is Asmodai now?' demanded Sapphon.

'He is… addressing these issues with the prisoner.'

'Call him off, brother. If Astelan chooses to cease cooperation now Asmodai will bring about the fate he suspects. We need time to marshal a response to this development and only Astelan can buy us that time.'

'By continued masquerade?' Belial grimaced. 'Words are poor replacement for gun decks, and we simply do not have enough to match this force.'

'Words can lure this fleet within range of Tharsis's orbital and ground defences,' said Sapphon. 'No number of guns can force that.'

'We cannot face this fleet in open space, so our options are either to depart now or take station within the orbital defences,' said Sammael.

'Or a third option,' Sapphon said. 'The moment one of Anovel's fleet detects a strike cruiser in the system our prey will know our intent. Tharsis is well-defended and I see no reason why he would prosecute an attack he did not expect rather than simply turn and leave. If we use the blind spots created by Tharsis's moons to cover ourselves from the enemy sensor arrays we can keep our presence hidden.'

'Your supposition ignores another possibility,' said Belial. 'If Anovel came to Tharsis expecting a world to dominate he might decide to take by force that which he thought was offered. Even with the system defences it is not certain we could prevent him attacking. If what you say is true, by revealing our presence and forcing the enemy to reconsider we could prevent an attack from ever starting.'

Sapphon could not refute the Grand Master's reasoning. An immediate show of force, and the threat that other Dark Angels vessels might be close at hand, would almost certainly prevent any offensive action by the traitor fleet. It would also completely destroy any chance of capturing the Fallen.

'It is a simple choice we face,' said Sammael. 'We must weigh the risk to Tharsis against the gains to be made by capturing Anovel.'

'I know from report of Thyestes that you are not above such considerations, brother,' Belial said, referring to the Ravenwing leader's use of that world's Imperial commander as bait in a similar trap.

'Such exploit did not end so favourably,' Sammael confessed.

'I disagree,' said Sapphon. 'Though sacrifice was made, Methelas now inhabits cell at the Tower of Angels. The plan was a success, and so we will gain victory here.'

'I will bring the remaining Deathwing to the surface, to counter any landing attempt,' said Belial.

'And what of the Imperial commander and other authorities of Tharsis?' said Sammael. 'The Adeptus Arbites, Administratum and others will be concerned by our arrival. Deployment of troops would excite suspicion further.'

'I am not a novitiate in such matters,' growled Belial.

'My tongue might not wag so well as that of Brother Sapphon but I will state a reasonable case to the Imperial commander.'

'What of Asmodai?' Sammael asked.

'He is absent from conclave, his opinion does not matter,' said Sapphon. 'Brother Belial, you must stop him from inflicting more harm to our cause.'

'He is stubborn and not without right,' said the Deathwing leader.

'I have not known you to baulk at task simply because it threatens challenge.'

'Save such mind-games for the Fallen, Sapphon,' said Belial. 'But I will turn effort to this task also.'

'Much will depend upon Astelan, are we sure that we wish this?' said Sammael.

'A doubt, brother?' said Sapphon. 'Already we have placed much of our fate in his hands. It would seem odd for him to betray trust now that we have the advantage. Asmodai stands ready with threat of execution. If Astelan wished to make some move for freedom I feel the time has passed.'

'A moment of cautious reason,' answered Sammael. 'If we are to fall to folly, let us be aware of the risks.'

'I have been long aware of such concern,' said the Master of Sanctity. 'Nothing has changed to dissuade me from this course.'

'Let it be done, as we have agreed,' said Belial. 'Move the strike cruisers out of possible detection and we shall see if we can lure the enemy into range.'

And as it was ordered, so it was done.

WARMONGER

The new palaces of the Imperial commander, whilst functional and sparse in aesthetic, had been well-equipped by the Adeptus Mechanicus. The vox-network and scanning systems were almost the equal of a fortress-monastery, although the forces at Tharsis's disposal were lacking. The central command dome was familiar in layout – it had once been the bridge of a decommissioned starship. Orbital augurs and manned interplanetary relay stations ensured a steady flow of data to building-sized cogitator banks that filled the underbelly of the palace. Nearly three dozen servitors and as many officers of the planetary defence force and system fleet kept track of the incoming intelligence, updating holo-maps, passing data-slates back and forth and transmitting logistical updates to the various space, orbital and surface installations and forces.

Since the arrival of the traitor fleet every scanner, surveyor and eyeball had been stretched to the limit analysing their strength and approach, feeding this information through matriculating prophet programmes, using Logistarix and Lexmechanics from the Adeptus Mechanicus to determine likely courses of action and probabilities. Immense data-counting machines spat out proposed counter-manoeuvres, corollary actions and emergent protocols to the militia commanders and fleet liaisons who then submitted their reports, recommendations and orders to the Imperial commander's war council.

Belial and Asmodai monitored the whole thing with passing interest, their primary responsibility for the time being to keep watch on Astelan. Only once the Deathwing and Ravenwing were in a position ready to commit to action would they take a more vocal role in the proceedings.

The Fallen seemed to be very much enjoying his role as chief strategic advisor, and there was no doubting his natural and trained capabilities. He marshalled the heavily gunned defence monitors, intra-system ships and orbital platforms with the ease of one accustomed to command. For their part the local militia and system defence officers were happy to defer to the Space Marine's judgement.

With an experienced eye, Asmodai could see what Astelan had been doing. Outlying ships had given way before the approach of the incoming ships, collecting in flotillas at strategically important locations, shadowing the other vessels without doing so in any obvious manner. The Chaplain suspected that Anovel was not fooled by appearances, but the arrivals had made no effort to engage or otherwise interfere with the mustering of the fleet. On the face of things they had the advantage not only of numbers but firepower; the two strike cruisers standing in-system from Tharsis would be enough, combined with the advantages of surprise and orbital defences, to tip the balance against the traitors when the time came.

'This might work,' Asmodai said to Belial, begrudging every word.

'Of course it will,' said Astelan. Standing a few metres away. 'Subterfuge is a very effective weapon and I have used it many times before.'

'I do not plan to start making recitations and hanging out the celebration banners just yet,' replied the First Company Grand Master. He looked at the immense hololithic display at the centre of the chamber. At its heart was a rotating representation of Tharsis and the space around out to two hundred thousand kilometres. Defence stations and ground silos were marked in blue sigils, as was the Imperial commander's palace. Sub-projectors showed schematics of the capital city around the palace as well as other nearby system sectors where the defence fleet was gathered. 'The next few minutes will be revealing.'

'Indeed,' said Astelan.

The foremost ships of the enemy fleet, two light cruisers, were almost within high orbit, slowing to take up position. A course correction a few hours earlier had taken them closer to the northern polar region, while other elements of the incoming flotilla had broken off to the south.

Astelan growled, something not to his liking, and approached the display to inspect it more closely. Asmodai followed like a shadow.

'Something amiss?' asked Belial.

'Perhaps,' said Astelan. Red light flickered from his black gauntlet as his hand passed into the hololith, pointing to a cluster of ships a few thousand kilometres behind the light cruisers. 'This group is keeping very close together for some reason.'

'Bad pilots?' suggested Belial. 'We are not dealing with Naval-trained officers, I expect. A lacklustre attention to formation protocol is understandable.'

'No, that is not it,' said Astelan. He manipulated the controls of a sub-display, trying to focus on the group of ships. There were four, cruiser class, all within a few hundred cubic kilometres. At Astelan's bidding the image switched into reverse, winding back half a day. He set the vid-display into motion again. 'See, they came together just outside the scan range of our orbital platforms.'

'What does it mean?' said Asmodai.

'It means we are going to be betrayed,' Astelan said quietly. He glanced at the other command staff and then erased the sub-display he had highlighted.

'What do you mean?' demanded Belial.

'I have seen this before. At extreme range, the energy signature of several ships can be used to obscure their numbers.' As he spoke he indicated various features of the display. 'There is a competent commander in charge of this fleet. The lead elements are already moving into position to exploit the Thurlmann magnetopause, whilst the main force is on a timed intersect course to enter orbit directly above us, and a secondary wing, these three frigate-class vessels here, are manoeuvring for static orbit over the equatorial defence stations.'

'Thurlmann? What are you talking about?' said Belial. 'I see standard fleet dispersal for orbital berth separation, nothing more threatening.'

'Castagor Thurlmann, fleet primus commander of the Iron Hands,' Astelan said with a lengthy sigh. He looked at them and shook his head. 'So much has been forgotten.

The polar magnetosphere of a world interferes with the arrays of orbital surveyors and augury stations, making the poles a blind spot. Of course, there is little on the poles of most planets to attack, and the effect is equally disruptive to ships in orbit, preventing any targeting, so the deficiency is usually negligible. Castagor Thurlmann devised an approach pattern that allowed a ship to hit the boundary of the magnetosphere in such a way that its void shields and navigational fields would effectively create a minor vortex through the magnetosheath.'

Astelan stopped, his explanation obviously complete. Asmodai was no wiser to the Fallen's concern than he was thirty seconds earlier, but was not going to betray his ignorance. He waited for Belial to comment.

'That negates the scanner-blocking effect?' the Grand Master ventured.

'Yes!' Astelan expelled an exasperated breath. 'These two flanking forces are on a Thurlmann intersect pattern. They'll breach the magneto-shielding effect and will have about five minutes of effective firing without reply.'

'Are you sure?' said Asmodai, intrigued by the possibility and appalled that he knew of no such phenomenon. He looked at Belial, but the Grand Master said nothing to contradict the Fallen's appraisal of the situation.

'I spent over a century attacking worlds in the Emperor's name, fighting alongside the finest strategic minds and tacticians in the Imperium.' Astelan spoke slowly, his tone patronising and infuriating, but Asmodai tempered his anger. There was a time and a place to unleash the rage, but thanks to Sapphon's weakness and Astelan's manipulations Asmodai found himself in a position where neither was appropriate. 'I know what a fleet converging to assault formation looks like. More so, it confirms again that Anovel must be present. If you do not remember such manoeuvres, it is unlikely anyone who does not share a similar... history to me could conduct them.'

'Do nothing,' Asmodai snapped. He motioned for Belial to accompany him as he stepped away, out of earshot of Astelan and the Tharsian officers.

'You do not trust him,' said the Deathwing commander.

'Do you?'

'His explanation is plausible. I must confess that I am ignorant of the detail, but his interpretation may be correct. A fleet approaches – it is difficult to tell whether their intent is hostile or otherwise.'

'What of this ship cluster masking its numbers?'

'I cannot see what they would hide when the rest of the fleet is so obvious to detect,' said Belial. 'We have already identified the source of the earlier transmission as a grand cruiser, at the centre of the main detachment. If Anovel is aboard, it must be the flagship. What else would be worth concealing?'

'How can we believe anything he says?' Asmodai glared at Astelan, the look unseen behind his helm. 'He is a treacherous snake. Every act here could be intended to deflect our ire while weakening our defences. See how we are already at a disadvantage? Our ships are out of range and we rely upon his word to decipher the enemy's movements.'

'We could remove him from command,' said Belial. He shook his head, countering his own words. 'No, that makes no sense either. He must know that the moment his c– '

'Incoming transmission from approaching fleet!'

The call from one of the communications technicians cut across the debate. Asmodai hurried back to Astelan, who had been watching the Chaplain and Belial.

'We should open fire,' said the Fallen.

'A warning to your comrade, perhaps?' snapped Asmodai. 'A signal just before he places his head upon the axeman's block?'

'A pre-emptive strike, you fool!' Astelan's vehemence shocked Asmodai for a moment. He quickly regained his equilibrium, realising that the Fallen might be trying to knock his judgement off balance with forced and hasty decisions.

'No,' said Asmodai.

'What of the transmission?' said Astelan.

'No, you do not have any further contact with the enemy,' Asmodai said flatly. 'Any attempt to establish communication and I will kill you.'

Astelan thumped a hand against the hololith generator in frustration, denting the metal edging and causing the image to flicker for a moment. The Fallen turned towards the Tharsian attendants.

'Monitor group Vesalas,' Astelan called out. The ship liaison officer turned at the mention of his proxy command. Astelan interacted with the strategic schematic, which appeared on one of the tactical displays in front of the local officer. 'I want an immediate narrow-augur scan of this target group.'

The officer acknowledged the order and set to the controls of his station.

'What are you doing?' Asmodai demanded.

'Taking a better look,' the Fallen replied. Even with the modulation of his helm's external address system his scorn was obvious. 'I have been keeping the Vesalas squadron just out of direct scan range. Time to move them in. I want to know what Anovel is trying to hide.'

The next few minutes passed in tense silence as the

alerted flotilla of system monitors moved closer and actively scanned the vessels that had roused Astelan's suspicion. Asmodai was expecting any moment the announcement that the enemy fleet had broken formation or changed course; anything that would betray their knowledge of what was happening.

'Feed to the command display,' the Fallen ordered when the liaison officer announced that the scan results had been received. On the main hololith the bulk of the enemy fleet was altering course, now heading directly for Tharsis, at increasing speed.

'What are you looking for?' said Belial.

Astelan did not answer. The data-cluster from the monitors appeared as a series of overlapping energy waves, superimposed over a schematic of their gravity displacement and energy output. As he looked, Asmodai saw something that did not match the other patterns; a discrepancy in displacement that was too large to be powered by the energy signatures.

'An anomaly,' said the Chaplain. He tapped in a control sequence to separate the interweaving lines. 'What does it mean?'

'I know this…' Astelan leaned closer, as if to study the hololith in more detail. 'I have seen this before.'

'What is it?' Belial demanded. The Tharsians could hear the exchange between the Space Marines and many were looking to them with worried expressions.

'Throne of Terra!' exclaimed Astelan, straightening. He turned to the command officers. 'The *Terminus Est*! All stations, all battle groups, attack priority. Engage the enemy, full attack. Open fire, for the Emperor's sake, open fire!'

'Belay that!' roared Asmodai, drawing his pistol. 'Do not fire!'

'We have to defend ourselves,' hissed Astelan. 'They mean to attack. That is Calas Typhon's ship. I would know it anywhere. Emperor knows, I fought alongside it.'

'I have only your word for that,' said Asmodai.

Astelan leaned forward until his chin was just above Asmodai's hand, the bolt pistol pointing at his throat.

'Pull the trigger if you do not believe me,' said the Fallen.

It was impossible to see his expression but the lenses of his helm were directly looking at Asmodai, daring him, forcing him to make a decision. The Chaplain's finger eased onto the trigger of his pistol.

It was so tempting, to squeeze once and end this despicable affair right there and then. Just a simple muscular motion, a chemical reaction and then Astelan would be no more of a problem.

'Is this how it was, traitor, when you gave the order to kill the Lion?' Asmodai's voice was just loud enough for the Fallen to hear, no louder. 'Is this how you destroyed our primarch?'

'Yes, remarkably similar,' said Astelan. 'I regret nothing.'

Belial's hand fell onto the pistol, gently pushing it away before Asmodai could react.

'I believe him, brother,' said the Grand Master. Asmodai nodded and let his arm fall to his side as he turned to the vox-attendants.

'Open fire!' the Chaplain ordered.

BATTLE BEGINS

Guided by attack patterns created by the Dark Angels, the Tharsis defence fleet responded quickly to the call to arms. Slow but heavily-gunned monitors accelerated towards the incoming fleet, placing themselves between the approaching traitors and orbit around Tharsis. Surface batteries – defence lasers and immense cannons – fired at the ships attempting to make polar orbit, driving off the light cruisers. Orbital space stations spewed squadrons of fighters ready to intercept any potential torpedo launch while flights of bombers assembled beneath the guns of defence platforms in preparation for attacks against the arriving starships.

The traitors responded to the escalation by dividing their main fleet. A third of the ships, mostly frigate-class and destroyers, peeled away from the advance to tackle the monitors. The heavy cruiser flagship and its attendant escorts made full speed for orbit, loosing several salvos of torpedoes to clear its path to Tharsis. In their wake the

Terminus Est was revealed as the cruiser squadron masking the energy signature of the huge battle-barge split, taking up supporting stations a few thousand kilometres from the Death Guard vessel.

Aboard the *Penitent Warrior* Sapphon could discern very little of what was going on, other than a swift spike in communications traffic and massive bursts of radiation and energy betraying ship weapons firing.

'Shall we respond, Brother-Chaplain?' asked Lasla Chirpet, the senior officer of the bridge attendants.

'Not yet,' Sapphon replied. 'Establish a narrow-beam channel with the *Implacable Justice*.'

It would take a minute or two for the communications officer to make the almost invisible laser transmission to the other strike cruiser. Sapphon studied the blurred mess of the main sensor display. In order to keep their presence undetected the two Dark Angels ships were operating on minimal scanning, using only close range navigational augurs to ensure they did not crash. With their reactors almost idling, gun batteries dormant and flight bays locked, it would take almost an hour for the ships to come up to full preparedness, and nearly half that time to manoeuvre to combat speed.

'Grand Master Sammael,' reported the comms serf.

Sammael's voice came through clearly, but there was no picture – a tight-band vox-link over a few hundred kilometres would keep the ships undetected.

'Who opened fire first?' asked Sammael.

'I could not tell,' said Sapphon. 'It matters not for the moment. I do not think it is yet time to spring the trap. Anovel's flagship has not fully committed yet.'

'If we allow them any closer they will be able to start landing troops,' Sammael replied. 'It seems they intend to assault Tharsis.'

'Let them,' said Sapphon. 'They will be greeted by Belial and his Deathwing, not to mention a fully mobilised planetary defence force.'

'There is also the matter of the battle-barge, brother. I do not recognise the pattern but it is enormous, and comms tell me that it is issuing ancient Death Guard identifiers. After events at Thyestes and Ulthor we must expect it to be carrying a full complement of several companies. If they deploy, the First Company will need support.'

'The moment we reveal ourselves our last advantage is spent,' said Sapphon. 'We cannot risk alerting Anovel to our presence. It will take at least thirty minutes for forces to make planetfall once orbit had been gained. I suggest we slowly bring up reactors to nominal threshold and stand-by in readiness.'

'To what end? If we strike now we can still catch the heavy cruiser as it tries to make orbit.'

'And what when we have to board the traitor's flagship with its full complement? Better to let them begin to attack and deplete their defence before they understand the true threat.'

The vox hissed for a few seconds, leaving Sapphon wondering whether Sammael was displeased with this course of action and was going to intervene regardless. The Grand Master responded eventually.

'It is a big risk, brother. We have no means of communicating with Belial and Asmodai without betraying our presence.'

'They will understand our strategy,' Sapphon said, hoping he was right. 'Our silence for the moment communicates intent more clearly than words.'

'I suppose that is the case,' said Sammael. 'Still, I would not wish it to be thought we stood aside while our brothers were needlessly in peril.'

'Nothing we have done here is needless, brother. Remember that.'

'As you say, brother. By the Lion, we will bide our time for the moment. When we strike, we must be swift and sure of our aim.'

'Another cause for patience, Sammael. Anovel will likely lead the attack. On the surface your Ravenwing can hunt him down far better than aboard a starship.'

'Let us hope that Belial does not catch him first, as you say. Preparing gradual reactor charge. Thirty minutes. Transmission end.'

DROP WARNING

'Finally!'

It seemed to Annael that Sabrael's exclamation summed up the feelings of the entire company. For watch after watch Grand Master Sammael had drilled them, covering drop protocol, inter-squadron formations, joint aerial tactics and everything else that made the Ravenwing the most responsive, coordinated force in the whole Chapter. It had been clear that they were preparing for something but nobody had been sure why they had been waiting in orbit over Tharsis on full alert. The scenario had become even more baffling when the two strike cruisers had broken orbit and moved further in-system. It had concerned the Ravenwing veterans, appearing to be a move that indicated a fleet engagement rather than ground assault. It had looked likely that the Deathwing would receive the battle honours rather than the Second Company.

The blare of sirens that indicated drop preparation

GAV THORPE

sounded again, urging the Dark Angels to their bikes, aircraft and Land Speeders. Annael had been in the aft firing galleries, practising with his bolt pistol alongside the other Black Knights. Now they strode towards the armoury bays with purpose, even enthusiasm, the long wait until battle almost over.

'Any confirmation on the mission, brother?' Calatus asked Tybalain.

'Not yet,' replied the Huntmaster. 'We are moving back into drop range at full speed. Full company-strength combat deployment will follow.'

'On open ground?' Nerean asked hopefully. 'It would be good not to have another city fight. I want open stretches and sweeping attacks to fire the blood.'

'Unknown,' Tybalain said. They reached the bay doors and the Huntmaster stopped, holding up a hand to halt them. He unhooked his helm from his belt and looked at them sternly, his gaze lingering on Annael and Sabrael. 'This may be the culmination of the current campaign. The end of the Hunt.'

Excitement grew in Annael at the thought. It was quickly tempered by the Huntmaster's next words.

'Remember our purpose.' Tybalain glanced down the corridor at the other Ravenwing squadrons assembling in the bays further forward. His voice was quiet and steady. 'We locate the traitor and bring in the Death-wing for his extraction. Our job is not only to run down the quarry but also to cordon off the area from the rest of the company. They do not know the full nature of the faithless men we hunt and we have a responsibility to defend that ignorance. The target will be referred to only as Primus. The call-signal to the Deathwing will be "Hammerfall". When the target is found you will restrict all communication to squad-vox. Before then, watch what you say on the company channel. A loose tongue now could still bring disaster.'

'Understood,' said Annael. The others chorused their affirmatives.

Tybalain was not finished though. His next words were directed solely at Annael and Sabrael.

'Initiative and surprise are key weapons in the arsenal of the Ravenwing, but you will remain in formation at all times and you will respond to my orders without hesitation.' The Huntmaster stared hard at Sabrael. 'Honour is earned by the completion of the mission. All other considerations are worthless. Kill tallies are meaningless if the target escapes. Discipline is honour. Do I make myself clear?'

'Aye, brother-sergeant,' said Sabrael.

'Understood,' Annael said again, inclining his head in respect. 'Duty comes first.'

Contented, Tybalain led them to their waiting steeds. Techmarines and their attendants fussed around the bikes, making last minute checks and laying pre-battle blessings upon the machine-spirits. The fog of oily incense and the rumble of ammunition carriers filled the bay. The sights, scents and sounds stirred Annael, his hearts beating a little faster as he mounted *Black Shadow* and started his own preparatory rituals.

'To victory this time, faithful steed,' he said quietly, activating the scanning interface.

'Starboard drop cascade four,' Tybalain told them over the comm.

The announcement heightened Annael's excitement even further. No gunship deployment this time. A drop assault, lightning-fast and intense. He ran through the mantra of the Black Knights to steady himself. Find the target. Isolate the target. Seize the target. It seemed simple enough but in the heat of battle it could prove difficult to focus amongst the cut and thrust.

'Vox-check,' Tybalain said. The squadron sounded off in turn, the voices as clear in Annael's ears as if they had been standing next to him, despite the growing thrum of engines and a deeper rumbling from the deck that signified the *Implacable Justice* accelerating hard, heading back into orbit over Tharsis.

'Drop count initiated at forty-seven minutes on my mark,' the Huntmaster continued the litany of the company's pre-battle routine. 'Embarkation in twelve minutes. Assimilate geotelemetry.'

Annael opened up the comm-receiver of *Black Shadow* and waited while a stream of data uploaded to the navigational cogitator. From the schematics that scrolled quickly across the bike's display the primary battle zone seemed to be a close-built urban area.

'What joy,' Nerean muttered over the vox. 'Another city fight.'

DISTRACTIONS

'He is coming for me,' Astelan said quietly.

Asmodai said nothing. He had nothing to say to the Fallen. Belial had left the command centre to hold a briefing with his Deathwing Knights, leaving Asmodai alone with Astelan. The Grand Master had made it clear that the outset of a battle was not the time for the Master of Repentance to pursue his vendetta against the Fallen and as much as it pained Asmodai he was inclined to agree. Despite all of the Chaplain's misgivings, so far Anovel had been lured directly into the trap as planned.

'He is advancing on a single front, pushing towards the palace,' Astelan continued, pointing at the hololith display. 'Standard practice, to remove the upper command first.'

'You are not in command here,' Asmodai reminded the Fallen. 'I am.'

'I sought to explain the success of our ploy, not to take credit,' Astelan replied. 'However, command or not, you would have to agree that I have played the part of bait exceptionally well. Anovel races to put his head into the noose. He sees me as the greatest threat to his ambitions.'

'I do not have to agree to anything. Even without your presence, the Imperial commander's palace would be the logical target for an initial assault. As well as removing all command functions such action would seize the most advantageous high ground.'

'Yet there is an almost unseemly haste in the speed of his advance. As far as our foe is aware he will achieve orbital supremacy very soon. He can take the time to surround and attack the citadel from several fronts, but instead he chooses to make a lightning attack along a single axis.'

Studying the schematics, the flickering icons that updated the positions of the enemy troops every thirty seconds, Asmodai could see that Astelan spoke the truth.

'Anovel makes little attempt to secure his flanks or a supply line back to the landing grounds of his dropships,' Asmodai observed. 'There is no obvious line of retreat. He plans to capture the palace or die in the attempt.'

'It does appear that is the case. Perhaps Anovel is showing his strategic naiveté. He was, after all, only an Apothecary in the Legion. I am frankly amazed he managed to muster any kind of force at all.'

Something about Astelan's words gave Asmodai a moment of pause. It barely mattered to him what rank or role a Fallen had filled during the Horus Heresy, only the degree of their involvement in the rebellion against the Lion. Battle-brothers and Scouts were sometimes guilty of far more heinous deeds than Chapter Masters and Paladins. According to Astelan's testimony it had been Anovel's task within the grand scheme to secure gene-seed for implantation into new recruits located by Astelan. Methelas, the Librarian, had been responsible for commissioning the pirates of Port Imperial as a fleet, and for securing the star base as a mobile fortress. Astelan was to provide the recruits and, presumably, train them.

'You were to be the commander, were you not?' the Chaplain said slowly. 'Within your new regime, the rank of Chapter Master would be retained by you.'

'It was my assumption, yes, but it seems Anovel had other plans.'

'Yet by your testimony he is an inadequate command figure, but has shown surprising ability in mustering an offensive force capable of attacking Tharsis.'

'As he throws himself at our defences, his shortcomings may be soon proven.' Astelan walked around the strategic display. 'He approaches from one of the most securely defended directions, taking the shortest route but perhaps encountering the most resistance.'

'It is not Anovel's battleplan,' Asmodai said slowly, coming to a realisation. 'Another guides his actions.'

'But... Typhon!' Astelan slapped a hand against the side of the hololith table, fuzzing the image for several seconds. 'A superior commander, indeed. We have perhaps made a grave error.'

'I believe that has been true since we left the Rock, but how is this present situation confirmation of such fact?'

'This is not a treachery to the plan I created with Anovel and Methelas,' said the Fallen, pacing further around the display in agitation. 'This has become the design of Calas Typhon.'

'He is cursed by another name these days,' said Asmodai. 'Amongst those who know, he is called Typhus.'

'Typhon, Typhus, now is not the time for pedantry. We

have been proceeding on a false assumption. I believed Anovel sought to oust me from my position so that he could claim Tharsis and my recruits for himself. This has nothing to do with that vision. Typhon seeks to conquer the world for himself and is expending Anovel's warriors to do so. He is a bold commander but not a rash one. He saves his Death Guard to strike the final blow once Anovel's twisted scum have bled the Tharsians.'

'His warriors would make a sharper tip for the spear,' said Asmodai, unconvinced by Astelan's assessment.

'But such tip might be blunted in the effort,' Astelan replied. The Fallen tapped gauntleted fingers on the surface of the projection plate as he spoke. 'It does not make sense to you, but you are not a renegade. I am, and I have dealt with these types of warriors. They do not fight out of grand ideal or loyalty to the Emperor. They are selfish and bound together only by mutual need. The Death Guard follow Typhon because they choose to for their own benefit. There is not one amongst them that would set foot in the breach first for the safety of the others, whereas you would happily die if it brought victory. They are not battle-brothers as you understand it.'

What Astelan claimed made sense, from the perspective of the warped mind of a traitor. Over and over on the torment rack Asmodai had laid bare the self-serving and shallow nature of the Fallen and the same lack of duty and character was likely to apply to other renegades.

'Your deductions are logical, but to what end?' said the Chaplain. 'Anovel is still placed well for capture, no matter the motivations and objectives of our foes. How does that alter the final goal?'

'It means that Typhon will not join the assault until he is convinced victory is possible. If you can defeat Anovel and blunt his attack Typhon is likely not to prosecute further invasion. Anovel knows this and expends every effort, and warrior, in the attempt to secure the aid of the Death Guard.'

Asmodai had only a few seconds to consider this before his train of thought was interrupted by a panicked shout from one of the sensor array officers.

'We have two cruisers in low orbit locking weapons onto our location!' the attendant warned.

'Anovel does not need to storm the palace,' Astelan said hurriedly. 'Damn! He only needs to remove us as a threat. He advances quickly to storm the ruins, not to take control! We cannot stay here.'

'You do not leave this chamber,' snapped Asmodai, pulling free his pistol. 'Do not treat with me as a fool.'

A thunderous crack reverberated across the chamber, blanking out the hololith and filling downs of screens with static. Asmodai felt a tremor run through the walls and floor of the command hall.

'Direct lance strike!' reported the sensor officer.

'Two power fields knocked out,' added one of the men at the damage control station. 'Four banks remaining.'

'Where is our counter-orbital fire?' Astelan demanded, striding towards the communications platform.

'Remain at your positions!' Asmodai roared as he noticed several of the officers backing away from their commands, eyes turned towards the door. He raised his pistol. 'I will kill any man that attempts to leave his post.'

Another blast of energy from the second cruiser slammed into the energy shields shimmering above the palace. Deep within the citadel generators overloaded, blacking out more of the tactical displays. The main lights flickered off, to be replaced by the orange glow from the emergency plasma reactor buried deep beneath the fortification. Brighter light bathed the defence officers as screens glimmered back into life.

'Answer me!' Astelan stormed up and down behind the planetary defence officers. 'Why are we not firing back?'

'Targeting solutions have been calculated and communicated,' one officer reported. 'Silos four, six and seven are responding. We will return fire before the enemy can recharge their lances.'

'Too late,' said Astelan. Asmodai saw what the Fallen had seen. Atmospheric sweeps picked up a storm of projectiles descending on the city.

'Torpedoes,' growled the Chaplain. Normally the huge missiles were only good for ship-to-ship combat, but Anovel – or Typhon – had modified his ships' ordnance to make them suitable for ground attack.

'Sound bombardment warning,' Astelan commanded.

The next few minutes unfolded slowly. The defence lasers positioned around the capital opened fire, driving away the two cruisers. However, as Astelan had observed, this was too little and too late. The entire reason for defence silos and orbital gun platforms was to prevent such an attack. Asmodai had no idea how a gap so large had been allowed to develop and any recriminations were pointless for the moment. It seemed likely that it was the work of traitors within the Tharsian establishment – maybe even old sympathisers of Astelan – but there was no proof of a connection.

The incoming torpedoes separated into hundreds of cluster-warheads two kilometres up from the palace, concentrated on a few square kilometres.

The command centre was located on the southern side of the citadel, behind metres of plasteel and ferrocrete, but such armour was only good against land-based weaponry. The destructive might of a plasma torpedo would find these defences little obstacle.

Asmodai had a hasty vox-conversation with Belial. Fortunately the Deathwing units had already moved outside the palace, deployed to encircle the attacking force rather than meet it head-on. Belial had ordered the Imperial commander conducted to the secure bunkers beneath the palace but for other personnel there was little shelter.

Anovel's forces were only three kilometres away. The timing of the orbital attack was near-perfect, and would leave the palace defenders with no opportunity to recover before the ground forces were moving to overrun their positions.

'It is time to formulate a new strategy,' said Astelan. 'The citadel is compromised. If Anovel is capable of seizing the centre of the city we can be sure that Typhon and his Death Guard will join the assault. You have to stop the enemy from advancing and counter-attack now.'

'That would suit your ends perfectly,' said Asmodai. He pointed his pistol at Astelan, rage building at the thought that the Fallen could think him so stupid. 'The chaos and confusion of battle would give you ample opportunity to slip away and there is no bond I can place upon you that I can trust. I have postponed this moment long enough.'

The defence force officers were streaming away from their positions, taking advantage of the confrontation between the Space Marines to seek better shelter or perhaps escape. Asmodai did not let his aim waver for a moment, knowing his foe would need only the tiniest opportunity to act.

'I should have expected no honour from the likes of you,' Astelan snapped. 'I have delivered Anovel to you on a platter, but you are so twisted up in your paranoia and lies that you cannot believe for a moment that I might act in good faith.'

TRAITOR!

A moment of weakness spawns a lifetime of heresy, so the adage claimed. It burned Asmodai's soul to think of the compromises he had already made; his skin crawled at the thought of further bargaining with Astelan.

'No, I cannot. You are treacherous to the core, Merir Astelan. You have been given many years to see the error of your past and to confess your transgressions yet have shown no repentance for your acts against your primarch and your Emperor. I have no choice but–'

The first of the torpedo warheads hit the remaining power fields, detonating with a bright star of plasma that shook the palace to its foundations.

In the seconds that followed, more and more missiles slammed into the citadel and its outlying towers, turning masonry to slurry, releasing shockwaves that toppled the towers of the Cathedral of the Emperor Restored and flattened the other buildings around the city centre. A rippling tide of superheated air washed over the main plaza turning cobbles to liquid, incinerating anyone and anything in the open. Thousands of Tharsians, defence force and civilians alike, were immolated over the course of the next thirty seconds, not even ashes remaining to mark their demise.

The metal vaulting holding up the roof of the command hall screeched and buckled under torrential impacts, finally giving way amidst an avalanche of shattered ferrocrete and semi-molten plasteel. As Asmodai looked up a block the size of a battle tank dropped towards the Chaplain.

Astelan slammed into the Master of Repentance, fist connecting with the side of Asmodai's skull helm. A moment later the block hit the ground next to the Space Marines, shattering into hundreds of wicked shards. Asmodai was knocked back by the impact, separated from Astelan as dust billowed like smoke. A piece of ripped girder followed, careening off the Chaplain's left shoulder. As he toppled to one knee he saw more boulders falling on his attacker, until Astelan disappeared from sight.

The deluge of rubble continued for almost a minute, during which time all Asmodai could do was dodge as best he could, shielding himself from the heaviest blocks as broken masonry fell like rain. Shredded power cables arced lightning across the hall and command consoles exploded, sending a refuge of red and blue sparks into the darkness.

Every fibre of Asmodai's being knew that Astelan was not dead.

He surged out of the rubble pile, switching to thermal view in the darkness. The air gleamed with the afterglow of the plasma detonations, laying an ochre sheen across everything. Jagged edges of broken buttresses and pillars glowed radioactively in the Chaplain's infrasight while jets of energy looked like coronal ejections from a star.

And there was no telltale glow from the power pack of a Space Marine's war-plate.

Astelan was gone.

Stepping over the wreckage, Asmodai smiled to himself. The Fallen had finally revealed himself and there would be no more arguments, no more dissembling and schemes within schemes.

Astelan could run, but he could not hide. Asmodai activated his battleplate's transponder recognition systems and a definitive return pinged back from three hundred metres away. Astelan was making good speed,

already at one of the armoury garages, Asmodai sur-
mised. Even amongst the destruction of the torpedo
strike a groundcar or armoured transport would survive.
Fate sometimes worked that way. It did not matter; the
Dark Angels had swifter means.

He activated the command-vox.

'This is Brother Asmodai, contact for Huntmaster
Tybalain. New priority objective. Designate Target
Beta. Locate prisoner on transponder encryption alpha-
seven-four-gamma. Terminate immediately on contact.
No overrule, this target must be eliminated.'

'Understood, Brother-Chaplain,' came Tybalain's reply.
'Target Beta will be eliminated on contact.'

Vengeance was at hand.

THE PRICE OF DUTY

Contrary to Nerean's misgivings, the Black Knights did not find themselves sent into the heart of Streisgant. Instead the Black Knights drop pods deposited them within striking distance of the traitor landing fields outside the city.

Dozens of huge drop-ships were scattered across a swathe of agri-district, looking like squat keeps amongst cereal fields and flattened mega-orchards. Air defence turrets on the dropcraft streamed tracer fire into the cloudy sky, seeking out the flitting shapes of Tharsian attack planes and Ravenwing interceptors. Rocket pods belched their payloads into the city, levelling buildings to pave the way for the infantry advance while armoured transports rumbled from the bowels of the drop-ships, grinding thick-tyred wheels over burnt crops and splintered trees.

The first Ravenwing charge was heralded by the arrival of the Darkshrouds. Black shadow spread across the flat plain from the east, masking the approach of Sammael and the bulk of the company. Ground-attack batteries fired shells and laser into the encroaching bank of darkness, the random fire passing harmless over the swift bikes and Land Speeders closing under the cover of artificial night.

Tybalain and his squadron curved around on a flanking attack, leading the Black Knights towards columns of augmented soldiers surging into the city outskirts. Land Speeder Tornados supported the riders' attack with heavy bolter and assault cannon fire while Typhoons blanketed the outlying streets with missile barrages.

The Black Knights pressed directly into the midst of the foe, using their enemies' own numbers as a shield against incoming fire, bolters and plasma talons spitting death. Chem-boosted bodies and mechanical exoskeletons were no match for the fury and firepower of the Second Company as the Black Knights and skimmers carved a trail through the advancing infantry.

Stooping in to the attack from over low warehouses, jinking between huge grain silos, a trio of Land Speeders dived onto clanking troop carriers, slicing through armour with flares of multi-melta, ammunition and engine explosions turning the transports into crackling pyres for the men and women within.

Swerving through the banks of smoke, *Black Shadow*'s wheels juddering over rubble and corpses, Annael plunged into the thick of the foe with the rest of the squadron. He lashed out with his corvus hammer, cracking open crudely-welded exo-armour, pulverising flesh and bone. Leaving battered, scattered bodies in their wake the Black Knights burst out onto a side street, moving away before the enemy could muster any sort of counterattack.

Following the Huntmaster, they looped around, passing between close tenements to come at Anovel's warriors again from another direction, once more carving a bloody path through the invaders before zooming away. Over the vox Annael followed the reports from the landing fields: the Ravenwing were taking a heavy toll on the rear of the traitor army, herding the survivors into the city where the militia were waiting in prepared positions.

'Priority objective, brothers!' Sabrael announced gleefully as they swept out onto a broad boulevard on their third attack run. He pointed with his hammer towards the centre of the city, where a lightly armoured half-track transport was ploughing its way towards the inner citadel. Vox-antenna and scanner dishes dotted the armoured cab, indicating some kind of command vehicle. Las-fire from pintle-weapons manned by warriors in its open compartment spewed into high-fronted assembly plants to either side, paving the way for several dozen armoured infantry advancing in its wake. The traitors used the wrecks of vehicles as cover as they moved further into the city.

'Good eyes, Sabrael,' said Tybalain. 'We will circle around and come at the target from the right.'

Sabrael needed no more encouragement and surged a few metres ahead of the squadron, angling his steed down an alleyway barely wide enough for bike and rider. Tybalain led the others after him, brick walls rushing past Annael within the reach of an outstretched arm.

Braking hard, tyres squealing, they banked into a broad stretch of ferrocrete; some kind of marshalling yard overlooked by cranes and gantries.

'Emperor's mercy,' whispered Calatus. 'Look to the palace!'

Annael followed his battle-brother's instruction in

time to see a blur of projectiles hitting the crackling arc of the citadel's power field. For an instant whiteness filled his vision before his auto-senses blocked out the flash of plasma. When they cleared a half a second later, his sight still dimmed almost to nothing, all Annael could see was a fireball rising high into the air above the city. The towers of the palace had become pinnacles of flame, raining down molten debris like volcanoes.

As one the squadron screeched to a halt to watch the unfolding spectacle. The upper parts of the palace – all that could be seen over the intervening buildings – had become pillars of ash shot through with rivulets of molten metal. Annael looked on in amazement as a pinnacle three hundred metres high crumpled like a burnt log, turning into a blossom of flame and cloud before disappearing from view.

'We need to move to support,' said Nerean.

'Negative,' snapped Tybalain. 'We remain on-mission until new orders from the Grand Master. Continue the attack.'

'The first vengeance will be our honour,' Sabrael said as he accelerated away.

'No mercy,' Annael added, the shock of the orbital attack subsiding, replaced by an upwelling of hatred for the enemy that had unleashed such destruction. 'We cleanse Tharsis of this filth.'

A blast from Tybalain's plasma talon shattered the gate to the yard and they exited at speed, swerving around falling remnants of burning metal onto a curving street that joined the main thoroughfare just ahead of the command vehicle's current position.

'My steed lacks teeth to bring down such a beast,' said Sabrael, referring to the bolters fitted to the standard Ravenwing bike that had replaced the mount he had lost on Ulthor. 'I shall draw their ire while you strike.'

Without waiting for confirmation or permission from Tybalain, Sabrael sped away down another side road, heading directly for the traitor tank.

'Target tracks and weapon systems first,' the Huntmaster told his squadron as they continued around the bend of the street. The lead elements of the command vehicle's escort – lightly armoured scouts on foot – could be seen moving through the buildings ahead.

Tybalain had signalled for the Black Knights to spread out into attack formation when the vox crackled with a priority command transmission.

'This is Brother Asmodai, contact for Huntmaster Tybalain. New priority objective. Designate Target Beta. Locate prisoner on transponder encryption alpha-seven-four-gamma. Terminate immediately on contact. No overrule, this target must be eliminated.'

'Understood, Brother-Chaplain. Target Beta will be eliminated on contact.' Tybalain switched back to the squad-vox to address his warriors. 'Abort attack and set augurs for designated transponder signal.'

The Huntmaster slowed hard and banked his steed to the left.

'Brothers, it will take but a matter of moments to destroy this foe.' Sabrael was breathless with exhilaration. 'We are in perfect position to strike.'

'Negative!' snarled Tybalain. 'We have our orders. I will signal for a Dark Talon to make a strike against the target.'

Annael carried on as the other three Black Knights with him turned around their steeds and started heading away.

'Annael, my brother, give me support. A delay of moments.'

It seemed a waste of an opportunity to turn away when they could inflict a serious blow to the enemy advance. The transponder signal of the Target Beta was clear on the augur relay, almost halfway across the city. It would take some time to catch up with the new objective, a minute or two's digression would make little difference.

'Honour is earned by the completion of the mission. All other considerations are worthless. Kill tallies are meaningless if the target escapes. Discipline is honour. Do I make myself clear?'

The words of Tybalain came back to Annael and he remembered the oaths he had sworn, on becoming a Dark Angel, on his investiture to the Ravenwing and in completing the Seventh Rite of the Raven. He was a Black Knight and he had a purpose above and beyond simply military accomplishment.

Other words came back to him, spoken by Malcifer. He felt the corvus hammer heavy in his grasp.

'In taking up these weapons you are accepting a binding oath to the Chapter and the Emperor. You will swear that you will uphold the lore of the Black Knights of Caliban. You will offer up your lives in protection of the rites and knowledge of the Order. As Black Knights of the Ravenwing you shall be the eyes and ears of your Grand Master not only on the battlefield but amongst your brethren. You shall guard against heresy and rebellion with every fibre and be prepared to lay down not only your life but your honour in the prosecution of our ancient pursuit.'

He had a sacred mission to attend.

'No, brother, we have to go,' said Annael. He slowed and turned his bike after the others. 'The Hunt comes first.'

The bark of bolters reverberated along the streets,

swiftly followed by the snap of las-weapons and chatter of autoguns.

'Too late, brothers, they have seen me,' announced Sabrael. 'Committing to the attack! Lend me your ire!'

It wrenched at Annael's heart to slip away, doing nothing. For a moment he wanted to slew his steed around and ride to Sabrael's aid, but the instant passed and he carried on after Tybalain. The increasing din of the firefight followed him down the street.

'Brothers! We h–' Sabrael was cut off and a loud detonation reverberated down the empty street. In the seconds that followed the din of battle quietened.

'Brother-sergeant,' said Annael, thoughts whirling with disbelief. It seemed impossible that Sabrael could have succumbed. There did not seem anything in the galaxy capable of killing such a warrior. 'Our brother might not be dead. Sabrael's gene-seed, the machine-spirit of his steed… The Blade of Corswain. Are we to abandon them?'

'The Hunt, Brother Annael,' came Tybalain's stern reply. 'That is our only concern. These other things we will attend in time.'

Annael glanced back but could see nothing of friend or enemy, only desolate road and buildings. He turned his attention back to the augur return of Target Beta's transponder. The marker blip was moving away, leaving the city. Annael focused his frustration and anger onto the dot of red on the scanner display.

Sabrael's name had been added to the list of those that needed to be avenged and Annael would see retribution exacted.

TARGET ALPHA

The purges and persecution committed by Astelan's sacred bands and the retribution of the Dark Angels had not left much standing of old Streisgant, the capital of Tharsis. In the past fifteen years the city, and much of the world, had been built anew; prefabricated hab-blocks and ferrocrete roadstrip punctuated by grandiose Administratum tithe buildings, Mechanicus temples and local militia force barracks and garages. The central square was dominated on one side by the outlying fortifications of the Imperial commander's palace and by the Cathedral of the Emperor Restored opposite, facing each other across a red brick plaza almost half a kilometre broad.

Though not in the way he had intended, Astelan's brutal regime had wrought a huge change on Tharsis and brought new life and energy to the stagnating planet. On the fringes of wilderness space, overlooked by the Eye of Terror – a distant but malignant red blot in the sky day and night – Tharsis had been on the outskirts of the Imperium, troubled by warp storms and difficult to reach. Following the intervention of the Dark Angels, and their removal of any proof of Astelan's origins, the Imperium had responded in a manner of almost unprecedented haste in comparison to much of the galaxy-spanning empire's activities. In fifteen years Tharsis had been rebuilt from the cratered remains of a civil war-wracked ruin to a functioning world once more sending its tithes of ore, produce and men to serve the needs of their overlords on distant Terra.

Now the Dark Angels had brought war back to Tharsis and Streisgant burned again. The sky above the city was choked with columns of smoke from hundreds of fires set by shells and energy beams unleashed by the starships in orbit. Dozens of drop-ships, the size of city blocks, had already crashed down into the marshalling yards and open spaces of the capital's outskirts, disgorging hundreds of soldiers augmented by the twisted bionical and chemical practices of Anovel and his allies.

Though the traitors possessed orbital supremacy, the defenders of Tharsis claimed the air; fighter trails crisscrossed the cloudy skies as interceptors blazed with autocannons and despatched missiles at another wave of descending drop-ships. Ground-attack craft with reverse delta wings swept over the buildings occupied by Anovel's army, hovering on huge turbines as they pounded away with multilasers and rocket pods. From silos arranged across the city streams of defence laser fire erupted into orbit while the resounding boom of artillery rumbled across the city, heralding the scream of descending shells and tremors of detonations on the traitor landing fields.

Despite every advantage of the Tharsians, the attackers

made swift ground. In the block-to-block urban fighting the boosted bodies and stimm-induced speed of the renegades were of greater effect than big guns and armoured vehicles. In bloody close fighting and hand-to-hand combat the Tharsians stood no chance against augmented foes trained in Adeptus Astartes-style close combat.

The advance could have been halted at any moment by the intervention of the Deathwing squads and vehicles waiting near the inner citadel but Belial and Asmodai held their counter-attack. They needed to be sure of Anovel's position before striking; an untimely attack would expose the presence of the Deathwing too early and give the Fallen an opportunity to escape.

That was the last thing Asmodai wanted. He waited with Belial in the ruins of a tower on the edge of the commander's palace, following updates of the fighting over the local vox-network. There were also reports from the Ravenwing, who were driving the rear echelons of Anovel's army further into the city and making hit-and-run attacks against their landing sites.

'Hundreds of the Emperor's servants are dying because we desire to capture one man. Do you think it was right to bring war to Tharsis?' said Belial.

'Yes,' replied Asmodai.

'So do I.'

They continued to watch the unfolding battle in silence.

It was easy for Asmodai to justify the unknowing sacrifice of so many in such a secret cause. He had seen first-hand the damage that one Fallen could inflict. A corner of his helm-display was taken up with scattered vid-images being transmitted back from Tharsian recon units. Seeing the bastardised warrior-mutants Anovel

had despatched into the city, their unthinking zealotry and insane heedlessness of casualties, was another
reminder of why the Fallen were so abhorrent.

*The lowest regions of Cetis Albus's hive-moon Sigma were an
infernal warren of half-collapsed mine workings and barely
stable air ducts. The tunnel-rat defenders knew every crawl-
space, disused tunnel and half-finished delving and employed
such knowledge to great advantage.*

*The Dark Angels faced a near-constant series of ambus-
cades and diversionary attacks, but Sergeant Elijah would not
be swayed from the advance to secure flanks or rear.*

*'The only path to victory,' he told Brother Asmodai, 'is to
chop the head from the serpent. When the body is left to
thrash without guidance it shall be quelled.'*

*Brother Asmodai could see the sense of this approach. It was
a standard decapitation strike, to disrupt enemy command
and control. It seemed the natural solution. Sergeant Ishmael
and nearly two-thirds of the company had already succumbed
to the relentless numbers of the Ceti Albus rebels. To prolong
the war of attrition would see the Dark Angels all dead within
days, no matter that they were far superior man-for-man.*

*It was a source of some amazement to Brother Asmodai
that any leader other than the Emperor could inspire such
devotion as the rebel commander had instilled in the people
of hive-moon Sigma. Youngsters no more than twelve Terran
years fought alongside grey-haired grandmothers. Improvised
weapons, converted rock drills and las-picks were little match
for bolters and power armour but still the populace were willing to hurl themselves again and again at the Space Marines.
Tens of thousands were already dead, but that was just a drop
in the ocean of the hive's population.*

*Such tenacity was also key to the Dark Angels successes,
pressing on through the slaughter without mercy or hesitation.*

It had brought them to the brink of victory, just a few hundred metres from the enemy stronghold. The defenders became more and more desperate, and better-equipped. Heavy lifting gear almost equal in strength to Adeptus Astartes war-plate had been turned into battle suits with spinning chainblades, plasma burners and energy-wreathed mattocks. Tunnel-borers with melta-tipped drill heads speared into the Dark Angels, their drivers trapped in the cabs behind welded armour plates and bars. Teams with las-cutters buried themselves beneath rubble and grit, ready to burst forth to unleash blasts from their short-ranged tools, cracking open ceramite like eggshell before being hewn down by their foes.

And still Sergeant Elijah was adamant in his purpose; an example that Brother Asmodai followed without question. Even as more and more of the battle-brothers struggled forwards under increasingly suicidal and devastating attack, Asmodai was at Elijah's shoulder every step of the way until they finally breached the inner sanctum.

And then that was the moment Brother Asmodai faltered.

The enemy rabble-rouser, the demagogue that had turned half a billion people against the Emperor, confronted his attackers.

He was clad in ancient power armour, decorated with the sigils and crests of the ancient Legiones Astartes. This alone would not have caused Brother Asmodai a moment's pause. He had fought and killed traitor Space Marines before.

What stilled Brother Asmodai's hearts for a moment, the shock that numbed brain and hands alike, was the fact that Malvine Rhemell was clearly a Dark Angel.

The rebel commander did not hesitate. While Asmodai stared in disbelief, Rhemell sliced apart Sergeant Elijah with a gleaming powerblade. Brother Asmodai brought up his bolter as reaction started to overcome shock, but not soon enough to stop the former Dark Angel plunging his blue-crackling sword through the battle-brother's thigh.

Falling, Brother Asmodai was helpless, his leg collapsing under his weight. Rhemell loomed over him, eyes gloating, mouth opened in a vicious grin.

Rhemell let him live.

In that moment of total power, the renegade Dark Angel stared down contemptuously at Brother Asmodai and shamed him; to spare the Space Marine was to prove that he was no threat.

More Dark Angels pounded through the breach, but by then Malvine Rhemell had retreated, heading through an archway lined with mining charges. The explosives brought down the roof, but for one second more Brother Asmodai looked right at the traitor, who turned and lifted his sword in mocking salute moments before tonnes of ferrocrete, rock and plasteel cut off the pursuing Space Marines.

Not another Fallen would ever escape Asmodai, that had been his vow. It was more than principle. Asmodai was well aware that the event, and the traumatic fight back to the surface of the hive-moon that he alone had survived, had scarred his mind far more than his body. He possessed enough self-awareness to know his unforgiving nature and relentless, even psychotic attitude were the result of that catastrophic encounter.

But there was more to Asmodai's belligerence than revenge for being made to feel helpless. After his escape Malvine Rhemell had set the plasma reactors of the hive-moon to overload before departing, incinerating millions in the subsequent detonation.

The actions of Astelan and the countless deaths of others, either directly at the hands of the Fallen or as a consequence of their treachery, was proof enough that they posed a clear and significant danger not only to the Dark Angels but to all of the Emperor's servants.

Perhaps Asmodai was mad, but he was convinced there was a method to his madness.

It was thus with no small amount of satisfaction that Asmodai received a message from one of the Ravenwing Nephilim fighters patrolling over the city. Target Alpha had been sighted leading the attack against the western flanks of the governor's palace, no more than a kilometre from Asmodai and Belial's current position. The renegade seemed to be pressing for the breach made by the earlier bombardment, confirming Astelan's earlier assessment.

'We have him now,' said Belial, having heard the same report. The vox crackled as the Grand Master switched to the company-wide channel. 'All forces attack! Sensorium upload with Target Alpha data. Converge and capture.'

The two of them followed Belial's squad of Deathwing Knights up the boarding ramp of the Land Raider Crusader *Lion's Fury*. The massive assault tank's power plant growled into life and with tracks churning across shattered ferrocrete the war machine burst past the ruined curtain wall of the palace and onto the roadway leading west.

Belial stood at the command console located near the front of the compartment while Asmodai looked past the Grand Master at the cluster of digital displays. Green sigils that marked the positions of the Deathwing arrowed towards a red smear of the traitor forces, converging as one on the flashing rune that designated Target Alpha; Ravenwing overflights and scattered comments from the force's vox-casts confirmed Anovel's position on a regular basis.

Friend and foe alike were scattered by the charge of the Deathwing. Their Land Raiders were impervious to any weapon possessed by Anovel's ground forces and they forged along the streets towards their objective with autocannon shells ringing ineffectually against their hulls while plasma bursts sprayed harmlessly along the heat-shields of thick ceramite plates.

From the external vid-periscope feeds Asmodai saw hab-blocks with shattered windows and firestorm-scorched fascias speeding past. Looking at the rear view monitors he saw that the higher portions of the palace had disappeared, leaving only the spindle of the upper spire remaining as a glass stalagmite five hundred metres high.

Closing on Anovel's position, they ran into the forwards elements of the traitor assault. Warriors with adapted zero-g construction suits stood their ground behind a barricade of broken vehicles a hundred metres ahead. Flashes of las-fire sparked past and glanced without effect from the Crusader's slanted armour. A missile rushed from the enemy position and hit the track guard on the right side, showering sparks and shrapnel but causing no real damage.

'No delays,' Belial told the driver. 'Press on.'

The massive tank smashed into the upturned ground-cars and burning troop carriers at full speed, slamming past the tangle of metal and plastek without any loss of impetus. The burning wrecks were thrown into the augmented traitors, turning them to slicks of blood and twisted metal frames, shattered glass slicing through flesh and arteries.

The hurricane bolter systems in the sponsons burst into life as the *Lion's Fury* rumbled on, twenty-four bolt-guns spewing explosive-tipped rounds into the survivors.

'Target Alpha has withdrawn to a defensive position,' Belial told the other Space Marines. 'Lower storey of a food dispensary. Local air units are suppressing upper floors with strafing runs. Prepare for frag assault entry.'

Belial stood up and the four Deathwing Knights gathered around him as he moved to the forward assault ramp. From a side street another Land Raider cruised into view alongside the *Lion's Fury*. Its lascannons stabbed beams into the buildings ahead while heavy bolters unleashed a torrent of fire along the road. The Crusader's hull thrummed with noise as its main weapon system opened fire, adding salvoes of assault cannon fire to the barrage, annihilating anything moving between the bullet-pocked buildings. On the tac-display Asmodai could see another three Dark Angels squads arriving in Land Raiders from a parallel position.

'Target Alpha is to be captured. Mark targets before firing. All other targets to be eliminated.'

'We still have Tharsians in the area,' came a report from one of the sergeants. 'Orders, Grand Master?'

Belial looked at Asmodai. The Chaplain made a cutting motion across his throat.

'Total cleanse,' announced the Grand Master.

The driver swerved the *Lion's Fury* to the right, away from the target building, and then turned hard left. The vehicle's engines reached a new pitch of power as it accelerated across the broad avenue. The front of the Land Raider smashed through the wall of the dispensary as though it was made of children's building blocks, scattering hunks of masonry and jagged splinters.

Coming to a halt, the Land Raider discharged its frag storm launchers. The ground floor of the dispensary was filled with razor-sharp shards of red-hot metal, scything through the enemy warriors that had formed a perimeter around a stairwell at the centre of the ground floor hallway. Hurricane bolter fire chattered ceaselessly as the assault ramp dropped down.

Belial was the first out, his Deathwing Knights on his heel, their fire unerringly finding targets amongst the smoke and dust, guided by their interlinked sensorium. Asmodai followed a few steps behind and allowed the Chapter's elite to do what they existed to do.

Now and then he snapped off a shot with his bolt pistol but as more Deathwing squads converged from other directions, the number of targets swiftly dwindled away. Augmented and chemically-boosted foes lay scattered like rag dolls amongst the debris, bodies punctured by bolt-rounds, torn apart by assault cannon shells and incinerated by heavy flamers. Promethium still burned, slicked across the hard ferrocrete floor, burning overturned tables and chairs, turning meat counters and synth-bean stands to charred piles.

'Downstairs,' Belial announced. 'Sub-level.'

As the bionic warriors had outmatched the local milita, in turn they were outclassed and outgunned by the Dark Angels First Company. Blinded to their plight by stimms and lies, not a single man or woman amongst Anovel's guard tried to surrender. In the close quarters of the basement store rooms they were hacked down by power swords and lightning claws, pummelled with power fists and crushed by thunder hammers.

In a crate-filled cellar they ran Anovel to ground. Asmodai was there the moment the last of the traitorous bodyguards were cut in half by the Sword of Silence wielded by Belial. The Fallen's once-white armour was much stained, the paint little but flecks on the grey and brown ceramite, metal tarnished, old symbols of loyalty crudely defaced.

The desperate traitor snatched up a power maul from one of his dead warriors and launched himself at Belial. A Deathwing Knight intercepted him, his two-handed mace clubbing the Fallen to the ground with one blow, cracking open armour. Belial moved swiftly, directing a kick into the side of the downed Space Marine's helm.

Dazed, Anovel's struggles were instinctual as Asmodai tore off the Fallen's helm. He gestured to Apothecary Temraen, who flicked a dagger-like point from the narthecium built into his right vambrace. Temraen steadied Anovel's head and drove the point of the injector into the Fallen's neck, administering a sedative dose that would have killed any lesser man.

Eyes rolling up, Anovel slumped and a trail of drool spilled from his gaping mouth, the acidic saliva hissing gently as it spattered on the floor.

'Target Alpha is secure,' Asmodai announced. The words gave him a sense of achievement that bordered on ecstasy.

'This place is *not* secure,' said Belial. 'Tharsian forces are still in the vicinity even if the enemy are broken.'

'Signal the *Penitent Warrior* to stand in for teleport withdrawal. We will move to the palace and await their arrival.'

Belial seemed hesitant.

'Brother Sapphon reports that the *Terminus Est* is not yet committing to orbit,' said the Grand Master of the Deathwing. 'It would seem the fiend Typhus is not prepared to risk his warriors.'

'We will deal with him in due course,' said Asmodai. 'Anovel was our primary objective. We must secure the prisoner first. You will provide escort back to the palaces.'

'It seems poor bargain to exchange a world for one warrior,' said Belial. 'The Hunt is not the sole duty of the Chapter, brother. Your honour guard will be sufficient to provide security and protection for your withdrawal.'

'A single squad? What do you intend to do with the rest of the company, brother?'

'I intend to win the war for Tharsis.'

TELEPORT ASSAULT

'Lord Sapphon, we have been detecting a narrow band transmission from the enemy flagship,' reported Lasla Chirpet. The deck-captain saluted with fist on chest and handed a datapad to the Chaplain. 'It has been pulsing on and off for the last twenty minutes. The origin is definitely the heavy cruiser but we cannot locate the destination.'

'I am sure that the flagship is sending all kinds of signals,' said Sapphon.

'Yes, Lord Sapphon, but this one is too intermittent to be any kind of vox-channel. I would suggest a locator beacon of some kind, but not very powerful.'

'A teleport lock attempt?'

'I cannot say from this range, lord.'

Sapphon analysed the readings on the datapad and came to the same conclusion: too weak for a command-vox. There had to be some other purpose.

'If we move closer can we trace the signal to the surface?' he asked Lasla. The officer shook his head.

'Too much residual scatter from weapons fire and other transmissions, lord.'

The traitor heavy cruiser had moved out of direct orbit over Streisgant, driven off by anti-orbital fire. In its place the *Penitent Warrior* was preparing to enter low orbit over the city to teleport Asmodai and his prisoner. That was clearly Sapphon's priority but the enemy signal nagged at him.

The unknown of the darkness beckoned.

Sapphon inwardly cursed his curiosity but he could not ignore it.

'Set intercept course for the enemy flagship,' he announced. Lasla met the command with a look of shock.

'The teleport action, lord?'

'Suspended.'

'Your will is my command, lord, but we are a strike cruiser and they are a heavy cruiser. We are outgunned.'

'I do not intend to destroy them, deck-captain. I need you to bring down their void shields and take us close enough for a teleport attack. If we cannot trace the signal we must go to the source.'

'As you command, Lord Sapphon.' Lasla hurried away, snapping orders to the navigation and command crews.

'Comms, connect channel to Brother Asmodai, route through my vox.'

It took almost a minute until Asmodai's voice crackled in Sapphon's ear.

'Are you ready to bring us aboard, brother?' asked the Chaplain.

'Not yet. There is a situation developing.'

Sapphon explained his discovery and his planned course of action. Unsurprisingly it was not to Asmodai's liking.

'Enemy forces are currently surrounding the commander's palace, brother. If the *Terminus Est* commits its forces we may not be able to hold here. It is imperative that you bring us back aboard immediately!'

'Have you recovered Astelan?' Sapphon said, knowing that Asmodai would be burning with shame at the Fallen's escape.

'Tybalain and his squadron are chasing him down, brother. It is only a matter of time before he is in our custody once more.'

'Not if this signal is intended for him. Perhaps you were right and he has been in concert with Anovel for all this time, or perhaps he has found a way of making contact since he eluded you. Either way, it is possible that the transmission is to guide him to a means of leaving Tharsis. Do you wish to simply swap one prisoner for another?'

Static hissed and Sapphon imagined the anguish of the decision wracking Asmodai. It did not really matter what his Brother-Chaplain felt about the matter, they would follow Sapphon's plan. However, it would be better if Asmodai and his warriors were prepared for a lengthier wait until extraction.

'Your plan has merit,' Asmodai said at last. The admission was made with some effort, that much was clear from the Chaplain's tone. 'You are right to pursue this possibility.'

'Then we are agreed, brother. I will update you as soon as I can. Transmission end.'

Sapphon turned his attention to the rotating hololith strategic display depicting the orbital situation. The enemy flagship was being harried by two squadrons of small intra-system escorts that had manoeuvred into its aft region away from the main guns. Two cruisers were turning to drive off these harassing attacks but would have to take a circuitous route unless they wanted to dare a ring of gun and missile platforms that had survived the initial assault.

The *Penitent Warrior* burst through the cordon of system monitors pursuing the enemy flagship, arrowing directly towards the heavy cruiser. As they closed the range on the ponderous enemy the prow bombardment cannon, normally used for surface attack, opened fire. The ship shuddered every ninety seconds with each titanic shell launched at the traitor flagship.

On the main display Sapphon watched as the plasma warheads detonated against the void shields of the heavy cruiser, splashing white against a shimmering curve of blue and purple. More flares of plasma erupted along the length of the target ship; arrestor thrusters firing to speed its turn towards the incoming attack. A dorsal turret swung towards the strike cruiser, stabbing a beam of lance energy towards the Space Marine vessel. The display momentarily fogged with static and alarms sounded.

'Void shields intercepted the brunt of the attack,' announced Lasla. 'Alter three points to starboard and bring port batteries to bear.'

The bombardment cannon alone would not be enough to punch through the layers of void shields protecting the flagship, and that meant the *Penitent Warrior* was forced to slow to bring her main gun decks into the attack, exposing the ship to counter-fire. For the next few minutes only the enemy lance turrets could fire, scouring lasers along the length of the strike cruiser, rippling along the void shields with plumes of dispersing gas and energy. The regular pounding of the forward cannon was like the beating of a drum, every thunderous outburst met with a corresponding flare of power from the enemy ship's defence shields.

Missiles and shells streaked from the *Penitent Warrior*'s main gun decks as Lasla ordered a full broadside. The firmament lit up as the strike cruiser unleashed the full fury of its batteries. Void shields coruscated with plasma and shell impacts, sparkling and spraying across the display in actinic waves as the generators fought to shunt the incoming energy and mass of the attack into the warp.

'Enemy target lock,' announced a servitor at the scanner banks.

'Incoming fire,' Lasla warned, grabbing the edge of a console to support his wiry frame. Sapphon locked his power armour as deck after deck of the heavy cruiser's guns opened fire, illuminating dozens of buttresses and galleries along the length of the ship.

The fusillade slammed into the *Penitent Warrior*'s void shields. Warning klaxons blared and red lamps lit up across a handful of consoles. The main lights dimmed as power was siphoned to the void shield generators and the vid- and navigational displays pulsed and whirled as the ship's sensors overloaded with the outpouring of refracted laser and radiation splash.

'Void shield generator overloaded, enemy void shields also down,' Lasla announced breathlessly. 'All damage control crews responding.'

'Brothers,' Sapphon turned to his bodyguards. Caulderain had been watching the main display intently but turned and saluted at Sapphon's word. 'We go to the teleportarium.'

The Terminators fell in beside the Chaplain as he exited the bridge. Sapphon briefed them on the mission as they headed to the teleportation hall a few decks beneath the command chamber, whilst monitoring Lasla's reports over the command channel.

The *Penitent Warrior* was relatively unscathed but with both ships vulnerable it was only a matter of time before the heavier guns of the enemy flagship started to tell. With the cruiser's void shields down the Terminators could teleport directly into the enemy bridge, but they would only be able to remain for a handful of minutes.

'Registering energy output on enemy void shields, lord,' Lasla told Sapphon as the Chaplain led his warriors onto the marble-like pads of the teleportation ring. 'Estimate between four and seven minutes before their generators are recharged.'

'Which is it? Four or seven minutes?' snapped Caulderain. 'The margin of error is too broad.'

'It does not matter,' said Sapphon before Lasla could reply. 'Four minutes should be all we need. We strike fast, access the comm-network and then teleport back. That is the mission, nothing else.'

He looked at the tech-adept manning the teleporter controls and raised a fist in command. The red-robed serf acknowledged the order and bent over his console. Red forks of energy arced between the teleporter coils, turning the pale armour of the Deathwing crimson in their glare.

The *Penitent Warrior* trembled as a mighty barrage of fire slammed into the strike cruiser's upper decks.

'If we have a ship to come bac–' Decemius's quip was lost as warp energy suffused the teleporter.

An instant of dislocation and existential emptiness gnawed at the heart and soul of the Chaplain.

Sapphon opened fire before his conscious mind had recovered from the jarring effects of teleportation. His bolt pistol ripped open the torso of a bionically-altered woman standing next to the command throne of the flag-ship bridge. Around him the Deathwing honour guard blazed with storm bolters, cutting down the shocked command crew.

Most of the officers were augmented in some fashion like the soldiers on the world below; bionic harnesses, piston-driven exoskeletons supported stimm-contorted bodies. Bolts sparked from lacquered armour plates and metal rods, punched into sallow flesh and unnaturally bulging muscles. Dark blood and viscous hydraulic fluid sprayed across the deck.

'Secure the comms-panel,' the Chaplain snapped, turning his fire towards the main doors as he heard the pneumatic mechanism hiss open. Two men carry-ing bulky las-blasters were sent tumbling, missing their heads. 'Fidellus, Satrael – overwatch.'

At their leader's command the two Terminators moved to the doorway; Fidellus with his thunder hammer and storm shield, Satrael carrying an assault cannon. The rip of the heavy weapon firing announced the presence of more enemies outside the bridge.

'Signal source located,' said Caulderain. Blood spatters dribbled down the comm-panel screens as he prodded at runes, trying to identify the purpose of the transmission. 'Some kind of beacon pulse, but not strong enough for a teleporter lock.'

'Where?' Sapphon demanded, joining the sergeant. 'Where is the receiver?'

'Decoding now, Brother-Chaplain.'

The crackle of Fidellus's thunder hammer indicated that at least a few enemies had survived the ongoing bursts of fire from Satrael and had reached the bridge doors.

'Status!' snapped Sapphon. They were not here for a prolonged fight. It would be a matter of minutes, perhaps two or three at the most, before the traitor ship's engine crew restored one of their void shield generators. As soon as that happened, the Deathwing squad would be cut off from their homing signal, unable to teleport back.

'Enemy numbers increasing. Estimate fifty dead, that number again incoming,' reported Fidellus. 'No heavy weapons yet.'

'There you are,' announced Caulderain. He turned to Sapphon. 'I have the coordinates.'

Sapphon looked at the line of numbers on the main vox-bank display.

'Outside the city?' said the Chaplain. 'That makes no sense.'

'I remember those coordinates,' said Caulderain. 'That is the site of the old governor's palace – the fortress where we first captured Astelan.'

'Tybalain's squadron is already en route,' said Sapphon. 'Use the ship's channel to broadcast an update to their mission. Tell them what we have found.'

'What have we found?' asked Caulderain. 'If Brother Asmodai has Target Alpha in custody, who is the signal intended for?'

'A good question, brother. The Ravenwing will provide the answer.'

With the transmission sent, Sapphon ordered the squad to destroy as many of the ship controls as possible. With storm bolter and power fist they spent thirty seconds smashing and ripping apart every console, screen, runepad and cable. Under the cover of Satrael's assault cannon they convened close to the main doors.

'Sapphon to *Penitent Warrior*. Sending signal lock.' Sapphon checked his chronometer. Four and half minutes had passed since they had arrived. 'Bring us back!'

EPILOGUE

HUNTER AND HUNTED

The transponder signal was a blinking rune in the middle of *Black Shadow*'s navigational display, directly ahead of Annael and two kilometres away. The hab-lined plazas and wide boulevards of the city centre had given way to factories and depots clustered around the highways and magrail termini serving the capital's starport a few kilometres to the west.

Looking ahead, Annael saw a stretch of ramshackle ruins, several square kilometres of towers and broken walls sprawling to either side of the cracked ferrocrete road. It was an incongruous sight after the freshly raised blocks and newly laid roads of the city. Past the plasteel and ironworks of manufactories and power plants a flat expanse of bare ferrocrete surrounded the tumbled citadel.

Approaching from this direction it had seemed unfamiliar, but looking at the coordinates on the bike screen he suddenly realised that this was where he had dropped onto Tharsis with the Fifth Company fifteen years ago.

Back then it had simply been Objective Prime, though those the Dark Angels had liberated from its dungeons and execution galleries had called it something else: Slaughterkeep. The name struck a chord even now and brought back a flood of memory.

Tracer fire from staggered gun emplacements tore the night sky while airbursts lit the underside of the low clouds. Storming down the ramp of the drop pod, Annael watched as a pulse of lance fire spat down from the heavens, turning an armoured spire into vapour and slag in moments. The bass thunder of battle cannon fire from circling Thunderhawks drummed out the war beat in time to the pounding of his hearts.

Land Raider and Predator tanks had already formed a beachhead half a kilometre from the drop site. Lascannon and autocannon fire spewed from the tanks towards the ramparts of the outer curtain wall, slicing and smashing at gun slits and sandbagged artillery positions. A constant storm of las-fire streamed from firing galleries and a ring of bunkers surrounding the citadel, answered by the flickering bolts of the attacking Dark Angels.

Sergeant Rameus shouted a warning and directed the squad to the left where dozens of enemy soldiers dashed from trenchworks under the cover of staccato heavy stubber fire and the boom of mortar bomb detonations. Squad Hadrael were fifty metres ahead, advancing into the teeth of the enemy fire, lasblasts and shrapnel ringing from their armour. Beside them stomped the massive form of Brother Tarallean, the hulking Dreadnought supporting his smaller companions with blistering fusillades of plasma fire and heavy bolter-rounds.

Annael was right next to Sergeant Rameus when they reached the trenchline. As he plunged down into the trench he came face-to-face with the defenders of Tharsis. They seemed terribly young, most of them no more than teenagers. The face of each was marked by ritual scarring, a crude device in the shape of an eagle with outstretched wings covering nose, cheeks and forehead. Annael fired, the dark green, slab-like carapace armour of his target little defence against the explosive bolt, which punched into the soldier's shoulder before detonating, sending his arm spinning into the trench wall.

There was a lot of screaming, something Annael was used to, but this time it was fury and hatred, not fear. The men manning the trench hurled themselves at the Dark Angels, shrieking and bellowing. There was something berserk about them and Annael recognised the telltale signs of combat-stimms: bloodshot eyes, corded veins and tendons in the neck, mouths foaming with saliva.

He cut them down with his bolter until the press of bodies grew so thick he had to use his combat knife, hacking and stabbing his way along the trench with the sergeant while the rest of the squad advanced along the lip above firing further ahead. Those that fell but still lived were trampled underfoot, their dying breaths spent in howls of rage and frustration.

Seeing the broken remnants of that evil place brought a sense of satisfaction to Annael. Its empty windows and shattered domes had been left here as a testament to the horrors that had been unleashed; both a memorial to those that had fallen and a tribute to those that had brought deliverance. At the time he had never known who had been responsible for the death squads and slave camps. It had not seemed important once the battle had been won. He had assumed the enemy commander, the renegade that had led the planet in revolt against the Imperium, had been slain in the fighting, or executed when captured. Suddenly he was not so sure.

'Brother Tybalain, you were a Black Knight when we stormed Slaughterkeep, were you not?'

'I was,' said the squadron leader, his tone suggesting that like Annael he was reminded of the battle. 'What of it?'

'Was it one of the Fallen that led the rebellion?'

Tybalain did not reply immediately and Annael wondered if he had overstepped a mark with the question.

'Yes, it was,' the Huntmaster said after several seconds. 'He is called Astelan. The same renegade that we hunt now.'

'As I thought,' said Annael. The news did not surprise him, and that in itself was a revelation. He accepted the admission of this secret as normal and it did not offend him. The answer begged other questions – why Astelan had survived and how had he come to be on Tharsis again chief among them – but Annael knew that this was not the time to voice them. Many mysteries from his past that he had not thought to question he saw in the fresh light of recent disclosures and hoped would be made clear in due course: battles on the brink of victory abandoned; missions despatching his squad or company away from the fighting; contradictory manoeuvres and other hints that a hidden purpose had been fulfilled but not disclosed.

'When we find him, we kill him this time, yes?' said Nerean.

'Those are Brother Asmodai's orders,' said Tybalain. 'He was both specific and vehement in his command.'

'Good,' said Annael.

The outer works as Annael remembered them had been flattened, the curtain walls levelled, leaving only the broken spires and ramparts of the central citadel. The lock on the transponder was pulsing strongly, almost exactly overlapping the grid data transferred by Brother Sapphon. The two had to be connected; it was too much of a coincidence that the signal from orbit had been directed at the same place their quarry had gone to ground.

'Dismount,' Tybalain ordered as they passed between the shattered towers of a gatehouse into a high-walled courtyard. Annael remembered the blossoms of explosions as the inner gates had been destroyed by Vindicator siege tanks.

They followed the Huntmaster on foot, armed with pistols and corvus hammers. The ruins were utterly silent save for the crunch of grit underfoot, totally unlike the mayhem and cacophony Annael had experienced when he had last trod these corridors.

Calatus had a hand-held auspex and guided them through the long passages, past guard rooms and empty armouries. They advanced along galleries lined with murderholes, the stone and plaster of the walls still bearing bolt craters, bullet holes and las-marks. The Deathwing had led the assault at this stage, Annael recalled. At the time it had seemed tactically prudent, given the fighting conditions. Now he knew there had been a more significant but hidden motive for their deployment.

He hoped that the trail they followed would not lead into the sub-levels, to the cells and execution chambers. Annael had experienced many things, and until the horrors of Ulthor the victims of Slaughterkeep had been the worst. He expected aliens to be disgusting, but the barbarity that humans had heaped upon fellow humans had strained his faith to its limit.

'Through that archway,' Calatus announced, waving them to a cloister on the left.

As soon as he stepped out beneath the open sky, Annael saw the glint of light on black paint and knew their prey was still another step ahead of them. Pieces of armour were piled against one of the columns around the edge of the cloister, exactly on the spot where the transponder signal originated.

'Spread out, he must still be here somewhere,' said Tybalain. 'He had no more than thirty minutes advantage against us and taking off his battleplate would have used most of that time.'

Annael headed back inside, confident that their quarry had not eluded them yet. It was clear that Astelan had come here for a rendezvous, perhaps hoping to be teleported or otherwise conducted up the renegade flagship in orbit. Brother Sapphon's attack had cut off that escape route and the Fallen had been forced to discard his armour to confuse his pursuers.

It would be a short-lived freedom. Annael was certain that the renegade would not escape again and it would feel good to be responsible for bringing the tyrant of Tharsis to justice. Whatever had earned Astelan a reprieve from death would not save him this time.

Occupied by this thought, Annael reacted a half-second too late as a shadow moved in a doorway to his right. A warrior clad in nothing but the under-harness of power armour sprang at Annael, clubbing a boulder of broken masonry against the side of the Dark Angel's helm. The blow was just enough to knock him back a step, giving his assailant time to duck Annael's instinctive swing of his corvus hammer.

It was just the move his opponent had expected. As the stone block crashed again into the snout of his helm Annael registered the hardened layer of a black carapace beneath his foe's skin and knew he faced the Fallen, Astelan.

Annael's armour gave him a massive strength advantage

but it slowed him just a fraction enough to give additional speed to his foe, and Astelan used it well. Dropping the broken piece of ferrocrete, the renegade seized the Dark Angel's bolt pistol as Annael raised it to fire. The Fallen deftly twisted it from his grip, cracking ceramite and finger bones to do so. Annael blotted out the pain and swung his injured hand at Astelan's head, but missed again by a narrow margin.

The bark of the bolt pistol sounded loud in the confines of the passageway. A moment later Annael's left knee exploded with pain, the bolt showering out muscle and cartilage along with pieces of the joint seal behind his kneepad. As his leg gave way he swung his hammer, knowing that the merest touch of the disruption field would be enough to down his unarmoured foe, even if he was a Space Marine.

The corvus hammer cleaved only air and Annael toppled with a shout of frustration. He managed to stall his descent with his broken hand, rolling forwards. A bolt ruptured the tiled floor where his head would have been.

The Fallen was aiming his pistol for the killing shot. Out of the corner of his eye, Annael saw another black-armoured figure arriving behind the near-naked form of Astelan. A pair of muzzle flares lit the dim passageway and two shots rang out.

Astelan spun as the side of his head exploded into bone and blood. A trail of bolt propellant scorched past Annael's cheek, leaving a welt on his helm from nose to ear. The bolt detonated on the Ravenwing warrior's backpack, shredding splinters of ceramite into the neck seal.

The Fallen collapsed to all fours, still alive, but only just. He tried to turn towards his attacker. The bolt pistol slipped from his grasp and a moment later Astelan slumped forward; unconscious or dead, Annael did not know.

'A timely intervention, br...' Annael's thanks trailed off as he looked at his rescuer. Though his armour was black he did not bear the sigils of the Ravenwing. He had a bolt pistol in hand and a plasma pistol at his belt, and there was a longsword scabbarded at his waist.

'Do not be disheartened by this turn of events, your foe had many more years of practise killing Space Marines,' said the stranger. The black-armoured warrior looked down at Astelan's unmoving body and his tone turned grim. 'As have I.'

The sound of the others arriving caused the warrior to turn, dropping the pistols to the ground as he did so. He raised his hands in surrender as Tybalain and Nerean advanced, their weapons levelled. Annael glanced over his shoulder at the scrape of a boot on tile, to see Calatus closing in from behind him.

'The sword as well,' Tybalain demanded, stopping a few metres away. 'Disarm yourself.'

'I cannot do that,' said the stranger. 'I swore an oath to carry this blade until my death.'

'Refuse and your oath will soon be fulfilled,' said the Huntmaster.

'Do not be so swift to pass such final judgement. Your masters would be much happier if I remain with breath in my lungs.' The unnamed warrior gestured at Astelan. 'They have chosen dangerous allies of late. I feared you would not find me. They will want to hear what I have to say.'

'You claim you are known to them? You intended to be found?' Tybalain sounded uncertain. Annael had thought such a thing impossible. 'What is your name?'

'You may address me by my title,' said the Space Marine. 'Lord Cypher.'

The story of the Dark Angels concludes in
The Unforgiven.

ABOUT THE AUTHOR

Gav Thorpe is the *New York Times* bestselling author of 'The Lion', a novella in the collection *The Primarchs*. He has written many other Black Library books, including the Horus Heresy titles *Deliverance Lost*, *Corax: Soulforge* and audio drama *Raven's Flight*, as well as fan-favourite Warhammer 40,000 novel *Angels of Darkness* and the epic Time of Legends trilogy, *The Sundering*. He is currently working on a new Dark Angels series, *The Legacy of Caliban*. Gav hails from Nottingham, where he shares his hideout with the evil genius that is Dennis, the mechanical hamster.

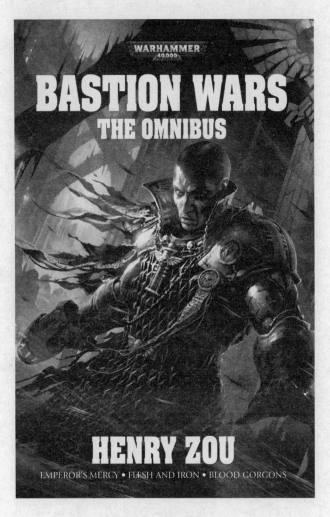